Louise Fuller was once a tomboy who hated pink and always wanted to be the prince—not the princess! Now she enjoys creating heroines who aren't pushovers, but strong, believable women. Before writing for Mills & Boon she studied literature and philosophy at university, and then worked as a reporter on her local newspaper. She lives in Tunbridge Wells with her impossibly handsome husband, Patrick, and their six children.

USA TODAY bestselling author **Natalie Anderson** writes emotional contemporary romance full of sparkling banter, sizzling heat and uplifting endings—perfect for readers who love to escape with empowered heroines and arrogant alphas who are too sexy for their own good. When not writing, you'll find her wrangling her four children, three cats, two goldfish and one dog…and snuggled in a heap on the sofa with her husband at the end of the day. Follow her at natalie-anderson.com.

Also by Louise Fuller

Royal Ring of Revenge
Business Between Enemies

Ruthless Rivals miniseries

Boss's Plus-One Demand
Nine-Month Contract

Also by Natalie Anderson

Billion-Dollar Bet collection

Billion-Dollar Dating Game

Convenient Wives Club miniseries

Their Altar Arrangement
Boss's Baby Acquisition
Greek Vows Revisited

Discover more at millsandboon.co.uk.

AFTER-HOURS TEMPTATION

LOUISE FULLER

NATALIE ANDERSON

MILLS & BOON

All rights reserved including the right of reproduction in whole or in part in any form. This edition is published by arrangement with Harlequin Enterprises ULC.

This is a work of fiction. Names, characters, places, locations and incidents are purely fictional and bear no relationship to any real life individuals, living or dead, or to any actual places, business establishments, locations, events or incidents. Any resemblance is entirely coincidental.

Without limiting the exclusive rights of any author, contributor or the publisher of this publication, any unauthorised use of this publication to train generative artificial intelligence (AI) technologies is expressly prohibited. HarperCollins also exercise their rights under Article 4(3) of the Digital Single Market Directive 2019/790 and expressly reserve this publication from the text and data mining exception.

® and TM are trademarks owned and used by the trademark owner and/or its licensee. Trademarks marked with ® are registered with the United Kingdom Patent Office and/or the Office for Harmonisation in the Internal Market and in other countries.

First published in Great Britain 2026
by Mills & Boon, an imprint of HarperCollins*Publishers* Ltd,
1 London Bridge Street, London, SE1 9GF

www.harpercollins.co.uk

HarperCollins*Publishers*, Macken House, 39/40 Mayor Street Upper, Dublin 1, D01 C9W8, Ireland

After-Hours Temptation © 2026 Harlequin Enterprises ULC

Billion-Dollar Baby Clause © 2026 Louise Fuller

Enemies Until After Hours © 2026 Natalie Anderson

ISBN: 978-0-263-41818-7

02/26

Printed and Bound in the UK using 100% Renewable Electricity
at CPI Group (UK) Ltd, Croydon, CR0 4YY

BILLION-DOLLAR BABY CLAUSE

LOUISE FULLER

MILLS & BOON

CHAPTER ONE

'Sir, just to let you know, we're about five minutes away.'

'Thanks, Frank.'

Looking up from his phone, Ares Konstantinou glanced out the limousine window. The interior of the car was pleasantly cool, but outside it was a warm July evening. Not the dry heat of Athens: the London air felt sticky and clogged. The roads were clogged too. But finally, the Clarendon Hotel in Mayfair was only a street away.

He was so tempted to tell Frank, his driver, to keep on moving.

Larry wouldn't mind if he skipped the party. Or at least he would say he didn't mind, he amended seconds later. But the Konstantinous had been using Milner's for the two hundred years the London law firm had been in business, and he was here to represent his family and celebrate the bi-centenary. In fact, he had promised his grandfather that he would do so, and this at least was a promise he could keep.

Not that Ares Sr was demanding he marry and produce an heir—he didn't need to. Ares knew that it was his grandfather's deepest wish.

And more than anything, he wanted to make the old man happy. Ares Sr was a rock. A constant in his life, as reassuring as the Pole Star to a sailor on a turbulent sea. But it was getting increasingly obvious that his star was fading. He got tired easily, forgot things and was anxious in a way he had never been. Particularly about his grandchildren and their futures.

A spiral of guilt twisted beneath Ares's ribs. Like his parents, his grandfather had never once condemned him for the wedding debacle that had made headlines around the world. But then the old man's disappointment would have been a bee sting compared to the trauma of losing his son and daughter-in-law the following month. Grief at their loss had hollowed him out. Even the business he loved no longer energised him as it once had.

Only one thing could do that. And it was the one thing Ares didn't know how to do.

His heart thudded sluggishly against his ribs, and he stared past his driver's head, battling the vortex of emotions stirred up merely by the thought of matrimony.

But right now, his own feelings about marriage were of less importance than his sister's, because unfortunately Ariana seemed to find the idea of walking down the aisle an altogether more tempting prospect than he did. He glanced back down at her latest message, which as usual was interspersed with exclamation marks and emojis that he didn't understand.

She was everything he wasn't. Romantic. Trusting. Impulsive.

Plus, she was ten years younger than him, and since losing their parents, he'd felt more paternal than fraternal towards her. Because she was his responsibility, even more so now that his grandfather's health was failing.

But clearly, he was sleeping on the job.

His frustration segued into panic as he remembered Ari's announcement last week. That she was engaged.

To a man she'd met just under five weeks ago.

It was ludicrous.

It was reckless.

It was not going to happen.

Not without a fight, anyway. But so far, and after several fights, nothing he'd said had made an atom of difference to Ariana. There were few people on earth as stubborn as his sister. But as his grandmother used to say, there were many roads to Athens. If logic and threats wouldn't work, an expertly worded prenuptial agreement should be enough to deter her young gold-digger from pursuing his claim. Setting that in motion was the main reason for his trip to London.

Thankfully Ariana had seen the prenup as a sign that Ares was accepting the marriage, and she had happily flown out to a health clinic in Oaxaca that was as remote as it was exclusive. And there she would stay until this prenup was watertight.

What the—?

His seat belt tightened across his body, and he grabbed the side of the car as the limo slammed to a halt and a sludgy green liquid spattered loudly against the windscreen.

A protester? Konstantinou didn't drill for oil, but they shipped it all over the globe. His brain was playing through hundreds of possibilities. Was it a diversion for a kidnap attempt? Some kind of street entertainment?

'Are you okay, Mr Konstantinou?' Stefan, his bodyguard, swung round in his seat.

'I'm fine.'

Frank's eyes met his in the rearview mirror. 'Sorry, sir. She just stepped out in front of me.'

She? 'Who?'

The answer was abruptly provided as a woman wearing sleek Lycra shorts and a cropped top smacked the driver's-side window.

His bodyguard was already uncurling and reaching for the door-handle.

'What the hell are you playing at? You could have killed

me—' The woman smacked the glass again. She glanced briefly into the back of the car, and he caught a flash of green, sharp like a shard of broken glass.

Interesting, he thought.

'Don't pretend you can't see me, buddy—'

Buddy. She was American? The raw anger in her voice had made that unclear, but *buddy* was not something people said in England.

'Stay in the car, Stefan. I'll handle this,' Ares said, and ignoring his bodyguard's protests, he pushed open the car door and stepped onto the pavement.

'Finally. Are you the organ grinder? Because your monkey almost ran me over.'

He felt a jolt of electricity as the woman's eyes narrowed on his face. He'd been wrong. They weren't just interesting, they were spectacular. Almost as spectacular as those cheek bones, that face. Framed by dark hair that was twisted into a complicated plait, she had the look of an artist's muse, but capturing her likeness would be hard. She would be hard to pin down.

His body hardened as his mind took a sharp, sexual turn into a bedroom that looked a lot like the one in his townhouse.

'Did you hear me?'

Her question cut across his thoughts. She was definitely American, most likely from the West Coast, although the chill in her voice could have blown in from the Arctic.

'I think the whole of Mayfair can hear you,' he lied, because she wasn't shouting or even speaking loudly. But people were turning to look. Probably they always turned to look at this woman. She was ballerina-slim with long lightly tanned limbs. Not fragile, though. She was toned, sexy. Angry too, although not in an out-of-control, hysterical way. And she most definitely wasn't a protester or a diversion. She was angry on her own account and was currently drawing attention to that fact. Which meant she was trouble.

Her glare blazed across the space between them, and he felt the pavement tilt beneath his feet just as if he'd downed several shots in quick succession. 'Oh, I'm sorry. Is this embarrassing for you?'

The shape of her mouth as she spoke made him momentarily lose track of his thoughts. Her lips were full and pink, and there was a slight crease in the centre of the lower lip. If he'd wanted, he could reach over and fit the edge of his thumb into it, and for one destabilising moment he half imagined he had done so, when he realised she was looking at him intently.

Wanting to distract her—and himself—Ares leaned forward and touched the goop on the windscreen.

'What is this?'

Her eyebrow rose in an arch, the glittering green cat's eyes narrowing infinitesimally. 'It's—it *was* an energy smoothie.'

He was suddenly conscious of the green smear on his fingers and how badly he wanted to use those fingers to unravel her plait.

'I can pay for a replacement.'

She stared up at him, and he wasn't a mind-reader, but he could hear her thinking *Jerk* so loudly it was almost audible.

'You're offering to buy me a smoothie? Your driver nearly ran me over.' Her forehead creased, and she reached down to pick up something from the road. 'And you broke my travel cup.'

It was certainly dented, probably from when it hit the windscreen. As she straightened up, she took a step closer and held it up for him to see. But he wasn't looking at the cup. Neither was she. For a second, they stared at each other, narrow-eyed. They were close enough that he could see flecks of the green liquid on her collarbone and the pulse jerking against the skin of her throat, and every single cell in his body was beating in time to that pulse.

'Sir.'

His bodyguard was on the pavement now, and it was enough to bring him to his senses. Or, rather, stifle them.

He reached into his jacket to retrieve his wallet. 'My driver was following the rules of the road to the letter, but as a gesture of goodwill, here.' He held out a fifty-pound note. 'This should cover your costs. Next time, though, perhaps take a moment to remember which country you're in. I think you'll find they drive on the other side of the road here. So you need to look right for oncoming traffic.'

The woman gave him precisely the withering stare that remark deserved and, ignoring the money he was holding out, she said quietly, 'You have a nice day.' Pausing, she leaned back on her heels so that she could meet his gaze, and his eyes followed the uptilt of her chin, mesmerised.

'Better still, may you live in interesting times.' And then without giving him the right to reply, she turned and walked swiftly away.

Five minutes later as he strode through the revolving doors into the Clarendon Hotel, Ares was still replaying that final exchange and finding new things that annoyed him about it. He'd half expected to see his tormentor sashaying down the street, but she had disappeared, and he found himself wondering where she had gone. Only, of course, because he would have liked to have had the last word. To pin her down more successfully—

'Ares.'

He turned and felt some of the tension leave his body. 'Larry. It's good to see you.'

The stocky man with ruddy cheeks and receding blond hair beamed at him. 'It's good to see you. Good of you to come. I know you're flat-out. We're in the ballroom.'

Ares gripped Larry Milner's outstretched hand, shaking it as they walked downstairs.

'I wanted to be here.' And seeing Larry's pleasure, it wasn't quite a lie. 'My grandfather is so sorry he couldn't join us tonight. He really wanted to come. He said he'd been in touch?'

'He has, and it's fine.' Larry tightened his grip. 'I wasn't expecting him. To be honest, I wasn't expecting you. I know how much you hate these things.'

'Milner's has taken care of my family for two hundred years.'

'And we're going to take care of this prenup for Ariana.' Larry Milner lowered his voice. 'I've put Nancy Kemp on it. She's tough. I mean, indefatigable.'

And *indefatigable* was what he needed, Ares thought, glancing idly across the room for a waiter.

Which was when he saw her.

It was maybe thirty minutes since she had tossed that curse in his face, and he hadn't expected to see her again, so it was a shock. But not as great a shock as the punch of heat that vibrated through him so hard and fast that he almost lost his footing.

For a moment he couldn't reconcile it—both her being here and looking so different.

She had changed clothes. The snug-fitting shorts and crop top were gone. In their place was a white dress that made his heart accelerate, although he couldn't say why, given that it was summer and women wore white dresses a lot in the summer. Usually something floaty and bohemian or a crisp structured cotton. The kind of dress Grace Kelly wore to seduce Cary Grant on the French Riviera.

But this dress was something completely different. It was long-sleeved with a high neck and a flippy knee-length skirt. If he'd seen it on a hanger he wouldn't have given it a second glance. Now, though, he was struggling to tear his gaze away.

His brain twitched as the woman turned to greet someone and the hem did a little shimmy.

She was not on the agenda.

And yet, it felt like they had unfinished business—

Ares Konstantinou let his gaze land briefly on the profile of the woman on the other side of the room. Her hair was in a different style now. Some kind of messy updo that made him think of waking up late in a tangle of sheets. A few stray strands curled at the nape of her neck, and he found himself fighting against an urge to walk over and wrap one around his finger.

'Nancy's fierce,' Larry said emphatically. 'She won't let anything slip through. Any prenup she writes will be ironclad. I've got your back, and Ariana's too.'

Ares dragged his gaze back to his friend, smiled, nodded. 'I know.'

'I know how important this is to you.'

Larry knew why it was so important. The Konstantinou family didn't need another marital crisis. Not one played out in real time on smartphones and TVs around the globe.

People talked about a twenty-four-hour news cycle, but at times over the last six years it had honestly felt as if the world would never move on. Even now, he knew some of the assembled guests tonight would be putting a face to the headline like some twisted game of Pelmanism.

The Runaway Groom
Konstanti-NO Leaves Bride at Altar
The In-Konstant Lover

His shoulders braced as if he was having to push back against the flow of headlines that had erupted in news outlets across the world after he'd abandoned his bride in front of eight hundred witnesses and the several hundred reporters and photographers who were jostling outside the church.

What nobody had witnessed, except him, was the sight of Zoe, his fiancée, writhing beneath another man on the bed they had also shared.

He had dropped by the day before the wedding with a sapphire bracelet, wanting to surprise her. Which was why he had let himself in. Why he hadn't called out to her. And he was so eager to see her that at first, he didn't understand what he was hearing.

A flicker of pain, and shame at his stupidity. Because naive idiot that he was, he'd actually thought that she was working out.

And then he saw them. In the days that followed, he would wonder why he hadn't done something, said something, shouted, raged, thrown vases, smashed plates—he was Greek, after all.

But he had done none of those things. Instead, he had reversed silently out of the bedroom, let himself out the way he'd come in and driven home, fully intending to tell his family that the wedding was off.

The Athens house had been awash with caterers and waitstaff and people arranging flowers. Even now the scent of roses made him slightly nauseous. And at the centre of all the chaos were his mother and father looking so happy and excited. And he couldn't bring himself to do it.

Until the following day when seeing Zoe's demure expression had flipped something inside of him. He could still remember it now. The blank oval faces of the people gaping at him. Zoe's wide-eyed shock and his parents' dismay.

And unspoken disappointment.

He still hated that they never knew the truth before their deaths. But in the aftermath of the wedding fiasco, they had been dealing with a hysterical Zoe and the moment passed. A month later, they were dead.

Pushing aside the memory of those terrible weeks, he clapped Larry on the back. 'It's a good turnout. So who's here?'

He let his gaze move oh so casually around the room, but inside he felt like an atom being split in two by some huge, unseen force. He wanted to listen to Larry. But his eyes kept moving of their own accord to the woman in white on the other side of the room.

She had turned again, now presenting him with her back, and his gaze dropped to the taut curve of her bottom, his pulse twitching as she shifted on her heels, and he wondered if her legs were bare. Or was she wearing hold-ups or stockings?

'Clients, like yourself. Partners, retired partners and associates. Some industry peers and people we work with closely like accountants and financial advisers. We've also got a couple of representatives from the charities we support. Which this year are a local arts foundation for disadvantaged kids and a mentoring service for women entrepreneurs.'

Larry's gaze flicked from a thirtysomething man wearing a vivid blue suit to the woman in the white dress.

So that's who she was. A woman fighting battles for other women. It made sense. It certainly explained why she hadn't been fazed or impressed by his driver and bodyguard. He caught a glint of green as she turned to snatch a glass of orange juice from a passing waiter and felt it unlock something inside of him.

He could go over. Make small talk. But he didn't want to talk. He wanted to touch—

Not happening.

So she was pretty. She had also cursed him in the street like some witch.

Was that why he couldn't stop thinking about her? Had she put a spell on him?

He replayed the moment out by the limo when they had been eye to eye, close enough to touch. It was a few half seconds at most, and yet it was like dancing on the edge of a volcano. He'd felt dizzy and elated and powerful.

But it had been a long time since he'd been controlled by his libido. And he wasn't going to start now.

Tucking a stray curl behind her ear, Willa Hamilton discreetly put down her glass of orange juice on a side table and asked a passing waiter for something the Brits called *Buck's fizz*. It was essentially a mimosa but with the ratio of champagne to orange juice reversed. In other words, two parts champagne to one part orange juice. Which was fine by her. She needed a drink right now.

Or better still a SWAT team to extract her from the building.

The room felt like it was running out of air. She couldn't believe it. What was *he* doing here?

When she turned and saw him, after the walls had stopped spinning and her heartbeat had returned to normal, she'd thought he'd followed her. Now, though, it seemed he was a guest.

This couldn't be a coincidence.

But coincidences must happen sometimes, otherwise why would there even be a word for a situation like this. Stay calm, she told herself, trying to still the jittery feeling in her stomach. That encounter in the street had happened outside of work. She wasn't even officially on the staff until Monday. And he might not even recognise her.

Could he be one of the A-listers that used Milner's for prenups and divorce settlements? A sports star, maybe, with those shoulders. Then again, there was something of the aristocrat about him, although Larry had told her that the firm currently had no royal clients.

He certainly had the arrogance of royalty, she thought, remembering his cool, grey gaze moving over her flushed, sweaty face. Back in LA and New York, she had handled plenty of wealthy clients. But this man was different. His authority wasn't rooted in money. Earlier he had been talking to her boss, Larry Milner, but now he was standing in front of one of the paintings, and there was something about the way he was standing at the edge of the room, apart from everyone and yet totally conspicuous. Like he was visiting the mortals from Mount Olympus.

His gaze suddenly snapped across the room, and she slid in front of the waiter, her heart beating in her throat. Why was he here? And given that he was such a jerk, why couldn't he look like one instead of a menswear model on a photo shoot?

He was too perfect, she thought irritably. It was bad enough that he had that jaw and those eyes that were the exact colour of the sky back home when the Pacific tossed up a storm. But he had to have that mouth too.

Resting, it was a beautiful shape, with a full lower lip and a slight downturn at the corners that was definitely designed to discourage unwanted intrusion into his space. But then he smiled at Larry, his lips curving slowly, reluctantly like petals unfolding for a winter sun and she wanted to drink in his smile, swallow it whole because it would taste like an old-fashioned, that perfect balance of sweet and spicy and smooth.

His kisses would taste like that too.

His kisses? What the—?

She breathed in sharply, swallowing Buck's fizz at the same time, and had to cover her mouth to stifle her choking.

'Having fun?'

She turned, her cheeks burning. It was Chloe, the associate who had shown her around the office on her first day. Willa had expected, been told, that the English were reserved. Chloe had taken that a step further and been wary and aloof. Now, though, she seemed to have thawed a little.

'Yes, it's a great party.'

Chloe held her gaze. 'There's an after-party too. Although, I don't know if the partners and the VIPs will go to that.'

Willa nodded, but she wouldn't be attending the after-party. She was here because she had been invited. Because not going would have meant having to come up with an excuse she didn't have and because nonattendance might mark her out, and as the only green-eyed brunette in a family of blue-eyed blonds, she had spent enough of her life already being marked out as different. Other.

But then, she was both those things.

Around her, the noise of the room receded like a tide pulling back from the shoreline.

Worse. She was a cuckoo in the nest. An impostor and an unwanted burden. A baby snuck into the home without permission to be incubated and nurtured and nourished. She'd always felt that there was something different about her. Right up until five months ago she'd assumed that it was because Amber wasn't her real mother. Not once had she thought Robert wasn't her real father.

Finding out the truth, the whole sorry truth about her parentage had been like standing on a fault-line as the earth cracked open. Sometimes she felt it would have been better if that had happened. At least then she could have slipped into the fissure and disappeared.

Instead, she was a living, breathing reminder of her mother's betrayal. A secret too awful to share with anyone. Except her father, Robert, who it turned out wasn't her father.

Her heart was thudding against her ribs heavily like someone pounding a door with their fist, and she took a sip of her drink, then another.

But thinking about that now was not an option. Otherwise, what was the point of being here? Not just at this party but here, in England. It had taken a lot of hard work to get this job. Becoming an associate at Milner's meant a new life in London. More importantly it had put an ocean between herself and the pain of the past.

'I'm sure it'll be fun either way,' Willa said diplomatically. 'Everyone seems very friendly.' Chloe blinked and then, as one, their gazes flicked across the room to where her unnamed nemesis stood, straight-backed and unsmiling again.

'Well, almost everyone,' she added, after a moment. 'I'm not sure if *fun* is part of his vocabulary.' She had a sudden, vivid memory of their showdown outside the hotel and of his face so dizzyingly close to hers.

Chloe shifted back on her heel, her gaze curious, perhaps even a little jealous. 'You spoke to him?'

'Briefly.' Willa revisited her encounter with the unnamed man. 'He's not my type.'

Chloe's gaze collided with hers, and then they both smiled, suddenly on common ground. The man on the other side of the room was every woman's type.

'Does he work here?'

Chloe shook her head. 'No, he's a friend of the boss.'

Great. That was just fabulous.

'I think they were at Harvard together.'

Willa let her gaze drift back to the talk dark-haired man. He was a lawyer. That scanned. Perhaps he'd rowed while he was at college, she thought. That would explain the shoulder and back muscles.

'So who is he?' she began, but Chloe's eyes had snapped to her phone screen.

'Sorry, I'm going to have to go. I told the doormen to let

me know when Nina Klein arrived. You know, the actress. We did her prenup, and her divorce. She's just out of rehab, so Larry asked me to babysit her.'

It was better that she didn't know his name, Willa thought as Chloe pocketed her phone. The less she knew, the looser the details, the easier it would be to forget him.

'It's fine. Go. I can mingle.'

Growing up as a Hamilton on the Californian island of Santa Catalina, mingling was second nature. The Hamiltons owned the only hotel on the island, and their festive events were a big deal to a small community.

But she had no intention of mingling now. Currently, her sole goal was to exit the ballroom without bumping into Larry's Harvard chum.

Which was easier than she thought because, for some reason she couldn't explain, even though she wasn't looking at him, she was aware of his place in the room at all times just as if they were connected by a thread. Avoiding him was like performing a complicated dance designed to keep her partner at arm's length, but finally, when her eyes were aching with the effort of not looking in his direction, she reached the door and made a casual, discreet exit from the room.

The woman had vanished. Again.

Ares let his gaze flicker around the room, but he knew she was no longer there. And he should be relieved. Her presence had been like a stone in his shoe, but now that she was gone, he felt...*thwarted*.

Not that he'd had any serious intention of—

Of what?

It wasn't as if he was into hooking up with random strangers. And besides, he was here to protect Ariana, to protect his family, and for that to happen, he needed to be razor-sharp and focused, not distracted by a pair of green eyes and some dazzlingly long legs.

Larry tried hard to persuade him to go out to dinner, but his stomach was still on New York time. And after six years of feeling people's furtive glances as he walked through a restaurant, of having to leave via the trade entrance to avoid the paparazzi, he still found it hard to eat in public.

As he walked back through the foyer, he heard the soft clink of ice on glass, and maybe it was the jet lag playing havoc with his head but quite suddenly he wanted a drink, and the Clarendon was exactly the kind of hotel that would have a top-notch selection of whiskies.

The bar was empty aside from a cluster of city boys with Windsor-knotted striped ties and an elderly couple who were sharing a bottle of champagne. A special occasion? he wondered and felt a pang as he remembered that if they were alive, his parents would be celebrating their fortieth wedding anniversary this year.

'Which Macallan's do you have?' he asked the bartender.

'We have a thirty-year-old, a forty-year-old and a 1964.'

'Which would you suggest? Be honest,' he added, because that was what mattered most to him, always.

'The forty. The '64 is for people with more money than taste,' his eyes flickered down the bar to the brokers. 'The forty has a beautiful burn.'

'Then, that's what I'll have.'

'Do you have a room number, sir?'

He shook his head. 'I'm just visiting.' Sliding onto one of the velvet-covered stools, he rested his elbows on the polished wood counter. Drinking in bars wasn't something he did often, but there was something oddly reassuring about watching the barman move back and forth in front of the glinting bottles and the huge mirror.

His brain blanked for a split second, and then he blinked, refocused.

Because she was here. The woman in white. He didn't turn to look at her. There was no need. He could see her reflection perfectly in the mirror. And he wasn't the only one looking at her. The young men in their striped suits were throwing furtive glances in her direction, curious no doubt to see a woman like her on her own. A beautiful woman. He could imagine their thought process.

Was she waiting for someone? Had she been stood up?

He knew because he was asking himself the same questions. But the weird thing was he knew the answers. His body tensed as, along with every other man in the bar, he watched her reflection slide off the stool with a feline grace that made everything in the room fade to a blur. Keeping his expression neutral, he watched her walk towards him.

It was almost unbearable. And then suddenly she stopped.

'You owe me a drink.'

He gestured towards the bar. 'Take your pick.'

She hesitated, on purpose, he realised a moment later. Playing with him like a cat. Imagining all the ways they could play together made the planet tilt sharply.

'Do you have any plans for the rest of the night?' she said then, her question as direct as her gaze, and he felt it snap tight between them, the thread that had made it easy for him all evening to know where she was in a room full of people.

'Why are you asking?'

She didn't answer. Instead, she slid her hand into his jacket and pulled out a pen from the inside pocket. His pulse twitched as she took hold of his hand and wrote something across the palm. 'In case you feel like watching the sunset.'

Ares stared down at his hand. She'd written a number. A phone number? Her room number? He looked up, intending to ask her, but she had vanished. Again.

The thought of her room, her bed, her on the bed made every hair on his body stand to attention, and he leaned forward, turning over his hand as the bartender approached.

'Yes, sir?'

'Is there anywhere in the hotel I could watch the sun set?'

'Yes, sir, the roof terrace. But unfortunately, it's already closed for the night. Can I get you another drink, sir?'

Ares shook his head. 'Just the bill.'

He took the lift to the top floor. Stepping out into the foyer, he spotted the door to the rooftop immediately. It had a keypad. Turning over his hand, he stared down at the number. He was suddenly unbearably conscious of the hammering of his heart.

This was insane. He didn't even know her name. And then he remembered the directness of her question. Her cactus-green gaze out in the street as she'd fronted up to him.

She was beautiful. Sexy. Honest. He liked that. Picturing her face as she'd asked him about his plans, he tapped in the number. There was a soft click, and he pushed the door, half expecting it to set off an alarm. But no bells rang. No lights flashed.

In the air-conditioned interior of the hotel, he'd forgotten the heatwave and now the warm air hit him like a wall. There was a fat crescent of sun still visible behind the London skyline, like an orange segment in a cocktail and there were lights, low-level ones that cast a soft glow across the roof terrace and the pool.

His blood thudded in his neck. And a similar glow across the woman in the pool.

Her hair was smooth against her skull, and he felt the shock of her beauty again as if they'd only just met.

'According to the bartender this terrace is closed.'

She didn't smile. 'That explains why it's so quiet.'

'But not how you got the security code.'

He felt his breath catch as she leaned back a fraction, her eyes glittering. 'Where there's a will there's a way.'

'I thought you wanted to watch the sun set. I didn't know you wanted to go for a swim.'

She watched him steadily as he walked towards the pool. 'It's still so hot, and the water's cool.'

He bent down and let his fingers trail through the water. 'It is. But I don't have anything to wear in the pool.'

There was a pause, and he watched, his pulse beating jerkily as she started to swim, moving gracefully into the shallow end of the pool. 'That's okay,' she said, and then he felt his body turn to stone as she rose up out of the water. 'I don't have anything either.'

CHAPTER TWO

HE HAD COME. She watched the man manoeuvre the line of loungers like a leopard cutting smoothly through the undergrowth, his dark, unyielding gaze tightening around her so that it felt as if it was wrapping itself over her skin.

Her naked body twitched. He could see everything. Not just see, she corrected herself as his pupils fattened: he was tasting.

Savouring.

Consuming.

Above the buzz of the traffic, she could hear Big Ben marking the hour. She felt like Cinderella. Only she had already scampered from the ballroom before midnight. And instead of leaving behind her slipper, she had stripped naked for her prince.

Her pulse jerked unsteadily in her throat as his gaze found her mouth.

At the party she had pushed back against the shimmering tension that filled the space between them, literally turning her back on him.

It didn't matter that she was more physically aware of him than she'd ever been of any other human. He was arrogant and off-limits.

Which was why she had kept moving in a carefully chosen orbit designed never to cross his path and had managed to leave that room with her pride intact. But he had gotten under her skin, crept through her bloodstream, snuck inside her head no matter how hard she tried to slide around him.

Her spine stiffened. She didn't do this. Men. Lovers. Boyfriends. Back at home, she hadn't dated much. She was famous for it, in fact.

The Ice Queen was one of her nicer nicknames.

She was never sure if the boys just wanted to date her because she was a Hamilton. Later she hadn't wanted to date anyone because she knew by then that she wasn't a Hamilton, and it simply reminded her that she was living a lie. Worse, it had made her realise that she didn't know who she was.

But tonight, and for the first time since she had found out the truth about her parents, she knew who she wanted to be. This man, this dark-eyed stranger, had cut through the doubt and all the lies she'd been told and all the lies she'd unwittingly lived.

And when he walked into the bar, it seemed less like luck and more like fate. A throw of loaded dice because she had wanted this man from the moment he'd stepped out of that stupid limousine with his storm-cloud eyes and those endless shoulders.

Hunger pooled in her belly, but she couldn't speak, and instead she turned and went back down the steps into the pool.

The water felt like a caress—or maybe that was his eyes. She could feel them following her, tracking the sway of her hips and she felt an ache in her pelvis that she hadn't felt in so long. Her lips ached too as if his gaze had pressed against them.

As she lowered herself into the water, she felt a rush of panic. He wasn't going to follow her. She had thought there was a connection between them, but she was so out of practice, maybe she had misread that heat in his eyes. Maybe it was just a simmering fury from what happened with his car. And things were different here in London. It wasn't just her accent. There were other things too that kept catching her out. Maybe this was one of those—

She sensed him before she felt the ripples as his body entered the water. Her breath somersaulted unsteadily in her throat, and then she turned her head to look over her shoulder, and—

Oh. My. Days.

Willa was conscious of her jaw dropping, of being not quite in control of herself and her reaction. The man was in the pool, close enough that if she reached forward, she could have touched him. Every nerve in her body felt alive with his nearness and his nakedness. Because, of course, he was naked too.

By the lights that ran at intervals along the interior of the pool, she could see the contoured expanse of his chest and the line of fine dark hair leading down to—

He was not fully erect, but he was aroused. Unmistakably aroused.

Nothing like this had ever happened to her. It was so intense and abandoned.

She tried to swallow. Her whole body was rigid with desire, and she considered moving closer to let him feel her eagerness, but now that he was here she wanted to just freeze time, drink him in slowly. Because there would be no repeats.

'It feels good,' he said then, and she watched his hands move across the surface of the water, slowly tracing a shape that made her skin itch.

How was he doing this? For so long, she hadn't wanted to be touched. To be touched was to be known, and she didn't know who she was, so how could anyone else?

But this man made her feel differently. He made her feel that not being touched by him would be appalling. Unbearable.

'The water. It feels good,' he repeated.

He would feel good too, she thought wildly, her eyes skimming over the smooth skin of his stomach. So much beautiful smooth gold skin. It had been a long time since she had touched any skin other than her own, and she realised that she missed it.

'The views are good too.' She half turned towards the London skyline to let her gaze drift across Big Ben and the Gherkin and the Shard. A fat, wavering strip of orange like a tiger's fur was melting into the buildings.

She was melting too, she thought as she glanced back to find him watching her in that intent way of his, as if she was a puzzle he was trying to solve.

'Yes, they are,' he said slowly, and she felt something inside of her loosen as his gaze drifted down to where her breasts were now exposed.

Her nipples tightened, then tightened again as she heard his sharp intake of breath. She let herself sink a little, floating beneath the surface. His gaze felt like a blow-torch, burning into her skin, softening her at the edges so that she could feel herself changing into something new.

'Is that why I'm here? So you could show me the view?' His voice, the hoarseness in it, made her legs part slightly. He was doing that too, and without even touching her, she thought with a jolt.

She shook her head slowly, feeling his grey eyes track the movement just as if he was using his hands.

'We didn't get properly introduced.'

'And this is how you introduce yourself?' He studied her face in that fierce, focused way of his that made heat slide under her skin like a hot knife through butter.

'No, normally I just say *Hi, I'm Willa*.' She didn't give him her surname. There was no need. 'And then you'd say—'

'*Hi, I'm Ares*,' he said softly.

Was that Greek? But she didn't need to know that either.

'So is that it? Are we properly introduced?'

'We are.'

'Then, what do you want to do now?' His mouth curled up infinitesimally at the corners into an almost smile as his question vibrated through her, and now she was holding her breath so that it was impossible to answer.

But she didn't need words for what she wanted to happen next.

She reached over and hooked her hands around his neck and kissed him, and panic, adrenaline, shock and relief at having done it spiked inside her as he kissed her back.

His hands were moving over her body. She could feel his cock pressing against her stomach, and the size and the hardness of it made her slip sideways a little, and then he was reaching under the water to lift her legs around his hips, taking the weight of her in his hands.

They kissed back and forth hungrily, tasting one another, and she had never kissed or been kissed like this. His mouth was possessive and devastating, and then there was the hard, insistent press of his erection against her stomach.

He scraped the hair from her neck, sucking her shoulder, and she moaned into the rhythm of his open-mouthed kiss, her fingers biting into his biceps.

'Easy,' he murmured against her lips, and then he was moving them both back into the shallow end of the pool.

Out of the water her breasts felt heavy and full, and a shiver ran over her skin as Ares sucked first one then the other into his mouth, circling the swollen tip with his tongue until she wanted to cry out. Not because it hurt but because anything that started had to end, and she didn't want this to end.

'Don't stop,' she panted, and he lifted his mouth and kissed her fiercely.

'I'm just getting started.'

He lifted her onto the shallow steps, his hands still cupping her bottom, and then he was spreading her legs, lowering his mouth to brush a kiss across the triangle of soft dark curls. Flattening his tongue, he licked the pulse beating between her thighs, and she arched against his mouth, moaning. He held her gaze, his grey eyes soft and light, sliding inside her as easily as his tongue was sliding back and forth.

And everything shuddered out of focus, and she was lost, adrift, spinning and splitting, her senses spiralling out of control, and yet she could still feel herself anchored to his mouth. He was holding her together and undoing her at the same time, and then she was rising up on the crest of a wave, and there was nothing but him, this man, this stranger and his tongue swiping inside her and his hands gripping her waist.

A few more strokes and she'd be gone, but she wanted to feel him, feel him lose control.

'Come inside me.'

She was pulling at his shoulders, his hair, so needy for him it hurt, scraped raw by her desire.

'Let me get a condom.'

'It's fine. I'm safe.'

Safe. Was that the word? For a moment the whole of it, all the pain and misery of finding out that as well as losing her past, she was to be denied a future, threatened to swamp her, but she pushed back against it.

'Please, I want you insi—'

But before the words were out of her mouth, he was kissing her, filling her with his need, and then he was angling his cock, sliding it in, and now he was filling her, and she was no longer conscious of anything but his nearness, and how big he was and how hard.

And he was kissing her as if he felt the same, and she jerked forward, her body no longer her own. She couldn't get enough of him, and she was almost climbing over his body, choking on a noise that rose from inside of her, losing herself in the fluttering heat as she contracted around him, and then he was moving too, urgently with a hint of impatience as if he had been holding himself in check not just for minutes but from when they'd met in the street.

His breath hitched and his hands splayed against her bottom, and he arched against her in a way that had her nearly sliding out of his arms, and then he made a sound that tipped her over the edge, and her pleasure broke her apart and she shattered around him, again and again and again.

Ares woke at exactly five fifteen.

It hadn't always been that way, but since the accident that had killed his parents, he woke without fail at the same time every morning.

At first, he had assumed it was a pattern that would shift with time, but when it hadn't, he'd seen a sleep therapist and learned that it wasn't just the brain that held memories. Trauma and shock could be absorbed into the fascia of the body, and basically his body was replaying that morning over and over, starting from when Iona, the Konstantinou's housekeeper, shook him awake in the darkness to tell him that the police were downstairs.

Of course, it was about more than just reliving the trauma. There was always a moment or two when he could pretend to himself that he could somehow change what happened. Or maybe do a better job of breaking the news to his grandfather and Ariana.

But on this occasion, it wasn't the past waking him but his phone, quivering in the darkness. His stomach folding in on itself, he grabbed it from beside the bed and stared down at the illuminated screen. It was a message from Ariana.

Guess what? I have a blue aura! Which means I'm powerful, peaceful and perceptive.

The message was followed by a couple of emojis. A face surrounded by hearts, which he understood, and a fire, which he didn't.

And now she was typing again.

I really love him, Ares. And I know you think that I'm too young and that he isn't The One, but he is.

Another emoji, this time of some praying hands.

His jaw tightened. Ari was young, too young to marry some chancer with puppy-dog eyes who carved driftwood for a living. But he needed her to stay at the spa while he got this prenup finalised, and so instead of saying what he really thought, he typed back

I know how you feel. But the whole point of you going to the spa was for me to deal with the boring bits while you unwind with Helena. So just try and chill. We'll speak tomorrow.

He hesitated, then added an emoji of a person in the lotus position.

Holding his breath, he watched the three dots dance in a bubble. Ari was his polar opposite. Mercurial where he was fixed. A shooting star bisecting the night sky, trailing light and laughter in her wake. Telling her that her parents were dead was the hardest thing he had ever done. To have made that light leave her eyes was not something he'd ever forget, and he'd sworn he would do everything in his power to protect her. Even if that meant playing with the facts a little and letting Ari think he was on her side.

His phone vibrated again. Another message.

My bad! I forgot I'm seven hours behind you here. ☺ Go back to sleep. I'll call later. Love you.

Ares switched off his phone. *Go back to sleep.* Ari made it sound so simple. And it was for her, because he hadn't woken her that morning. He had waited, wanting to let her sleep because while she slept, she still had her parents.

At least he had given her that.

Putting his phone down, he breathed out softly.

At this point, normally, he rolled over and switched on the light and then headed straight to the bathroom. Now, though, he stayed where he was: for once he didn't want to move. Moving would break the spell, and it would mean uncurling his body from the woman lying next to him.

Willa.

There was enough light in the room that he could see the outline of her hip, and it was impossible not to let his hand caress that curve. He felt his cock harden, and again it was impossible not to press into the soft cushion of her bottom.

Wake up, he thought, and he stared down at the small oval face, willing her eyelashes to flutter open and her eyes to find his in the darkness as they had done multiple times in the night. But Willa stayed sleeping, and he couldn't bring himself to rouse her.

But he would have to move because he needed a glass of water.

Or maybe it was lust presenting as thirst. Either way, he needed to move. Unpeeling his arm from across her body, he edged backwards and then rolled smoothly out of bed. He moved slowly, cautiously across the room.

'Skatá.'

He swore as he trod on something, grabbing at the back

of a chair as he lost his balance. There was a soft thump as something hit the carpet and he tensed, his gaze moving back instinctively towards the bed and the sleeping figure.

Willa shifted noiselessly, her arm flinging across the pillow, and he held his breath until he heard her soft, regular breathing.

Damn it. Reaching down, he massaged his foot, feeling in the darkness for what he'd trodden on. It was his belt, still looped through his trousers. Normally, he folded his clothes carefully, but nothing about last night had been habitual.

Everything had been frenzied, urgent, insistent, even when they'd made it back to her bedroom. It had never been like that with anyone before, and he still didn't know why it felt that way with Willa, just that it had. There was a need there that pulled him under like a rip tide. It was impossible to fight. He hadn't wanted to fight it.

And surrendering felt so good. So right. She fitted against him so smoothly, soft and yielding like petals curving over a stamen. Maybe he would ask her to have breakfast with him. Or maybe they could just stay here in her room and have breakfast in bed. Or stay and skip breakfast altogether.

Something flickered at the margins of his vision, and he crouched, leaning forward in the darkness, his gaze dragging down irresistibly. And then his pulse juddered to a halt.

His fingers trembled as they curled around the thin, gold chain. But it was the ring hanging from the chain that had turned his heart to ice.

Three diamonds jostling for supremacy on a slim gold band. Sharp-edged, glittering with a brilliance unmatched in nature, they seemed to light up the room, and smother the lightness in his chest. On the inside of the ring, he could just make out some words. *Just getting started.*

It must have dropped out of her bag when he knocked it off the chair.

He swallowed with difficulty because there was no mistaking what it was. It was an engagement ring.

It was also a betrayal of trust. He had been here before.

His heart jerked heavily against his ribs, and mechanically he picked up her bag, dropped the chain inside and hung the bag back on the chair. His shock was matched—no, swamped—by his anger, and he breathed in sharply, trying to push back against the choking swirl of adrenaline, striving for calm.

But how could he be calm?

He straightened up, the ache in his chest swelling like a wave. A better question would be how he could have been so stupid? Again? How could he have let himself be gulled like that? Again.

His gaze pulled towards the sleeping woman. He was such an idiot, letting vanity and lust blind him to the truth. He felt a hot rush of shame burn his face because the truth was that her hunger had flattered him into thinking she wanted him, and that had fed his desire. But it was the thrill of the illicit and the secrecy of an affair that had caused that feverish light in her eyes.

A ripple of nausea cramped his stomach as he remembered that day six years ago when he'd let himself into Zoe's apartment, the apartment she had insisted on keeping despite staying over at his most nights. It was for her parents' benefit, or that's what she'd said at the time, but he knew now that she'd needed a place to conduct her affair.

It was the ring that had stopped him in his tracks. He had seen it from the doorway, sitting on the top of her dressing table, glinting in the sunlight like a lighthouse warning of hidden rocks. But he was so trusting, so naive that it wasn't until he saw her body moving beneath her lover, that he understood what he was seeing.

And now it was happening again.

For a moment, the anger reared up inside him, blunt-edged and savage, and he wanted to stride over to the bed and wake Willa and demand answers, an apology, an explanation. But he hadn't wanted to hear Zoe's lies, and he didn't want to hear Willa's.

Instead, he dressed quickly and silently and without so much as a glance at the bed, he let himself out of the room and strode down the hallway to the lift.

'How far away are we now?'

Leaning forward, Willa watched the cab driver's eyes flick to the rearview mirror.

'Six minutes, tops.' He paused. 'So what did you do?'

'Excuse me?'

'Why do you need a lawyer?' He grinned. 'Fetter Lane. That's where all the lawyers are.'

She shrugged. 'Oh, I robbed a bank.'

He raised an eyebrow. 'Don't they have banks in America?'

'I've robbed them all.'

He laughed then, and after a moment Willa smiled. Her best smile. Not the glacial, keep-your-distance smile she had perfected as a child. A smile designed to combat the curiosity that most people felt on meeting the eldest of the four legendary Hamilton girls, the one with the tragic back story. The same smile that had earned her the reputation of being stuck-up and entitled.

Of course, she didn't know then that she wasn't one of the Hamilton girls. Not a Hamilton at all. She kept people at a distance because growing up she had felt like an outsider, and she was scared that if she let them get close, they might sense what she was feeling. Maybe even agree with her.

She had earned her reputation for being aloof. The triplet sisters, Carrie, Ruth and Kendall, had sleepovers and camp-outs and soccer shoot-outs on the beach, but aside from when she rode or danced, she was busy working, trying to hide that she was different—hard as a brunette in a family of blonds. Trying to earn her place as a Hamilton.

Later when she found out the truth and the difference was not simply a fear but a fact, she had fled. Because being at home made her feel guilty and fraudulent and alone.

But now she was in London.

Just another anonymous face in a megacity. Except here, she thought, gratitude and relief washing over her as she stepped into the elevator just as they did every time she walked into Milner's offices in Fetter Lane.

She liked the building with its marble columns and wood panelling. Liked her colleagues, even Chloe. Liked her boss. Liked her job.

Even liked the coffee which everyone back in the States had warned her about.

Because for once, the pain of being an outsider, a fraud and a burden had receded. She was here because Milner's wanted her. Because she was good at her job.

She even had proof. Her pulse did a tiny, triumphant dance. She had been on her way to court to sit in on a particularly complex custody arrangement when Maggie, the legal secretary she shared with Chloe, had called to tell her that Mr Milner wanted her back in the office immediately. Nancy was ill, and her client needed a prenup ASAP.

Willa felt a bubble of happiness swell against her ribs. *Her* client now.

Her first—in London anyway.

If only she had someone she could tell.

There was someone. Or rather she'd thought he might become someone.

Ares.

Her throat tightened. Maybe she didn't know his surname,

but there had been a connection with him that seemed to transcend the simple stuff of bodies and breath. Or that's how it had felt at the time. And she thought he'd felt it too.

But waking just before six, the bed was empty. He was gone.

It was stupid to care, and she couldn't explain why she did, even now, two weeks after it happened. It wasn't as if they'd made plans or promises.

Staring straight ahead, she pressed her thighs together, remembering how Ares had shaped her with his hands, pulled her hands above her head and licked her breasts. She'd had sex before, but it hadn't felt like that. Like wildfire lighting her up, consuming her and leaving her still smouldering.

She could have asked around to find out more about him. But that would have drawn attention to something that she wanted to stay private.

She had thought about searching for him online.

Her shoulders stiffened as she remembered waking alone in her hotel room. But why would she search for him?

He'd made it clear that he had gotten what he wanted. And what he wanted, all he wanted, was to use her body. But she had used his right back, so they were even.

'There you are.'

Maggie was waiting for her as she stepped out of the elevator.

Willa grimaced. 'Sorry, the traffic was a nightmare.'

'It's fine.' Maggie glanced at her watch. 'He's here already, but Mr Milner said to put him in the Zen Den.' That was Larry's nickname for the room used by the staff to discuss matters like prenups that needed a clear head. 'He wants to speak to you first. Here.' She held out a file. 'You won't have time to read it, but you need to look the part. Mr Konstantinou's family goes way back with the firm, so—'

So no pressure, then, Willa thought, her stomach tightening with nerves and excitement. But it was also more proof that Larry thought she had the chops for the job. 'So what happened to Nancy?' she said, tucking the file under her arm.

Maggie stopped midstride, clearly thrilled to be asked. 'Her appendix burst this morning. She was rushed to A&E about an hour ago.'

Willa felt her jaw tighten. A little over five months had passed since she was taken to hospital with suspected appendicitis. She still had her appendix, but the repercussions of that day continued to haunt her now, and it took a fraction of a second before she could speak.

Fortunately, Maggie was so excited to be the bearer of bad news that she didn't notice. 'It's awful, isn't it?'

Grateful to be reminded of how a normal person was supposed to react, Willa nodded. 'Awful. Is she going to be okay?'

She felt a pang of sympathy. Nancy was the partner who had sat in on her interview, and she'd liked her immediately. She was maybe a decade older. One of those English women with a flawless complexion and a soft voice who was whip-smart, no-nonsense. The kind of woman who in America would be called a *tough cookie*.

'She will be, but she's not going to be coming back for at least three weeks, maybe longer. Apparently, there was an abscess.' Maggie's eyes widened ghoulishly, enjoying the drama now that it was over. 'Which means that her caseload is being shared between the partners. But Mr Milner thought you'd be a good fit for the Konstantinou prenup.'

'I did, indeed. Thank you, Maggie,' said Larry Milner, in person.

Blushing, Maggie gave Willa a quick, encouraging smile, and then she was gone, heels tapping on the polished oak floorboards.

'Thanks for getting back here so quickly.' Larry gestured towards the end of the corridor. 'I take it Maggie's brought you up to speed on the Nancy situation.'

'Yes. It's awful,' she repeated. 'It's supposed to be very painful.'

More painful than the cyst on her ovary that burst. The one she had mistaken for appendicitis. But it wasn't the pain she remembered from that day. It was the furtive conversation between her father and the doctors and the tension in the air. It had felt like a wave curling over, suspended above her, waiting to break. And then it had, and everything she had thought to be true had been swept away. She was swept away too, spinning and swirling in the foaming water, dragged far, far out to sea, so far that she didn't know how to get back to land, to home.

Because she hadn't realised then what she knew now. That her home wasn't her home. It was just pretending to be a home like the set of a sitcom.

Larry winced. 'The pain's supposed to be terrible. Worse than childbirth, my wife said. And she's given birth twice, so she should know.'

But she would never know, Willa thought, biting the inside of her cheek and forcing a smile.

Of course, Larry had no idea that his joke had sent her back in time to that Californian hospital and the doctor who had taken away her future just hours before she lost her past.

It didn't matter how many times it happened, being reminded that she would struggle to get pregnant naturally was still a lot. There were options. Surrogacy. Adoption. IVF. All might give her a child one day, but maybe she wasn't supposed to have one. Maybe it was a sign, proof that she was meant to roam the earth alone.

Which sounded so like something her drama-queen, younger sister Ruth would say she almost laughed out loud, and for a few half seconds she felt the warm endorphin rush of being part of a tribe that was hardwired into the DNA of every human.

But the Hamiltons weren't her tribe. If her dark hair and green eyes hadn't made that obvious, finding out that her DNA was unrelated had. And the chances of her DNA being shared with anyone else, without a lot of intervention, were pretty much zero.

'Maggie said you wanted to talk to me about the Konstantinou prenup.'

Hearing the excitement of her voice, she felt a ripple of panic. It was a long time since she had allowed herself to show her feelings. Caring too much about anything was a risk. But this was different. This was work. So much had already been taken away from her. Work was her focus and her solace now.

'That's right. Nancy has set up a fine framework for the prenup, but obviously she is going to be indisposed, and this is a matter of some urgency.'

Willa felt her pulse stall as Larry stopped in front of the door to the luxurious office where the wealthier clients were taken to be interviewed. Now he turned to face her, his expression suddenly serious.

'But also, some sensitivity. The client is a high net-worth individual, but he's a friend. Our families go back a long way, so it's important to me that we do this right.'

Willa ignored her somersaulting stomach. 'That's all I ever want,' she said firmly.

'Good. I know this must feel a little daunting, but I feel confident that you are a good fit for the client.' Smiling, Larry opened the door. As Willa followed him into the room, she caught a glimpse of the seated man's dark hair and broad shoulders.

'Ares. I thought I'd drop in and say hi and introduce you to Nancy's replacement.'

Ares?

Willa felt her smile freeze to her lips. Her heart was suddenly banging. *Ares?* She had probably misheard. It couldn't possibly be her Ares.

Her Ares? She was still reeling from her use of a possessive pronoun in front of any name, let alone the man who had left her sleeping after sharing her bed for five feverish hours two weeks ago.

But then he got to his feet, and she saw the flicker of shock play across his features, and her heart stopped beating and the floor beneath her feet opened up and she was dropping into a sharp-edged void. Because it was him.

Ares Konstantinou was her one-night stand.

Only he wasn't hers.

And now that she knew his surname, it all made sense that she had woken alone. Because this man wasn't a keeper.

He was the runaway groom.

And he was furious.

CHAPTER THREE

WILLA STARED AT the man in front of her, mute with shock and sheer disbelief.

He looked, if anything, even better than he had that first night in another of those custom-made suits that sat somewhere between armour and a work of art.

Reluctantly, she let her gaze graze his face.

He really was astonishingly good-looking. Beautiful in that way only very masculine men could be. But then, as someone a whole lot wiser than her once said, beauty was only skin-deep. Ares Konstantinou might have the face of an angel and the body of an Adonis but for once the media was right. He was every bit as arrogant and ill-mannered and ruthless as the man in the headlines.

So why was her body acting as though he was the human equivalent of catnip? Why did she feel flustered and twitchy and cornered all at once?

Probably because she was struggling to reconcile how the man she'd slept with two weeks ago could also be a billionaire heartbreaker.

And more crucially, the newest and most important client of her career.

She had thought about Ares so often these last two weeks. Too often. Mostly at night but sometimes when she was strap-hanging in the tube, she would remember the weight of his body and his hot breath against her throat as she canted her hips up to meet his, and her face would burn. Other times she had imagined coming face-to-face with him and telling him exactly what she thought of his shoddy behaviour. But it had never crossed her mind that they would meet like this, here in her new workplace, with her new boss beaming beside her.

Resentment and confusion and frustration swelled and swirled in her stomach, making the fact that his attention was focused on shaking her boss's hand both another insult and a tiny, temporary act of mercy.

Larry turned towards her, still smiling. 'Willa, this is my good friend, Ares Konstantinou. Ares, this is our newest associate, Willa Hamilton. I'm not sure if you caught her name in the message I left you.' He screwed up his face. 'I was coming out of an underground car park.'

As Ares tilted his head in her direction, Willa was ready for him, and meeting his gaze she saw that he was ready for her too. That in the time it had taken for Larry to make his introduction he had regrouped and was now staring at her steadily, taking in her new status.

The slight narrowing of his eyes suggested that the change pleased him less than it did her. But why? He wasn't the one who'd been made to feel like a fool.

'Ms Hamilton.' He paused and held out his hand, and she took it because not doing so would have looked weird, but it was hard not to jump out of her skin when his fingers curled around hers.

Two weeks ago, his touch had burned her. No one had ever touched her like that. Even the memory of his hands moving on her belly and on her hips and between her thighs made her breath knot in her throat because Ares Konstantinou had a great sense of touch.

Precise. Measured. Intuitive.

Now, though, his grip felt just a fraction too tight as if he wanted to pull her close and demand what she was doing there.

'Willa's a new recruit.' Larry smiled. 'She was actually at the anniversary party, but I'm guessing you two didn't cross paths.'

'No,' she lied.

'No.' He spoke a fraction after her, and the sensation of his voice overlapping hers made Willa's body stiffen, and she had a sudden flashback to the moment in the pool when he'd thrust inside her and they'd both cried out at the same time.

Larry's glance ping-ponged between them. 'Well, as I said in my message, I know you're going to be as impressed as I am with Willa's skill and care, but I also think in relation to Ariana she has a kind of superpower. Being around the same age as Ariana makes her uniquely placed to get inside your sister's mindset.'

Glancing over at Ares's taut jaw-line, Willa was willing to bet her entire annual salary that he was wishing he had a superpower of his own that would allow him to turn back time and erase her from his life.

'But she doesn't need me giving her the hard sell, so I'm just going to leave you in her capable hands.' Reaching out, Larry clapped Ares on the shoulder. 'Don't forget we're having lunch.'

There was a taut silence like a held breath as the door closed behind him, and suddenly they were alone. Again. Just like they had been on the roof of the Clarendon.

Time stalled, each second creeping forward in slow motion, and she felt his gaze, the stinging intensity of his focus.

'Is this some kind of a joke?'

His voice snapped across the space between them like the crack of a whip, and she met his gaze head-on. Because even though he was a high net-worth individual and a family friend of her boss, she refused to kowtow to a man who didn't even have the decency and good manners to say goodbye. Even if it was just sex.

She met his gaze. 'I don't know. Do you feel like a punchline?'

The grey of his eyes darkened to black. 'Don't get cute with me, Ms Hamilton.' His gaze dropped to her ring finger momentarily as if to check her marital status, and watching his face harden, she knew that Larry's hard sell hadn't found a buyer.

There was a beautiful malachite and ormolu clock on the mantelpiece to the left of Ares's shoulder, and she watched the second hand tick forward before saying crisply, 'Then, don't get snippy with me, Mr Konstantinou. I didn't ask for this. Or make it happen. Unless you think I can miraculously burst someone else's appendix by the power of thought alone.'

He was staring at her as if he couldn't quite believe what he was hearing, which was understandable because she couldn't quite believe what she was saying. But why was he making out that this was something she had engineered?

Her heart thumped dully in her chest as he stared down at her, his expression hardening. 'You seem to have forgotten who you're talking to.'

With another man, another entitled member of the one percent she might have taken his words at face value, but there was something in his eyes that arrowed into her, stirring up memories of their night together. Because that was what this was about. This strange, weaving tension between them, part anger, part frustration, part lingering contrail of heat.

She had broken the rules by turning up in his life like this.

She lifted her chin. 'I haven't forgotten.'

'I see.' His voice was terse. 'So do you talk to every client like this?'

Client. She fought the wild beating of her heart as the word echoed ominously inside her head. But whatever he had been before, that was what he was now.

'No, I don't.' She didn't sleep with them either. The memory of his body slanting over hers in the pool made everything tilt a little, and she reached out to steady herself on the back of a chair.

'But obviously I didn't expect to see you here.' Didn't expect to see him again, period. 'It was a shock. For both of us.' She glanced towards the door, longing to escape, but there would be no escape unless she could come up with a reason for not wanting to work with Ares—other than the truth, of course.

Maybe his thoughts were following the same path, because his eyes narrowed on her face. 'I take it you didn't know who I was when you invited me up to the roof?'

Was that why he was so annoyed with her? It was tempting to dismiss his question as some kind of paranoia, but when Larry had told her who they were meeting, her mind had gone there too.

It felt too staged, too unlikely to be a coincidence, the two of them meeting like this. But now she had all the facts, now she knew that Ares was both a friend of Larry's and a client of the firm, it was still an unwelcome shock to find herself face-to-face with her one-night stand. And yet, it felt less surprising.

But that didn't mean she had known about the surprise.

Briefly she replayed that first encounter on the street. There was a moment of recognition, but truthfully, she just hadn't put two and two together until she'd heard his surname a moment ago.

She hadn't followed the Konstantinou/Gilmour split story at the time. There were other, bigger things happening in her life, but she could remember their names being clickbait for months. Because who didn't love a story about a bride jilted at the altar? It was basic Schadenfreude, and of course it had no doubt helped that the bride and groom looked like something out of a telenovela.

No wonder she had woken alone in her hotel room.

Any man who could walk away from a woman in a bridal gown with several hundred witnesses watching was going to have no trouble hitting and splitting without a word. And yet—and she knew she was being ridiculous—it still stung that it hadn't been what she'd thought. That she had misread the signals so spectacularly.

'No, I didn't,' she said, after a moment. 'I mean, yes, your face looked familiar, but that's the trouble when you move to a new city. Everyone's a stranger, but they also look like someone you know back home.' She hesitated. 'I didn't know you were a client. I would never have slept with you if I had.' The sceptical look on his face made her want to throttle him with his silk tie. Instead, she said firmly, 'I want you to know that's not something I do—'

'How old are you?' His voice cut across hers, but it wasn't the abruptness of his question that startled her but the way he was looking at her, as if he was seeing her as a woman again, not his lawyer.

'I'm twenty-nine.' It made her feel nervous, exposed, him wanting to know things about her, and she told herself that was why it was suddenly hard to breathe, and why her body felt taut and achy and hot—

She bit the side of her cheek as he closed the gap between them, and she found herself in the gravitational field of his body. For a moment he held her eyes captive just as he had up on the roof of the hotel. As if he was hungry and fierce and unstoppable and that urbane, civilised exterior was just a veneer.

Her toes curled up in her shoes as he reached into his jacket and pulled out his phone. Swiping across the screen, he held out the phone. It was a photo of a young woman with glossy dark hair and bee-stung lips that were pulled into a smile that made the camera's flash unnecessary because her beauty was luminous.

'My sister, Ariana, is twenty-four, but she's particularly young for her age, for which I am partially to blame. I am her guardian, and she's grown up protected and indulged by everyone around her so she is unusually trusting and naive, enough to believe that she is in love, and perhaps she is.'

There was a tension to him now that hadn't been there before, as if instead of talking about love he was picking his way through a field of landmines.

Then again, that was probably how love made him feel; otherwise, why would he have fled so publicly from his bride?

'Perhaps she is,' he repeated, this time placing an emphasis on the *she*. 'Which is why I've sent her to relax at a spa in Mexico with her godmother. But—' more emphasis '— as for her *beau*, I would imagine David Arteta's affections are more deeply stirred by the trust fund she is set to inherit on her twenty-fifth birthday in just under seven months. Of which he is, no doubt, fully aware.'

There was a coldness to his voice now, and she felt a shiver run down her spine—and something a little like pity for David Arteta. Ares Konstantinou would be a formidable opponent.

She cleared her throat, took a breath. 'And there's no possibility that she could be pregnant?'

His profile was like a granite cliff face. 'None. She did a test at the spa. They insist on it because some of the treatments are not recommended for pregnant women.'

'It's good to have that confirmed. And how old is Mr Arteta?'

He frowned, seemingly surprised by her question. Or perhaps it was merely being reminded that she was his lawyer.

'Twenty-three.'

They were both young, then. Did that mean David Arteta was a gold-digger? Possibly. But if she had to guess, judging by the photo of Ariana, the money was probably just a potential bonus right now.

She met his gaze. 'In my experience, young love is often oblivious to real-world matters.'

He stared at her, his mouth curling into something almost like a sneer. 'A lawyer who believes in love. You surprise me. I wouldn't have had you down as a hearts-and-flowers kind of woman.'

Her shoulders stiffened. Did she believe in love? Once upon a time, absolutely and unsurprisingly. Her mother's tragic death and her father's status as a grief-struck widower with a tiny baby more or less demanded that their love be the real deal, till-death-us-do-part type of love. A love that had defied death through her.

But then she'd had that terrible conversation with her father and her view had changed.

Everything had changed.

The foundations of her identity had been smashed to rubble, and it was impossible not to look at the world around her and see only its fragility and falsity.

And her perception of the world wasn't the only thing that had changed. She felt different. There was a hollowness at the heart of her, a lack of certainty. Loving someone, being loved, felt suddenly out of reach, because how could you love or be loved when you weren't even sure of who you were?

But the scabs had hardly healed on those wounds, and now was not the time to be picking at them.

She met Ares's narrow-eyed gaze. 'I'm not. But even if I was, love is as irrelevant to the law as your sister's and her fiancé's ages, given that both are legally old enough to marry.'

'She will not be marrying him,' he said, and there was an

authority to his voice, a reminder that he was a man used to getting his own way. 'Whatever my sister might think, that is the true purpose of this prenup. To deter. To discourage. To dissuade her lover by making it absolutely clear that it will not be financially worthwhile for him to pursue her down the aisle.'

Was that why *he'd* bolted from her bed? From his wedding? Had he overlooked a prenup for himself and fled to protect his finances? Was that why he wanted to get everything watertight for his sister?

Leaving those questions unasked, she nodded. 'I understand. And there are clauses and conditions that can help with that.'

Flicking open the folder, she scanned the document.

'Given the short time between your sister meeting Mr Arteta and the two of them getting engaged, I would start by suggesting an extended cooling-off period. Typically, twenty-eight days is considered the bare minimum between any prenup being signed and the marriage. As a rule, I always push for longer. It will give your sister pause for thought, and Mr Arteta may well lack the patience to wait. But if they do go ahead and the marriage fails, the court will be satisfied that both parties entered into the agreement of their own free will, which makes it more likely to uphold the terms of the prenup.'

She took a breath and braced her shoulders, but there was no point in prolonging this agony. 'But this is something you can discuss with my replacement.'

There was a short, unpleasant silence. Ares's expression didn't alter, but there was an undercurrent of hardness in his voice as he said, 'Your replacement?'

She lifted a hand to her throat, feeling her pulse jerking under the tips of her fingers, and automatically, to calm herself, she reached beneath her blouse to touch her mother's engagement ring. His gaze followed the movement of her hand, his pupils drilling through the thin fabric.

Now, the chill in the air had nothing to do with the air conditioning. His gaze was so harsh and unwavering she felt as if it was turning her to ice, and she had to force the muscles in her face to smile stiffly.

'Obviously I'm not suggesting we need to discuss what happened between us after the anniversary party.'

A sense of foreboding snaked down her spine as Ares straightened his shoulders, and she wondered if she should have kept quiet. But that was why she had come to London. To stop hiding, to stop pretending. She didn't want to live like that anymore. To be the skeleton in someone's wardrobe.

She forced her chin up.

'But I would also prefer to be transparent—'

'Transparent?' He stared down at her, his mouth curving into what could only be described as a mocking smile, his gaze rolling through her like storm-clouds so that it was suddenly hard to catch her breath, and she wondered if her heart had ever beaten so loudly.

She cleared her throat. 'Yes, transparent. Given our…history, I think it goes without saying that another lawyer would be a better fit for you,' she said carefully. 'So what I would recommend is for the two of us to come up with a suitable explanation for why that should be the case. For example, you could say you would prefer to deal with a partner as opposed to an associate. That's just an idea, of course. You might have your own thoughts.'

Staring down at Willa Hamilton, Ares felt his whole body tense.

It had bugged him for weeks now. Not knowing her full name. Even though it was better that way. It made that whole crazy night easier to file under *Miscellaneous*. Or that was the theory, but the reality was that he couldn't let it go.

Couldn't let *her* go.

She was captive inside his head, still naked, the smell of her damp, warm skin playing havoc with his thoughts, making his own skin twitch like a dog with fleas.

And now she was here and, apparently, she was his lawyer.

Getting to his feet when Larry came into the room, he hadn't registered the woman at first. Partly because he was focusing on Larry. And partly because it hadn't occurred to him that Nancy Kemp's replacement might be the woman he'd slept with two weeks ago.

He stared at Willa, disbelief vying with fury, except fury didn't really do justice to the sheer scale and breadth of what he was feeling, what he'd felt when he found that ring. It shouldn't hurt so much. He'd told himself that at the time, and it was even more true now, and yet it did. It felt like a betrayal. That she could lie to him, that her body had lied to him—

Their night together had been a new kind of pleasure. The heat of her and his own pulsing hunger had made something charged and unparalleled shimmer through his body.

How could that have been a lie?

But it wasn't just that he felt betrayed physically.

She'd been so direct that night, so explicit, never mind that she'd felt even better than she looked or that her body had fitted with his in all the right ways. He had trusted her, believed her, and that was what hurt.

His head was spinning. Or maybe that was the walls.

Why had she picked him? Why was she betraying her fiancé? How did she live with herself with such apparent sang-froid? He'd wanted answers to those questions. He still wanted answers. One way or another, he intended to get them.

And maybe in the moment, he'd gotten confused into thinking their night together had somehow forged a connection beyond bodies and breath. But he'd been wrong.

She'd been wrong too, to think that she was in charge here.

'I don't think so.'

He let his gaze rest on her face, wanting to see her reaction. He was not disappointed.

She frowned. 'What does that mean?'

'Your recommendation. I've decided to ignore it.'

Her eyes slammed into his, and he felt as if he'd been kicked by a horse. Her irises darkened, he realised, when she was angry and frustrated.

And aroused.

His teeth were suddenly on edge, his body so tense he felt as though he might explode. But also, for the first time in a very long time, he felt alive, stimulated. Invested.

'It's inconvenient, and I don't like to be inconvenienced.'

She was staring at him in confusion. 'Surely you can't want to work with me. And you don't have to. You're an important client. You can call the shots on this.'

'I can, and I am,' he said with deceptive casualness. 'I want you to work for me.'

She took a step forward, her hands clenching around the folder she was holding. 'You are joking, aren't you?'

'You tell me. Do you feel like a punchline?' he said in that same taunting way she'd asked the question.

'Very funny.' Her smile looked as if it was stretched to breaking point. 'I'm glad you find this situation amusing, Mr Konstantinou.'

He shook his head. 'Nothing about this situation amuses me, Ms Hamilton. Naturally I would prefer not to have slept with you.' That jolted her, he thought, watching her chin jerk up, but he told himself he didn't care. Had she been honest with him, he would never have slept with her, and if she didn't like the truth? Tough.

'I've already lost one lawyer. To lose another would be not just inconvenient but careless, and I don't do careless.'

At the back of the offices, Milner's overlooked one of those private parks that stippled London, and there was a silence as she stared past him at a fluttering canopy of green leaves. Regrouping, he thought, or maybe just buying time, and he hated that there was a part of him that couldn't help admiring her stubbornness.

Of course, he was being stubborn too. Contrarian, in fact. But he was not done with this woman. There were questions he wanted answered. And on a pettier note, it pleased him playing puppet master and jerking her strings to make her dance.

'Why are you doing this? I mean, you couldn't get away fast enough two weeks ago.'

'And what exactly would I be staying for?'

The shock on her face threw everything into sharper contrast, the green of her irises startling against the pupils. And then she recovered, her fury cool, and ice-tipped as if it was studded with diamonds.

'As if I'd want you to stay.'

'Enough.' He spoke more harshly than he intended, and he heard a sudden silence outside the door as if the life of the office had paused.

He took a breath, steadied himself. 'This is getting us nowhere, and you are wasting your time and, more importantly, mine. You will work for me because I am an important client, which means I call the shots.'

Her eyes fixed on his face. 'There are lots of very experienced, very effective lawyers at this firm, Mr Konstantinou.'

He shrugged. 'But none are both female and the same age as my sister. But if you are unwilling to do your job, then of course, I will find another lawyer.' He held her gaze. 'Just not at this firm.' He was bluffing. He had no intention of letting Willa escape the punishment she deserved for up-ending his mental state. And the complexities of the various overlapping family trusts had already turned what he'd hoped would be a cut-and-paste job into a frustratingly long process. But he couldn't stall Ariana indefinitely.

There was a pulsing silence.

'You wouldn't do that.' He saw her hands ball into fists. She had given up trying to smile.

'I wouldn't want to. Larry and I are friends. I trust him implicitly. But given our *history*, as you so charmingly put it, I feel it would be only fair to let him know why that trust is wavering.'

'Is that a threat?'

Staring at her with a calmness he didn't feel, he shook his head. 'I'm merely being *transparent*. You are, of course, free to make your own decision. But I will need you to make that decision before I leave this room.'

Emotions he couldn't read flickered across her face, and he hated that, even now when he had her cornered, she remained so opaque to him.

'I'll take that as a *no*.' He turned towards the door.

'Fine. I'll do it.'

Her words made him stop midstep, but he made himself wait, made Willa wait a good twenty seconds before he spun round to face her.

'That wasn't so hard was it?' he said softly.

His blood thudded as her gaze sharpened on his face. Not scared. Defiant. 'You haven't exactly given me a choice, Mr Konstantinou, but just so we're clear, what happened at the

Clarendon will not happen again. I don't want there to be any confusion. Any crossing of boundaries.'

'I'm not the one who needs reminding about the limits of our relationship. Of any relationship.'

She stared up at him in silence. Outwardly she had recovered her composure. Nobody walking in on them would suspect that a battle royale of wills had just taken place between them. Or that she had been vanquished. It was quite a skill at her age to be able to present a perfect shopfront like that.

But then, no doubt it was one she'd perfected; otherwise, how else would she be able to do what she did? What she had done with him at the Clarendon.

A memory of her body coming apart uncontrollably beneath his.

Her pupils flared, and he wondered if it was just temper or if she was remembering it too. Could she feel it swelling up inside of her? If he touched her, would he feel it burning beneath her skin?

He didn't know when he'd drifted into her orbit, just that he had. All it would take was for him to reach across the space between them—

His palms itched. The air was changing, growing taut, and despite trying so hard to pretend he couldn't feel it, that pulsing, electric thread between them twitched like the tail of a kite in a gust of wind.

For a moment, neither of them moved, and then the light in her gaze sharpened, and he saw it again, that flicker of light on the floor. Diamonds were supposed to be forever. But not for this woman.

'One last thing, I have business in Athens, so you'll have to fly out to meet me there to thrash out the final details.'

Her face, her whole body stilled like some small animal spotting the shadow of a bird of prey.

'No. I never agreed to that.'

'I don't require your agreement. Just your compliance.'

'But I could do the work remotely until the prenup needs to be signed.'

'I prefer to do it in person. But if that's a problem—'

He waited again.

Finally, reluctantly, she said stiffly, 'It's not.'

He watched her pulse hammer against the pale skin of her throat, saw her fingers tighten around the folder to leave crescent-shaped imprints in the cardboard.

She was angry but curbing her emotion, and he felt another tiny flicker of admiration but also frustration, because time had rewound and they were back on the street again, and the barriers in her eyes were as high and impregnable as a forest of thorns.

And yet as he turned and walked out the door and down the corridor, he felt calmer than he had in days.

CHAPTER FOUR

WILLA WAS RUSHING AGAIN. Or trying to. But Heathrow was the busiest airport in Europe. Apparently, it averaged around a quarter of a million passengers a day. And right now, it felt as if most of them were trying to get to her boarding gate.

It was the second time in a little over a week that she had found herself at the beck and call of Ares Konstantinou. Although, to be fair, it was Larry who had summoned her the first time.

But Ares was still the reason she'd had to hail a taxi and hotfoot it across London that day, she thought irritably.

Hot was apt. She felt her cheeks tingle, remembering her flushed face and general air of coming apart at the seams as she'd walked into the meeting room and seen Ares. But he seemed to have that effect on her.

She replayed the moment when she'd agreed to stay on as his lawyer. At the time she had told herself that the taut, quivering thing inside her was fury. It was her fury with him, and with herself for giving someone power over her that was making it hard to breathe, making her skin prickle. And by *power*, she meant the power to hurt her.

It was one of the reasons she'd found it so hard to date. That need to keep a part of herself separate, hidden. But Ares had broken through her firewalls. His touch had ignited a spark, and suddenly she was a forest fire burning out of control. It was like trying to hold back a tsunami with her hands. She hadn't known it was possible to feel how Ares made her feel.

But perhaps her overuse of natural-disaster metaphors hinted at what was to come, she thought sourly, because afterwards he'd got up and left while she slept. As if none of what happened had mattered. As if she didn't matter.

Which was pretty humbling. Or at least humbling enough to immunise her against the pull of his dark eyes. Except for that moment when she felt as if it was going to start up again and she'd been so terrified that he might see her body's response. That it was as visible from space as the bright lights of Las Vegas.

She shivered. And now she was going to be stuck in Athens with him.

But twenty minutes later, the memory of that prickly, air-choked meeting at Milner's was long forgotten as she tried to wedge her bag into an overhead locker. It was the first week of the school holidays, and the flight to Athens was rammed with parents and children. In fact, she might be the only single passenger on the flight. Then again, all the working people would be in business class.

Where she would have been too if Ares had not flexed those metaphorical muscles of his.

As if to demonstrate that he was indeed calling the shots, he had changed the time of their meeting twice, and the second time the only available flight out of London to Athens had one seat available.

Which was why she was flying economy rather than stretching out in business class. She had hoped to work on the prenup, but it would take more than noise-cancelling headphones to block out the excited first-day-of-vacation hum, and instead she had decided to try and read her book.

And yet despite the noise, and the crying that was no

doubt the result of too little sleep and too much sugar, she couldn't help envying her fellow passengers.

They were going on holiday. To have fun in the sun. Whereas she would be spending two days in the company of a man who had only hired her out of some deranged sense of revenge.

The one positive was that Larry was delighted. 'This is a great opportunity for you to be seen in the right circles. The Konstantinou name will open doors for you.'

Which was undoubtedly true, but frankly she would rather be slamming the door in Ares's beautiful, arrogant face.

'In you go. Go on. Mummy's coming.'

Willa glanced up and smiled mechanically at a tired-looking woman holding a baby in a sling and the hand of a sticky toddler who was staring at her curiously.

It was around the twenty-minute mark into the flight when the little boy, who was called James, dropped his car off the side of the drop-down tray for the twentieth time since take-off.

'Here, let me.' Leaning forward, she picked up the car and held it out to him. His mother, who had the baby sitting on her lap, had picked it up the previous nineteen times, and Willa had wanted to help but was worried it would look a little pointed.

The woman smiled. 'Thank you. Say *thank you*, James.'

The little boy mumbled something, then hid his face. His mother screwed up her face apologetically

'I'm sorry. You were probably hoping to sit back and relax with your book.'

'It's fine.' Willa smiled reassuringly. 'It was an impulse buy, and it's not very gripping.'

'I booked this holiday on impulse. At half past three in the morning when this one had me up in the night.' The woman grimaced as the baby tugged at her hair. 'Sleep deprivation makes you do crazy things.'

Willa laughed. 'You're making memories. That's not crazy. And going on holiday on your own with a toddler and a baby is impressive.'

The woman laughed. 'Oh, I'm not on my own. My husband's just over there'—she nodded across the aisle—'with this one's twin sister.' She pressed a kiss on top of the baby's downy head.

'You have twins.' Willa glanced back to where a man who was the spitting image of James was clutching an identical blond baby. 'My younger sisters are triplets.'

'Wow! Triplets.' The woman's eyes widened comically. She looked both admiring and appalled. 'Your mum must be a legend.'

Willa felt her body tense. But obviously this stranger didn't know her back story. Didn't know that Meg Hamilton's tragic, early death had turned her into a local legend back home.

But like all legends, the facts had been made to fit the fiction. Her mother was a composite of other people's memories and observations, the majority of which were based on lies they had been told and unwittingly believed. Her father, Robert, was the only person who knew Meg, the real Meg, and she couldn't bear to ask him, to hear more about the woman who had deceived him and left him with the ultimate rock-and-a-hard-place choice: to tell the truth about his wife and be revealed as a cuckold, or keep her secret and be forced to raise another man's child as his own.

He had picked the latter because he was a good man. But that wasn't to say he had no regrets, and she couldn't bear to watch them play out on his face or hear them in his voice. It was why she had left home and not gone back.

As for Amber, she had inherited Willa when she was ten

years old. She wasn't a wicked stepmother, but the triplets were her focus, and ironically, she was worried that Willa had a special place in Robert's heart because of Meg dying.

Willa gave a small gasp of surprise as the baby launched herself into her lap. She clutched at Willa's shoulder as her mother tried to lift her off.

'Oh, I'm so sorry,' the mother said. 'I can't believe she did that. She can be tricky with people she doesn't know, but you're obviously a natural.'

Ignoring the sting of pain that sentence produced, Willa smiled. 'I'm glad I can help. And on a selfish note, it's good for me too. Babies are the best distraction.'

The woman frowned. 'Are you scared of flying?'

She wasn't someone who chatted to perfect strangers about her private life, but suddenly Willa felt the oddest desire to share why she needed to be distracted. To explain that her anxiety had nothing to do with flying and everything to do with what was waiting for her in some glittering, high-rise office in Athens.

Or rather *who*.

Because that was why her stomach was performing somersaults. It was the thought of having to spend time with Ares.

She wasn't afraid of him. She'd worked with other men who had made her feel uncomfortable. Seen for the wrong reasons. Those men with their inappropriate and overstepping attention were the reason she'd started wearing her mother's ring on her hand instead of around her neck. But with Ares, it was less about his behaviour than hers. She didn't like how being in his orbit made her feel so out of control.

So pagan.

The remaining two hours of the flight passed with surprising speed, and Willa was shocked to feel the wheels hitting the runway at Athens airport, but not as shocked as when she stepped through the open door. After the air-conditioned chill of the plane, the heat was almost solid to the touch and the dazzlingly bright sunlight had her reaching into her bag to find her sunglasses.

She nipped to the restroom so that she could apply some sunscreen to her face and tidy her hair, but everything else could wait until she arrived at the hotel. By the time she emerged, the queue for passport control had shrunk to a handful of people and she felt a sudden frisson of excitement when she stepped out of the terminal back into the sunlight.

Could she smell the sea? Almost certainly not, but the air smelled different to the London air. Or maybe her senses were on high alert.

Now all she had to do was find a taxi.

'Ms Hamilton?'

She turned, frowning to find a tall, grey-haired man with wire-rimmed glasses standing behind her. Next to him were two other thick-set men with identical dark suits and blank expressions.

'My name is Demetrios Kyriakos. I work for Mr Konstantinou. Welcome to Athens. If you would follow me, we have a car waiting.' Sensing her confusion, he frowned. 'I spoke to your PA, Maggie. She said she would let you know.'

At that moment, Willa felt her phone buzz repeatedly as her wireless provider changed networks and message after message tumbled into her inbox. Including one from Maggie.

Konstantinou car to collect you at the airport. ☺

She could feel the legal secretary's excitement pulsing down the phone. But as she turned and followed Demetrios, she felt more exposed than excited as the hustle of the airport stilled around her. Tucking a strand of hair behind her ear, she tried to ignore the covert but concentrated gaze of the other travellers, and she was grateful when they left the main concourse and walked into another smaller waiting area. There were fewer people there, and the air was scented with something light and floral and expensive.

Outside, there was not just one car waiting for her, but three heavyweight SUVs with blacked-out windows. The car in the centre had another blank-faced man in a dark suit and dark glasses standing in front of it. It was a formidable welcoming committee.

Except, it didn't feel welcoming.

She felt her stomach somersault. Was this supposed to remind her of her place in the scheme of things? As if dragging her halfway across Europe hadn't already ticked that box.

'Is everything okay, Ms Hamilton?'

'You tell me,' she said crisply.

Demetrios smiled politely. 'It's standard security logistics. Mr Konstantinou always travels with three cars.'

Her pulse skipped a beat, and she felt her chest tighten. Mr Konstantinou? But he wasn't here. Was he?

In answer to her unspoken question, the man standing by the SUV turned smartly and opened the door of the car, and her gaze pulled towards the man stepping onto the runway just as if he was a new moon and she was some spring tide.

As Demetrios melted into the Greek sunshine, she felt her legs stutter to a halt, the sight of Ares Konstantinou acting like some unseen brakes even as her heart began to race.

It wasn't fair that each time they met, he looked even better than the previous time.

Make that *spectacular*, she thought, her eyes narrowing on his face.

Unlike everyone else on the runway, he wore no sunglasses, but then, he had no need of them. He was brighter and more brilliant than the sun. As she stopped in front of him, she reluctantly removed her own glasses, suddenly conscious of her flushed face and the stickiness of her skin where she had recently applied sunscreen.

'Ms Hamilton.'

He inclined his head like some modern-day Alexander the Great greeting a subject. He wasn't a king, but there was something that set him apart from other men. She'd noticed that in London, at the party. In a room crowded with the wealthy and influential, his presence had been a commanding thing.

'I hope your flight was comfortable.'

'It was.' She inclined her head, matching his imperious gesture. 'It's very thoughtful of you to meet me, Mr Konstantinou. I hope you didn't go to any trouble on my account.'

His hard, sensuous mouth dipped at the corners as he shrugged. 'My flight came in from London at the same time as yours, so it was no trouble whatsoever.'

His flight?

'I thought you'd already left England.'

'My schedule changed,' he said casually. 'One of the perks of having one's own ride.' He gestured towards the sleek white jet that sat gleaming on the runway behind the line of cars.

Willa blinked. How had she not noticed that plane?

But she knew how. All her focus, every atom of her being had been pulled inexorably towards that second dark car as if by some invisible force.

Sadly, Ares Konstantinou wasn't invisible.

He was here. Large as life. Larger, she thought peevishly. Even in heels, he was still two inches taller than her.

'I would have offered you a lift. But I know how strongly you feel about crossing boundaries.'

She felt a sudden, strong urge to take off her shoes and hurl them at his handsome head, but instead she said with an admirable coolness given the provocation, 'I do. So perhaps I should sit in one of the other cars.' It would certainly be a lot less unsettling than being cooped up with his lean, muscular body.

As his dark gaze flicked to her eyes, she felt the absence of her sunglasses. She had learned to hide her thoughts, her feelings, to hide a truth which could blow apart the lives of so many people. But three weeks ago, at the Clarendon, she'd let this man get close. She'd let herself be seduced by his beauty and masculinity.

She'd let down her guard.

Let him in.

And yes, it was *just sex*. But whatever anyone said about casual sex, there was nothing casual about taking someone inside your body.

It took trust.

She had trusted him. And in the intense, flickering focus of his dark grey gaze she hadn't felt as though she was concealing who she was. Or pretending to be someone that she wasn't. She was eager, honest, uninhibited, inexpert. And he'd liked who she was.

More than liked. She'd had sex before, and no man had ever looked at her so intently or touched her so feverishly.

Her breath twisted in her throat.

But she'd misunderstood his intensity, that feverishness. He wasn't seeing her. He was simply cutting loose, enjoying the freedom of no-strings sex with a stranger, and it was stupid—irrationally so—to care that he hadn't wanted more. They'd barely spoken, let alone made plans or promises.

But what kind of man woke in the early hours of the morning and just left? And then insisted on making you work for him.

It was not just ill-mannered, it was brutal.

Not that Ares cared what she thought. He was too busy

holding a grudge against her for turning up in his life again without permission.

Stomach tensing, she lifted her chin. So they were both holding grudges.

'I'm afraid that won't be possible for security reasons. On the plane you were just a random passenger, but here in Greece you are my guest,' he said smoothly, but there was an edge to his voice. An accent too, faint but discernible, as if being here had stripped away some of that urbane, ultra-high net-worth exterior to reveal the man underneath.

'Is that why you had me escorted from the airport? It was quite a show. I felt like I was under arrest.'

Ares was staring at her in silence, and she was torn between wanting to keep staring back at his fascinating face and turning and running as fast as she could in the opposite direction. 'Is that something you're familiar with?' he said finally.

'I have an imagination.'

His pupils stilled, snapping outwards to swallow up the grey of his irises.

'Yes.' He paused, and the tension in her stomach wound tighter. 'You do. But whatever you're feeling is all in your head. Unless, of course, you're guilty of something.' Her breath spiralled in her throat as he stared at her steadily. 'Is that true, Ms Hamilton? Are you hiding something you're ashamed of?'

She knew her face was pale, that it was impossible to hide. But she couldn't imagine sharing that moment when her whole life unravelled with anyone, much less the beautiful, cold-eyed man gazing down at her.

'Everyone is hiding something.'

He didn't reply, just pushed the door a little wider, and she slipped past him, altering her trajectory enough to be certain that they didn't touch. But any hopes she'd had of retaining that level of control throughout the journey were swiftly extinguished.

For starters, the car's blacked-out windows kept nudging her brain back towards a memory of the darkening sky above London, and it took all her willpower and muscle resistance to stop her brain and body from replaying that night. And then—

'Here. You can keep it.'

She stared at Ares in confusion. He was holding out a crisply ironed handkerchief, his gaze hovering on her shoulder and glancing down, she frowned.

'Oh, she must have brought up some milk. The baby.'

He frowned. 'The baby?'

'There was a baby on the plane. I offered to hold her for a bit.'

'You offered?' His grey eyes fixed on her face, and feeling all fingers and thumbs, she dabbed at the stain.

'Do you like babies, then?'

'I have younger sisters.' She felt a wrench, and folding the handkerchief, she leaned back against the door-frame, trying to put distance between herself and his all-seeing gaze.

Sisters. Was that what they were?

Was that how they would feel if they found out the truth? She hated lying to them. Hated not seeing them too, but she couldn't risk letting something slip. Something that would change her relationship with them forever as it had changed her relationship with Robert. It didn't matter that their bond was forged in a shared history and affection. She was a cuckoo in their nest, and they had every reason to resent her and push her out.

Blanking her mind to that destabilising thought, she reached into her bag for a phone. 'I have the name of my hotel. Shall I give it to your driver?' Hell, what was it? She knew what it was, but being in such proximity to Ares had apparently short-circuited her brain. 'It's called the—'

'Minos.'

She frowned. 'Yes, that's right. How did you know that?'

'Are you seriously asking me that?' Now he frowned. 'You're here, in my city on Konstantinou business. Clearly I expect to know where you're staying.'

My city. She gritted her teeth, but he wasn't exaggerating. She had done her research; although, in all honesty, clicking on page after page of photos of Ares Konstantinou at various events surrounded by countless beautiful women was not so much research as torture. The photos of him on his yacht were both unsettling and unnecessary. She didn't need to know what he looked like in swim shorts to write his sister's prenup.

Not when she knew what he looked like without them.

But aside from photos of a semi-naked Ares, her research had been both informative and somewhat daunting. She had grown up feeling well-off, but he was dizzyingly wealthy. And his family's status in Greece, particularly in Athens, was similar to that of royalty.

'I see,' she said, stiffly.

'But as I said earlier, there was a change to my schedule, so my people cancelled your reservation.'

She stared at him in disbelief. 'Why would you do that?'

'You are here on Konstantinou business, which means that my name is your name by proxy, and I cannot allow my family's name to be associated with somewhere like the Minos.'

She blinked. Was he for real?

It was on the tip of her tongue to ask him, but as she opened her mouth to do so, he said abruptly, 'Do you understand how important this prenup is to me, Ms Hamilton?'

'Yes, of course I do.'

'No, I don't think you do.' He persisted. 'For you, Ariana's inheritance is just numbers on a screen. A list of assets. They don't mean anything. They're just data. To understand why this prenup matters you need to do more than read about what's at stake. You need to feel it. And the only way that can happen is if you experience it for yourself. Which is why you'll be staying with me on Kallos.'

Kallos.

The Konstantinous' private island. Or rather, *off-limits*. No one outside of the family and only a few trusted, close family friends were allowed on Kallos.

Willa was neither, Ares thought as they arrived at the helicopter launch pad.

He met her gaze, dared her to look away. She didn't, and he found he couldn't look away either, and for a moment they just stared at one another. And it was intoxicating, having her look at him so intently.

Was that why he was acting like this?

Because it was unheard-of behaviour. Incomprehensible and out of character. And yet it was happening. He had decided it had to happen. Just like he'd decided to wait for Willa's flight.

To wait?

His shoulders stiffened against the cool leather upholstery. Waiting, like queuing or carrying a coat, were not part of his life. And yet he had waited for Willa. And while doing so, he'd found himself impatient to see her again.

It was three weeks since he had been inside Willa's body. They had spoken on the phone over the course of the past week, and every time she had been polite but seemingly unaffected by that charged meeting at Milner's, where he had more or less blackmailed her into working for him. Almost as if she had forgotten.

Now though, there was a faint flush of rose like blusher

along her cheek bones, and he knew she remembered every second.

'Kallos is your island,' she said slowly as if she was talking to a child or someone who didn't speak English fluently.

'It is.'

'But Ariana has no claim on Kallos. It will go to your children.' There was a tension in her voice.

'If I have children, yes. Which currently I have no plans to do.' No plans ever. How could he, when to do so would mean having to take a wife? To let someone get close.

Close enough to slide a dagger into his heart. As Zoe had.

Picturing her face as she'd turned towards him in the church, he felt the blade twist. Her deceit was as unexpected and calamitous as a meteorite crashing to earth. It wasn't just that she had betrayed him. The Konstantinou clan had embraced her too. Zoe was at every gathering, invited to the most select family events. Everyone had assumed that they would marry and wholeheartedly approved of the match. That she could so casually deceive them had shattered some fundamental belief in love itself. The forever kind that his parents and grandparents had so effortlessly achieved so that where once he had seen certainty and candour, now he saw insecurity and duplicity.

'My family owns several properties in Athens. But Kallos is where our family began. That is who we are. It's a short flight. Twenty minutes by helicopter. Which, as you can see, is ready and waiting for us.'

The flight took nineteen minutes. Willa made no attempt at conversation, but as they reached the island, he watched her lean forward, and he too leaned forward, wanting to see her reaction.

'Do you own the whole island?'

He nodded. 'All two hundred and fifty acres.'

'It's beautiful,' she said quietly.

'If you're agreeable to the idea, I thought we'd have a light lunch, and then I could show you around. It's a little too far to walk on foot, but we have ATVs or horses.'

'You have horses here?' Her eyes softened, and he was suddenly so aware of her that it was like they were one person.

'Can you ride?'

She nodded.

Even before she swung herself expertly into the saddle, he could see she was relaxed around horses in a way that only happened if they were a regular part of your life. She looked the part too, in some of Ari's jodhpurs and boots and a loose-fitting T-shirt.

'When did you learn to ride?'

She was silent for a beat, using the moment to tie up her hair in the same unthinking way that Ariana did. 'Pretty much from when I could walk,' she said in that cool, neutral way of hers that worked in tandem with those barriers in her eyes to keep her one step removed at all times. But he had seen her naked, caressed her skin. He knew where to touch her to make her squirm and arch against his body. It was why he felt so on edge, why he kept pushing back with this woman. She was an iceberg that he wanted to melt.

'We have horses at home,' she added.

He watched her lean back in the saddle, her fingers collecting the reins, and he had to remind himself that he was showing her Kallos to make her understand what it meant to be a Konstantinou. To prove to her, and himself, that whatever power he'd surrendered to her that night was an aberration.

'There were about a dozen families living here originally, including the Konstantinous,' he said as the horses slithered down a rock-strewn hill to the dusty track that followed the island's irregular coastline. 'They left for the mainland, for work. For marriage. After than it was uninhabited until my great-great-grandfather bought it from the Greek government in 1901, and then it was sold to pay death duties when I was ten years old. I bought it back seven years ago.'

He'd thought it would be a place to raise his family. He had built the house wanting to fill it with children. But for that he needed a wife, and he had failed abysmally to pull that off. Of course, there was no shortage of women willing to enter into a marriage of convenience for the right price. But children needed more than money. They needed loving role models, not actors, for parents.

'Have you talked to Ariana about your plans for Kallos?'

He frowned. 'Why would I? She's not married, let alone pregnant.'

'But she is engaged.'

'Not for much longer,' he said tersely. 'If you do the job you're being paid to do.'

Her green eyes were cool. 'I'm being paid to advise you. Not validate a knee-jerk, emotionally charged response that results in an unwieldy, unworkable legal document.'

'Careful, Ms Hamilton.'

'It is you who needs to take care, Mr Konstantinou.' She was frustrated. He could hear it in that slight huskiness when she said his name. Feel it, too, in the wrong places.

'You're assuming David Arteta will be the one to walk away. But what if Ariana chooses not to sign the prenup?'

'She will. She's not a fool. And for all her impulsiveness, she is also very traditional. And smart. She knows what she stands to lose.'

'Which is what? You? Her family? Her wealth? Are you going to disown her? Leave her penniless?'

'It won't get that far. She'll come to her senses. She just needs time to think, which is why I need the prenup to slow her down.' He frowned. 'What?'

Willa was no longer looking at him but at a point somewhere past his left shoulder. 'There's someone waving at you,' she said after a moment.

He turned and swore softly. He hadn't planned on coming this way, but he was so distracted that he hadn't been paying attention, and the horses had simply followed the path. And now it was too late, he thought, lifting his hand to wave back at the elderly woman.

Thea was his mother's former housekeeper. He couldn't remember a time when she hadn't been there. She had loved his mother. And she doted on Ares. Which was why after her retirement, he had built her a home on Kallos.

'Who is she?' Willa sounded curious.

'Her name's Thea. She was our housekeeper for years. She was more than that,' he added, although he didn't know why he felt the need to share that fact. Because it was the truth, he told himself a moment later. And he felt suddenly angry with Willa, remembering the lie her body had told him.

'Hey, Toula.' Dismounting, he greeted the black-and-white sheepdog that had bounded up to greet him with an enthusiasm that was matched by Thea's delight. And after he'd made the introductions, Thea insisted that they stay for coffee and a slice of honey cake, as he knew she would.

'Your favourite.' She beamed at him, and he smiled as she handed him a plate.

'This is absolutely delicious.'

Watching Willa smile at the older woman, he felt something like envy. She had been polite at lunch but only ate a little of the meze prepared by his cook. But she seemed to genuinely be enjoying the cake.

'Is it thyme I can taste?'

'Yes, *thymari*.' Thea nodded. 'It grows here on the island. Do you like to cook, Willa?'

'Actually, I do.'

'Your mother, she taught you?'

'My father.' She hesitated as if she'd said too much, and he wondered why. Boundaries, he thought with a flicker of irritation, and it shouldn't have annoyed him because he wanted boundaries too, and yet it did.

'He's the cook at home. He loves cooking outdoors. Building a fire on the beach. That's his favourite. Mine too. Oh, hello—'

Toula had pushed open the door to the sitting room and was pressing herself against Willa's leg.

'I'll take her out.' Ares got to his feet.

'It's fine. Honestly. I love dogs.'

And her love was reciprocated. Toula seemed smitten with her female guest, resting her head on Willa's thigh and gazing up at her with soulful brown eyes. Which was unusual. Normally, she didn't leave his side when he visited, but even when he clicked his fingers softly, she didn't look over at him. He had a sudden, sharp sense of déjà vu, but as he was trying to pin it down, a bee got itself trapped against the inside of the window, bumping noisily against the glass. To his surprise, the dog got to her feet, growling softly, before returning to Willa's side.

'She's in a funny mood today.' Thea was staring at the dog. 'She reminds me of Lefki. Do you remember, Ares? She was just the same with your mother when she was pregnant with Ariana. She wouldn't leave her alone.'

That was it. That was what he remembered. He was about to nod politely when he caught sight of Willa's face. She looked young, distracted. Like his sister when he used to help her with simultaneous equations. He could almost hear her counting inside her head—

Another bee was trapped against the window, and he got up to let it out, but the buzzing stayed inside his head. The room seemed to be shrinking, air pressing against him just as if a storm was brewing.

And then Willa looked up and her gaze found his, he saw shock and panic in her eyes and a dawning recognition of having found the answer to a very particular question.

And it was like a rain cloud breaking over his head.

Because he knew what she was counting. And why he was part of this particular equation.

CHAPTER FIVE

WILLA FELT THE room tilt sideways. She was dazed, dazzled. Dumbfounded by the swerve the day had taken.

For a moment it was as if she was breathing in water not air, and she was back in the private room at the hospital with Robert looking at his hands, looking anywhere but at her face as he admitted that he wasn't her father.

Trying to stem the rising tide of panic, she made herself focus on solid shapes in the room. The pale wood of the window frame. The curving rim of the teacup.

No, she thought, as the dog continued pressing her head against her leg. She was being ridiculous. She had multiple follicles on her ovaries. The infected one she'd had removed had left scarring. And she wanted to tell Toula that she was mistaken. That whatever it was the dog thought she sensed, she was wrong.

She wasn't pregnant. She couldn't be.

A sudden, vivid memory of Ares's body surging inside hers in the pool, and before that, a conversation of not-quite asked or answered questions.

'It's fine,' she'd said. 'I'm safe.'

But was she?

Like most women, her periods had been a little erratic when she'd started menstruating. They'd settled down, although they were light, but then she did a lot of dancing and riding. And then she'd gone on the pill and forgotten about periods, although she did get a tiny amount of bleeding and some cramping. But nothing that a couple of painkillers and a hot bath couldn't make bearable, until six months ago when the cramping had gotten so painful she'd gone to hospital. She'd thought her appendix was about to burst, but the surgeon had spotted something on her ovary.

Polycystic ovary syndrome. PCOS for short. Not a death sentence or anything like it, but the doctor had spoken bluntly about the implications of the diagnosis. The infertility rate for someone with PCOS was fifteen times higher than someone without it. Treatment to remove a cyst could result in removing the ovary.

After the diagnosis she had stopped taking the pill, stopped having sex.

Because she felt unsexy, and let down by her body, and obviously someone was trying to tell her something. Why else would she have had her future taken away on the same day as she found out that her past was a sham? That her so-called family was not hers. Or not in any absolute way. There were no blood ties. She was connected by shallow, ephemeral things like living in the same house and sharing a surname.

She felt something misshapen pressing in her throat so that it was hard to swallow. Since coming off the pill, her periods had stayed regular. So if her math was right, she was slightly late. A week maybe.

But a week was nothing. Look at what had been going on in her life. She'd had a long-haul flight and started a new job. And been blackmailed. Her stress hormones were probably stratospheric. It didn't mean she was pregnant. The opposite, in fact.

Her hands clenched. Because she couldn't get pregnant. She couldn't.

Because if she was, there was only one man who could be the father—

'We should probably be getting back, Thea. Ms Hamilton and I have a lot to get through before she returns to London.' Ares's voice cut across her panicky thoughts, and glancing up she smiled at the older woman.

'It was lovely to meet you, and thank you so much for the delicious tea and cakes.' Her voice sounded fine, she thought, easy, relaxed, not even a flicker of anxiety, but she felt a sudden and urgent need to get outside.

The horses were where they had left them.

'Hey, there,' she said, catching Chiron's bridle. 'Did you have a siesta?' she crooned as he lifted his big head to nuzzle her shoulder. 'Are you ready to roll?'

A hand clamped on the bridle next to hers. 'He might be, but you won't be riding him.'

She spun round, frowning. 'Why ever not?'

'The terrain here is the same in any direction. And he almost lost his footing on the ridge.'

'So did Agrius.'

'True.' The sun was in her eyes, and she couldn't see his expression, but she could hear the tension in his voice. 'But I'm not the one who might be pregnant.'

She could feel her legs swaying slightly in the sea breeze.

'I'm not pregnant.'

'You can't know that.' He was being reasonable—or what a billionaire used to people jumping through hoops when he so much as blinked thought was reasonable. But to her, it felt intrusive. It was bad enough having these thoughts in her head, she didn't need him giving them some kind of validation.

'Toula is a dog. Not a gynaecologist. And this conversation is completely inappropriate. There are boundaries. We agreed, remember?'

'I haven't forgotten. But there is always a case for making exceptions. And this is one of them.' For a moment with Thea, he had relaxed a fraction. But now his voice had shifted back into that familiar autocratic way of speaking, the one that assumed everyone would simply and obediently take instruction. 'You're on my land, you're my responsibility. And I take my responsibilities very seriously.'

There was the hum of an engine, and an SUV appeared, crunching over the pebble-strewn driveway. As it stopped, two of the stable hands climbed out, and she watched with a mixture of disbelief and fury as they mounted the horses.

'Ms Hamilton.' Ares paused. 'Could you get in the car?' He waited, and his will was like a living thing, but she stood her ground literally, and after another few pulsing seconds, he said quietly, 'Please, would you get in the car, Willa?'

For a moment she imagined storming away from him across the rugged hillside, but he would insist on coming with her. At least in the car they wouldn't be alone, and the journey would take less time.

And what was the alternative?

Ares was going nowhere. He was standing there, tall and straight-backed like a Greek column made of flesh and blood and muscle instead of marble. And he would stand there for all eternity if that was what it took.

It took seven minutes to get back to the villa, and Willa spent every one of those minutes trying to steady her thoughts. There was no reason for her to be getting so het up. Thea was very sweet, but it was just a random, throwaway comment. And as for Toula…

Yes, the dog had been oddly attentive, protective even, but maybe Toula thought she was someone else or that she would give her some cake. Which weren't good reasons to go into a tailspin like this. She was here to do Ariana Konstantinou's prenup. Everything else was a distraction.

Including the man sitting next to her.

She had thought Ares was going to start in as soon as they got in the car, but his interest in her appeared to have waned as swiftly as it had caught fire. As they walked into the villa, he was typing something into his phone.

But her relief was premature and short-lived. His housekeeper, Iona, came out to the entrance hall to greet them, only for Ares to snap something in Greek, and she melted back through the doorway. Now he turned to face Willa.

'We need to talk.' His eyes found hers. 'About what Thea said.'

'No, we really don't.' She turned and walked swiftly away from him. The layout of the villa was still so new she had no idea where she was heading, and she found herself in a sitting room that on any other occasion would have stunned her into silence with its uninterrupted view of the Aegean. Now though, she felt...

Unmoored.

Panicky.

Blurred at the edges.

Inside her head, she could hear Robert's voice, a memory now but clear like an audio file, hear the pain, the shame, and it was her pain, her shame. And now as then, she wanted it so badly not to be true.

'We had unprotected sex.' Ares had followed her into the room as she knew he would, but she was still unprepared for the bluntness of his words. 'You said you were safe,' he said tersely. 'Ten minutes ago, your face said otherwise.'

'I was surprised.' She did her best to keep her voice level.

'You think it's a possibility—'

'I don't,' she lied.

He held out his phone. 'I looked it up. Dogs can smell the hormonal changes of pregnancy before mothers test positive.'

Her chest and throat tightened so that it was hard to speak.

'Are you saying you trust a dog more than you trust me?' She shook her head. 'Maybe you should get Toula to do Ariana's prenup.'

A muscle tightened in his jaw. 'I'm saying that you seem very on edge about something you claim is impossible.'

'I didn't say it was impossible,' she snapped.

And only realised as she did so that she had effectively self-sabotaged her own denials. The sudden narrowing of his gaze told her he'd reached the same conclusion.

'So you could be pregnant?'

She hesitated. If she said *no*, it would mean telling him about herself, revealing things that she had never revealed to anyone. And he didn't deserve to know anything about her, she thought, muted by the memory of waking alone, her confusion and that crippling feeling of stupidity at having got it so wrong.

'Yes. Maybe. I don't know. But it's all supposition.'

'Currently, yes. But there's an easy and highly accurate way to find out for sure,' Ares said, and that statement as much as the intensity of his gaze made her feel suddenly weak and loose inside, and she understood on a visceral level just how unrelenting he could be.

'No.' She shook her head. The idea of doing what he was suggesting, here, now, in his villa was horrifying. 'I won't be doing a pregnancy test because your former housekeeper's dog was friendly to me. That's crazy.'

'You're overreacting.'

'And I'll stop overreacting when you stop overstepping. Just because we had sex once does not mean you get to have an input in my private life.'

'You can't hide from this, Willa. You can't hide it from me.'

'I'm not hiding anything.' Except, she was. That was why she had taken the job in London: because work was a place to hide. At work, there were no kudos earned by sharing personal information. On the contrary, staff were encouraged to keep their private life private. Which meant it was easy to deflect questions about herself. And work was work. There was no shortage of emails and documents and meetings and court appearances to occupy the space that would otherwise be filled with picking at those scabs.

She'd tried to leave them alone. For five months she'd held the truth close, smothering it against her body, lying to her sisters, ignoring Robert's calls. And when that hadn't worked, she had fled from it.

But how could she flee from herself?

Something of what she was thinking must be showing on her face, because Ares was shaking his head.

'You know, people have often said to me that lawyers lie as easily as they breathe. I never believed that. Until I met you. How do you live with yourself? Have you just gotten so good at lying to people that you don't know when you're doing it?' he said, and she didn't know whether it was the partial truth of his accusation or the contempt in his voice that shook her more.

The air thumped out of her lungs, and she stared past his shoulder at the line of the horizon which appeared to be shaking. Or maybe that was her.

But Ares Konstantinou didn't get to judge her life. And this wasn't some moral crusade. He was just lashing out because she had the temerity not to jump when he clicked his fingers.

'Oh, I think of the two of us, you're the expert on lying to other people. I mean, you're the man who left his bride standing at the altar in front of hundreds of people,' she said hoarsely.

His grey gaze didn't flicker, but a different muscle worked

in his lean jaw, and she felt a shiver of apprehension as he took a step towards her.

'You are such a hypocrite.' His beautiful face was a blank-eyed, bronze mask. 'If you're done talking about my fiancée, then perhaps we could talk about yours? Is he the father? Were you having unprotected sex with him too? If so, how can you be sure it's not mine?'

For a moment she was so focused on the cool contempt in his eyes that she didn't take in his words. And then she was shocked to stillness and silence. Even her heart seemed to stop beating.

Because his accusation made no sense. She had no fiancé. She had an ex-boyfriend. But most women had one of those, and she had ended things with him eight months ago. Since then, she hadn't dated anyone. Hadn't so much as touched a man.

Aside from Ares.

'I don't know what you're talking about.'

He took a step closer and leaned forward, his dark, powerful gaze, a sweep of steel blocking out the light, swamping her world, holding her captive, and every single cell in her body tightened so sharply that she almost lost her footing. But it wasn't pain, it was just her body reacting to his proximity.

She took a breath and dug her feet into the floor to stop herself from turning and running. 'I know you think your word is law, but you seem to have got your wires crossed,' she said icily, except beneath the ice her fury was churning like lava. 'Because I don't have a fiancé.'

'Then, why are you wearing an engagement ring on a chain around your neck?'

Her fingers moved automatically to the outline of the ring. How did he know about that? She had taken it off that night out by the pool, hiding it in her purse. Of course, she could have told him that it was her mother's engagement ring, but at that point she didn't even know his name. And by the time she did, talking would have changed the atmosphere, slowed things down, and she had been scared that if there was time to talk, there would be time to think, and he might change his mind.

Or she would.

His eyes were fixed on her face. 'Or are you going to lie about that too?' he said softly, and she felt the steel and warning of his words slice through her like a blade.

'It's not what you think.'

'Then, why did you take it off before we got together? Why did you hide it in your purse?'

She could feel the heavy thud of her heartbeat. Her hands were suddenly shaking.

'Did you go through my things?'

He hadn't. Even before he spoke, she could feel his shock.

'What kind of man do you think I am?'

The kind that left a woman looking like a fool in front of all her family and friends and the world's media. The kind that snuck off in the middle of the night because sharing a bed until morning smacked of a commitment that repelled him.

'You basically blackmailed me into working for you and into coming out here to Greece, and you've spent the last half an hour trying to bully me into taking a pregnancy test because your former housekeeper's dog sat too close to me. So you'll forgive me for thinking you might have looked in my purse.'

'I didn't. I was thirsty in the night. I got up to get a drink and I knocked your bag off the chair. It must have opened when it fell.'

She could picture him moving in the darkness of the room, negotiating the unfamiliar layout, then colliding with the chair. She could hear the soft thud of her bag and then his fingers curling around the diamond ring.

Was that why he'd left? But she knew without asking that it was. That his pride had been pricked.

Screw his pride, she thought savagely.

It was the only thing she had of her mother's. A slim gold band connecting her to the woman who had brought her into this world and then left her with nothing but unanswered questions and a life based on lies.

She let out a small, brittle laugh.

His eyes narrowed. 'What's so funny?'

'Nothing.' She sobered up abruptly. Because it wasn't funny. But she had felt perilously close to tears, and it was either laugh or cry, and she'd stopped crying when she realised that it couldn't change any of the things she wanted to change. 'I don't have a fiancé.'

She glanced over his shoulder to the rippling blue sea. Hamilton blue.

'It was my mom's ring. She died when I was very young. My dad gave me the ring when I was eighteen.' That was mostly true. Aside from the fact that Robert wasn't her dad, but she wasn't about to reveal that crushing, admittedly major detail to Ares, a man who already thought so little of her. How was that wound ever going to heal if she kept scraping away at the scabs?

'When I first started working, I had a few…encounters with male colleagues which were uncomfortable, and one of the other women at work told me that she had the same problem at her old business. She'd started wearing an engagement ring, and it stopped.'

'What kind of encounters?' Ares's voice was neutral, but the muscles in his shoulders seemed to have expanded outwards.

She shrugged. 'The usual kind. Inappropriate comments.

Getting too close. Once I was kneeling down to unplug a printer and one of the other juniors made this crack about how he'd like to see me like that outside of work.'

'Did you talk to HR? Your manager? And what did they say?' he said, and she nodded twice.

'They had a word. But it happens so often, you can't always go running to the grown-ups.'

'Because then you become the problem.' Something dark moved in his gaze.

'Yes.' That was how it felt. How it was. But a lot of men simply didn't understand that. They thought that, because there were checks and balances in place, sexually suggestive and inappropriate language and behaviour was no longer a problem.

His face was still and unreadable, but when he spoke his voice had softened. 'I'm sorry about your mother. Losing her so young must have been hard.'

It was just the first of many losses—and the easiest as it turned out.

'I don't remember her. I have a stepmother, Amber. She married my father when I was ten.'

'And you have sisters.'

'Yes. Three. Triplets.' Her words reminded her of Robert's fridge-magnet poems, and she felt a flicker of homesickness.

'I'm also sorry that you had to deal with those kinds of men.'

He was, she realised, but it was more than that. He was angry. She could hear it in his voice. But for the first time, he wasn't angry with her but *for* her. And it made her own anger collapse like a sandcastle, and she felt it unfurl inside of her, that same feeling of being safe, of having someone by her side that she'd felt lying in his arms in her hotel room.

Obviously, it wasn't real. She'd felt like that at the Clarendon because she hadn't been intimate with anyone for months, and sex was a game of smoke and mirrors when it came to intimacy.

As for the here and now, she was feeling hounded, literally by something a dog had done. Which for some unaccountable reason, this man was accepting as evidence that she was pregnant. But now, he had backed off, taken her side. She was relieved, grateful.

And clearly suffering from some form of Stockholm syndrome.

Stifling her relief and gratitude, she met his gaze. 'It's nothing I couldn't handle, but I didn't want to have to handle it. To handle them. So I started wearing my mother's ring. And it worked. When I wore the ring, men spoke to me like a peer instead of trying to be flirty or showing off.'

Ares was staring at her intently, listening too as if her words mattered. 'So why did you stop wearing it?'

Because it was a lie. Another lie. And she'd had enough lies by then. But she'd also been unsettled by how easy she'd found it to mislead people. Was that how her mother had started? With white lies? Had those white lies made it easier for her to slip into the deceit of an affair?

'I didn't need it anymore. I was older and more confident.' That was true. 'I stopped wearing it just before Larry interviewed me.'

London was going to be a fresh start. A new life. Moving across an ocean to another country was not just about progressing her career, it was about shedding her old self. In England, she could stop pretending, stop living a lie. She could leave the baggage of the past behind.

Only now the past had caught up with her.

Or was it the past repeating? The idea that she could be pregnant like her mom had been, carrying the baby of a man who neither loved her nor wanted her, made her feel suddenly sick.

Her stomach cramped. But it couldn't be morning sickness. Could it?

What if it was? She shouldn't have let it happen. She'd been warned about daydreaming about her future, but she had ignored the warnings. She had let herself get lost in Ares's dark-eyed beauty, and now she was adrift in the present.

'Why did you say you were safe?'

Willa let her gaze drift back to the horizon. It was steady now. Unlike her heart, which was beating fast and hard and arrhythmically like a jazz drummer's improv set.

It was no wonder that Ares had turned a profitable family shipping business into a global behemoth. He was intelligent and determined. But it was that ability to focus on the details when a hurricane was uprooting everything around him that made him exceptional. He would be a formidable opponent.

Would he be a good father?

Not going there, she thought, and blanking her mind she met his gaze. 'Are you saying you believe I'm not engaged now?'

'Yes, but you haven't answered my other question.' He waited. 'Did you think you were safe because you were using the pill?'

'That's a complicated question so I'm not sure I can give you a clear and accurate answer.'

'And I'm not sure a judge would agree with you.'

His lips curved up infinitesimally at one corner, and she felt her senses shift entirely to the shape of his mouth.

'So you're not acting as judge, jury and executioner anymore. That's progress.'

'I'm not a tyrant, Willa.'

'And I didn't lie to you. I'm not engaged. I've never been engaged. I don't even have a boyfriend.'

'But you could be pregnant.'

She smiled stiffly, trying to spin out the role-playing. 'Objection. Badgering the witness.'

'You weren't a witness, though, were you?' His eyes locked with hers, and she felt it low in her pelvis, a sharp, compelling tug of desire. 'You were a participant. A willing participant.'

'You were too.'

He shook his head slowly. 'Not willing. I was impatient. Hungry.'

Hungry.

The air stirred in the room. Why had he said that? After the Clarendon, she'd bolstered herself against the world. Against him. But now he'd taken a wrecking ball and smashed her defences as easily as if they were made of papier mâché so that there was nothing between them. Nothing to stop this gravitational force that seemed intent on pulling them ever closer.

But gravity was supposed to be the weakest of the four natural forces. She just needed to come to her senses—

They both snapped at the same time. His hand was in her hair, and she was gripping his shirt, pulling him closer, and she felt hunger and relief swell inside her as his mouth found hers. It felt so good, so right, so honest.

Be honest, then, she thought desperately, as heat slipped over her skin. Because soon she would be too warm to think, to speak—

'I wasn't on the pill.' Her voice vibrated against his mouth, and she shivered as his fingers moved lightly over her ribs. 'I wasn't using contraception.'

She felt his hands still, and then she was shivering again, but this time it was because he was disentangling himself.

'What do you mean?' His eyes were dark and impregnable. He was just inches away, but he was so out of reach to her now he could be standing on the moon. And his removal made her feel scooped out, discarded. Superfluous. 'Are you saying you knew you could get pregnant? Was it deliberate?'

'No, I didn't do it deliberately. I never thought it could happen.'

He was too smart. Too relentless. If she said more, there would be another question and another and another, and when he had all the answers, he would see her for what she was. An empty shell. A phony with a stolen past and no future. And a present filled with nothing but lies. Because she didn't belong anywhere now.

She felt as if she was dissolving. There was a tightness behind her eyes that felt like tears. But she didn't cry. 'I can't do this. I can't—' She stepped back to the side of a sofa.

'Willa—' He reached out to steady her, but she shied away.

'Just leave me alone.'

She stepped past him, half expecting his hand on her wrist, but then she was out of the room and scampering up the stairs and into the bedroom and—she felt a rush of relief—there was a lock on the door, so she turned the key, then stumbled across the room to the bed and hugged her knees to her chest. Because if she didn't, all of it would spill out of her, and then there would be nothing left at all.

Ares woke with a jolt, breathing in sharply, his body twitching beneath the sheets, his cock hard, a sense of disappointment creeping over his skin because, of course, Willa was not in his bed. And there was a twisted justice to that feeling of loss and frustration. Now that he had all the facts, it was clearly payback for how he had acted that night at the Clarendon.

Maybe that was why it felt so real. Why she felt real. He could feel the heat of her skin and the soft press of her fingers, and he had to steady his breathing and recalibrate all his senses.

He could see her now, naked, legs curled underneath her body, watching him, staring at him intently, watching, waiting, just out of reach—

Remembering Willa's small, wary face, he felt his jaw tighten. After yesterday, saying she was *just out of reach* was something of an understatement.

He had hassled, hounded and hectored her. Accused her of lying in about fifty different ways. And then he had kissed her.

In his defence, he had been caught off guard. Her admission that she wasn't and had never been engaged was a haymaker that was quickly followed by a second, knockout punch: that she hadn't been using contraception.

In other words, Toula was right. She could be pregnant, and he could be the father.

He realised he was holding his breath. A father, to a baby conceived from a one-night stand with a woman he had met three weeks ago who he had blackmailed into working for him.

That she was currently writing Ariana's prenup because he had been so furious with his ditsy sister for getting engaged to a man she had met a couple of months ago now was less an irony than a cosmic joke—on him.

Picturing Ariana's expression, his skull felt like it was going to explode.

Could Willa have done it deliberately? Had that supposed accident in the street been anything but accidental? Logically, the answer to that was *possibly*, at least. And yet he knew that it wasn't. That she was as stunned as he was. Unflatteringly, aside from the sex, he got the feeling that she saw him not as a catch but a complication.

The room felt suddenly like it was closing in on him. He needed to get out of here. Get some air. Move. Run.

Throwing back the sheet, he got to his feet and made his way to the window and pushed open the shutters. There was enough light. All he needed to do was get dressed. And then he would run and keep running until the ache in his lungs offset the one in his chest.

CHAPTER SIX

STUPID, STUPID, STUPID.

Willa pressed the heels of her hands into her eyes, blocking out the daylight that was creeping in through her window, wishing she could as easily block out the memory of that kiss.

She had been awake for about an hour and spent most of that time wishing she could go back to sleep. At least asleep, she didn't have to deal with her stupidity.

As if everything wasn't enough of a mess.

What she should have been doing was containing it, shushing it into submission so that she could get on with her job. Instead, she had thrown fireworks into a bonfire.

His mouth on hers.

Her breath mingling with his.

At some point early yesterday evening, either of her own accord or because Ares had sent her, Iona knocked on her door with some freshly squeezed peach juice, and she had taken the opportunity to excuse herself from supper by claiming that she had a migraine. She hated lying, but she'd had more than enough of Ares Konstantinou for one day.

That was one way of putting it.

She felt her cheeks burn as the kiss swelled up inside her again, and she touched her lips, remembering how he'd bent his head and fitted his mouth to hers. She should have pushed him away. Or slapped him like the heroine in an old black-and-white movie. But instead, she had kissed him right back, unthinkingly, as if it was something they had done a hundred times before. As if he hadn't spent the last week making her jump through ever-higher hoops.

But it wasn't all her fault. He was so close. Close enough for her to see the hunger in his eyes, to feel the pull of his desire. And it felt real, more real than that first time because now they had done more than kiss. They had talked, argued, made accusations, and then suddenly it was as if the storm had blown through and they had survived it. And it was just the two of them alone, and it had felt right in the same way it had on the roof of the Clarendon.

Except, it wasn't right. Or real.

Up until yesterday, she might have kidded herself that it was both, but she couldn't do that now. Not having seen his face, the way it changed, that shuttered expression as she told him that she hadn't been using contraception.

It told a story all of its own, one that would end without a happily-ever-after.

Not that she was expecting one. Her future was as unmapped, as unmappable, as the rest of her life. In the short term however, it was obvious that no matter what she had reluctantly agreed to do in London, she needed to get out of here as quickly as possible. They both needed some space—she did, anyway, and she could speak to Ariana without Ares being there.

Because he wasn't going to forget what Thea had said. Particularly as she had as good as admitted it might be possible. She could be pregnant.

And if she was, then Ares was the father. She'd as good as admitted that too.

Her shoulders tensed as she replayed his reaction. But what had she thought? That he wanted her to be pregnant with his baby? Aside from the fact that they barely knew one another, less than a day ago he'd told her that he had no current plans to have children.

But why was she even thinking about this? Why had she let Ares and his random logic get inside her head? She threw back the sheet in irritation. The chances of her being pregnant were slim to none.

Standing up, she walked into the dressing room, blinking as the lights fluttered on.

There was a full-length mirror at one end of the room, and she tugged her T-shirt over her head and stared intently at her naked body.

Obviously because she was weak-minded, she had looked up early changes in pregnancy, and it was easy to convince herself that her breasts ached. That she was exhausted and breathless. But then arguably, all of those symptoms were also caused by being in proximity to Ares Konstantinou.

She stared at her reflection. She knew they weren't, but her breasts definitely looked bigger. And her hair looked glossier.

Stop it.

Turning away from the mirror, she stalked across the room to the window and pushed the shutters slightly apart. There was no breeze, but she could smell the salt from the sea, and there was a faint hint of thyme.

Thymari.

She breathed out unsteadily, feeling the soft press of Toula's head, her all-seeing brown gaze.

This was going to stop. She was going to get dressed and get this prenup written and then get the hell out of Dodge and—

And what? She glanced across to where her mother's engagement ring sat on the bedside table.

Ignore the possibility that she might be having a baby? Live yet another lie?

Misery stabbed her stomach. She had left California to stop having to lie to everyone around her. Yet now she was thinking about lying to herself. Acting like a child shutting her eyes and thinking nobody could see her. If she was pregnant, then wasn't it better to know?

Something moved on the terrace below, and she felt her body stiffen, nipples tightening as Ares walked out into the soft morning light.

He was wearing shorts and a T-shirt that fitted his contoured upper torso like a glove. Her breath hissed through her teeth. He was the most beautiful man she had ever seen. He was also ruthless and uninterested in marriage or children. Did she really want to find out if she was pregnant with his baby?

Yes.

Because then she would know for sure, and knowing anything for sure right now felt like a big deal. She watched as Ares began to jog away from the house, and then she quickly got dressed.

Making her way downstairs, she headed for the kitchen. Iona was talking quietly to another woman who was folding napkins. As Willa walked into the room, they both turned towards her, smiling.

'Good morning, Ms Hamilton. I hope you slept well.'

'I did, thank you,' Willa lied. 'I wondered if you could help me?'

'Of course.'

Something of the tension in Willa's body must have been visible, because Iona turned and said a few quiet words to the other woman, who instantly retreated, and now it was just the two of them. But where to begin?

She cleared her throat. 'It's a little awkward. I need to get to the mainland. There's something I want.'

'I understand.' The older woman nodded. 'But perhaps

that might not be necessary. If you'll excuse me for one moment?'

'Of course.' Willa stared after the housekeeper in confusion as Iona walked across the kitchen and disappeared through a doorway. When she returned, she was holding a padded envelope. 'I think this might be what you need.'

Her smile was neutral, polite.

Willa took the envelope, opening it a fraction. Pregnancy tests. She breathed out unsteadily.

'I don't understand—' And then she did. Because Ares Konstantinou didn't do careless, and it would be the definition of *careless* for him to let Willa leave this island without knowing for sure if she was pregnant with his baby. Or pregnant, at all.

'Actually, it's fine. You don't need to explain, but thank you.'

As she left the kitchen and made her way back upstairs, she wondered what Iona was thinking. The older woman seemed completely unfazed, but then she was a trusted family employee. She lived with the Konstantinous and was witness to their private lives. Who knew what she had seen? Maybe this was just what she called a typical Wednesday.

Twenty minutes later, Willa was staring in shocked silence at the array of plastic wands resting on the side of the bath. There were five tests in the envelope, and she had used all of them. Although, she could have stopped after the first three because the result was irrefutable.

Pregnant. 2–3 weeks.

The bathroom was warm, but she was shivering. She could feel her shock beating in her throat, hard, an actual physical thing as if her heart had relocated. And beneath it, tiny but fierce like a match striking, a flare of joy.

Pregnant.

She had told herself this morning that it was better to

know for sure. And now she did. But she had never allowed herself to imagine this moment. She knew first hand how hard it was to give up something you had. Better to just accept what the doctors had said. That conception would be challenging. Not impossible, but highly unlikely.

And yet, here she was, pregnant.

Pressing her hand against her mouth, she breathed out shakily. Because now came the hard part. She picked up the last test and stared at the result. Was this how it had started for her mother? A chance encounter. A kiss that felt imperative. Sex that burned like wildfire.

And then a plastic wand revealing a life-changing future.

Had her mother told her father—her birth father—that she was having his baby? If so, how had he reacted?

She shivered again. Had he denied it? Was that why his name wasn't on the birth certificate? Had she put down Robert's name out of spite? Or despair? Or, more likely given that she was married at the time, had she not known for certain? And rather than rock the boat, had it been simpler, safer to tell herself, tell the world, that Robert was the father?

So many questions that would never be answered. So many lies, because there was never just one lie.

Her eyes slid down to the test. She could lie to Ares. Tell him the tests were negative. He would be relieved; he would want to believe it was negative.

But then what?

Because there was never just one lie.

Speeding up, Ares took the hill at a sprint. It was a bit risky. The ground was dry and uneven, with loose stones that slithered treacherously beneath the soles of his trainers. But he needed to make his lungs burn. Burn off the anger and that feeling of being out of control.

And then his legs were slowing, and it took a moment for

him to work out why, another moment for his brain to catch up with his eyes, and then he felt it: that faint shiver like a breeze but not, a feeling of rain falling on his skin, even though it wasn't raining.

Willa was sitting on an old tree stump.

She was wearing a simple linen dress, and her hair was tied up in the same low ponytail as before, but there was something about her posture, a kind of tension like a deer in a clearing who had heard the soft, unmistakable tread of a predator. And he wished then that she hadn't seen him so that he could simply gaze at her for a moment and absorb her unfiltered beauty.

But her shoulders were already bracing, and she was getting to her feet.

'You were right,' she said stiffly. 'I'm pregnant.'

He had expected it. Known it all along. Except it turned out that he hadn't, because his brain couldn't seem to process what she was saying.

She had done the test. Five, in fact. They were all positive. She was holding something out. A plastic wand.

Pregnant. 2–3 weeks.

Two to three weeks. The words repeated on a loop inside his head.

'The *two to three weeks* is from conception. But you date pregnancy from your last period so I'm about five weeks pregnant.'

He had a sudden, sharp flashback to school and the diagrams in his biology textbook. They had seemed so one-dimensional and lifeless, but this was the beginning of life itself. A new life.

And he felt so unprepared. How could he be a father?

'And you want to keep the baby?' He phrased it as a question, but a knot in his stomach loosened as she nodded her head imperceptibly.

'So what happens next?' There was a harshness to his voice: he heard it before he saw it in her eyes. But he was still trying to ground his breathing.

'I suppose I go to the doctor. And obviously you'll want a DNA test.'

Her words made his chin jerk up sharply. He could remember the expression on her face when Thea had made that remark about his mother's pregnancy. There was no doubt there or confusion. If she was pregnant, Willa thought he was the father.

'I don't want there to be any assumptions made.' She paused. 'And just for the record, I don't have any expectations about how this should work.'

'Expectations?'

'For your involvement. With the baby. I just want you to know that I'm not expecting anything from you.'

It stung more than it should. More so than when he woke up at the Clarendon and found her ring and thought that she was engaged. He'd been wrong about that—the ring part anyway. But not wrong apparently about Willa seeing him as nothing more than a fleeting pulse of pleasure.

That night in her hotel room flickered across his mind. It was a bubble of pure, distilled ecstasy. A fever dream outside of time. But things were different now. That pleasure had blossomed into a timeline which would end with the birth of their child.

'The last time I checked, it takes two to make a baby, Willa.'

She stared at him steadily, and the forest of thorns was back. He could feel her withdrawing, but she couldn't hide everything, he thought, his eyes snagging on the pulse hammering against the delicate skin of her throat. His body tensed as he imagined pressing his mouth against it. Would he be able to taste what she was feeling?

He certainly wasn't going to hear it from her lips. She gave him one of those cool, precise looks of hers that gave off Cleopatra-on-her-throne vibes, and despite his irritation he found himself admiring her poise. He couldn't imagine Ariana being half as composed in the same situation.

Ariana.

He felt a stab of guilt because, truthfully, he couldn't remember the last time he had thought about his sister or her prenup.

'There will be plenty of time for us to discuss how to move forward,' she said after a hard pause that left his teeth on edge because it was a lawyer's answer.

But she wasn't supposed to be acting as his lawyer right now.

As if she had read his mind, Willa cleared her throat and looked pointedly back at the path leading to the villa. 'And we will discuss it, but I'm here in Kallos as your lawyer, Mr Konstantinou, and I know how important it is for you to get this prenup wrapped up, so we should probably get back to work.'

Mr Konstantinou? That annoyed him.

Only she was right about needing to get back to work. That she should be the one to point that out was more annoying still. He was normally the one who had no trouble compartmentalising his life. But now Willa was doing it for him. Compartmentalising him, he thought savagely as they walked in silence back to the villa.

They worked in the sitting room, which in principle should have been the perfect venue. It was light and spacious. Except it didn't feel spacious, largely because the recent past, *their* recent past, kept nudging his consciousness as they bent over their respective laptops. It was distracting to say the least, and almost as frustrating as Willa's mission to scrutinise and counter his suggestions as to how the prenup should be amended. By midday, he'd had enough.

'You do realise you're working for me and not David Arteta?' he said, after Willa had challenged him yet again.

'Yes, of course.'

She didn't look up from her laptop, and his frustration increased. 'Your predecessor approved that clause. In fact, she wrote it.'

'It's a standard clause. I've written it myself in countless prenups. But if Nancy was here, I'm certain she would be amending it. As I said before, this version of the document is simply a template. We use it as a framework, a starting-off point for the process of going through the prenup line by line and making it personal for the client. In this case, your sister, Ariana.'

'You think there should be little hearts above all the *i*s?'

Now she looked up, her eyes narrowing at his face. 'I know you see this agreement as a means to deter Mr Arteta from pursuing Ariana, but we have to write the prenup with the reasonable assumption that he and your sister will sign it. So I have one question for you. Do you think Ariana will sign this in its present form? Because I have to say it feels unlikely to me.'

It was on the tip of his tongue to tell her that she didn't know his sister. Only, she did.

That was the difference between Willa and Nancy Kemp. They were both methodical and thorough. That was to be expected at this level.

But Nancy was more process-driven. For her, Ariana's personality was the sum of her property portfolio and other assets coupled with the status afforded her by being a Konstantinou. In contrast, Willa asked questions about Ariana's life, her degree, her interests, her previous relationships. She wanted to know who his sister was.

Larry was right, he thought. She was good at her job.

Shifting back against the sofa, he shook his head. 'I doubt it, no.'

She stared back at him, and he had a sharp flashback to that moment on the Clarendon's roof.

'Then, I suggest we attach a note to this clause.' She leaned forward to type into her laptop, highlighting the offending paragraph in their shared document. 'I can come back to it later when I've talked to Ariana.'

He frowned. 'You want to talk to Ariana.'

'I would have thought that goes without saying.' Now she frowned. 'This is her prenup. I need her input. You need her input.' Willa cleared her throat. 'Prenups are not legally binding. But in the vast majority of cases, a judge will uphold them if they meet three criteria.'

She ticked them off on her fingers. 'Was the agreement freely entered into? Did both parties have a full appreciation of the implications of the agreement? Is it fair to hold the parties to the agreement? In other words, the best prenup is one Ariana feels is a choice she is making, willingly. So yes, I need to talk to her. Is that going to be a problem?'

There was an edge to her voice.

'No.' It was. He felt suddenly disorientated. The idea of Willa meeting Ariana seemed seismic. Of course, Ariana wouldn't know that Willa was pregnant with his baby, but still it made him feel vulnerable, and he didn't do vulnerable. Hadn't allowed himself to feel vulnerable since Zoe had betrayed his trust.

The memory of that afternoon, of Zoe's hands splayed against her lover's shoulders, made his breath snarl in his throat. He felt a sudden need to push back, to reassert his authority over this woman and her opaqueness, and leaning forward he flipped his laptop shut. 'No, that won't be a problem. I'll text her now. Just out of interest,' he added casually as he typed out a message to his sister, 'why did you think it wouldn't happen?'

It was a non sequitur. It shouldn't make sense, but he knew from the sudden tension in her spine that she understood. Knew that she had been hoping this whole time that he wouldn't circle back to what she'd said yesterday.

Her eyes were still and wary and very green. She shrugged. 'Statistically, it was unlikely.'

As answers went, it was entirely plausible. He'd done some research last night before he fell asleep, before he knew for sure that Willa was pregnant and the chance of pregnancy from a single act of unprotected intercourse was roughly one in twenty or twenty-five percent, assuming the act occurred during the fertile window. Which presumably it had.

Of course, it had been more than one act, which might skew the probabilities a fraction.

Either way, he knew Willa wasn't telling him the truth.

'And that's what you were thinking about, was it? When we were up on the roof, by the pool. When we were both naked. Statistical probabilities?'

She licked her lips. He could feel the thorns rising up, tangling around her, but he was done with simply gazing up at them. It was time to bring out his metaphorical sword and start hacking a path through.

'Willa?'

'I don't remember.'

'I think we both know that's not true. That night is seared into my brain. And I know it's seared into yours just like I know that you weren't thinking about statistics.'

He got to his feet a second after she did. The difference was that Willa was clenching and unclenching her hands and shifting her weight onto the ball of her front foot as if she couldn't decide whether to punch him or turn and run.

Fight or flight.

The most basic, evolutionary response to threat or danger. But there was no threat. He was just asking a question.

'Then, you're wrong.' There was no emotion in her voice, and her eyes were devoid of anything other than hostility. 'Like you were wrong about me hiding that I was engaged.'

'I was wrong about that,' he agreed. 'But you're hiding something from me now.'

Against the sudden pallor of her face, her eyes were sharply green. 'Yes, I am. I'm hiding how appalled I am that someone as arrogant and ruthless and vengeful as you should be the father of my baby.'

She was lashing out but not because she was angry—or if she was, her anger was driven by something bigger and more powerful. Fear.

His ribs suddenly seemed too tight.

Was she scared of him? No, that wasn't it. He replayed their conversation, tracking the changes in her manner from defensive to aggressive. This was about her. About why she thought she couldn't get pregnant, even though she wasn't using contraception.

I didn't do it deliberately. I never thought it could happen.

He glanced over at Willa, her words echoing inside his head, and it was suddenly obvious why she would think unprotected sex would be so unlikely to result in a pregnancy. And then he felt her gaze, and he knew that his hunch was right. Knew, too, that she knew that he had connected the dots because she was backing through the door and onto the stone slabs of the terrace. But he couldn't let her leave alone this time. He couldn't leave her to deal with her anger and misery and fear on her own. Like he'd had to.

She was moving swiftly across the terrace, past the manicured lawn, ducking under the branches of the olive trees that covered the slope away from the villa. He caught up with her as she was crossing the flower-strewn hillside.

'Please, Willa, wait—'

Now she turned, making a pushing-away gesture with her hands. 'I don't want to talk to you.'

'Then, don't talk. We can just walk.'

Her eyes blazed. 'Don't do that. Don't act like you're the reasonable one here. Or have you conveniently forgotten that you forced me to work for you? Forced me to come to your stupid private island.'

'I was angry.'

The simplicity of his words or maybe their truth cut through her anger and panic, and he felt her hesitate. And he wanted to push forward, corral her like he'd been doing ever since she walked into that meeting room at Milner's and upended his life. But he didn't do or say anything. Instead he waited, again, like he had at the airport. Because this was a choice he needed her to make willingly.

And it cost him to wait, to not demand, to not order or cajole, but he waited in the upbeat Aegean sunshine that seemed distractingly at odds with the intensity of the drama playing out beneath it. And he kept waiting, until finally, she said quietly, 'About five and a half months ago, I had a pain in my side. I thought it was appendicitis, and I went to the ER.'

He let his gaze move briefly over Willa's profile. She spoke with the calm, steady voice of an adult reading a story to a child. But there was something about the set of her shoulders, as if she was struggling to hold up an unseen weight. Had been struggling to hold it up for some time.

'But it wasn't? Appendicitis?' he prompted after a moment.

She shook her head, stared away.

'They thought it was at first, and then they thought I might have an ectopic pregnancy. But then they did a scan, and that's when they found the cyst in one of my ovaries.

They're not actually cysts. They're follicles and they found a lot of them. But only one of them was infected. That's what was causing the pain.'

'Did it need surgery?'

It took a moment for her to reply.

Finally, she nodded. 'It did. It was a bit of a mess. Afterwards I spoke to an endocrinologist, and she said that I had Polycystic Ovary Syndrome. I have some of the symptoms, but I did a lot of riding and dance, so I'd put them down to that.' A pause. He felt her stiffen. 'Anyway, she told me that I would struggle to get pregnant. So to answer your question, that's why I thought I was safe.'

He could still hear the traces of shock and hurt. No wonder she had been in denial.

'I was on the pill before that, but I went off it then. It just seemed pointless, and it felt cruel, you know? Taking something to prevent getting pregnant.'

She breathed in sharply. 'This daily reminder that I was a failure. Pretending I needed contraception when there was no risk of conception. It made me feel like a failure. A fraud.'

He heard her swallow, and her eyes seemed suddenly over-bright. With tears?

A muscle ticked in his jaw. Seeing Willa vulnerable was worse even than feeling vulnerable himself. It made him feel furious and frustrated. It made him want to uproot the ancient olive grove with his hands. It made him want to hold her close.

Reaching out, he caught her wrists.

'You're not a failure or a fraud.'

Willa felt the vibration of Ares's voice crackle down her spine. He sounded fierce enough that it could have cut a fissure into the rock beneath her feet, and she felt as if the expression on his face was carved into her skin.

'You have a great job at a world-renowned legal firm. And for the very good reason that you are an excellent lawyer. But you're also pregnant, so your body hasn't failed you. It's done everything right despite the odds.'

She swallowed.

That didn't stop her from being a fraud. But Ares didn't know that up until a little under six months ago, she had been living a lie. She wasn't entitled to any of it. Not her father or her stepsisters and stepmother. Not her home or all those family lunches and Thanksgivings and Christmases. Not even her surname. All of it had been dishonestly acquired twenty-nine years ago. She was the unwitting accomplice to the longest of long cons.

And there was a price to be paid. A sentence to be served. Only now that sentence had been commuted. Or had it? Her panic closed around her, and she was shaking her head,

'You don't know that. What if the test was wrong?'

It was the reason she hadn't wanted to talk about the pregnancy with him. Why she couldn't allow herself to think forward even two weeks to the DNA test. Everything felt so fragile.

'You did more than one test, didn't you?' His hands tightened a fraction around her wrists as if the question might cause her to bolt.

'Yes. And they were all positive, but—' She bit her lip. How could she explain how surreal it felt to read the word *pregnant* on a test wand? The impossibility of it. Like someone finding a bottle on the shoreline with a message addressed to them personally inside.

'I don't know anything about Polycystic Ovary Syndrome,' Ares said, 'but I can have an expert fly in tomorrow from anywhere in the world.'

Willa felt her heart lurch against her ribs. His words, the

certainty of them, the intensity of his expression would never leave her, she thought, and she felt suddenly close to tears.

'Why would you do that? You don't even know if the baby's yours.'

The air was suddenly so still she could hear the leaves from the olive trees as they fluttered onto the baked earth.

Before, when she was telling him about her PCOS, he'd looked unfazed; now though, he seemed off-balance. 'Because,' he said slowly, 'I don't want you to keep feeling appalled that someone as arrogant and ruthless and vengeful as me might be the father of your child.'

A faint flush of colour spread across her cheeks. 'I shouldn't have said that.'

His mouth curved up minutely at the corners.

'As my lawyer, probably not. But outside of our professional relationship, I think I deserved it. I shouldn't have said the things I did either. I regret them.'

She felt his fingers tighten reflexively against her skin, and then her breath caught as they softened to caress the inside of her wrists, and his warmth seeped into her.

The world blurred. She cleared her throat. 'What, even *Hi, I'm Ares*?'

'Maybe not that.'

Her head was spinning. She was seeing stars, which made no sense because they were standing in bright sunshine. But then she realised they weren't stars but the tiny gold flecks in the grey of his irises.

He was so beautiful. So steady and immutable, and he was still holding her wrists. Her pulse dipped with panic that he would suddenly realise and let go, and she thought wildly for a reason for them to stay standing where they were.

She half twisted her head towards where the sun was slipping down towards the blue Aegean. 'It's a beautiful view.'

There was a silence, and she assumed Ares was looking out to sea, but turning she found his eyes locked on her face.

'Is that why I'm here? So you could show me the view?'

His words pulsed through her, followed like a shadow by a memory of the night when he asked her that exact same question. And she felt it simmer between them, this conspiracy of two. And she took a step closer, close enough that she could feel the press of his erection against her stomach.

He felt it too.

'No,' she said hoarsely, and she held her breath and watched the stars dance in his eyes, and she was still watching them when he leaned forward and kissed her.

CHAPTER SEVEN

WILLA WAS GLAD that Ares's hand was solid against her back because in the slithering unsteadiness of the moment she would have lost her footing. She felt loose and soft at the edges as if she was dissolving into the brilliant sunlight and the heat of his mouth on hers.

Her pulse was shivering, because she had lost her mind. He had too.

This was crazy, ridiculous, foolish, but his mouth was warm and urgent, and his hands were moving deftly over her skin. He was literally reading her like a map, and she clutched at him feverishly, the certainty of his touch giving her permission to embrace her insanity.

He was touching her face, her throat, her shoulders, and each caress was a flame licking over her skin, accelerating her desire, and she moaned against his lips.

His fingers tightened in her hair, and she felt something liquid and electric skate down her spine as he began nuzzling her throat, tasting her skin with hot, open-mouthed kisses, breathing her in, and she had to grip his shoulder to stop her legs from buckling.

Now he found her mouth again. 'Do you want to go back to the villa?'

The hoarseness in his voice jolted her back to real time, and she saw that his face was taut with muscle and concentration, and she knew that he was having to keep himself in check. There was a tantalising power in seeing him so aroused, in knowing that she was the reason it was such a struggle.

'No.' She frowned. 'Do you?'

But he was already moving both of them backwards up the slope, his hunger a living force she could feel vibrating through his body into hers.

His hands shifted to her shoulders, and then he was pulling at the straps of her dress, and she felt the fabric slip over her body, snagging on her taut nipples. Already they felt more sensitive than before, and she tugged the bodice of the dress past them.

He grunted, and the sound jolted her nerve endings, made her think of hot, damp skin and the flat of his tongue moving between her thighs. She could feel pleasure fluttering over her abdomen like a bath spilling over, and suddenly she wanted to make him shake, to feel him lose control. She tugged at the button on his waistband, fingers clumsy with need, and then she was unzipping him, her fingers pushing past the fabric on his trousers to take his cock in her hand.

Was he this big last time? Her breath caught in her throat. He was smooth and hard, the skin taut over the straining flesh.

'Let me taste you,' she said hoarsely, and his pupils fattened so that his eyes were pure black, and he let her push him backwards onto the springy grass, his hand moving to tangle through her hair as she dropped down between his legs and moved her mouth over the head of his erection.

She could sense his yearning, and then his fingers moved to caress the curve of her bottom, and she felt her blood sing, and finding his hand, she pressed it between her thighs.

His cock twitched and swelled in her mouth, and she felt him shudder against her as he slid his fingers beneath the damp cotton of her panties.

He was lifting her slightly, holding her up, holding her together almost with his fingers, and her thighs trembled uncontrollably. Her pulse was beating against his hand as she rocked against him. His other hand moved to clutch her hip, and the pressure inside of her lurched outwards.

Maybe he was feeling it too, because he was pulling her hips backwards and kissing her hungrily, his fingers pinching her aching nipples. She squirmed in his arms, wanting more contact, more flesh, more skin, desperate for friction, certain that she would die if he stopped what he was doing.

The roar in her ears was getting louder. She felt like she was melting. Her fingers twitched against his chest as he sucked her breasts.

'*Se thélo*,' he said. She didn't speak Greek, but the raw hunger in his voice almost tipped her over, and she was arching against him wildly so that he had to clamp his hands on her hips to steady her.

'Ares,' she breathed out.

Beneath them, the grass-covered slope was starting to spin, the flowers nothing more than a swirling kaleidoscope of pink and yellow and violet. His hands cupped her bottom, lifting her again so that he didn't enter her too deeply. And she was moaning against his neck. His skin was feverishly, beautifully warm, and his cock was rock-hard. He started to move deeper inside her, and the first jolts of pleasure hit her so hard that she bit into his shoulder. And even though she was anchored to his body, her own seemed to lift out of itself, and there was a sharp brightness like a match striking, and she was blooming and burning and flickering in the white heat, not blood or breath but a flame.

His hand clamped around her shoulder, and the sound he made in his throat made her vision narrow: there was nothing but Ares and his shuddering breath and her own thundering heartbeat as he surged inside her.

For a moment, she was unable to move or speak. She was outside of time. This Willa existed only in the shade of this olive grove. A creature of raw need, lost to rational thought, uncaring of her semi-dressed state. Half-wild.

All his.

And he was hers. And it was the sweetest, most terrifying feeling. And she knew better than to say it out loud. But she couldn't stop herself from thinking it, just for a moment.

She had expected Ares to pull away, not because he'd done so that last time. He hadn't. But this was different than before. Now they had a past. And a future?

Her breath shortened. She wasn't going to think about that now. Most likely Ares didn't want that anyway. After all, he was still in limbo, waiting for confirmation that he was the father. And she hadn't forgotten what he'd said about his children inheriting Kallos.

If I have children. Which currently I have no plans to do.

No plans. But this baby wasn't planned.

'What are you thinking?'

Ares's voice cut across her thoughts, and she rolled towards him, tilting her head back to meet his gaze. 'Nothing, really,' she lied. 'Usually, I have so much going on in my head. I find it hard to tune it out. But here it's easy just to get lost in the beauty of all this.'

He shifted her weight so that she was resting against the crook of his shoulder. 'That's what Kallos means. *Beauty.*'

'It is beautiful.' She let her gaze move across the gold-drenched, flower-covered slope, taking in the grove of silvery-leaved olive trees and the clumps of wild thyme.

'It's aesthetically pleasing.' Reaching out, he picked a petal from her hair, and then almost on impulse, he leaned in and stole a kiss that had her forgetting how to breathe. 'You're beautiful,' he murmured against her throat, and she made herself look away because she wanted to look at him so badly and keep looking so that she could remember this moment in time when everything was perfect between them.

'You don't have to compliment me. We've already slept together.'

'You think I compliment women to get them to sleep with me?'

It was more of a statement than a question, but there was an intensity to his grey gaze now, as if her answer mattered.

'No, I don't.' It seemed unlikely that he would need to. She couldn't imagine there were many women who would refuse Ares Konstantinou, and the thought stung a little. 'I'm sure you get by just fine doing the whole brooding-Greek-hero thing.'

His mouth pulled up at one corner. 'The brooding-Greek-hero thing?'

She rolled her eyes. 'Don't pretend like you don't know what you're doing. Standing on your own at Larry's party had a definite Achilles-sulking-in-his-tent vibe.'

He laughed, and suddenly her pulse was thrumming, and she was weightless, soaring high like a bird or a kite with a fluttering tail because his laugh was not just aesthetically pleasing, it was beautiful, and all she could think about was how she could make him laugh again.

'I wasn't sulking. I was trying to think of a suitable counter-curse for you.'

'So, you did see me.' Willa sat up to look at him, tugging her dress up to cover her breasts, trying to ignore the way his pupils narrowed as she did so. 'Why didn't you come and talk to me?'

'Why didn't *you* come and talk to *me*?'

'You nearly ran me over. And then you mansplained how to cross the road.'

'I was looking out for you. I didn't want you to get hurt any more than I want you to miss another meal.'

Lost in the sudden easy familiarity of what was probably the closest she'd come to banter in her entire life, it took her a second to realise that Ares was glancing at the sky. Or, more precisely, at the sun which was well on its way to the dark line of the horizon.

'I am actually quite hungry,' she said quickly. She wasn't. But she didn't want him to think that she was trying to prolong what was essentially the dotting of an *i* in a final edit.

They dressed quickly without touching, but as they walked back up the slope, Ares's fingers grazed hers, and after a moment he caught her hand and held it firmly.

Only to stop her slipping, of course. Which was why he let go as they reached the villa.

Iona had set the table out on the terrace. It was an unashamedly romantic setting. The sky was streaked with pink and orange, and a pale moon was starting to creep upwards like a shy sister peeping into a ballroom.

'I usually eat outside, but if you'd rather—'

'No, this is lovely.'

She had been too tense yesterday to do more than pick at the meze at lunchtime. But eating had been tricky for months now. Food was a big part of life in Santa Catalina. And when she was working in LA, when she still thought that she had a place in her family, she'd gone home most weekends for a Sunday barbecue or a cookout on the beach.

And then she'd found out the truth about who she was and she had moved to New York, and whenever she thought about food, there were just so many things she couldn't eat because they reminded her of home. Reminded her of everything she had taken for granted, when none of it had been hers to take.

'Then, let's eat,' he said simply. And maybe because he made it sound that simple, she found to her surprise that she hadn't lied earlier. She was hungry.

And the food was astonishingly good. Hamilton's had an excellent chef, but this was a cut above the beach barbecues the hotel was famous for. There were green beans with grilled apricots and goat's curd. Sliced tomatoes flecked with tiny black olives and samphire. *Bonito carpaccio* with cucumber and *boukovo*. And to finish, caramelised *tsoureki* pudding with pistachio and ice cream.

'That really was incredible. I think I could eat that ice cream every day, all day.'

'Have more, if you want.'

'No, it's fine.'

He raised his hand languidly. It was a mark of wealth, moving like that. Her family were comfortably off, but they owned one successful hotel, not a global empire. And although they had staff, they mucked in. But the super-rich didn't muck in or rush or wave at people to get their attention. Someone was always watching them attentively, poised and ready to swoop in and meet their every need. Now Iona appeared as if she had indeed been waiting in the wings.

'Another ice cream for Ms Hamilton, please, Iona. And an espresso for me.'

'Do you always eat like this?' she asked as the housekeeper disappeared into the villa.

'I usually skip dessert unless my sister is here.' His face softened. 'She has a sweet tooth.'

Iona returned, and they waited as she set down another bowl of ice cream and a cup of coffee.

'But you don't?'

This conversation was a first, she realised watching Ares's lips close around the rim of his cup. Every other interaction had been fraught with tension. Combative. Weighted. Even at Thea's, he had only relaxed momentarily. Now though, she wondered if this was Ares when he wasn't focused on trying to protect his sister. Or his family name. Or his empire.

'My preferences are a little more complex.' His grey eyes rested steadily on her face. 'I like sweet and hot and something with a little bit of bite.'

She felt her body tighten, remembering how she had nipped his shoulder, her teeth shuddering against his skin as she arched against him. They hadn't talked about what had happened in the olive grove on the way back to the villa. But what was there to talk about? It wasn't planned, but nor was it random. It had been building for days, weeks really, like a wave far out at sea. At some point, it had to come crashing onto the shore. That was what waves did. It was inevitable, an irresistible law of nature in action.

Her pulse twitched. Ares felt like an irresistible force of nature. Especially when he was sitting so close to her.

Picking up her glass, she took a sip of chilled sparkling water. Time to change the subject. Time maybe to reinforce those boundaries and remind herself why she was here. Time to put on her metaphorical wig and gown.

'I was wondering, did you manage to arrange a time for us to talk to Ariana? I know she's still in Mexico, but it would speed things up if we could get her input.'

'She was being a bit vague about when would work, but I'll try and pin her down today.'

And then it would be time to return to London.

Her throat tightened around the lump that kept forming every time she allowed herself to think about that. The lump was part of a wider set of symptoms that felt a lot like homesickness. Which showed how destabilising elevated hormones could be.

She nodded. 'Thank you. In my experience, nobody likes paperwork. At this stage, a lot of clients get impatient with the process. They just want to get the prenup signed and get on with their lives. Which is why this is the riskiest period. In their rush to get to the finishing line, people lose sight of what's at stake. I find talking it through, step by step, making it real can be very sobering. And as I said before, this is Ariana's prenup, for her marriage.'

His cup made a tiny chink as he placed it back on its saucer.

'It is. But it isn't Ariana's marriage that I want to discuss right now.' There was an expression on his face that was familiar but jarring. It was serious, meditative. And then she remembered where she had seen it before.

Robert had looked like that when he'd sat down with her at the hospital and told her he wasn't her father.

Her heart felt spongy like the driftwood that sometimes washed up on the beach back in California.

'I should warn you that I don't work on a Write One, Get One Free basis when it comes to prenups.' It was a joke. But he wasn't laughing, and she felt suddenly unanchored.

'Whose marriage do you want to talk about, then?'

She knew the answer before he replied, but it was just so many levels of crazy that her brain wouldn't process it.

'Ours,' he said quietly. 'I want to talk about our marriage.'

It wasn't on her to-do list. Even before she started to shake her head, Ares had known that by the stunned, incredulous expression on her small oval face.

'Our marriage?' There was an infinitesimal stammer in her voice. 'We're not getting married.'

She meant it as a statement of fact, and in that sense she was right. But he had meant it as a statement of his intentions. And walking back from the olive grove it had all made perfect sense. All of it, that night in the Clarendon, forcing Willa to work for him, bringing her to Kallos, finding out she was pregnant, it was not who he was. Before she had walked into the road in front of his car, his life had been as ordered and smooth as the swing of a pendulum.

Now it felt like a ball spinning on a roulette wheel.

'You don't know that you're the father.' She spoke slowly as if her words were pearls she was stringing together to make a necklace.

He shrugged, knowing it was important to stay calm. 'Judging by your reaction at Thea's, I'm guessing that the DNA test will be a formality. And obviously if I'm not the father, then there will be no need for us to marry.'

'There's no need if you are. This isn't the Middle Ages, Ares. Women don't marry men because they're pregnant.'

'Some do. Others marry out of duty. For others it is a strategic decision to forge an alliance. And then, there's love.'

Love. The word was a serrated blade against his skin. All his family made it look so easy. His grandparents, his parents. Even Ariana. But for him, love was a foreign language written in an entirely different alphabet. And whenever he thought about loving someone, it would take him straight back to Zoe's apartment in Athens and the engagement ring he'd given her glittering treacherously in the afternoon sunlight.

Willa was staring at him. 'But you don't love me. And I don't love you,' she added as if he had accused her of doing so. 'Honestly, I can't think of a single reason why we would marry.'

'How about that it's the right thing to do?'

He pictured the noisy, laughter-filled meals at the summer house in Ekali; his father teaching him to sail; his mother showing him how to hold Ariana when she was a baby; his grandfather reading him *Jason and the Argonauts*. Memories now, but no less magical.

'Children need parents. They need to know where they come from. They need to belong. We both had that ourselves, and we know that its value is incalculable. For what reason, therefore, would we deny our child that same experience?'

And not just their child.

Like any disaster, Zoe's betrayal, and his handling of it, had hurt more than just the people at the epicentre. There had been far-reaching consequences for his family. Painful, shaming consequences. There was nothing he could do to atone for the pain he had caused his parents, but this was his chance to give his grandfather and Ari the happily-ever-after he knew they craved for him.

And then there was Willa.

His pride would never allow him to admit it aloud, but with Zoe, he had been hapless and blind to what was going on. But he and Willa had found out at the same time that she was having a baby. They were feeling their way in the darkness together.

Only it was more than that. From that very first meeting in that sunlit street in London, he had wanted to pin Willa down. Then, as now, she evaded him. She was an itch he could never quite scratch.

Marriage would bind her to him.

And that was different too. With Zoe, he had slipped into getting engaged unthinkingly, just as if he was climbing into the first cab at a taxi rank. With this proposal, he was making a conscious choice.

None of which he was prepared to share with Willa. Instead, he said firmly, 'You are carrying my baby. That makes you my responsibility.'

Her face stiffened, and he could almost see her retreating back into her forest of thorns.

'I don't belong to you. We've had sex. Twice. And currently I am rewriting your sister's prenup. That is the extent of our *relationship*.'

'So you admit that we have a relationship?'

She held his gaze. 'You know you can't keep doing this.'

'Suggesting we marry?'

'No. Pushing me into doing things I don't want to do. Things I'm not ready to do.'

'Pushing how? You gave me the code to the roof terrace at the Clarendon. You had sex with me without contraception.'

She flinched, then steadied herself, but he could read the hurt in her eyes. 'That's not fair.'

It wasn't. But he didn't feel fair. He felt thwarted and out of control.

'Yeah, it's really unfair being offered an all-expenses-paid way out of single motherhood.'

The air snapped tight. This time Willa didn't flinch. Or maybe she had retreated so far from him that he couldn't see it.

'Tell me something, Ares. If Ariana had sex twice with a man who got her pregnant, a man she was working for temporarily, would you be encouraging her to marry him?' Her eyes jerked to his. 'No, I thought not.'

He watched as she started to eat her ice cream, his gaze following the rhythmic progress of the spoon, momentarily mesmerised by the movement of her graceful hands.

'It's not the same.'

'Of course not. She's your sister.'

He pushed his coffee cup to one side and leaned back in his seat. 'How long did you wear your mother's engagement ring on your hand?'

Frowning, she pushed the bowl away. 'I don't know. Two years maybe.'

'You were happy to do that. To pretend that you were engaged.'

'Not *happy*. I told you why I wore it. It made my life easier.'

'And wearing my ring for real will do that too. It's just a different ring, Willa.'

She was giving him a *what are you talking about?* stare.

'It's a lie is what it is. Or are you planning on telling the world that the reason we're married is because you knocked me up in a one-night stand?'

'That wouldn't be quite how I'd phrase it.'

Her eyes clashed with his. 'In other words, you wouldn't tell them the truth.'

'We would know the truth,' he said slowly. 'The rest of the world is unimportant.'

'But your sister isn't. And your grandfather isn't. Most important of all, our child won't be. Is that who you are? Are you happy to lie to the people you love? To make them co-conspirators to our lies?'

The sun had set, but there were solar-powered lights in the trees that edged the terrace and now they cast shadows across Willa's cut-glass features so that she seemed to be disappearing into the darkness.

'I don't understand you. We've just spent the better part of two days finessing Ariana's prenup so that she won't marry some random man she's only known for a couple of months, but now you want to marry me, and we only met three weeks ago.'

'The difference is you are pregnant.'

She had, he noticed, stopped mentioning the DNA test. Which meant he believed it was his child.

Now she took a breath. 'How long were you engaged to—?' She left space for him to supply the name.

After a moment he said as calmly as he could, 'Zoe.'

Her name tasted strange in his mouth. It was such a long time since he had said it out loud. Years, and he felt a rush of anger with Willa for forcing him to do so now.

'And we were engaged for eighteen months.' They had known each other a lot longer. Her parents were friends of his parents, and she came to every family event, first as a friend, then as a girlfriend.

'You must have known each other very well.'

Ares felt his body tighten as if it was being stretched on a rack. At the time, he had thought he knew Zoe as well as he knew himself. Now though, he wondered if he had simply made assumptions.

'We did.'

'You knew each other for a long time, and you loved each other, and yet you still walked away from her. Which makes you either cowardly or cruel. Right now, I'm not sure which one best applies.'

He had been neither.

His lungs felt as though they were full of lead. For some reason Willa's words hurt more than Zoe's betrayal. More even than his parents' deaths.

Pushing back his chair, he tossed his napkin onto the table and walked past her towards the gardens. He had no idea where he was going, just that he needed to be in a space large enough to contain the ache in his chest. And nowhere near the olive grove.

Which was why he found himself on the beach.

The tide was in, but there was a strip of sand, cool and pale and powdery like confectioners' sugar. He sat down to watch the tumbling waves, breathing in the salt breeze. Normally, he found it calming to watch the rippling water, but tonight it felt overwhelming, as if the sea was mimicking the chaos inside his chest.

A chaos he had wanted to contain by getting Willa to agree to marriage. To living a lie. To lying to his family and hers. To their child. Only, in answer to Willa's question, that wasn't who he was. Not that she would believe him. Or care.

She probably wouldn't care if she never saw him again.

'You know, even if we don't marry, we're going to have to get to a point where one or the other of us doesn't storm off in the middle of every difficult conversation.'

He glanced up, his heartbeat blunt with confusion. Willa was standing beside him. Her dark hair was very dark, and her skin looked silver in the moonlight. She looked nervous but defiant.

'Although, I suppose technically it was your turn.'

'Is that how it works?'

'I don't know. I don't know how most things work. Particularly us.' She sat down beside him. 'I wasn't expecting a proposal. I didn't handle it very well.'

'No, you were right to say what you did. It's better that we're honest.'

She glanced away. 'You were trying to do a good thing, and I know people get married for all kinds of reasons, but no good will come of you forcing yourself to do something that you clearly don't want to do. If you felt trapped with Zoe, how are you going to feel with me?'

A wave rose and tumbled at the shoreline, but he wasn't really seeing it. There was nothing but the dark-haired woman sitting quietly, patiently, beside him. She had come to find him so that they could finish this conversation.

The idea that she would do that went some way to soothing the turmoil in his chest

So finish it, he told himself.

'I wasn't the one who felt trapped.'

He had never said those words to anyone. Not his family. Not the media. And in the past, the idea of revealing Zoe's infidelity would have felt like ripping out stitches with his teeth, but as Willa's gaze shifted from the sea to his face, he felt nothing but relief.

'Then, why did you leave her at the altar?' she said quietly.

'I went to Zoe's apartment on the day before the wedding. We'd agreed not to see each other, but I'd bought her a bracelet.' He glanced down at his hands. 'I let myself in. The lock was stiff, but I'd learned how to open it smoothly. If I hadn't done that, I might never have found her.' A pause. 'I wanted to surprise her, but it was me that got the surprise.' Was that the right word for a gut-wrenching betrayal? 'Zoe was there with a man. They were having sex.'

In the silence that followed that statement, he felt Willa's shock and confusion, but when she spoke, her voice was matter-of-fact, calm. 'That's awful,' she said simply. Because, of course, it was undeniably and emphatically awful. And it felt liberating to acknowledge that, finally.

'What did you do?'

'Nothing.' He frowned. 'She'd taken off her engagement ring, and I just kept staring at it, and then I left. Honestly, I felt like I was drugged. When I got in the car, I couldn't remember how to drive.'

'You were in shock.' Willa's eyes were a soft green like wet grass after summer rain. 'You didn't want it to be true.'

'I didn't.' But it was. 'I wanted not to have seen it. Only I had, and I knew I couldn't go through with the marriage. I went back to my parents' house, and I was going to tell them. I was going to call the wedding off. But they were so happy and excited. And they loved Zoe.'

Far out at sea, a red light was blinking in the darkness. A yacht, port side, cutting silently through the water like Zoe's betrayal had sliced through his heart.

'I didn't plan to leave her. I was going to go through with it right up until I got close, and then she turned and smiled, and my legs just wouldn't move—'

He could still remember Zoe's face. She'd looked beautiful. But all he could think about was how good she was at lying.

'You did the right thing.'

'Did I?' He felt his heart twist. 'I humiliated Zoe, hurt her family. And my family.' It still gutted him now, that look on his father's face. His mother's tears. 'I turned our lives into a circus for years. And they died thinking I was that man on the front of all the tabloids.'

'They knew you weren't that man.'

There was a fierceness to her voice now that pulled him back from that same dark place he'd been in those terrible months after the wedding, and then he felt the soft touch of her fingers on his hand, and after a moment he twisted his hand round to clasp hers. She tightened her grip, anchoring him.

'Sure, you have faults. You're stubborn and bossy and too smart for your own good.'

'Don't forget *arrogant* and *ruthless* and *vengeful*?'

Her eyes gleamed, still fierce. She wasn't fighting him now, but fighting in his corner. It made something flare inside of him, called something back to life.

'You're not any of those things. But you are determined and loyal and kind. I know that, but more importantly, your parents did too. They knew you better than anyone, and they would have known that you had a reason to do what you did because they loved you and trusted you enough to make you Ariana's legal guardian.'

'I would have told them, but I waited too long. Then later, there didn't seem any point in bad-mouthing Zoe, so I let people think I was the villain. And in a way I was. I let her be humiliated in public.'

'You had no choice.' She squeezed his hand. 'The alternative would just have been to lie and keep lying because there's never just one lie. Trust me, it's better to rip the plaster off than to do it gradually.'

'You're very wise for someone so young.'

There was an expression on her face, a flickering emotion he couldn't catch. And then it was gone. 'It's the job. It's very ageing.'

There were smudges under her eyes, and he got to his

feet, pulling her up beside him. 'I've kept you up so late. You must be exhausted. Let's go to bed.'

His words replayed inside his head during the ten minutes it took the two of them to walk in silence back to the villa. Willa seemed lost in thought, or maybe she was revising her opinion of him again.

As they reached the bottom of the stairs, he stopped and cleared his throat. 'Just to be clear, I didn't mean my bed. I wasn't assuming—'

'Weren't you?' She was staring up at him, her absinthe-coloured eyes steady on his face. 'I was.' And then she took his hand and led him upstairs into her bedroom, pulling him against her hungrily as he pushed the door shut with the flat of his hand.

CHAPTER EIGHT

Willa woke first.

For a moment, she didn't know why. And then she heard it. Faint, but imperative, buzzing somewhere in the room.

An alarm? No, a phone. Her phone? No, her phone was downstairs, somewhere. Whereas she was upstairs, in bed with Ares.

Her cheeks burned as she repeated that to herself. She was here, in bed with Ares. He was next to her, his dark head beside hers on the pillow, his arm curving possessively across her waist.

She had forgotten to close the shutters fully, and breathing out unsteadily she lay in the soft, morning light, working through all the possible interpretations of this new state of affairs, and then he was shifting against her, his eyelashes fluttering open.

Her stomach tensed, half expecting to see regret in his grey eyes, but instead she saw confusion, then desire. And she couldn't help herself, she couldn't stop the smile from pulling at her mouth as his hard body spooned around hers just as if they were the married couple he'd suggested they become.

'You feel wonderful,' he murmured against her throat, and he pressed closer, and she felt his cock twitch against the cushion of her bottom. And then he was tugging her round, and his mouth found hers at the same time as the slightly roughened pad of his thumb found her already-hard nipple and her breath hitching, she let her eyes drift shut—

There it was again—

Her eyes snapped open as the buzzing sound echoed around the room, punctuating the soft thundering of her heartbeat, and gritting her teeth, she broke the kiss.

'I think that's your phone.'

His mouth was seeking hers again.

'They can wait.'

'It might be important. I heard it a minute ago too.'

Abruptly the ringing stopped. And then it started again.

He groaned, a *V* forming on his forehead. 'It'll be Ariana. She's probably in bed, bored, and she's forgotten the time difference. She can be very demanding.'

'Family trait?' she said softly.

He rolled away from her, then stopped, rolled back and kissed her hungrily, and she knew that it was stupid, she was being stupid and reckless letting her body open to his so easily, but he was so hard to resist. Even more so now after last night.

She felt a pang as he pulled away again, and then her pulse shivered as he stood up and she stared at the glory of his nakedness. His cock was not fully erect, but it stood starkly proud of his body. Her mouth felt suddenly dry. He was utterly gorgeous. Muscular but not overdeveloped like some comic-book hero. Just lean and hard and toned, and with all that tempting, smooth golden skin.

'You're making it very hard for me to concentrate,' he said huskily.

He was searching through the clothes they had stripped from one another as they made their way across the bedroom, but now he turned to face her, and her pulse stuttered as his eyes met hers and she saw the breadth of his pupils.

'Do you want me to help?'

She sat up, letting the sheet fall away from her body, feeling her skin tingle as his eyes narrowed on her breasts.

'I think you know that isn't helping,' he said hoarsely, and she felt her nipples tighten again and a thrill of power as his cock stiffened. '*Skatá*. Where is my phone?'

Willa caught a flash of light from across the room. 'It's over there, under the armchair. It must have dropped out when we were getting undressed.'

Falling back against the pillows, she pressed her thighs together as she remembered the feel of his hands as he'd unpeeled her clothes from her body. The sex was different last night. He had been different last night. Before there was intensity to his lovemaking, a gentleness, too, that second time out in the olive grove. But until last night he had never let down his guard.

Ares had found his phone, and she watched him answer. As he started speaking rapidly in Greek, her heart twisted.

At first, when he'd walked off and left her sitting alone on the terrace, she'd felt relieved. His marriage proposal— although, it had felt more like an assumption of marriage than a proposal—was so unexpected it had thrown her off balance.

But it was nowhere near as unbalancing as what had come next.

She had followed him down the beach, spurred on by frustration and fury at the cruel and disdainful economy of his accusations. Her hands were shaking as she walked, her breath too. She'd lost sight of him a couple of times, but she didn't need to see him. She could find him wearing a blindfold. His body pulling her to him by magnetic force or maybe something less scientific.

And then she had seen him sitting on the sand, his head bowed over his hands.

He'd looked lost, and in pain.

He was both. And it hurt to know, to see, to feel his pain.

No wonder he had been so easily convinced that she was playing him. She could imagine how he must have felt finding her engagement ring like that. The shock. The repeated sense of betrayal. For a man like Ares, so certain, so proud, so beautiful, it would have been less of a shock than an earthquake shaking the foundations of his world, his identity.

And of course, that initial revelation was only the start. Afterwards, you had to react, to continue living even though you were bloodied and blinded by pain. She had focused her energies on work. Ares had tried to go through with his wedding.

Because he still loved Zoe?

Her fingers tightened around the sheet. It suddenly hurt to breathe. It was another reason why she couldn't marry Ares. Or maybe it was the same reason as not wanting to be his burden but just looked at from a slightly different angle. She had lived her life feeling like an outsider. Six months ago, that feeling had been explained, and she had left Santa Catalina rather than live a life of pretence. But if she married Ares, knowing he loved Zoe, she would simply replace one set of lies for another. And spend every day being reminded that she was not entitled to love, just a duty of care.

Of course, Ares hadn't said he loved Zoe. Probably he couldn't or wouldn't admit that out loud to Willa, so he transferred the emotion to his parents. But why else had he shouldered the burden of guilt? He could have thrown Zoe to the wolves. He'd had every right to do so. But instead, he had taken the blame. He had let the world, his parents, his family think he was a commitment-phobe, a heartbreaker who left women at the altar.

Of course it had backfired.

Lies always did.

They had unseen repercussions that crossed time and

oceans, rippling outwards, on and on, multiplying and swallowing up everything in their path.

And the only way to escape was the hardest to take: to tell the truth. It sounded so simple. Something you would say to a small child. But some truths were just too destructive, too toxic to inflict on others. It was why opening Pandora's box was rarely given a positive spin. Sometimes it was better for everyone to keep the lid tightly shut.

'S'agapó, ta léme.'

Ares tossed his phone onto the armchair, tension visible in every line of his superb body.

She wanted to ask him why. It was the kind of thing you did as a couple. But were they a couple? They were having sex and sharing a bed, and he had sort of proposed but—

'Problem?'

He glanced down at her, his shoulders filling the room. He seemed to have forgotten he was naked, or perhaps he didn't care. Which was understandable, given that his body was nothing short of miraculous.

'It's Ariana.'

He wasn't upset. Not hurt. Just angry. Her stomach lurched sideways with panic. 'She hasn't got married, has she?'

'What? No.' He shook his head. 'Thankfully, even my sister is not that impulsive. She is, however, back in Greece.'

Willa frowned. 'I thought you texted her yesterday. Wasn't she in Mexico then?'

'She was. But when I asked if she could talk to you, she thought it would be better to do it in person. She flew out of Oaxaca yesterday afternoon and arrived back in Athens about a half an hour ago. She wants to meet around four.'

'Won't she be feeling a little jet-lagged?'

'My sister is a seasoned traveller. She'll have slept on the flight. But we don't have to do it today. Ariana is used to having my attention, but if you want to do it tomorrow or the day after—'

Tomorrow? The day after?

The lump in her throat was back. She had been here before on a different island, in a different sea, living a different fantasy. But you couldn't fight reality. The day after was a fantasy.

Of course, that wasn't to say she wouldn't miss all of this. Not the luxury. That was great, but she had grown up with wealth. Admittedly, not this level of wealth, but she knew the downsides.

By *all of this*, she meant Ares.

It wasn't just that the sex was transformative. She had meant what she'd said on the beach. He was a good man. Determined and loyal and kind. And brave. It would have cost him to reveal something so shaming as Zoe's infidelity. She knew because she couldn't reveal her shame.

She couldn't bear for him to see the real Willa. The daughter of a woman who had gotten pregnant by her lover and told her husband he was the father. It sounded so overwrought and melodramatic using language like that. And maybe it was. It was also one step removed from her, but once Ares knew, he could never unknow the truth.

She couldn't bear to be just another heavy burden to another good man. And what else could she be?

Her stomach cramped as she remembered Robert's face. It had been a word cloud of bad feelings. Shame. Sadness. Hurt. Regret.

So why ruin things with Ares? She was in a good place with him. It would never get any better than this.

Now though, she needed to face up to reality.

'Today would be better. I'll talk Ariana through everything,' she said quickly. 'When I get back to London, I'll add in any amendments she wants to make, and then if you're both happy I'll send that draft to Mr Arteta's legal team.'

The silence between them stretched and widened and swelled to the edges of the bedroom. His face didn't change but the air felt suddenly charged. 'You're going back to London today?' A question, not a statement. As though it was negotiable.

'I'll pick up a late flight. Those flights always have seats.'

His eyes locked onto her face like they had in the Zen Den. 'Why the rush?'

It was like being hypnotised. Suddenly it felt there was nothing else in or outside the room that mattered aside from Ares. With an effort she dragged her eyes away from his. 'There's no rush. But I put aside two to three days for working through the prenup with you, and this is my third day. Larry will be wondering if I've gone native.'

She cleared her throat. 'I'm looking forward to meeting Ariana. Like I said, it's always good to meet a client in person... Or maybe it isn't,' she said when Ares didn't reply.

'Yes, it is. It's good.' He nodded, but she knew that he was replying as much to the rising inflection in her voice as the question itself.

'*I am large, I contain multitudes.*'

There was a beat of silence, and his eyes found hers. 'Why are you quoting Walt Whitman to me?'

'Because for me *good* is generally something positive or favourable or satisfying, but when you said *good* a moment ago, it felt like there were a whole other bunch of meanings that I was missing.'

He smiled then, and some of the tension left his body, and it was stupid, but she couldn't stop herself from feeling disproportionately pleased that she could do that.

'I'm not going to talk to Ariana about us. Is that why you don't want the two of us to meet? A *yes* or *no* will suffice.'

'Yes. No. Yes.' His pupils snapped out to swallow his irises. 'I don't think I can have a conversation with you about my sister when you're naked.'

'Do you want to talk about something else? Or we could talk later.'

There was a different kind of tension to him now. She could almost see his skin tightening. And he was hard again.

Her pulse flickered as he walked back towards her, dipping as he knelt on the mattress and pulled her slowly towards him, and even though she was there on the bed, she felt like she had lost her bearings.

'Let's talk later.' He spoke softly, his voice caressing her skin so that something hot and liquid pooled between her legs.

'Yeah, let's.' The words had hardly stumbled from her mouth before he was leaning forward, licking her breasts, his warm breath flooding her with heat and hunger and a hazy, indescribable wonder that anything could feel this good.

And by *good* she meant *positive* and *favourable* and *satisfying* in every sense of the word.

They arrived back in Athens at a little after three o'clock.

As the SUVs made their way through the Athens's traffic, Willa found it hard to pull her eyes away from the view through her window. Three days ago, she had been too distracted by Ares's unexpected appearance to fully take in the city, but now she marvelled at the mash-up of classical and contemporary architecture. The Parthenon might dominate the skyline, but it was part of a living, breathing, modern macrocosm of tightly packed apartment blocks and streets lined with shops and cafés.

The city was proud of its past, proud period. But also pulsing with energy. No wonder Ares called it his city.

'Do you like it?' Ares was watching her intently as

though her reply mattered. As though he cared about what she thought.

'I think it's amazing,' she said truthfully. 'I've never been anywhere like this. London's old to me, but this is—'

'Ancient,' he suggested, his mouth curving into one of those small smiles that turned her into something unthinking. All she wanted to do was stare at him and try to imprint a memory of his beautiful, architectural face into her brain.

Because it would never be like this again. Not with him. Not with anyone else either. If it was hard to think about leaving him, it was impossible to imagine replacing him. There would never be another man like Ares. They might only have spent a few days under the same roof, but they had passed through fire together. Exposed their flaws, revealed their secrets.

Not all their secrets. Ares thought she had shared everything, exposed her underbelly like he had. But her biggest secret was like an open wound that hurt to touch. And he was the last person on earth who would want to see it.

The Konstantinous had no title or family crest, but they had an unbroken, traceable lineage, and Ares was understandably proud and protective of that. But for him, it was about more than being a Konstantinou. He was an Athenian and Greek to the core. A member of a civilisation that stretched back thousands of years.

Whereas half of her was unknown. Undocumented. Nameless. The unplanned consequence of an affair. A love child whose birth father hadn't loved her enough to even see her be born.

How could Ares understand that? A man raised in a city where the past and the present and the future all happily coexisted. Where the different strata of history were visible and validated. He couldn't know what it felt like to be a blank slate. To feel that you mattered less than other people. Because the inequality between them was not just economic. It was to do with being wanted and loved.

She smiled. 'I wish I'd seen more of it.'

'So stay. Another day or two won't hurt.' He spoke casually, but there was an intensity in his gaze that made her feel muddled and off balance.

'But we're here in Athens. I'm already packed.'

He shrugged. 'So unpack. We can stay in the townhouse, or if you want to see the summer house, we can head out to Ekali. It's only a twenty-minute drive from the centre. Then tomorrow I could show you my city, and when you're ready to go back to London I'll give you a lift.'

Willa felt her head swim. It was tempting on so many levels.

'I think Larry is expecting me back.'

'I'll talk to Larry,' he said easily. He was making all of this too easy. She needed obstacles. Boundaries. She almost laughed out loud. They would need to be higher than the Parthenon and wider than the Aegean.

'It's just a few days, Willa. Last bit of pushing, I promise. Think of it as a reward for all your hard work.'

It would only be a few more days.

And a few more nights.

'Another time, maybe,' she said quickly.

He held her gaze momentarily, then inclined his head. 'As you wish.'

The SUV was slowing. She glanced out of the window. They had left the clogged city centre, and the car was moving smoothly down a broad street dotted at regular intervals with sycamore trees.

'Are we not going to the office?'

Ares shook his head. 'I did think about meeting there, but Ariana is very sensitive to her environment. She is a shareholder in the business, but it is very much my company, and I didn't want that fact to overshadow the discussion... What?' He raised an eyebrow. 'I know I was reluctant before to get my sister involved, but I can see now that she needs to be.'

'Hence the use of *discussion*.'

'Correct.' She felt light-headed as his mouth curved into a small, warm smile that reached his eyes. 'Which is why I suggested we pick somewhere she feels in control. Ergo, her apartment.'

Somehow, she doubted that Ariana's apartment was going to have the same effect on her, Willa thought as she stepped out of the lift into a beautiful, high-ceiling entrance hall.

'Ares—'

A beautiful young woman burst into the hallway. As she launched herself at her brother, Willa only caught a glimpse of her long tanned limbs, bare feet and painted toenails, but Ariana was instantly recognisable from the screenshot on her brother's phone.

Her long glossy dark hair swung in a shimmering arc as he spun her in a circle. 'It's so good to see you.'

Gently lowering her to the floor, Ares kissed her on both cheeks. 'It's good to see you too. Although, I wasn't expecting to see you quite so soon.'

Ariana's lips pulled into a pout. 'There are only so many hot-stone massages you can have. And Helena is lovely, but you know that house she bought in Paris? She's having it completely renovated, and it's all she talks about. Honestly, I could practically smell the paint.'

'We can talk about Helena's renovations later.' Taking his sister's shoulders, Ares turned her towards Willa.

'Ariana, this is Willa Hamilton. She's been working on your prenup. Willa, this is my sister, Ariana.'

Willa felt her eyes pull automatically to Ariana's ring finger, but it was bare. Following her gaze, Ariana reached under the collar of her dress and fished out a pretty diamond ring on a chain.

She felt Ares tense beside her as his sister turned the ring to show off the stones. 'I'm not wearing it on my hand until we've told Pappou.'

'It's lovely, and it's lovely to meet you, finally.' Willa smiled. 'Ares has told me so much about you.'

Ariana screwed up her flawless face. 'I'm guessing it was all bad.'

Ares was right. Ariana didn't come across as the same age as her. It wasn't just her bare feet or her candour. There was something fluid and unfixed about her, in contrast to the solidity of her brother.

Willa nodded slowly. 'It was. Sorry.'

Ariana frowned, and then she burst out laughing. 'A lawyer with a sense of humour. I can't tell you what a relief that is. I've been so nervous about this prenup—'

'You don't have to be nervous. I might be a lawyer, but you're not on trial. And all we're going to do today is talk through your options. And they are your options. Ms Konstantinou. Not mine. Not your brother's. Not your fiancé's.'

'Call me Ariana.' The young woman grimaced. 'Ms Konstantinou is what my old principal used to call me.'

'I think the less said about that, the better.' Ares stepped forward. 'Let's go through, shall we?'

The sitting room was another jaw-dropping reminder of the Konstantinou family's wealth. It was light and spacious, and the beautiful furniture was arranged in that effortlessly oh so casual way favoured by the wealthy. Most impressive of all, there was an unimpeded view of the Parthenon.

'This is a lovely room.'

'It is. I love that I can see the whole of the city, but mostly I love that my mum rented this exact apartment before she married my dad. That's why you chose it, wasn't it?' Ariana's face softened as she turned towards her brother. 'Ares gave me the apartment for my twenty-first birthday.'

Ares nodded. 'They had their first date here. She cooked him chicken souvlaki—'

'And she burnt the chicken,' Ariana said.

Willa felt her heart twist as the siblings smiled at the punchline to what was clearly one of those family jokes. They were close, but it was obvious that even though he was her brother, Ares had stepped into the void left by their parents' deaths.

As the coffee and sparkling water arrived, Willa cleared her throat. 'You said you were nervous, Ariana. Did you have a specific reason?'

Ariana shrugged. 'Just that the last time I had to deal with a lawyer was after the accident. They were all locked in a room with Ares, and I didn't really know what was going on.'

Ares leaned forward. 'You were very young, Ari.'

'I know. I'm not blaming you.' Ariana's eyes were suddenly over-bright. 'How could I? You took care of everything. Of me, and Pappou. Even though you had all that other stuff with—'

Her eyes darted to Willa, and she broke off, biting her lip.

'You're my sister. You and Pappou came first. You always come first.' Ares spoke firmly but there was an ache beneath the authority, and Willa wondered if he had processed his own grief. Most likely, he had put the needs of his sister and grandfather first, even though he was still reeling from Zoe's betrayal.

'In my experience, the legal system has a rather polarising effect on most people,' Willa said carefully. 'When they don't need it, it feels elitist, intentionally overcomplicated and intimidating.'

'And when they need it?'

'It feels intentionally overcomplicated and intimidating.'

She smiled, and then Ariana smiled, and the tension in the room eased fractionally. 'When it comes to prenups, it gets even worse. The law is seen as pragmatic and unromantic. Undermining marriages before the vows have even been made.'

'Exactly.' Ariana glanced pointedly at her brother.

Willa took a breath. 'But I disagree with that view. I've met countless couples, and honestly, I would say that a prenuptial agreement is the best way to start your marriage in a spirit of openness and honesty.'

Her stomach tightened as she spoke. She felt like a hypocrite. How could she preach openness and honesty when her whole existence was based on a lie?

'So you'd get one, would you?'

'I would. Prenups aren't jinxes. Or predictions. They deal with the unromantic aspects of a marriage, so you can focus on the romance. Why don't we all take a breath, and then let's get your prenup written.'

It took just under three hours. But most of that was spent simply reading through the document and explaining each clause.

Slumping back against the sofa, Ariana blew out a breath. 'What happens now?'

'I get this written up. You then reread it with your brother and make sure you're happy, and then I send it to Mr Arteta's legal team, and we wait for him to respond.'

Ariana frowned. 'Davey doesn't care about any of this.'

'You said.' Willa nodded. 'And if he has no amendments to make, then you can both sign it as it is.'

'Thank you, Willa,' Ares said quietly. Their eyes locked for a moment, and her chest felt tight as if she was holding her breath.

'Yes, thanks, Willa. I feel so much better now. Actually,' Ariana groaned, 'I feel famished. We should go out and eat. And celebrate?'

'It's not finalised yet, Ari—'

'I know. But I've been drinking green smoothies for what feels like forever.' She sighed theatrically. 'Look, I did what you asked me to. I went to the spa so you could get the prenup sorted, and now I want to have an actual drink with alcohol in it. And I want to eat fatty and salty and sugary food. So could we please all go out to dinner? You'll come, won't you, Willa?'

'Well, I—' Willa began, but Ariana was grabbing Ares's hands, tugging them like a child. 'We could invite Pappou too. He'd be so thrilled.'

Ares nodded. 'Okay, but you can't discuss the engagement with him.'

'I know that. And I promise I won't. Now, can you please get someone to book a table at Pláka. Let me grab my shoes.'

She returned a moment later wearing a pair of beautiful, beaded sandals.

'Okay, I'm ready.' Glancing up at Ares, she frowned. 'You look different.'

'I look exactly the same, Ari.'

'You still dress like Pappou, but there's something different. Your hair maybe?'

Ares sighed. 'I thought you were famished.'

Turning to face Willa, Ariana rolled her eyes. 'He hates being late. But it wouldn't matter if we turned up at midnight. Everyone in Athens loves Ares because he's done so much for local people.'

'Ariana—'

'What? It's true. You've invested loads of money in local businesses. And you've set up countless charities.'

He had? Willa frowned. 'I had no idea.'

'That's because he likes to keep a low profile. For *low*, read *submerged*.'

She wanted to ask more, but Ares was pressing his hand

into the small of his sister's back. 'The car's here, Ari. Let's go.'

They met at the restaurant. He was frail but straight-backed and handsome with a mass of white hair and the storm-coloured eyes that his grandson had inherited.

'This is my grandfather, Pappou, and this is—'

'My friend, Willa,' Ariana interrupted. 'She's a lawyer.'

'Given that Ares and I share a name, it might be easier if you called me Tino to save confusion.' Ares Sr smiled at Willa. 'Which area of the law are you in, Willa?'

'Family.'

He nodded slowly. 'In my day, that used to be unfashionable. Among the male lawyers, anyway. As often happens in life, they needed women, like yourself, to show them what matters. And what matters more than family?'

'Pappou is very pro-women.' Ariana squeezed her grandfather's arm.

'Did you always want to be a lawyer?'

Willa blinked, caught off guard by Ares's question. He had been speaking to the waiter, but clearly, he had been following their conversation.

'From when I was about fifteen. But only really because I loved *Suits*. Do you know the show?'

Ariana grabbed her hand and squeezed it with excitement. 'Same. I love that show.'

'No other lawyers in the family, then?'

Back to Ares.

Ariana was talking to her grandfather. Maybe that was why her brother's eyes felt so intense, why Willa could feel his curious gaze probing her. Beneath the table, her fingers scrunched up the napkin in her lap.

'They run a hotel. In California.' It sounded so mundane, and she suddenly felt defensive of the beautiful old hotel with its arched veranda and red-tiled roof. And of her family too.

Not her family, she thought quickly as she felt another stab of homesickness. Because it was so hard to give them up. So hard not to know, just as if she was there, what time it was on Santa Catalina. What were they doing right now? Were they having breakfast on the terrace? Had Robert been for his morning swim?

'I'd love to have my own hotel.' She felt a rush of gratitude as Ariana's voice cut off her thoughts.

'What would it be like?'

'It would be like a cross between Chateau Marmont and the Gritti Palace.'

Ares rolled his eyes. 'You mean filled with reprobates and sinking into the sea?'

Ariana rolled her eyes back. 'Willa knows what I mean.'

Willa smiled. 'Of course. Classic but with an edge. The hotel equivalent of a dirty martini.'

'Exactly. We should go into business together.'

'Did you never think about it?' Ares was picking up his water glass, but she knew he was watching her. 'Going into the family business.'

Yes, she thought with a pang. Often, as a small child. But after the triplets were born, her relationship with Robert had changed in the way that a landscape changed when a glacier melted. Things revealed themselves, but they had always been there beneath the carapace of ice. But it was only six months ago that she had understood what she had been seeing.

Thankfully before Ares could ask any more questions, the food arrived.

As she started to eat, it became obvious why Pláka was the restaurant of the moment among the Athens in-crowd.

The food was sublime. The diners even more so. But even in a room full of luminously beautiful people, none shone more brightly than Ares. He should have been called Apollo,

Willa thought, as her eyes darted over to him beside her. She couldn't let herself look too closely. It made her feel dizzy, and she wasn't even drinking alcohol.

'I fly back tonight,' she'd explained when Ariana had suggested cocktails. 'Sparkling water's fine. Truly.'

Ariana made a sad face. 'Let me know if you want something buzzier. But they do great mocktails here too.' She seemed more relaxed now. Ares, less so. But no doubt, he was not convinced that a giggly Ariana was going to keep her promise of not mentioning the engagement.

He was sweet with his grandfather, speaking clearly and steering the conversation to matters that were dear to the old man's heart. And when Tino started to tire, Ares insisted on seeing him home.

'It'll take me ten minutes door-to-door.'

'Which is why I'm coming with you. It means I can walk back and have space for dessert,' he said firmly when the older man protested.

'What did you think of Kallos?' Ariana asked as the two men left the restaurant.

'I thought it was beautiful.'

Leaning forward, Ariana rested her elbows on the table. 'You know you're very privileged. I don't think Ares has ever taken anyone there outside of family. Not even Zoe. You know about Zoe?'

Willa nodded. She felt something like jealousy. 'Did you know her?'

Ariana nodded. 'They were childhood sweethearts, kind of. Zoe was like a cousin. They knew each other for ever before Ares proposed. Not like me and David.' She bit into her lip. 'You'd like David. He's not driven and intense like Ares. He's more like Daddy. And he gets me. I just want Ares to like him,' she added wistfully.

'I'm sure he will.'

Ariana sighed. 'Maybe. He's so hard to please. I love him. I mean, he's the GOAT. But all he does is work. He needs to find someone who gets him. That's what Pappou wants too. We just want him to be happy. He hasn't been, you know. I think he's forgotten how. He's too busy thinking about me or Pappou or his charities. But he's not had anything for himself. Not since Zoe.'

When Ares returned, they finished the meal and then dropped Ariana off at the apartment and returned to the townhouse.

'Did you have fun?'

Ares seemed surprised by the question. 'I did. I don't often go out impulsively like that.'

'You have a very lovely family.'

He was pleased. 'Ari is a handful but she's a sweetie, and my grandfather is a legend.' He hesitated. 'They love you, by the way. My grandfather couldn't stop talking about you. And Ariana texted me. She wants to take you clubbing. You're *fire*, apparently. I'm not invited, by the way. It would be too *cringe*.'

Willa laughed. 'That's exactly what my sisters would say. When they were about six or seven, they went through a phase when they thought I was *fire*. Now I am definitely *cringe*.'

She was still laughing when a thought occurred to her, and her stomach clenched. What would her sisters think of her if they found out the truth? It would be way worse than cringe, surely?

'When are you planning on telling them about the baby? Or have you already told them?'

Ares's question, the casualness of it, coming on the back of thinking about another, bigger truth, caught her off balance.

'No, I haven't.' Her fingers found the ring around her neck. 'I don't know when I'll tell them. They're very young.'

'How old?'

'Thirteen.' Fourteen in a month's time. She turned the ring quickly, rolling it back and forth.

'But you'll tell your father, your stepmother?'

His question made something sharp and smooth slide through her. 'Why does it matter to you?' She stepped backwards unsteadily as Ares stared at her.

'It doesn't. I was just asking—'

The faux reasonableness of him, standing in front of her was suddenly terrifying. 'Well, don't. You don't get to pry into my life. Or tell me what to do. You're such a hypocrite. I mean, you haven't even told your family the truth about Zoe.'

It was a low blow, but if Ares felt it, he didn't show it. Instead, he held her gaze. 'And that's why you're not telling your family that you're pregnant?'

Objection, leading question, she thought, as her hand made a small, unformed gesture of its accord.

'I'm not telling them because I can't.' She had reached for anger; instead, she felt a surge of hot, swirling panic as his eyes dipped to her face.

CHAPTER NINE

Ares watched as Willa's hand fell still. Everything in her seemed to still.

She looked small and young and unsteady as if something fundamental inside her had been compromised.

It was a shock, seeing her like that. In the past, when they had argued, she had fought back. Or fled. But now she seemed to be frozen in her own body, trapped and taut and expressionless.

'Willa?'

He said her name softly, and he wanted to touch her, to take her in his arms and unfreeze that rigidity from her spine, but he was scared she might break apart if he did so.

'You're right,' he said then, to give her space and turn the focus away from her stunned face. 'I am a hypocrite. I don't want to be. I want to tell Ari and Pappou the truth, but you saw my grandfather. He doesn't need to be upset by something he can't change. And Ari feels things so keenly. After my parents died, she was devastated. In pieces. I can't risk triggering all those feelings of loss again. Actually, I can't face it. It's easier to keep lying, because I'm selfish—'

'You're not selfish.' She looked up at him, as he'd hoped she would, and the pain in her eyes felt worse than any pain he was feeling now. Any pain he'd ever felt on his own account.

'I saw how you are with Ariana and your grandfather.

You walked him home. You bought Ariana your mother's old flat. You're protecting her future with this prenup. You're looking out for them.'

For a second the pain retreated, pushed back by her sudden, partisan ferocity, and then she glanced away, and he saw that her vehemence had loosened other emotions, and he said slowly, 'So why won't you let me look after you?'

For a moment, she didn't reply, she just looked away from him to the window, and he followed her gaze to where the Parthenon was illuminated in the darkness.

'You don't know me. Not really. And if you did, I think you'd pity me.'

'Pity you?' He stared at her, his brain spinning. 'I don't pity you, Willa. I'm in awe of you.'

Her eyes jerked back to his.

'You're a billionaire. You run a global business—'

'Which I inherited. I got my job because of my surname. Okay, I've increased our profitability. But do you want to know a secret of the super-rich, Willa? It's almost impossible to mess up. It's not like the old days. There's so many checks and balances in place, and money isn't stockpiled in one business. It's liquid. It's in real estate, investments, stocks, bonds, private equity.'

'You make it sound so easy.'

'It's not. But it's easier if the business has already been up and running for several centuries.' He took a step forward, still not touching but closer.

'But you got your job on your own merit. In a competitive industry, you fought to get where you are. And you got there because you're talented and brave. Look at how you moved to a different country on your own.'

'I didn't go to London on my own because I was talented and brave. I came on my own because I don't have anyone—'

His throat thickened and he stared down at her, shocked

into silence not so much by her words but by the dullness in her voice. Those weeks and days when they were apart, he'd pictured her flawless face, the supple curve of her body, the smooth gloss of her skin. But it had never satisfied because nothing in his imagination could conjure up that energy she brought into any room.

Willa was a comet blazing across an ink-coloured sky. A lightning fork igniting a line of trees. A spinning sparkler. There was a vivacity to her, a life force.

Now life and colour seemed to have left her face.

More than anything he wanted to make her eyes sparkle like gemstones, but he had no idea what to say. Not least because her words made no sense. Her mother had died, but she had talked about her father, a stepmother. There were younger sisters, triplets who thought she was cringe. He remembered her telling him how her father had taught her to ride. Surely if something had happened to them too, she would have mentioned it.

There was only one way to find out.

'Your family—'

'They're not my family.' Her hands were trembling.

Again, her words made no sense. He felt a stab of frustration and fear. He'd never wanted to learn another person from scratch. He'd never needed to. He had gotten to know Zoe organically: they had grown up in the same social circles, grown closer by osmosis rather than intent. After Zoe, he was careful to keep a distance emotionally with the women he dated. To never get close enough to care. And it was easy to do just that. Leaving was easy too.

But leaving Willa was the last thing on his mind. He wanted to hold her and heal her. Because he cared, really cared. And the newness and the expanse of what he was feeling was terrifying. Because this was different than what he'd felt for Zoe. He had loved her like he loved everything that was familiar and known.

Now he knew that it was a pale imitation. A forged Picasso. A souvenir model of the Parthenon instead of the towering original.

He thought back to when he'd told Willa about letting himself into Zoe's apartment. *If I hadn't done that, I might never have found her.* Now though, all he could think was that he might never have met Willa.

And even thinking that made him shake inside.

Because he loved her.

He knew because he was terrified. He knew because he felt young and stupid and bumbling and desperate not to lose her now to this terrible chasm that was cracking beneath her feet.

Knew too that it was why he had proposed. That the baby was only a part of it. That he wanted her in his life. Wanted to tell her that his love was unquantifiable. Immense and immeasurable. That it swallowed up the universe. And that she didn't need to fear whatever it was that was making her tremble because he would slay her demons.

'Who are they, then?' he said softly.

'They're good people. Kind people. They took me in under false pretences. They think I have a right to share their lives, but I don't.'

He'd never had a conversation like this, where questions created more questions rather than answers, more confusion rather than greater clarity.

'Are you saying you're adopted?'

She bit her lip. 'It's complicated.'

He thought about how long it had taken him to tell anyone what happened with Zoe. And yet with Willa, the sentences had felt fully formed as if they'd been waiting for her to come along. He cleared his throat, then took her hands in his. 'Most things are. Until you take a second look, and then I find they're often quite simple to unpick.'

She didn't answer, but maybe she was remembering their conversation too, because a moment later her shoulders shifted a little as if the burden had lightened just a fraction.

'My mom died when I was two years old. She had pancreatic cancer. It was very aggressive, and she only survived ten weeks after she was diagnosed.'

'I'm so sorry, Willa.'

He felt her fingers tighten around his.

'I don't remember her. My dad didn't talk about her much. I thought it was too painful for him, and so I didn't ask about her. And then he met Amber, and they got married, and she had the triplets. And things changed. Got worse. My dad was always tense with me, but after the triplets, he never wanted the two of us to spend time together. I thought it was because of my stepmother. I blamed her. And then when I was working in LA, I ended up in hospital with the suspected appendicitis.'

There was an unpleasant twist in his throat. He knew this part. Why, then, did it feel as if somebody was playing Grandmother's Footsteps behind him?

'I called my dad, and he came to the hospital. I wanted him to be there.' Her voice trembled, and his fingers tightened around hers. 'I thought if he came to the hospital, it might go back to how it used to be. But instead, it wrecked everything.'

She fell silent, but this time he didn't prompt. He had pushed enough. He would accept how much she was prepared to share.

After a moment, she started speaking again. 'I don't know why he decided to tell me then. Maybe it was being in the hospital. Maybe it reminded him of when I was born. He'd brought me grapes and one minute he was handing them to me, the next he was telling me that I wasn't his daughter.'

Whatever he had expected Willa to say, it wasn't that.

'My mother had had an affair just after they got married.' She gave him a small, tight smile that looked painful. 'When she realised she was dying, she told him the truth. I think it was quite close to the end. And then she died, and he was left with me.'

Now her smile was a mess. 'It all made sense then. How he was with me. I don't look like him. I must look like my biological dad. Every time he looked at me, he must have seen her betrayal.'

'Her betrayal, not yours. You weren't to blame—'

'Not intentionally, no, but I ruined his life. After my mom died, what choice did he have but to keep me? He had no idea who my dad was. He's not on the birth certificate. Robert is.'

'And you're sure he's not your dad? I mean, could your mum have lied?'

She was shaking her head. 'I have type B blood. Robert is an A, and my mother was an O.'

Ares pulled her against him. Her pain felt like a stake digging into his heart.

'What happened after that?'

'I left. I'd applied for this job in New York, and I got it, so I packed up my stuff and took the first flight to JFK.'

'Have you talked to him since?'

The silence that followed that enquiry was full of tears and impossibilities.

'No. I send a text every week, but I don't—I can't talk to him. I know he'll tell me that he wants me to come back, because he's a good man. But he doesn't owe me anything. I'm not related to him. I'm not related to anyone. I have no one.'

She was crying now, and he held her against him, stroking her hair with bone-deep relief and a love that felt like the most natural thing in the world.

For him.

But Willa was not ready. And he could wait. He'd waited his whole life to feel this love. This love that captivated and consumed.

'You are related to someone.' He pressed his hand gently against her stomach. 'You're having a baby, Willa.'

'It's your baby too,' she said then, and now her tears were softer, her voice was too.

'And you're not alone.' His heart was beating too fast, and he willed himself to be calm. 'You have me. I'm not going anywhere.'

She pressed her hand against her mouth, and she was nodding, clutching at his shoulder with the other hand.

He pulled her with him onto the sofa and onto his lap, and she curled her arms around him, and he stroked her hair until her heart was beating calmly again.

'I'm sorry for being such a cow earlier.'

'I like cows. They're very underrated. People think they're dopey, but they're very smart and kind. And they're good listeners, apparently.'

She laughed then, and a beat later he did too. It was that or tell her he loved her. And it was still so new to him, this feeling of closeness and wanting to become one.

From somewhere outside the window, the city's churches rang out the hour, their chimes overlapping, and he remembered hearing the sound of Big Ben from the roof of the Clarendon.

'Is that midnight?' Willa seemed stunned.

'You can't go to the airport now. Stay the night. I can take you in the morning.'

She nodded, and he waited for her to refuse his offer or insist on leaving now, but she didn't move. Instead, she kept staring at him, her irises bright against the pink rims of her eyes, the lashes clotted with drying tears.

'Will you come upstairs with me?'

His mind blanked. He was unthinking. A Vantablack void of desire. Yes, he thought, I will go anywhere you ask.

They undressed, and as they slid into bed, she reached for him, and they made love slowly, hungrily, teasing out their desires, building a world all of their own. Afterwards she lay in his arms, stroking his skin.

'You're making it very hard for me to let you go—' Ares said softly.

Her eyelashes fluttered open. 'I was going to talk to you about that. I thought I might stay a little longer. But only if Larry agrees, and I don't want you asking him. I'll do it. I'll call him first thing.'

'And what's going to be your reason for staying, Ms Hamilton?'

She bit into her lip as his hands closed around her waist. 'The truth, of course. That Mr Konstantinou is very demanding and is still not completely satisfied.'

'In that case,' he pulled her closer, his cock twitching, 'for the sake of authenticity, let me show you exactly how demanding I can be.'

Willa woke in a room she didn't recognise with a man she would never forget. And she didn't have to, for at least another day. Or two.

Changing her mind had been not just easy but freeing, as if a burden had lifted. Because she couldn't bear to part from him just yet. Because for the first time in her life she wanted to pretend. To hope?

Larry had been entirely supportive of her staying, and despite teasing Ares about what she would say, she had ended up telling the truth. That Ariana had flown in from Mexico unexpectedly and that she was still amending the prenup. And Larry himself had suggested she take some time to look around Athens.

What she hadn't told her boss was that she was sleeping with one of his oldest friends and an important client of the firm.

Ares frowned in his sleep. A lock of hair had fallen across his forehead, and holding her breath, she brushed it away.

They had made love on and off most of the night. Their need for one another had started high but escalated exponentially every time they touched, igniting and soothing in turn until they finally fell asleep just before dawn.

A part of her wished Ares would stay asleep so that this day would never start, because then this would never have to end. Whatever this was.

Three weeks ago, when it had all started, it was sex. Lust. Desire.

For her, at least, it was a chance to take back some part of what had gotten lost in that hospital room in California. Because so much had been lost that day. A father. Three half-sisters. A family. She had felt adrift. And then she had walked out in front of Ares Konstantinou's car—she could admit that now, to herself anyway—and for the first time in months everything she had lost was forgotten.

Nothing mattered except the beautiful man with storm-coloured eyes, and in the space of one day their paths had collided three times. Seriously, what were the chances of that?

And each time they met, her heartbeat grew ever rougher and more impassioned.

No wonder they had ended up in bed.

But now it was so much more than sex. She was pregnant with his baby. And that judgy, impatient man, whose will was like a many-headed hydra, had shown himself to be not the runaway groom demonised in the tabloid press but a kind, fiercely protective brother and grandson who had shouldered the blame for his fiancée's infidelity.

And paid the price.

She remembered his gaze as she tried to hold it all together downstairs. Everything had been snarled inside her chest, and her panic was choking her, suffocating her slowly.

But Ares had slowed things down, and suddenly she could breathe. And talk. For the first time in months, years really, she had talked openly, revealed her fears and her secrets. Her whole body felt lighter.

Even though it was not just her body now. Her fingers caressed the curve of her belly. Ares was right: she was related to somebody. She was a mother now, and—

You have me. I'm not going anywhere.

His words tasted sweet on her tongue. He meant them, she was sure. He would do the right thing. Even if Ariana hadn't told her so, she knew that now. She'd seen it, lived it. It was why he'd proposed, even though he was still in love with Zoe.

But could that change? It was stupid to hope. She had no claim on his heart.

Just his body.

Her breath caught as his eyelashes fluttered and his grey eyes rested drowsily on her face, and she thought he would fall back to sleep. But then his pupils flared into stars, exploding with a hunger and a need that was unmistakable because he was feeling it too, and she felt her blood thicken as he pulled her against him, his mouth seeking hers.

They finally made it out of bed and downstairs just before lunch. Ares was wearing dark glasses to block out the glare of the Athenian sun, but it seemed unlikely that he would be able to pass unnoticed in the street.

Her suspicions were confirmed as three women in succession glanced at him with open admiration. Not that he noticed. He seemed only to have eyes for her, and she felt suddenly happy that she had stayed on.

'What do you want to do first?' he asked. 'We can grab lunch. Or we can do some touristy stuff? Or are you itching to hit the shops? It's your day. Your choice.'

'Let's do the Parthenon, and then I will buy you lunch, and then we can play it by ear.'

'I love your ears,' he whispered, leaning in to nibble on the lobe under the pretext of guiding her through a chattering group of teenagers.

Later, as she gazed up at the halva-coloured columns of the Parthenon, Willa got goose bumps. There were plenty of world-famous sites that didn't live up to the hype, but the sheer majesty of the monument and its palpable sense of history didn't disappoint.

'How old is it, again?' she asked, ducking into the shadows to watch a cluster of tiny birds dart in and of the columns just as if they were playing tag.

'Over two thousand four hundred years.'

'It just feels insane to think that there were people like us walking here so long ago. It's really humbling, but I find it reassuring. Their life would have been so much more challenging on a daily basis, and yet they built this.'

He nodded. 'It's why I love Athens. Kallos is a retreat, but here you have to embrace what life throws at you. Like you do.' Pulling her into the shadows of a column, he kissed her softly, and she felt her heart flip over. He liked her, and that was a starting point. Something to build on. Maybe together over time, if she stayed longer, they could build their own Parthenon.

She took some photos and sent them to the private group she and her sisters used, and then it was time to leave.

Back in the city, they grabbed some takeaway souvlaki from one of Ares's favourite places to eat, which turned out to be not a three-star Michelin restaurant but a tiny café on one of the side streets in Monastiraki, where the owner welcomed him like a long-lost son.

'How do you even know about this place?'

'I live here.' He sounded amused.

'Yeah, but you are you. I mean you're a Konstantinou. People like you don't eat street food.'

'My dad used to bring me here for lunch, and then we'd go and sit and talk. He wasn't a big talker, my dad. Especially in crowds he was quite shy, but he learned to manage it—'

'Because he was a Konstantinou?'

Ares nodded. 'It's a job in itself. You go to a lot of events. You're the patron for a lot of charities and on the board of countless institutions. I'm not complaining. I live a privileged life. But it's not all parties on private yachts. At least, not since I was your age.'

She felt her cheeks burn, remembering how she had scrolled over those photos of him in swim shorts. She had focused on his nakedness, but he was clearly younger in those pictures.

'Are you okay? You look a little flushed.' The concern in his voice made a lump swell in her throat. 'I keep forgetting you're not a local.'

It was just a throwaway remark, but it made her glow inside.

'Let's get out of this heat. Are you happy to go back to the townhouse?'

'You think there'll be less heat there?' she teased.

His eyes were dark pulses in the sunlight.

'No, but at least you won't be wearing clothes.'

They walked slowly back through the old town, stopping when Willa got distracted by some trinket in one of the shops.

'Most places stay open all day. We can come back later if you want—'

'I want you.' The words escaped from her mouth, and he stared down at her, silent, transfixed, and then he fitted his mouth to hers, moving into her and she felt how hard he was, and the hardness of him fed her hunger.

'I want you now,' he said, and his voice was a raw scrape of desire.

They ran up the stairs of the townhouse like teenagers. The sex was frantic, fully clothed and shockingly fast. The second time was naked and slower, the third slower still. Finally, they lay sated and sweaty, their heartbeats overlapping.

'Where are you going?' Willa frowned as Ares started untangling their limbs.

'You need some water. And I do too.' He yanked on his trousers and pulled a shirt over his head.

It was inside-out, and she was on the verge of telling him so, but it was sweet that he was so distracted.

'Stay right where you are,' he said, leaning in to kiss her on the forehead, and then the mouth, and then—

'Ares, go,' she ordered. He gave her one of those smiles that sent a current of electricity through her veins, and then he was gone.

She rolled over and pressed her face into his pillow, breathing in his scent. None of this felt real. But it was. He was here. He was hers. For now, anyway. And maybe they could make it work for longer than now.

For life?

His proposal was never far from her mind, but that had not been a proposal. It was a solution to a problem. But if he asked again, for real—

Her phone vibrated, and she reached over and picked it up and walked into the bathroom.

It was a message from Little Women, Cali Style, the group

she and her sisters used to message each other. A video, to be precise, and as she waited for it to load, she brushed her teeth and splashed some cold water on her face.

'Hey, Willa.'

She glanced at the screen and smiled as her sisters started to dance and sing.

'Triple threat, listen up, it's a beach day call,
Our fourteenth's here, we're gonna have a ball!
You know the date, the place, sand and sun's the scene,
Just us four sisters, living the dream.
So, RSVP, yeah, you know what I mean!'

As they collapsed, laughing onto the sand, Kendall, the extrovert, grabbed the phone. 'It doesn't quite scan, but you can't not come. Tell her, Dad.'

Her fingers tightened around the phone as the screen swung shakily to the left and Robert's face appeared. He was smiling but there was a tension to his mouth. 'Of course you must come, Willa.' As the girls clambered onto his back, four pairs of blue eyes filled the screen.

Switching off the phone, she stared at her reflection, her heart beating jerkily. She missed them so much it hurt. But how could she go? That would hurt more. She didn't want to lie to her sisters, but she couldn't tell them the truth. And Robert. Her throat tightened as she remembered his face, the tautness of his skin across his cheek bones. As if he was wearing a mask. But she couldn't keep forcing him to act a part.

'I thought you might be hungry too.' Ares was back, sliding a tray onto the top of an antique chest of drawers.

'I brought some fruit and olives and some *kritsinia*. For energy.' He hesitated. 'My grandfather left a message. He's invited us to lunch with him tomorrow at his club, and Ariana just called. She wants to take you shopping.'

Her head was pounding slow and hard. His shirt was still

on inside-out and he looked sweetly dishevelled, and she wished that she could just pull him onto the bed and lose herself in the heat of his hunger all over again.

It wasn't fair. For months now, she'd felt hollowed-out and inchoate. Ares had changed that. She had told him the truth, and the world hadn't ended. He hadn't looked away; instead, he had pulled her closer and filled her with his body and his certainty. That unwavering Konstantinou immutability that was as constant and enduring as the Parthenon.

The worst part was her own stupidity. All day she had been blinkered, bolstered by his presence. She'd actually believed that she could be like other people. That talking about the past meant it was boxed up, safely stored out of harm's way.

She had been incredibly naive. But who was she trying to kid? Her gaze moved to the city outside the window. The past wasn't something you could file away. You could only live with it.

Except, she wasn't. She couldn't. She had taken something that didn't belong to her, and she would never be free of that debt.

Ares was free. He didn't need to take her burden and make it his. But he would. She knew that he would bear any burden. But she didn't want to be that. Be a burden to him. She didn't want to be his responsibility.

'She doesn't have to do that.'

'She wants to. She really likes you. They both do.' He hesitated, and she felt a thump in her stomach as his eyes met hers. 'I do too, Willa. I care about you. A lot.'

It hurt, and she tried pushing it away, tried not to see it. But it turned out that the truth was harder to hide than a lie. And the truth was that Ares was kind and strong and loyal, and he did the right thing. Which was why she loved him.

But all those reasons for loving him were also the reasons she couldn't stay. No matter what he said or did, she had to stop this fantasy now. As a child she'd had no say in Robert's sacrifice, but she was not a child anymore. And she didn't want Ares to save her. She didn't want him to be with her out of duty. She wanted his love.

She shrugged. 'And I really like you. I love your body and how you touch me. And we have fun. But I think I need to get back to London. Today.'

His expression didn't change, but she felt the impact of her words ripple across the room.

'We can do that. Or I could talk to my grandfather and Ari. Get them to back off a little. I know they can be a lot.'

'They're not a lot. This is. We are.'

Now his face altered, and she wanted to break the laws of science and rewind time so that she could stop the confusion in his eyes.

'We're just having fun, Willa.'

'Are we? Or is this some big seduction? You know, showing me around your city. Getting your family to cosy up to me.' She was being unfair, but she had to stop this now. She wouldn't be to him what her mother had been to Robert. A burden to be borne.

'That's not what happened.'

'Isn't it?' She breathed out shakily. 'I'm pregnant with your baby, and I know you, Ares. You like to get your way. And this is just another form of pushing, and you're going to keep pushing until I agree to marry you.'

'You already turned me down.'

'And that's it, is it? You're never going to ask again...'

He stared at her in silence. 'Would it be so bad if I did?'

'I'm not one of your charities. I don't need rescuing.' She was pulling on clothes now.

'Maybe I did feel like that before. Not so much like you

need rescuing, but I felt responsible. But that's not why I'd ask you to marry me now.'

'And why would you ask me now?'

The air stilled. His face, his beautiful face was taut. 'Because I love you.'

'No, you don't, Ares. You still love Zoe. That's why you didn't tell everyone why you left her at the altar.'

'I care about her, yes. Like I care about Thea. She was part of my life. But look around you, Willa. There's evidence of the past everywhere, and yet life moves on. You have to accept it. Just like you have to accept that I love you.'

It took a second. She had to force herself to breathe, to swallow, to stop from breaking down or, worse, reaching for his proudly masculine body. Ares was saying he loved her. It was what she wanted to hear, and she wanted to believe him. But maybe he needed her to believe it so that she would agree to marry him. Because he wanted to take care of her and the baby. He was that kind of man. The one who did the right thing. Like Robert.

But accepting his love would mean being his responsibility. And it would mean more lies. Ares would have to live a lie. Lie to their child as she had been lied to.

The thought turned her stomach and hardened her resolve.

'But I don't love you. And I'm not my mother. I'm not going to marry a man I don't love.'

'I don't believe you. I think you love me with every atom of your being, but you're scared of the past, of making it your present.' He took a step forward. 'But we're not your parents.'

'We're not yours either,' she said flatly.

'But I am the baby's father.' There was no softness to his voice, no trace of a curve to that beautiful mouth. Just a dark, flickering light in his grey eyes that made her heart flip.

Thankfully, she was dressed now, and that focused her

thoughts and smothered those unsustainable fantasies that she and Ares could create their truth, build their world.

She'd forgotten who she was. Her limits. The limits that were unswervable.

But now she'd remembered.

'And I will make sure you're a part of the baby's life. But I don't want you to be a part of mine.' She glanced at the bed with its tangle of sheets. 'This was just sex. That's all it was. And it's great sex, but it's not love.'

'Say it to my face. Tell me you don't love me.' His voice was scratchy. 'Say it.'

'I don't love you. I could never love you.'

For a few seconds, neither of them moved in the shattering silence that swallowed up her lie, and then he turned and walked out of the bedroom. She heard his footsteps on the stairs and the unmistakable sound of the heavy outside door shutting, and then slowly, moving like an automaton, she started to pack.

CHAPTER TEN

LOOKING UP FROM his screen, Ares blinked.

He glanced up at the clock on the wall, out of habit more than because he needed to know what time it was. Time was indeed a construct. Obviously, he respected it for the sake of other people. But for himself, it had ceased to matter eight days ago.

His gaze drifted to the windows. His office had enviable views in all directions, and now he let the chair revolve slowly, taking in the panorama of the city. Athens was always hot in July, but for the last few days, the city had been baking in the grip of a heatwave. The roads and pavements felt spongy, and even the Parthenon seemed to be affected by the blistering sun, appearing to sway in the heat shimmer at the top of the Acropolis.

Or so everyone was saying.

He hadn't noticed. He went from the townhouse to the office and back again on a loop like some pit pony in a mine.

He rarely went into Athens.

He couldn't. The city he loved was no longer his city.

It was her city. Willa's.

At the edges of his vision, he saw her move. And he stared straight ahead until he felt her retreat. It was easier to do that here. Here, she was only in his head.

But it was different outside of the office. Everywhere he went, he could see her in the shadows. He felt like an archaeologist, but instead of broken pots and rusting arrowheads, he found traces of Willa imprinted in every stone. This corner was where they had stopped to look at a dress in a shop. That street was where he had taken her hand and towed her back to the townhouse.

His spine stiffened painfully against the leather upholstery, and he got to his feet, needing to move, to shift the memory of Willa's body curving against his.

He had many memories like that. Most he could banish to the recesses of his mind if he focused on work. Or ran on a treadmill at the gym, forcing his body to keep striding until his muscles burned and his brain blurred with fatigue.

But there was one memory he couldn't shift.

Willa, her eyes fixed on his face, her voice clear as spring water as she said *I don't love you. I could never love you.*

His fingers curled into fists.

He'd told himself she was lying. That she was scared. That she needed space. So he'd left. And he'd been right. She did need space. More space than Athens, more than even Greece offered, presumably. Which was why when he'd returned two hours later, she was gone.

Chest tightening, he flicked the headrest of the chair, sending it spinning. He'd felt like that chair when he walked back into the bedroom. For a few agonising seconds he hadn't understood that she was gone.

And then he had, and it felt like an earthquake.

He let go of the chair, ran his hand over his face.

She had packed her things and presumably taken a taxi to the airport. There was no note. But then she'd said everything she needed to say.

He could have gone after her. Could have followed her back to London. But he was no stalker, and anyway his brain had been offline, and his body felt as if it was made of glass.

And then the pain started. Heartache. It wasn't real.

Hearts had nothing to do with love—he knew that logically—but still his heart ached as if it was being squeezed by a giant hand.

It was so much worse than what he'd felt with Zoe.

That had been pride, he realised now. A bruised ego. And shame, and anger with Zoe, and with himself. Because he hadn't loved her.

He had wanted to love her. Wanted their relationship to mimic the love stories he'd been told about his parents and his grandparents, and so he had pushed the marriage agenda. And it was easy to do. Zoe was beautiful, and she was already part of his life. And he'd thought that was enough.

No wonder she had looked elsewhere. Zoe had acted wrongly, but at least she had been self-aware and honest, in a way. She understood what love looked like. What it should look and feel like.

He'd had no idea, despite speaking a language that offered countless words for love.

And then he met Willa. And the world had swerved off its axis just like his car had swerved on that London street. What was it he'd said to her? *I call the shots.*

Not after he'd walked into the bar at the Clarendon, he hadn't.

He had become a creature of obsession. Pursuing her, then pushing her into working for him, into coming to Kallos, pushing and pushing—

Until he'd pushed her away.

He glanced over at his laptop. She had emailed him a copy of the prenup. But aside from that, Willa hadn't reached out once.

Could he blame her? He could. But he also blamed himself. He hadn't learned anything from what happened with Zoe. Instead, he had compounded those errors with a few additional ones.

There was a tap at the door.

'Mr Konstantinou.' It was Christina, his PA. She was staring at him anxiously as she had been doing for the past eight days. But then, he had practically been living at the office. One night he had even slept there.

'I have your sister on the phone. She's been trying to get hold of you on your mobile. Shall I put her through?'

Ariana. She knew something was wrong. Typical Ariana, she had asked him directly if it had something to do with Willa. With Willa leaving. He had denied it, but she was persistent. She would keep asking and asking. Pushing, he thought dully.

He was so bad at love. The rest of his family made it look so easy. Was this how Willa felt? Was she still feeling like this? But even before he pictured her slim, tense body, he knew the answer to the question, and he realised he was braced on the balls of his feet. Not to flee. He was done with running. But Willa needed someone on her side.

'Tell her I'm on another call and that I'll call her back. And then get hold of Andreas and tell him to get the plane ready.'

Christina frowned. 'Were you going somewhere?' She tapped on the screen of her tablet. 'I had you down for a meeting with the mayor this afternoon.'

'Cancel it. In fact, cancel everything for the next few days. There's been a change of plan.'

'If you can sign off the file-D for the Leilani case, I'll send it to Katie Godfrey.'

Willa looked up from her screen. 'Thanks, Maggie.'

It was Friday. She was sitting in Chloe's office with Maggie. This meeting was Chloe's idea, a chance for the three of them to go through their overlapping schedules. And it was a good idea. Not that she was much of a judge, Willa thought, as the legal secretary got to her feet.

A shaft of sunlight cut through the blind and as she blinked, she saw Ares's face in the moment before he turned away and walked out of the bedroom, and for a second, she couldn't feel her hands, her breath. It was as if she was floating.

'And you should be going.'

Maggie's voice pulled her back to Chloe's office, and hoping that nothing of what she was thinking was visible on her face, she frowned. 'Go where?'

'You're doing that interview with Andrew Kilroy.' Maggie frowned. 'From the law society. Larry set it up—'

'I thought that was tomorrow.'

'It's in twenty minutes.' Maggie glanced at her phone. 'The taxi is already here.'

'I thought it was tomorrow.' Willa felt a flush of panic as Maggie left the room. She hadn't prepared anything.

As if she could read her mind, Chloe did one of those dismissive hand gestures she so excelled at. 'It's fine. They do them all the time for the website. They don't ask any hard questions. It's a puff piece. You praise your previous firm but also say how much you love working for Milner's. Talk about London being the birthplace of the law, mention someone who changed your life.'

Shaking her head, Willa smiled stiffly. 'I don't know what's wrong with me.' That was a lie. Obviously, she could write a short dissertation on what was wrong with her. Or compile a new dictionary, starting with *A* for *Ares*.

'Really?'

Glancing up, she felt her smile freeze on her face. Chloe was looking at her incredulously.

'Isn't it obvious? I mean, you're only human, Willa, and it's a lot for one person to process.'

Willa felt her heart drop through her stomach. Her feet were rooted to the ground, but her brain was racing like a sprinter so that she felt almost breathless. Was Maggie talking about the pregnancy or Ares? Only, how could she know?

'Does everyone know?' she said hoarsely.

'Of course. We might be British, but just because we have stiff upper lips doesn't mean we're entirely without feelings.'

Chloe sighed. 'You've moved across an ocean. You left your family behind. It's a big deal. But you're not on your own. If you ever just want to grab a beer or go catch a film, just ask.'

To her horror, Willa felt her eyes flood with tears. 'Thanks, Chloe. I'll do that.'

As Chloe had predicted, the interview was straightforward. The only time she stumbled was when Andrew Kilroy asked who had changed her life.

And all she could think about was Ares.

How he had held her hand, coaxed her out the cage she had built around herself. Made her feel solid and seen and safe. How much she loved him. But she had already trapped one man into looking after her. And she could remember Robert's face. That helpless tangle of emotions. She never wanted to see Ares look at her that way.

But at this point it seemed unlikely she would ever see him again anyway. She had sent him a copy of the prenup, and he had thanked her. Although, most likely it was his PA who had written the response. Aside from that, nothing. Not even about the DNA test.

With every passing day, it felt more and more like a dream.

She let herself into her rented apartment, fighting the impulse to cry, again. It was the hormones.

Except it wasn't. It was knowing that Ares would one

day find someone else, and she would have to live on the same planet.

She wanted him to be involved with the baby, but if it all felt like a dream to her, maybe it felt the same way to him.

It was an effort to cook. If she wasn't pregnant, she would have simply eaten cereal for every meal. But having managed to scare off the baby's father completely, she was determined to do everything right nutritionally for them. And after a shower and a fusion-inspired Cobb salad, she felt less unhinged.

Maybe she needed to follow up on Maggie's suggestion. Not the beer, obviously. But a movie would be nice. And she should start to unpack. She had moved in a few weeks ago but had left to go to Greece soon after, and since getting back, she hadn't had the energy—

She frowned as the sound of her door buzzer startled her.

Who could that be? Hopefully not someone campaigning for the upcoming local election. She had got stuck with a candidate the other day who couldn't seem to understand that she was in London on a work visa and had no right to vote in the UK.

Oh, seriously!

The buzzer cut into her thoughts, and scowling she got to her feet.

'I didn't order anything, I'm not eligible to vote, and—' She yanked open the door, and her rant was silenced mid-flow. There was a man standing on her doorstep

'Hello, Willa.'

'Dad.' The word was automatic, and she pressed her hand against her mouth. 'I'm sorry, I know you're not—'

'Not biologically, no. But if I had my choice, you would be mine,' Robert Hamilton said quietly. And there were tears in his eyes that matched the ones in hers as he pulled her into a hug.

'What are you doing here?' she said finally as he released her and she led him back inside.

'I came to see my daughter.'

'Would you like some coffee? Or tea? Have you eaten?'

'Yes, no and yes.' Robert gazed admiringly around the sitting room. 'This is nice. Amber would love that fireplace. And that ceiling rose.' He took a sip from the mug Willa had handed him. 'Coffee's not bad either.' He took another sip and breathed out shakily.

'I've been so worried about you. Amber too.'

'Does she know?' Her stomach clenched. 'Did you tell the girls?'

'The girls don't know. We'll tell them when you're ready. But I had to tell Amber. She's my wife. She knew something was upsetting me more than just you leaving. And I should have told her before. I didn't because I hadn't told you.' He shook his head. 'I waited all that time, and I made such a mess of it.'

'Is there a right way?'

'Maybe not. But when I got to the hospital, I was in such a panic. I sat waiting for you to wake up from the anaesthetic, and the doctor came in to talk about the operation, and I just kept thinking that at some point you would find out.'

His hand found hers, and she squeezed it hard. 'I'm glad it was you that told me.'

'I wanted to tell you, but you were so young, and after I married Amber and the girls were born, you were so anxious, and I was worried if I told you, you'd feel pushed out.'

'I thought I reminded you of her. Of mom. I felt responsible.'

'I know you did. But you weren't. We were the grown-ups. Me, Meg, your dad. It was our mess.'

Willa bit her lip. 'Did she ever want me?'

'Always.' Robert's voice was gentle, but his hand was

firm around hers. 'I did too. Even after she told me. I think I already knew there was a chance you weren't mine—'

'And you still took me in. You had all those years when it was just the two of us, and I wasn't even yours.' She felt a rush of anger towards her mother. 'Why would she do that? Why would she give you that burden?'

Robert was silent for a long time.

'You weren't a burden, Willa.'

'I thought I was. And then when the triplets were born, you seemed so much easier with them than me, and then when I found out that I wasn't yours, I understood why—'

'It was easier. Because I knew what I was doing. Because of you. And you did get left behind, Willa. I knew that at the time. And I should have done more, said more to reassure you. But I was exhausted, and Amber was exhausted, and I knew if I said something it would be a lot for everyone to take in. But I wish I had said something. You deserved the truth. You needed to know that you were never a burden. You were a gift—you are a gift. More than that. You saved me.'

His words made something delicate and warm unfurl inside of her like petals opening to the sun. 'I couldn't save your mom, even though I loved her. And I did love her. She loved me too. Just not the way I wanted her to. Like I made the world tilt.'

Like the love she felt for Ares.

'But I knew how she felt, and I married her anyway. She was beautiful like you, Willa. But you're your own person. You always were. I could see it when you danced and when you rode. I always knew you'd fly.'

He hesitated. 'I should have come after you. I thought you needed space, but when I told Amber she said what you needed was your father. I came up to New York once a month hoping I'd see you. I went into all these law firms and showed your photo at the reception desk, but they wouldn't tell me anything.'

'How did you find me, then?'

'I was hoping you wouldn't ask me that.'

'Why?'

'He asked me not to say. But I think there's been enough lies and half truths between us.' Her dad's face twisted into something was part smile, part grimace. 'I had a visitor. He turned up two days ago. Sat me down and told me that you needed me and then he offered to fly me to London.'

He? Who? But she knew who even before her father said quietly, 'I refused. Told him I could pay my own way. But he's a hard man to say no to, your Ares.'

'He's not my Ares,' she stammered. 'He wanted to be, but I turned him down.'

'You did? I don't think there are many people who would do that.'

The stunned expression on her father's face made her start laughing, and then quite suddenly she was crying. But then, she was always crying these days.

'Sweetheart, don't cry.'

'He doesn't love me. He thinks he does. But he just wants to do the right thing.'

'The right thing?' Her father was staring at her, and she could almost hear him replaying her words. 'Are you—?'

She bit her lip. 'I'm pregnant. He's the father. He asked me to marry him, but I couldn't—'

'It was too much like what happened with your mom and me,' her father said after a moment. 'And I can see why you might think that. It's the same as thinking a redwood looks like a giant Sequoia. Except they're not the same tree and you're not your mother and I'm not Ares Konstantinou. But you and this little one growing inside of you are Hamiltons.

If you don't love him, you don't need him because we love you. Both of you.'

How was it possible to feel so happy and unhappy at the same time? Her family loved her and wanted her. It was what she had wanted to hear her whole life and yet—

'But I do love him,' Willa whispered. 'And I've lost him.' And the crushing impossibility of it all overwhelmed her, and she started to cry again.

Her father rested his hand against her cheek. 'Then, go find him. Like I found you,' he said, as if that was the simplest thing in the world to do.

And for the first time since Ares walked out of her life, she felt a flickering hope flare up like a pure, painless flame.

'Shall I bring some juice and water out onto the terrace, Mr Konstantinou? Or would you prefer to stay in the sitting room?'

Looking up from his laptop, Ares frowned. Truthfully, he would rather be left alone, but Ariana had finally tracked him down at the office and insisted that they spend the weekend on Kallos because she wanted to swim and sunbathe without being bothered by the paparazzi. And have lunch with her brother to get his opinion on something financial.

It sounded like an excuse. It probably was. But she was worried about him, and giving in to her and proving he was fine would be a quicker way to persuade her than trying to argue it out.

'The terrace, please. Ariana's hoping to top up her tan.'

He heard the thwomp-thwomp of the helicopter, and shutting his laptop he headed outside, holding up a hand to shield his gaze.

'Thanks, Iona,' he said as the housekeeper appeared with a tray of juice and water.

As she disappeared back into the villa, he heard footsteps.

Pouring out two glasses of water, he turned to greet his sister. 'Before you say anything, I am going to go swimming—'

But it wasn't Ariana walking across the terrace. It was Willa.

She was hovering on the step down to the terrace, her eyes steady and unblinking. And for a moment he thought he was hallucinating, and he wanted to ask if she was real. But he couldn't speak. His breath was gone.

'Hi,' she said quietly. Her voice was slightly hoarse as if she had been shouting. Or perhaps it was hard for her to speak too.

Why are you here? Had he been able to form sentences, that was the question he wanted to ask, but the answer he wanted to hear might not be the one she gave.

'Hi.' He paused. 'I'm expecting Ariana. Or maybe I'm not,' he added as Willa swallowed audibly. And that hurt. That Ariana could do that to him.

'I'm guessing you haven't locked her in a wardrobe, so she's in on this, whatever this is.'

His pulse quickened as she stepped onto the terrace. 'She wasn't at first. She was very angry. But then she was. She is.'

His throat tightened.

'Did you tell her about the baby?'

Her eyes flared, and he felt her anger like a balm. She still cared enough to fight.

'Of course not. I wouldn't do that. Any more than you would tell my father.'

Robert. He had told him not to say anything, but how could Robert lie to Willa?

'He found you, then.' A statement, not a question, but she nodded, taking another step closer as she did so.

'He came to my apartment. We talked about my mom and

him and how I felt, and everything's okay. I wanted to thank you for doing that. For me.' She touched her belly. 'For us.'

His disappointment was shattering: it hurt to look at her, to share the earth and know she wasn't his.

'That's not all, Ares.'

The air was hot around them, pressing in like it had that day in London when it all started. But now it had ended.

'I'll do the DNA test on Monday,' he said before she could. 'And then you better get a lawyer, and we can sort out a financial agreement.'

'I don't want your money.' Her voice was tight and trembling.

'Then, why are you here?'

'Because I can't not be.'

'You can be. You left. What's changed?'

Willa stared up at Ares's beautiful, taut face. He was angry, and his anger helped ground the panic that had been swirling inside of her since she'd arrived in Athens.

'Nothing. I just didn't have the right words to say what I needed to say. I still don't know if there are words for what I feel for you. For how much I hate not seeing you. For how much it hurts not to be able to touch you or hear you laugh or watch you smile. For how much I loved waking up with you and falling asleep with you. And I know you've probably had second thoughts. Honestly, I wouldn't blame you. I said horrible things to you. Hurtful things because I wanted to hurt you. I needed to hurt you because you have such strong arms and you're so stubborn—'

'*I'm* stubborn?' His pupils narrowed.

'You are. We both are. You push, and I push back. I've been pushing back so long I got lost in the momentum, and I pushed you too hard. Because I didn't want to be a burden to you like I thought I'd been to my father.'

'You think I don't know that? You think this is news to

me?' He looked furious, impatient as he had that first day in London. 'I thought you needed space. I didn't realise that meant leaving the country.'

'I thought I'd gone too far. Because I'd said those things. But they weren't true. I lied because I thought that it would make you hate me and then you would let me go.'

'I let you leave, Willa. There's a difference between letting someone leave and letting them go. And I never let you go.'

Willa pressed her hand against her mouth to stifle a sob, and then Ares closed the distance between them, and he was taking her into his strong, surprisingly shaky arms.

'I'm so sorry for what I said, for how I acted.'

'I'm sorry I let you leave. I never hated you. I wanted to. But I couldn't. And I kept seeing you everywhere. I was going crazy. I kept replaying what you said about it being just great sex.' He loosened his grip, his eyes finding hers. 'You weren't lying about the sex being great, were you?'

She laughed, then started crying. 'I'm not crying because I'm sad. I'm so happy. It's the hormones.' She reached around her neck and undid the chain with fingers that shook slightly. 'But mostly it's you. You make my world tilt, Ares Konstantinou. So would you do me the honour of being my husband?'

She held out her mother's ring, held her breath as Ares stood there gazing down at her, a stunned look on his face.

'You want to marry me?'

'I do, and I know it's not traditional and probably not what the Konstantinous do, but—'

His *yes* stumbled against her mouth, and then he was kissing her as the sun shone, kissing her until she couldn't think or breathe or see, and she was weightless and soaring with a love that was as precious as it was perfect.

EPILOGUE

Eighteen months later...

GETTING TO HER FEET, Willa shielded her eyes from the sun beating overhead, her green gaze scanning the sky.

Of course, there was no sign yet of the quivering outline of an incoming helicopter. The guests were not arriving for another two hours for the surprise birthday party she had arranged for Ares. It was just family and Thea, who was as good as family. But there was still a schedule of sorts, which meant that she had to persuade her husband to come out of the sea. Her stomach flipped over as Ares glanced back towards the beach. Because it was still there, that invisible thread pulsing between them. Of course, he had noticed her getting up.

He noticed everything.

Not quite everything, she thought, her hand moving lightly over her stomach.

She watched, heart swelling as his lean, muscular body cut through the waves like some mythical sea god, their son clutched firmly against his chest,

Alexander Robert Konstantinou.

Named for both his grandfathers, dark curls framing his face and dark blue eyes that changed almost overnight to match his father's and great-grandfather's. Her love for Alex, for Ares was immeasurable and absolute. And it was reciprocated. Of that, she had no doubt.

'Hey, there, little man,' she crooned, cocooning him in a towel as he reached out for her, and buried his petal-soft face against her throat, babbling excitedly.

'We saw some fish.' Ares leaned in to kiss her. 'Did you see? He got so excited. I think he knew what they were.'

She nodded, smiling at the pride on his face. They had been reading to Alex for months now. At first it was more about creating a routine and the baby had simply tried to eat the books, but recently he had started to show a preference for certain stories and *Ten Little Fish* was by far his favourite.

'He's smart. Like his daddy.' She kissed her son's head.

'Like his mummy, too. He's a lucky boy. Luckiest little boy in the world to have you as his mother. And I'm the luckiest man in the world to have you as my wife.'

'So it was luck that brought us together?' she teased him. 'I thought it was my poor understanding of British traffic rules.'

His grey eyes rested on her face, soft but serious now. 'Luck had nothing to do with it. If you hadn't stepped out in front of my car that day, we would have met anyway. I would have found you because we were—we *are*—meant to be together.'

She knew that he wanted to reassure her, that once she had needed that reassurance. But she didn't need it now, because she knew that he meant each word with every beat of his heart. She knew because she felt the same way.

And she still hadn't quite gotten used to these feelings. Maybe she never would. Maybe they were just so fathomless and overwhelming and all-consuming that it wasn't possible to get used to them. Maybe the preciousness of it would always remain because that was what real love was supposed to feel like.

Reaching out, she pressed her hand against the contoured muscles of his stomach and his pupils snapped outwards to swallow the grey of his irises as he pulled her closer, nuzzling her throat, and it felt like flying, knowing how much he wanted her, needed her.

She felt him tense. 'Is that the helicopter?'

'It is.' She took a breath. 'We've got some guests for lunch. Your family and mine. Oh, and Thea's coming too. I know it's not a big birthday, but I wanted to get everyone together. Ariana told me about your family celebrating things. Celebrating life, and I thought that sounded so lovely. It's my birthday present to you.'

There was a short silence, and then he nodded slowly, and he cleared his throat. 'It's a beautiful idea. I love it.' He kissed her gently. 'I love you.'

'And I love you, so very much.'

Her gaze rested on the platinum band on her ring finger. They had married fifteen months ago in a tiny white-painted chapel, with just their close family in attendance and no media. Ariana had been her maid of honour, and the triplets had been her bridesmaids. Robert had walked her down the aisle.

Thanks to her hormones, she had been close to tears all day, but it was only when she saw Ares waiting for her, his grey eyes soft with tears of his own, that she had cried. But they were tears of happiness and gratitude.

She was still grateful now. How could she not be? She had everything she'd ever wanted. The love of her family. All her family, because her sisters knew the truth now, and instead of weakening their bonds, it had strengthened them. She and Amber had forged a new alliance too, based on truth and acceptance.

And then ten months ago, she had given birth to Alex, bringing chaos and an even sweeter contentment.

They made it back up to the villa in time to greet the three blonde teenage girls as they burst onto the terrace, shouting excitedly at the top of their voices.

The rest of the day was spent eating, drinking and talking.

It was the perfect birthday, Ares thought, his gaze travelling over his expanded family, resting momentarily on David Arteta.

He felt a sudden urge to cross the terrace and shake David's hand to thank him, because David was the reason he and Willa had met now rather than later. His early antagonism towards the younger man had faded, partly because David had agreed to a two-year engagement. But mostly because David was clearly smitten with Ariana.

'Admit it. You like him, don't you?'

His sister poked him in the ribs, one eyebrow raised in challenge.

'More than I thought I would,' he admitted, smiling.

'Good. Because I have good taste in more than just shoes,' Ariana said, glancing down to admire her embellished leather sandals. Her face softened a little, and she leaned in to press her cheek against her brother's shoulder. 'You have good taste too.'

'You mean that?'

'I do. I think she's cool and funny and smart. But what matters is that she loves you.' Ariana bit her lip. 'She properly loves you. And that's good enough for me.'

He had told Ariana and his grandfather the truth about Zoe, and although they were both angry with her, their anger was tempered by his deep and grounded happiness.

And he was happy. He still loved his work, but the lure of the big deal had faded. His eyes flickered across the noise-filled terrace to where Willa was laughing. She was doing some complicated dance routine with her sisters, and she was concentrating on her feet. Then, as if she could feel his gaze, she looked over at him, her mouth curving into a smile that knocked the air out of his lungs.

As he watched her peel away from the dancing girls and walk towards him, he took a moment to marvel at the woman who was his wife and the love of his life, feeling his body tense as it always did, feeling the air change.

'Having fun?' She kissed him softly on the mouth.

'I am, yes. Thank you for arranging it all. I've never had a surprise party before.' He pulled her closer.

'I was a bit worried about not telling you.' She was biting her lip, and he knew why, and that she cared so much made his heart hammer against his ribs. 'I know you don't like surprises.'

'I do now. What the—?' Ares glanced down, frowning as Toula nosed her way between them.

His heart jerked as the dog pressed her muzzle against Willa's thigh, looking up at her adoringly, and he felt Willa's hand curl softly around his forearm.

'Why is she doing that?' His body was vibrating because he knew the answer to the question even before Willa said quietly, 'The party was one of my presents. I have another, but I think Toula just spoiled the surprise.'

'Are you...?'

'Yes. I did a test. Well, six actually. This morning before you woke up. I was waiting for the perfect moment to tell you.'

'This is perfect. You're perfect.' His voice was husky with a love that he had no choice but to feel. A love that would be complicated and sometimes hard. A love that would bind them tight and keep them strong.

He moved his hand to caress the curve of Willa's belly, and then she was kissing him, and his heart was a tangle of love and wonder and happiness. Perfect happiness.

* * * * *

Were you blown away by Billion-Dollar Baby Clause*?*
Then why not explore these other dazzling stories
by Louise Fuller!

Reclaimed with a Ring
Boss's Plus-One Demand
Nine-Month Contract
Royal Ring of Revenge
Business Between Enemies

Available now!

ENEMIES UNTIL AFTER HOURS

NATALIE ANDERSON

MILLS & BOON

For Deb

CHAPTER ONE

MIA SIMONINI GLIDED along the polished wooden floors of the gleaming office, humming her favourite song. First to arrive, last to leave; that was her mantra and she was killing it. Admittedly, for most of the ten days she'd been working here, the office had been more than half-empty so maybe that wasn't that much of a claim, but she had a plan to tempt the creative and coding geniuses to come and work in person for at least a few more hours each week. Small things could have big impacts—not that Mia herself was small. Nor quiet. But as she was alone right now, the latter didn't matter and the former never had. She bit into her cannoncino, savouring the silky rich cream and the light, flaky pastry, and her hum became a guttural moan of gastronomic delight. The thing was sheer buttery joy. She'd discovered the best pastry shop in Rome, and calling in her order on her way to work was her reward for these early starts and diligence. She set her coffee on her desk but as she took another bite of pastry, a dollop of cream plopped onto her shirt.

'Damn.'

Not *quite* killing it. But if it weren't for her boobs the cream would have landed on her keyboard, so there was a marginal silver lining to the snafu. Mia never had mastered the art of sitting down to eat tiny portions slowly—'like a lady'—as her jerk of a father had frequently harangued her to. He'd not liked her appetite. Nor her enthusiasm. Honestly, not anything much about her. But he was no longer around and Mia didn't know why she allowed his judgy words to echo within her still.

Get it together.

Mia was used to jobs where having some food on her clothing was an occupational hazard and thus if not quite acceptable, then at least understandable, but this gig wasn't one of them. She was temporary office manager for a tech start-up incubator that clearly had too much money to throw about, given the luxury refurbishment of the historic building in central Rome where it was housed—and the fact that half the staff never bothered to show up to use it. Including the boss. She'd had doubts about taking on this contract for her dear friend Adele; tech was not her sector—truth be told, she barely understood what some of those apps did—but she hoped that managing a bunch of genius programmers wasn't unlike managing any other bunch of strong-minded individuals. Because Adele had been desperate. She'd needed immediate cover so she could care for her husband, who'd suffered a serious medical event, and as luck would have it, Mia had opted to pass on her next cruise ship contract and so was able to step in. It was a weird set-up, though—gleaming and new and clearly successful…just run by ghosts. Though at this moment, the staff all being absent was a good thing. Mia snatched her spare top—it was hardly the first time she'd spilled food on herself so she kept one at work—and nipped into the private bathroom in the CEO's suite as it was nearest. Of all the AWOL staff, he was the one who was never there. But she needed to move because the stalwarts who did show up daily—company lawyer Paolo and his property team, plus the chief financial officer Carla and her two investment analysts—would arrive any second.

With her fresh shirt wedged in the crook of her arm and the remaining pastry held between her teeth, Mia unbuttoned her blouse, still humming her tune of the day as she walked through the empty office to the bathroom and turned to the mirror.

'Who are you?'

She whirled, the two halves of her cream-smeared blouse splaying wide with the speed of her spin. She stared, utterly unable to answer and not because of the pastry hanging from her mouth like an oversize cigar. Sweet mother of mercy. There was a man already in the bathroom.

Not just any man. He was about as bare chested as she—while his shirt was on his arms and shoulders he was still in the process of buttoning it up, which meant she saw flexing pecs and washboard abs and a seemingly endless expanse of lean, bronzed skin and a light smattering of dark hair that arrowed down into tailored dark grey suit trousers that emphasised his narrow hips and long legs and—

'Who are you?' he repeated in rapid Italian.

Who was she? Who was *he*? Mia froze on the outside and melted on the inside. He was tall, dark and very much looking like he'd just stepped out of the shower. The scent of soap tantalised her suddenly suffocating lungs. The single trickle of water slipping its way down his finely muscled torso was too fascinating and she snapped her attention up to his face.

Oh. Oh *my*. He'd freshly shaved and that simply highlighted his sculpted cheekbones and square jawline that screamed to be touched while his hair was slightly too long and too unruly for the pristine carved perfection of the rest of him.

Good Lord, the man was gorgeous.

Her brain refused to compute. At all. But there was something familiar about those bottomless, dreamy brown eyes.

Was it possible that she knew him? Was it possible her brain would ever work again?

She removed the end of the cannoncino from her mouth and quickly licked her lip, certain there'd be an errant flake of pastry; there always was. Too late, she realised her struggle to breathe was because of the lingering steam in the air. He'd definitely showered in here. And *that* meant—

'You're the boss,' she muttered.

The guy who'd been absent for over a week. The one her friend Adele adored and wanted Mia to protect and do everything for without question.

'Who are you and why are you here?' He switched to English immediately.

So much for thinking her Italian had improved. She'd lost most of her first language when her mother had died and she'd had to go live with her father in England, but she'd been working on it and—

'Are you the cleaner?' he prompted, his gaze grazing down her body.

She grabbed her blouse with her spare hand, but there was a lot of Mia to cover. A polite man would avert his eyes. This man was not polite. This man took his time to scrutinise every inch of her exposed skin, and given his forbidding expression he was not impressed. He could not stand more ramrod straight. Or still. Or look more grumpy.

'Did one of the coders hire you as some kind of inappropriate entertainment?' he growled.

OMG—had he just mistaken her for an exotic dancer? *At seven o'clock on a Monday morning?*

Mia straightened as best she could given the gaping blouse issues, determined to recover some dignity. 'I was hired by Adele.'

'What?' He cocked his head and stepped closer. 'Why?

When?' His bottomless soulful gaze turned icy. 'To do *what*?'

Mia didn't answer. He still looked disturbingly *familiar* and if only she could get her brain to work, she might rake up why. But surely, she would remember if she'd ever met a man this ridiculously hot?

'Who are you?' He took another step closer and his voice dropped to sub-zero temperatures—perfectly matching his frigid glare.

Mia was used to far worse than disapproving looks and quelling glances and being told to be quiet because once again she was being too much. This jerk's supercilious ability to look down his nose at her was nothing on the acid that streamed from her father's tongue. This ass and his not-so-silent distaste could take a hike.

She stared back at him. Hard. And shoved the remainder of the pastry into her mouth. It wasn't the first time she'd stuffed in food to stop herself saying something she shouldn't, but it was the most stupid.

Because suddenly she placed his face. More precisely, his *eyes*. She finally remembered those meltingly deep brown eyes. And now she didn't want to answer any of his questions. Now she needed a moment to recover.

Adele had referred to her boss only as Santo—Saint. Mia had figured it was some kind of inside joke given Santo Antonio was the name of the software company. Mia had gotten full access to Adele's email, and her boss had only his first initial on the email address and he signed off with simply an S.

She'd had only a day and a half with Adele in a frantic handover before the older woman had needed to get back to the hospital. Mia had listened and not questioned anything unless it had been essential because Adele was already struggling and Mia hadn't wanted to stress her more. So Mia had simply assumed—*wrongly*—that the 'S' in all those emails stood for Santo. It didn't. It was Sante with an 'e.' She knew *exactly* who he was and she was no longer warring between melting and freezing; she was numb.

He stood more rigid than ever, glaring at her with that outrageously square jaw while she chewed. It took a while before she could swallow because it had been a good third of the pastry that she'd shoved in there. The tragedy was she'd couldn't even taste it anymore. It could've been cardboard for all the pleasure it brought. Of course she shouldn't have done it, but she'd needed to buy time to work out how on earth she was going to deal with the devil before her.

Sante Trovato couldn't decide if he was hallucinating or this was real because apparently Venus herself had materialised in his bathroom. *Bountiful* was a word. *Magnificent* another. Half-dressed and luscious and looking *him* up and down with hungry, wide blue eyes as if he…

His mouth dried. He'd visually drowned in acres of creamy skin and ample curves, in the tempting richness of the long chocolate-brown hair cascading over her shoulder. As for her consumption of that custard pastry—she'd inhaled the remainder like some sex goddess. She was *all* goddess and—

He could not be thinking these thoughts.

Gritting his teeth, he slammed the brakes on his brain, but still couldn't help absorbing her beauty. With high heels she would look him almost straight in the eye, and he was tall. She was all curves and straights and *fascinating*. Sante could only stare.

Was he in a dream he couldn't wake from? He'd returned to Rome late last night, come straight to the office, gotten stuck in to a problem and worked through the night. He thought he'd woken fifteen minutes ago with a minor headache and a dry throat, figured a quick shower would help, but here he was still asleep and—

'Tell me who you are,' he muttered in a strangled voice.

The only way to be sure she was real was to reach out and touch her. His muscles tensed in anticipation of pleasure. He gritted his teeth harder as she licked another scrap of pastry from her lower lip.

'Would you mind turning away?' she said.

Her tone was absolutely frigid.

Sante instinctively rebelled. He'd seen her looking at him with heat and hunger so what had caused the sea-change in her emotion? For a split second he stared longer, then reality jolted and he stalked out of the bathroom. He stood in the centre of his office and buttoned his shirt to the collar.

What had happened? What had she suddenly thought that made her turn to ice? He stiffened as the old defensiveness swept over him. He hadn't been verbally disciplined in a decade but she'd spoken with the same cold tone of the English school principal of the boarding school he'd been sent to. He remembered the day his hopes for a life-changing education had been destroyed. Sante had rejected the sought-after university scholarship before the offer could be rescinded. He'd been blamed for an accident. His innocence was irrelevant. Sante had *always* been blamed. Guys who came from backgrounds like his always were, no matter the truth. Which was why he'd built his own company. Why he still operated alone as much as possible. He had a few property and investment assistants for his portfolio and recently gathered a small group of techs to work through the ideas that wouldn't let his brain rest. But none spoke to him the way this woman just had. No one did. Not *now*. Not since he'd taken complete control of his life and expunged his past. So who was she and why was she taking off her blouse in his private restroom? His brain didn't actually care. His brain just wanted to go back in there and drink in her luscious curves. He'd been caught off guard and he was stupid tired…

No excuses. He was at *work*. He would focus on her prim disapproval, not her succulent body. Not that smear of cream on her shirt nor the appetite with which she'd demolished the pastry. He would not think about the slide of her tongue across her full lips and not her radiant, smooth skin that his fingertips itched to touch. He wouldn't focus on any of that. He wouldn't allow such a distraction to destroy his equilibrium or his reputation. He planted himself in front of his desk, legs apart, arms folded, and glared at the door, waiting for her to emerge.

'Who are you and what are you doing here?' he demanded the second she walked out.

Her new shirt was buttoned to the base of her creamy neck but the copious material didn't hide the curvaceous body beneath. He made himself focus on her face, blinking as a vague thought stirred in the back of his still-distracted brain. Yes, her mood had gone from hunger to hatred but there was something about the set of her eyes that made him pause. Not just their stunning clarity but—

'Adele hired me to run the office while she attends to a personal matter,' she said in that annoyingly precise and prim way. 'She didn't want to disturb you. Apparently, you don't like that.'

'What?' He frowned. There'd been fewer emails from his office manager than usual but Adele knew his preferred method and frequency of communication. 'I've been at a conference—'

'That ended five days ago. Weekdays that is,' the curvy

brunette interrupted icily. 'There's been a weekend in the middle as well.'

He stiffened. Who was this woman to judge his routine? Sante loathed judgement of all forms. He often was away for days at a stretch, and he relied on Adele to keep things ticking along as she had for nearly the past *nine years*. This was normal for them and why he'd given her full oversight over the office. But if there was a problem, Adele would've definitely made contact. Admittedly, he'd gone deep into a contemplative hole this past week but the fact that his assistant hadn't bothered him surely meant that whatever the problem was, it couldn't be that bad. 'How long does she need off?'

'Adele hired me to act as office manager for the next three months.'

He reeled. *That* wasn't happening. He couldn't have this walking distraction near him for that long. 'And I'm supposed to just take your word for that?'

'If you'd bothered to come into the office, or even, I don't know, picked up your phone to personally talk to any one of your staff, then you'd already know.'

Her chastening tone irritated him. He *had* missed a call from Adele a few days ago and he'd not had a chance to return it. He'd emailed through various instructions as normal, though. And gotten a reply. But now he wondered who the reply had been from. He swallowed uncomfortably. Why hadn't Adele emailed about this? Or tried calling again? The older woman had been his first hire and still was his most reliable, loyal employee, so much so he'd given her leeway in the office set-up. She'd directly hired half those young techs and her instincts were usually good. The last thing he wanted was to lose her. She sorted any office issues before they were even brought to his attention. But maybe that was what she'd tried to do here.

'Adele was almost as worried about inconveniencing you as she was worried about Bruno,' the brunette beauty added in his silence.

Any last lingering haze of sexual arousal still enveloping Sante evaporated in a blink. 'What's wrong with Bruno?' he snapped.

'He's had a stroke.'

'*What?*' Sante leaned back on the edge of his desk, his legs emptying of strength in the shock. Why hadn't Adele been in touch when it had been this serious? 'When?'

'Adele can't have any more stress or *she'll* become unwell,' she added. 'If you knew her, you'd know that.'

Of *course* he knew that! 'She should have come to me. I would have given her—'

'And if you *really* knew her, you'd know she wouldn't ever ask for or accept your charity.'

But he did know that, too, because he *did* know his very efficient executive. Okay, perhaps not all that well personally because that was how both he and Adele preferred it. She was efficient, discreet, reliable. She worked exact hours—she never would have turned up as early as this—yet she got absolutely everything done. Always. Adele was the perfect employee. Or she had been until hiring *this* woman as her temporary replacement in the office. He was not the bad guy here.

'Or is leaving people to suffer alone your forte?'

Sante went very still as his pulse suddenly roared in his ears. The creamy-skinned brunette was unnaturally still, too. He mentally repeated her soft accusation several times until it sank in. Then he stepped forward and grabbed her arm because he still needed to be sure. '*What* did you just say?'

Mia shouldn't have said it but her tongue had run away before her brain could catch it. She *hated* this man. With her heart and soul she hated him. Sante Trovato had ruined *years* of her brother's life. Because of him her brother Dario had *suffered* so much. He'd endured physical pain, emotional betrayal and he'd lost so much time. And now Sante was her temporary boss and looking every inch the ruthless billionaire that he was. His presence was shocking enough, but that she'd felt an appallingly intense moment of sexual attraction to *him* was horrifying.

'Who are you?' His voice was still barely above a whisper, yet every menacing word reverberated to her bones.

Except it wasn't only her bones that responded. She was so weakened by him she didn't even try to jerk her upper arm free of his grip—and he wasn't even holding her that tightly. His strength was leashed and he still held back from giving her the oddly disconcerting feeling of being too close yet distanced. The insane thing was for a split second she wanted him *closer*. He was unbelievably handsome—no wonder it had taken her a moment to recognise him. Sante had gone from a lanky teen with close-cropped hair to a tall, muscular man whose tousled hair had an untameable life to it.

Mia cleared her throat, trying to rationalise that her attraction was merely from the surprise—she'd not expected to see a bare-chested man in the office, definitely not such a built one, and as she'd not seen let alone touched a guy in a long, long while, that moment had simply been a basic physiological response to masculine beauty. Animal instinct. She was over it already. Except she needed him to release her and step back. He didn't. He just stepped closer still.

'*Who* are you?' He ground the question, a muscle jumping in his jaw.

She was filled with remorse for not asking Adele all those finer details. For being arrogant enough to assume she could handle a job she was barely qualified for. But *this* man was even more arrogant. He thought he could do whatever he wanted and get away with it. He was a cold-blooded, avaricious ass who cared only about himself and his money. Most of all, he was a *coward*.

And she would not cower before him. She stiffened, trying to tug her arm free. 'Ms Simonini. I'm your new office manager.'

His eyes narrowed and he still didn't release her. She knew he wouldn't recognise that surname—it was her maternal grandfather's; she'd rejected her family name the moment she'd turned eighteen.

'Okay, Ms Simonini, what did you mean about me leaving people alone to suffer?'

'What do you think I meant?' She swallowed.

He put profit and prospects before people. Before loyalty. He was a *user* and he would cheat to win.

'You're English.' He dropped his hold on her so suddenly she had to take a step back to keep her balance.

She immediately rallied and stepped forward again. 'Actually, I'm half Italian.'

He stared into her face. His brain ticking over. It took him so long to place her it was almost an insult.

'Mia,' he muttered. His head lifted and he snapped. 'You're not Simonini, you're... *Lorenti*. You're Dario Lorenti's sister.' He inhaled sharply. 'You can pack your things and leave immediately.'

'Why?' She held fast. 'Does my presence cause you guilt? Shame, perhaps? I should hope so.'

Her brother would completely freak out if he knew who she was standing in front of now. Which meant he wasn't about to find out. This was only a three-month contract and she was never letting Sante Trovato intimidate her out of here just because her presence prickled his conscience. So it damned well should.

He folded his arms across his chest and glared at her. 'Whatever offer Adele made you, its terminated.'

Yeah, no. Mia didn't let anyone tell her what she could or couldn't do. Not anymore. And she was not going to make this easy for him by walking out of here and not looking back. She was not doing that to Adele. She was not doing that to her brother.

'*I'm* not going anywhere.' She stepped close, suddenly determined to thwart the jerk.

While she and Dario weren't as close as she'd like, the opportunity to be the thorn in the side of his sworn enemy was too good to pass up. She'd been too young to defend Dario properly back then. Or to be an ally against their horror of a father. But she was different now and this was one fight she wasn't backing down from.

'I signed a fixed contract with Adele,' she said. '*You* can't simply terminate it.'

That muscle ticked in his jaw again. 'I think you'll find I'm—'

'Obliged to observe employment laws just like everybody else.'

'No.' He inhaled sharply. 'You're done. Don't worry, I'll ensure you're paid until the end of the week.'

Of course he thought he could just get his way. He *always* got his own way. He was the most selfish man in existence. He even trounced her father in that arena, which was really an achievement.

'You're dismissing me on what grounds?' she asked.

There were a few tense moments as he glared at her.

'Gross misconduct,' he eventually bit.

'What?'

'Stripping in the office. This is no place for sexual impropriety.'

Oh, he had to be kidding! Mia lifted her chin. She'd been slut shamed by her father simply for developing breasts and she wasn't having it here. 'Says the man who was *equally* undressed.'

'Because it was *my* office bathroom. You walked unannounced in there and started stripping.'

'Only in your wildest dreams would I have done that had I known you were there.'

For a split second an unreadable emotion flickered in his eyes. It almost looked like amusement. 'Okay, then you're suspended on suspicion of corporate espionage.'

'Excuse me?' Mia gaped at him.

'You're in here spying for your brother.'

Well, that was the most outrageous and infuriating thing she'd ever heard because Sante Trovato was the true *thief* around here. 'My brother doesn't need to steal anything from you.'

'Because he has all that inherited wealth?' Sante said acidly. 'That wouldn't stop him trying. People like your brother can never have enough.'

She was speechless. Sante Trovato was the greedy one. He was the morally dubious. *Never* her brother.

'There's no other reason for you to be in my private domain,' he added.

'I had no idea it was your private domain. If I'd *known* I wouldn't be within fifty feet of anything, anyone or any *place* to do with you,' she said scornfully.

'So much ferocity merely confirms my theory that you're in here spying.'

'I came in here to change my shirt.' She ground her teeth.

'That's your convenient excuse in case you were caught.

The likelihood of which would be low given how early you're at work. Quite the enthusiastic assistant, aren't you? So *eager* to please. It's a very good facade for falsehood.'

'The likelihood of my being caught is only low because neither you nor your supposedly genius workers like to actually show up to work.'

'So you admit you're in here snooping.'

'Of course I *wasn't*. I just wanted to change my shirt—'

'Because you're a messy eater?'

'Sometimes, yes. Absolutely.' And she wasn't ashamed nor afraid to admit it.

He blinked. 'There's another bathroom for the workers. This one is mine.'

'As I'd thought the boss was permanently AWOL, I figured it was okay to change in here. The other bathroom is ages away from my desk and I didn't want to traipse all the way through the office dropping more cream.'

'Why don't you use your true surname? What are you trying to hide?' he asked.

'Unlike you I have nothing to hide.'

He looked furious all over again.

Good. Mia used a different name because she didn't want to be associated with her father—not that he'd ever bothered to bestow *his* name on them legally. But she didn't want to ride on her *brother's* success, either. She preferred to avoid the assumptions when people found out her connections. She liked her independence. But now she smiled. 'Maybe I'm married.'

Fire flashed in his eyes and he quickly glanced at her unadorned hands. 'Constantly lying to my face really isn't going to help your employment case.'

'Don't you ever read your emails?' she asked coolly, determined to get this conversation back on track.

She was even more determined not to leave. She would happily cause his conscience problems for a few weeks with her presence. She was a connection to his past and he immediately wanted to get rid of her. Too bad for him.

His lips thinned. 'How bad is Bruno?' There was a beat. 'Adele should know I would h—' He broke off and cleared his throat.

At the starkness flashing in his eyes, Mia could *almost* believe he was genuinely concerned. But she already knew the man had neither conscience nor heart.

'Why didn't she get in touch with me?' he asked quietly after a moment. 'She only called once.'

'If you hadn't disappeared off the planet, maybe she would have tried again. But you'd vanished and apparently when that happens, you can't be disturbed—no matter the circumstances. It's written all in caps and underscored three times in the tip sheet she left for me after our handover here.'

He blinked. 'You had a handover here?'

'Of course I did. Adele loves this job and she did the best she could in the time she had because she was afraid of disappointing her insanely demanding boss.'

She completely failed to understand why Adele would want to work for him—but clearly, Adele didn't know what Mia knew. The truth.

'How long have you been working here?' he asked.

'Almost two weeks.'

He looked both horrified and apoplectic. 'You've had access to this office for two weeks?'

'Plus Adele's email. Yes.'

'That's a gross breach of confidentiality.'

'Oh? Why don't you want your new office manager to access company data? What have you got to hide?'

She'd seen his emails. They were unbelievably devoid of

any human element. It was lists of tasks. No praise. No personal chat. Nothing remotely nice or supportive or checking in that Adele and the rest of the staff were okay.

'Oh, I know.' She smiled viciously. 'You don't want the world to know what a traitorous jerk you really are. Is that why you keep your name so discreetly hidden from all company documents?'

He simply stared at her. Not rising to her provocation. That Adele had referred to him as Saint was too ironic.

'You don't want anyone to find out your shameful secret,' she said, her fury rising.

'What secret do you think that is?'

Was he serious? Did he really want her to spell it out? She'd *been* there. She'd witnessed it all. But fine. She'd play his game.

'That you're a fraud.' She locked her knees to stop them trembling. 'You're a liar. You're a cheat. And you're a callous coward.'

He didn't move. He just whispered. 'And you know this because…'

'You caused the accident that almost killed my brother. You ran away, leaving him trapped, injured, alone. And then you stole his ideas to make your first billion using my father's blood money as your seed capital. You like a payout, Sante. And all the while he was suffering. Dario suffered for *years*.'

Sante reared back as if she'd whipped him.

Good.

Mia breathed hard. Her brother Dario *still* suffered. What had happened back then had changed him. It had changed everything. And it was entirely Sante Trovato's fault.

Her fury unleashed, Mia jabbed her hand on his chest to emphasise her words. 'You're a shark who'll destroy anyone who gets in your way. But not this time. You're *not* getting rid of me.'

CHAPTER TWO

SANTE TROVATO TENSED as rage ricocheted through him. Again. If he didn't hold himself on lock he'd forcibly manhandle her out of the building or, worse, silence her in another diabolically inappropriate way involving their mouths. He was giving in to *neither* of those impulses.

Stolen her brother's idea? Taken blood money from her father?

She was utterly deluded. But her accusations stirred memories he'd ruthlessly suppressed for years, and his head spun as he struggled to catch up on a catastrophe he'd not seen coming.

'Is that what you think happened?' he muttered tightly.

'It's what I know happened. I was there.'

Hatred radiated from her. Dario Lorenti's little sister was hissing like an aggravated kitten, fury pushing her not only to provoke him, but punish him as well. To make him *pay*.

Just over ten years ago, he'd been at boarding school in the UK with Dario. They'd been friends then. As close as Sante had been to anyone. They'd busted out of school one weekend—gone to a music festival. But Sante had gotten lost on a back country road in Wales. It was black as pitch and he'd slowed—but not enough. He'd lost almost everything in that instant. But what Mia thought had happened was a shockingly far-fetched twisted version of the truth.

He hadn't taken her damned father's money, but he *had* been the driver in the crash that had almost killed her brother and smashed his leg. And no, it didn't matter that Sante had modelled the physics of the crash on a computer over and over again and knew, fully *knew*, that there was no way he could have avoided it, he still felt guilty about it. He would always feel guilty about it. Just as he would always feel guilty about not protecting his foster brother years earlier. Those facts proved he wasn't meant to be around people much, but he was too on edge, too defensive, to explain any of that to *her*.

'If I'm such a monster, why do you want to work for me?' He glared at her, ignoring the intense pull he felt towards her on a molecular level. He was not touching her again. Never *ever*.

'Let me repeat it for you one more time. Slowly.' She glared back, adding an even more patronising inflection to her irritatingly precise intonation. Her Italian was laced by that posh English accent, instantly giving away her status. 'I'm not working for *you*, I'm working for Adele. *She's* the reason I'm not leaving.'

As if she were some holier-than-thou saviour stepping in to protect his best, most highly paid, most trusted until *now*, employee from his appalling treatment?

'*I* won't let *her* down,' she added, tightening the screws.

Mia couldn't claim the moral high ground. She was a *Lorenti*, and the greed and ruthlessness she'd just assigned to him was nothing on that of her own family. A fact which made Sante certain that playing protector to Adele *wasn't* her only motive now. Bitten as he was by the urge to toss her onto the street, he would find out her intentions first, then neutralise her.

He scooped up his phone. 'Then let's see what she says.'

He'd initially thought that as Adele hadn't pushed to get

hold of him, it meant that whatever had happened wasn't that bad. Now he knew the truth was the total opposite. Bruno had to be desperately unwell because while Sante had given her a lot of power, Adele would never normally hire someone to step into the office without at least consulting him.

He stared at Mia as he waited for Adele to answer, trying not to feel a hit that Adele hadn't confided in him. But he didn't have *personal* relationships with employees. Not with anyone, in fact. He'd dated on and off over the years before remembering that he hated the prying into his past that inevitably eventually occurred. So now he was a misanthropic loner who had the occasional one-night stand and that was the way he liked it. He had plenty of projects and properties to occupy him. But Adele had been his only employee for the first few years, and she'd stuck with him all this time and she hadn't told him she was in trouble.

Of course she'd stuck with him only because he paid well. But he paid her well because she was intelligent and reliable. Until now, when she'd hired the sister of his enemy. Not that Mia was a threat to him in any kind of murderous way, but her presence forced Sante to revisit a deep injustice he couldn't stand to consider let alone resolve. Adele wouldn't have known anything about that when she'd contracted Mia. Sante—and Mia's father—had worked in their own very different ways to ensure that.

Adele finally answered his call and the second she did he heard the strain in her voice. He immediately regretted doing this in front of Mia. He'd wanted to see her squirm; instead, he was the one feeling wretchedly uncomfortable. He met Mia's cool blue gaze as he offered what he could for Adele—money, more resources—and clenched his teeth when Adele distractedly assured him everything was okay and that she just needed time and that she was so sorry for letting him down but that she knew Mia would be doing a wonderful job for him. Hearing her anxiety, Sante could only bite harder before confirming that indeed Mia was, and that he would be in touch again soon.

Mia's chin lifted in triumph. But Sante couldn't contradict Adele or subject her to a barrage of questions when she was so obviously masking her distress. He ended the call, even more frustrated. Adele wouldn't accept direct help. He'd have to figure a more creative way to ensure she had all the support she needed. He would also have to discover all he needed to know about Mia directly from her. Given her attitude, he was going to have to watch her every move.

'Did you find out what you needed to know?' Sparks flickered in Mia's eyes, enhancing their blue.

Sante surveyed her defiant stance with bitter, fatalistic amusement. 'Not everything. I need your résumé.'

'I'm already hired.' She folded her arms across her chest.

Sante wished she hadn't. It had been a defensive gesture but all it did was enhance her glorious shape.

Focus. He cleared his throat and distracted himself by picking up a pen. 'For now, but I'd like to understand exactly what Adele saw that she thought you'd be such a perfect fit.'

She took another step into his office—filling up all his vision and causing maximum discomfort.

'Adele has worked for you for almost a decade and never let you down.'

'She didn't know who you *really* are,' he muttered acidly. 'You deceived her.'

'You still think that was some elaborate plot?'

'I don't believe she told you how long she's been with me but didn't tell you my name.' He stepped forward to expend just a smidge of the extra energy racing round his body.

'She only ever refers to you as *Saint*. It's like a bad joke.'

Sante glared at her. Adele did call him that and it *was* a joke between them. About the only one they had.

While it ought to be unbelievable that Mia hadn't known who she'd be working for when talking with Adele, it was *possible*. Sante fiercely guarded his privacy—everything personal about him was locked down both online and off—but not for the insulting fabricated reasons she'd inventoried earlier.

'I still want a copy of your résumé,' he said coldly.

Mia Lorenti came from a family of users who thought money could buy them anything they wanted. Why did she even need to work? Hadn't her jerk father left her a few million when he'd died a few years back—making Dario some pretentious duke or lord or the like? It galled Sante that he even knew this much. Maybe Mia had partied her way through her inheritance already. Well, she wouldn't be in his offices by the end of the day. *He* would pay *her* off if he had to—whether he'd have to buy out her entire contract or offer more, he didn't care. The Lorenti family was all about money, so it was only a matter of meeting her greed. Then she would be gone and he would forget that searing moment of sensual attraction.

'I'll email it as soon as I have a minute.'

'You have a minute now.'

She pinned him with those ice-blue eyes and lowered her voice. 'Try to make life difficult for me and I'll sue you for constructive dismissal.'

He almost smiled. 'I see you have your father's negotiation skills.'

'I'm *nothing* like my father.' Stiff with outrage, she stalked out.

Sante stared after her. Well, *that* got a reaction. Scoring a hit felt good because her fictional list of *his* supposed failings earlier had bruised. Why should he care what she chose to believe? He rubbed his temples and turned back to his desk.

In the bathroom before, he'd seen fury bloom in her eyes as it had slowly dawned on her *who* he was. She'd eventually *recognised* him. Because they'd met before. He forced himself not to consider the curves he'd glimpsed, but to think back to the eighteen months he'd spent in the UK that had changed his life.

He'd spent one summer at Westwick, her father's stately pile in Wiltshire. At the time Sante would have said it was the best summer of his life—certainly, it had been his *only* holiday. The only time he'd had away from the boarding school aside from sports tournaments. A few months before the accident in their final school year, it had been a summer of freedom. He and Dario had spent the afternoons training for sport, learning to code on Dario's computers half the night and spitballing app ideas—the more ludicrous the better. He'd naively believed he might finally have a future he could look forward to. Dario had been his best friend— hell, he'd have considered him the brother he'd never had apart from—*no*. He slammed the door on that earlier, even more devastating, memory. He could *never* go there.

Dario's father had come home twice during that summer and his presence had instantly changed the atmosphere of the place. But there'd been another occupant in the house aside from the stand-offish, clearly disapproving, staff. Mia Lorenti. At least five years younger than Dario, she'd been a rambunctious kid with long, messy hair, loud laughter and who sang as she skipped down the long corridors of the manor. He'd not interacted much with her, he'd been busy plotting with Dario, but he finally let himself remember the last time he'd been face-to-face with her. She'd been in the reception area of the hospital when Sante had finally made it there a full twelve hours after the crash. She'd been tired, tear-stained, so young and he'd asked her how Dario was. She'd not known.

But she'd clearly believed whatever she'd been told about him since.

Stolen idea... Blood money...

He swallowed the bitter betrayal at the scope of the lies her father had spun. Sante had no real *need* to defend himself, yet he felt oddly compelled to. It would be a futile undertaking. It wasn't as if he could just tell her and expect that she would believe him. People *always* believed the worst. And he refused to have her opinion matter.

She wasn't a kid now. Now she was tall, curvaceous, utterly beautiful and utterly unable to be ignored in any way.

He wasn't actually attracted to her. He'd just experienced a basic bodily reaction to copping an eyeful of breasts spilling over lace bra cups—unexpected, and his reaction had been visceral. Automatic. Frankly, animal. Because he'd had barely any sleep and his brain had gone primeval on him because of it.

Frustratedly, he refreshed his email. No CV. So much for the efficiency everyone was raving about. Still, the longer she took to fulfil his request, the better, right? If she failed in her duties he could get rid of her even more quickly.

In that instant his email pinged a notification. Mia's CV. He read the document five times and was no less apoplectic by the end of the ninety seconds that it took. He snatched up the phone again.

'Get back in here,' he ordered gruffly.

She appeared in the doorway in moments. Chin high, the epitome of spiky defiance.

'Do you order all your employees about with such devastating charm?' she asked. 'No wonder none of them like to make an appearance in the office.'

Sante chose to use few words at the best of times but to be actually rendered speechless was new, even for him. And he pushed against it.

'Close the door.' He cleared the gruffness from his throat.

Her eyebrows lifted.

'Unless you want everyone to overhear how spectacularly unqualified you are to work for me,' he elaborated.

'We both know I'm far *too* qualified.' She closed the door and leaned against it. 'Aside from the lawyer to keep you out of jail, your accountant to track your ill-gotten billions and an older woman you take advantage of because she's desperate to support her unwell husband, you only employ university dropouts and ex-hackers—none of whom are actually present right now.'

Sante gaped, then clamped his mouth shut. It seemed Mia had no problem in using many words—albeit unwisely. She was being deliberately and outrageously provocative and to his utter bemusement he suddenly felt the urge to laugh. *Not* an appropriate reaction, and he dragged up an element of severity. 'You were a *nanny*.'

Amongst an assortment of other temporary and vastly different jobs in a variety of places. But Mia was basically British aristocracy, so why had she spent the past five years working an assortment of weird and frankly low-paying jobs using an alternate surname?

'Yes.' Fire flickered in her eyes and she lifted her chin proudly. 'I was a very good one. I have the employer recommendations to prove it. Feel free to phone and check them.'

Mia crossed her fingers behind her back. Sante Trovato was calling her bluff but she was bluffing right back. Still smarting from the humiliation of standing in front of him while he'd spoken with Adele, she wasn't letting any weakness show.

Adele had made her 'saint' of a boss sound ancient and somewhat infirm. She'd said he spent a lot of time working from his private estate and that he needed gentle handling. It was complete rot. Sante Trovato was an absolute villain. He'd left her brother trapped in a smashed-up car on a country road in the middle of the night. He'd been Dario's friend, then taken so much from him.

She *did* have exemplary references from every job other than the first. She'd fudged the embarrassing end to that one but she'd learned her lesson. Never again would she make the mortifying mistake of having an affair at work.

Ordinarily, she would be the first to admit she wasn't perfect. As a child she'd been full of mischief, but after her mother's death she'd moved to her father's home in England and become 'always makes mistakes Mia.' As the old jerk had repeatedly berated, she was too boisterous, too capricious, too loud, too much. But while she was well used to never pleasing authority figures, *Sante* was no saint and his searingly obvious judgement stirred her full rebellion.

Mia had long ago accepted there was no real way to ease the pain Dario had suffered, but maybe she could make Sante pay just a little.

He rose and walked around his desk, slowly advancing upon her with a thoughtful expression in his eyes. 'My employees are not toddlers.'

'No, but they have some traits in common with the little darlings,' she said. 'They like to nap. Take time out to play. Have the occasional tantrum.'

His lips twisted. 'Are you stereotyping my coders?'

She shrugged. 'I've managed recalcitrant children. I've managed egotistical genius chefs in a five-star restaurant and exhausted crew on a ship coping with overly demanding wealthy clients in the middle of a ten-week luxury cruise. I can handle your teenagers.'

His jaw flicked. Was he about to *smile*?

The man had a shocking amount of magnetism despite his grumpy demeanour. Good-looking even when frowning, his rare flash of a smile was electrifying. Looks like his were actually a weapon.

She stiffened even more. 'I can pull people together.'

'You think I want you to pull them together?'

'Adele said that you wanted to get your workers into the office for the same two days in a week, isn't that correct?' she asked. 'I'll create an environment in which they can thrive.'

Mia was neither daunted nor fazed by that challenge. She knew how to treat spoiled children. But Sante Trovato was more than spoiled. He was selfish and he had no empathy.

He blinked. 'That was something she and I discussed.'

'Well, it might be helpful if the CEO were to lead by example.'

'You're saying you want *me* in the office?'

'I've been here ten days and this is the first one you've bothered to show up.'

He glared at her. 'I have no immediate travel plans. You have ideas for bringing them back in?'

'I have a plan,' she fudged.

'Talk me through it.'

'I prefer to show, not tell.' She was fully employing delaying tactics.

'Actions over words?' He cocked his head. 'Do you really think I'm going to let *you* do whatever you want with my workers?'

Why did that sound inappropriate? She arched her eyebrows at him. 'Maybe you should. Give me rope to hang myself, right? Then you can fire me legitimately without having to resort to threatening behaviour.'

'How did you meet Adele?'

'I was the activities coordinator on a cruise she and Bruno were on a couple of years ago.'

'A cruise?'

She bristled at his obvious distaste. No doubt Sante would hire a luxury yacht and ensure he never had to see any staff, the supercilious jerk.

'A big one with a lot of customers and a lot of activities to coordinate. I'm extremely good with spreadsheets and rosters.'

'It was a cruise to Norway.'

'Yes.' She was taken aback. She'd not had the impression he would know anything about it. 'We got on very well. I always thought it a shame that she had to work most of the time she was on board.'

Sante's lips twisted into a small cynical smile. 'I paid for that cruise outside of her usual remuneration. Adele only accepted on the proviso she would work while she was away. Adele loves her job. She's been with me for years.'

'I know. It's a true mystery as to why.'

His lips twisted. 'Perhaps I'm a good boss.'

'Well, you *are* out of the office more often than not...' Mia mused. 'I suppose that would be a bonus.'

'Just so you know, I barely bothered her during that cruise. I didn't actually ask her for anything while she was away so any work she did, she did out of her own sense of responsibility. In fact, in the end I had to get one of my techs to lock her out of the company intranet for a couple of days just to be sure she would actually have a break, and even then she was on the phone to me complaining about it. That cruise was the only way Bruno was ever going to see the Northern Lights,' he muttered. 'I offered her the jet but as you already know, not only is Adele extremely good at her job, she's irritatingly proud. She wouldn't just take a gift. She wanted to earn it and pay for it all herself but his medical costs were draining her savings, so that was the compromise we agreed on. She's my best employee and I would—'

He broke off and growled.

Mia stared as he ran his hand through his hair and turned away from her. He looked and sounded sincere and for a moment she almost believed him. Adele was important to him. Yet, he'd gone off for days with no word and Adele hadn't wanted to bother him?

He turned that hard, bottomless gaze back on her. 'So you befriended Adele on board?'

Straight back to sceptical and suspicious.

'Actually, I made friends with Bruno first. He's an absolute gentleman and in her view that put her in my debt.'

He nodded.

'So we both want her to focus on him now and not worry about what's happening in here,' Mia said.

He studied her. 'Are you able to set aside your loathing and work for me?'

'I'm able to do my best for Adele. Also your workers. They deserve that.'

His eyebrows lifted. 'You feel sorry for them?'

'You only want your disparate group of brilliant coders and creatives to work together more so they'll spit out more ideas for you to add to your billions. Like some kind of genius factory.'

'Because you think I'm incapable of having my own ideas?'

'You stole them in the past. I guess at least here you're paying them.'

His eyes kindled. 'Why do you need to work at all?' he asked softly. 'Didn't your father leave you millions?'

She'd never taken anything from her father. Not even in his death. And she flared against the suggestion that she ever would. '*You* took more money from that man than I ever did.'

'Did I?'

'Yes,' she hissed. 'He paid you off after you crashed the car and ran away leaving Dario for dead.'

The difference between her and Sante was that he would take money. It was all that mattered to him. He would jettison any person to get it and keep it. But Mia needed autonomy and independence and to earn her own. She'd rather starve in the streets than take anything from her father. A few times she almost had.

Sante didn't seem to move. 'Is that what he told you happened?'

She didn't need to be told. 'That *is* what happened. I was there.'

'You *saw* me take your father's money?' he asked dryly.

She stiffened. No, she hadn't actually *seen* the actual transaction. But that didn't mean it hadn't happened. 'You're telling me it didn't?'

'Why would I bother? It's not like you'd believe me.'

Right. Because Mia hadn't just heard things. She'd *seen* things. She'd been there back then and he couldn't deny they'd happened just by turning his soulful brown eyes on her.

'You ran away from the accident,' she said. 'You ran,' she added. 'I *saw* you when they finally caught you and brought you to the hospital—'

'I ran to get *help*,' he interrupted bluntly. 'I just ran in the wrong damned direction.'

Mia froze at the underlying fury in Sante's goaded tone. Dario hadn't remembered anything about the accident. Her father had relayed to her brother what the doctor had said. What the police had said. What their school principal had said. Her father had been the filter for *everything* both Dario and she had known about the accident and the aftermath. Except for what Mia had actually seen, and she *had* seen Sante that terrible morning. He'd been scared. He'd sounded guilty. He'd kept saying he was *sorry*.

She dragged in a breath. 'You were pale—'

'I was *fine*.'

She might've been young but even she'd known Sante was anything but fine. He'd come to stay at Westwick for the summer only a few months earlier. He'd taken up all Dario's time and Mia had been left on her own. She'd hated Sante for that. But honestly, she'd also been fascinated by her brother's dark-eyed, quiet friend. At the hospital she'd initially been pleased to see him. She'd been alone in the reception area for hours. Lonely. Hungry. Not understanding how unwell Dario really was but afraid he'd disappear from her life like their mother had. That everything would change again and she would be alone for good. Because her father was no real father.

When Sante had been brought in she'd been too young to ask the right questions, to even understand what was going on. But she'd noticed his bloodied socks. The dried sweat and dirt, his pale face and the panic in his eyes.

'He said you caused the accident,' Mia muttered.

'Dario—?'

'Dario couldn't remember anything about that night. My father said that's what the police said.'

His gaze didn't waver from hers. 'Then why wasn't I charged over it?'

'Because Dad wanted to protect Dario from the stress of a trial. He needed time and space to recover.' Including from her. 'My father told the police not to prosecute you.'

'And you think he was powerful enough to influence justice like that?'

Yes. But her breathing grew uneven. Her father was wealthy—might have thought he could control everything—but perhaps he *didn't* have that power? The police would have charged. In fact, knowing her father, he would have *insisted* on it. Which meant he'd have been even more angry if there were no case to answer.

'He said you were expelled from school. He said you took the money. That you agreed to stay away from Dario.'

'*I* left the school before they could expel me. I didn't take a cent from your father. I would never let someone else dictate who I could be friends with.'

She couldn't believe him yet his assertiveness seeded the smallest of doubts.

'Did Dario say I'd stolen his idea?' Sante asked tightly.

'You talked about coding and ideas all the time that summer.'

'Not my app. He lied if he said we discussed that.'

Mia stared at him. Dario had been in recovery a long time. She'd been kept away from him. Ultimately, he'd become distanced from *everyone*.

'He doesn't talk about you,' Mia admitted.

'So you came to that wildly inaccurate conclusion all by yourself,' Sante said acidly.

'My brother and I are separate people,' she said stiffly.

'So he really doesn't know who you're working for?'

'*I* didn't know who I was working for until just over an hour ago,' she reiterated with annoyance. 'Dario has no idea where I am. We haven't spoken in a few months.'

'Why not?'

She gritted her teeth because she'd not wanted to open

up as much as she had to him. 'Adele and I have independence in common.'

'You mean you won't do whatever it is he wants you to.'

Given his audible judgement of Dario, she didn't want to admit that Sante was right. But Dario wasn't anything like her father. He wanted what was *best* for her.

Sante watched her dispassionately. 'Are you going to tell him you're working for me?'

'He doesn't need to know. He's not my keeper.' She needed to move forward, to get enough space to think all this through properly. 'Dario is irrelevant now. As is my father. There's no need for us to discuss anything personal ever again.'

He looked sceptical. 'Can you work for me if you believe I would take a pay-off?'

'My personal opinion of you won't impact on my ability to do my job,' she said. 'I can be professional.'

Slowly, he stepped towards her.

'But you don't want me here,' she muttered, annoyance growing as he towered over her. 'Because you don't want anyone to know the truth about your past.'

'Is this the part where you demand payment for your silence?'

She stayed still, refusing to be intimidated into backing away from him. 'That's your playbook, not mine.'

'So you're not here to do anything other than—'

'Help Adele. I made a commitment to her and I'm going to see it through. I'm going to do a good job.'

He stopped an inch away from being too close. 'I'll give you one week to prove it.'

'You'll give me my entire contracted time and I'm not the one with innocence to prove.'

'But, Mia.' He shot her a bitter smile. 'Isn't it *guilt* that normally requires proving?'

CHAPTER THREE

MIA ROLLED HER eyes and stalked to her desk. The nerve of the guy; he was totally guilty and they both knew it. Almost the second she'd sat down, her phone rang. It was a stressed Adele, checking Sante was okay and telling Mia not to let him try to do anything for her and Bruno. Mia couldn't understand how Adele could work for someone as soulless as Sante let alone be so desperate not to cause *him* any additional trouble. She just managed to stop herself calling out the older woman for *coddling* the jerk and managed to reassure her instead. She would take care of it. But the way they treated him was ridiculous. Mia wasn't about to do the same. She would work hard, but she wouldn't succumb to whatever spell he'd put on all his other workers. It seemed the coders were clearly affected. Mattia was the only one who'd arrived this morning, but the second he'd seen Sante was present he'd sent out an alert. Four more had arrived in the past hour. They didn't look scared. They were *excited*. It seemed *everyone* in the office was amped that Sante had finally shown up. But the man stayed in his office, his door imperiously shut firm. However, as the office was all wooden floors and exposed brick and glass, a procession of staff wandered past, peeking to catch a glimpse of the rare and magical creature. Sante Trovato was apparently a unicorn. He'd somehow manipulated them into thinking he was something wonderful. No doubt his looks helped. The lean youth who'd taken her brother away had matured into an impossibly handsome man with unruly hair and bottomless brown eyes. The sharp cheekbones, sculpted jaw and loose-limbed, rakish moves added to his 'lost boy' air. Even in the perfectly tailored suit, there was a wildness about him that seemingly fascinated everyone. But not her. She would never succumb to those looks—the grumpiness and mystery he exuded was a deliberate ploy. She checked but there was nothing on the company website about him. He hid the truth from *everyone*. No wonder he didn't want her here—he couldn't hide his true self from her and he knew she wouldn't let him get away with projecting this false front.

But she *would* do a good job—just to spite him. She would get the office full and moving. She would get those shy coders in and despite her cynicism, Mia realised his employees' obvious interest in him could be useful.

What he'd said about that cruise made a lot of sense. Bruno *had* been forever reminding his wife that she didn't *have* to work while on holiday. Worse, Sante's questions about his and Dario's accident made conflicting, confusing doubts rise. Mia knew that what she remembered wasn't always a complete picture of the past. Sometimes she'd leapt to conclusions. She'd *assumed* things because she'd not had anyone close enough—who cared enough—for her to ask the truth from. And that included her brother Dario. The carefree times *Mia* remembered from when they'd lived in Capri with her mother—when they'd had picnics in the gardens and devoured leftover luxury hors d'oeuvres—had in reality been engineered by her brother Dario, who'd scavenged them from the kitchen. Mia had only figured it out when he'd let a clue slip one day in a temper. It had taken too long for her to see her mother's absences for what they really were—the neglect of a woman desperate to find pleasure however she could. Dario had always staunchly defended their mother, but eventually it had become clear how much he'd protected Mia from her neglect.

So had what she remembered about Sante also been wrong?

No. Since the accident, Dario had kept a lot to himself but *he* believed this about Sante. Yes, he was distant and wouldn't discuss it but her brother knew better than anyone how awful their father could be. So for Dario to believe the worst of Sante, then *some* of it had to be true. Even though she'd fought with Dario when he'd wanted to correct the terms of their father's will, she knew her brother had always wanted to protect her. Now she would protect him in return.

Frustrated by her distraction, she went to the swanky office kitchenette and poured a glass of filtered water. She leaned back against the counter to sip it, almost choking when Sante walked in, still looking tense. He checked his step but then headed to the coffee machine. His guard was clearly up and he was deliberately maintaining distance.

Full-of-mischief Mia couldn't resist challenging him on it.

'You worked through the night?' She studied him.

He looked annoyingly good for such lack of sleep. That tallied with his general physical perfection. As a teen he'd been tall and broad and fit. Blessed with athleticism and intelligence. It was incredibly annoying.

'You must be very tired.' She hoped he was. Because if he had inhuman stamina that would just be too much.

'Working long hours is normal for me,' he snapped dismissively.

She barely refrained from rolling her eyes at his grumpy abruptness. But he saw and she was provoked into sarcasm.

'So you feel the need to prove yourself smarter, stronger, fitter, faster?' she queried. 'In that total alpha male way of enduring discomfort and extreme suffering better than anyone?'

He sipped the scalding coffee without a wince and regarded her steadily, which made her all the more irrepressibly determined to provoke him into a response.

'Well, at the very least you must be very hungry,' she added.

She knew there was nothing in that gleaming fridge other than milk for the coffee. Replenishing it with more supplies was on the extensive list of questions she'd compiled for the boss if he ever made an appearance.

'I am,' he acknowledged with almost a whisker of a smile. 'That cannoncino you demolished earlier looked delicious.'

'Then you should go get yourself one,' she said with a sharp smile. 'Stretch your legs if you've been asleep at your desk. The fresh air might do wonders for your temperament.'

His jaw dropped.

Amused, her smile widened. 'I'm here to manage your workers in the office, not be your personal slave.'

There was a moment of silence in which Mia regretted her unruly tongue as she watched Sante's expression change from disbelief—and disapproval—to a look she didn't trust.

Was he almost *smirking*? And why was she suddenly gripped by the awful vision of being helpless in his hold? And could he read her mind? Because he looked like he could and would and so would she.

OMG. If he looked at her like *that*, she'd do *anything* he asked. When he smouldered he was horrifyingly tempting. *How* could she be remotely attracted to Sante Trovato?

'I thought you were going to create an environment in which my staff will *thrive*,' he drawled.

'Your staff, yes. I'll make other purchases for them accordingly now I know you're happy for me to.' She shot him a faux smile. 'I wouldn't make purchases without prior approval.'

'You might think you have all the answers, Mia, but know this. I don't trust you. I'll be keeping a close eye on everything you do here.'

It was a threat, not a come-on, but that wasn't how her body reacted. It was a terrible idea to provoke him, but that impishness within Mia still wouldn't be silenced.

'Go ahead and watch me all you want,' she murmured.

The atmosphere shimmered. She reminded herself that he was a callous user. He was the ruthless, money-hungry one. He was the one unworthy of *trust*. But she'd been in his presence for mere hours and her system was going haywire already.

Sante stared as colour swarmed in her cheeks and the cobalt-blue of her eyes deepened. She regretted that last, he knew. She also couldn't move. In truth, nor could he. They were locked in a moment of awareness that was completely...completely...

He blinked. He could get rid of her. Of course he could. He was still in charge for all her bluster.

She broke eye contact and cleared her throat. 'These are very nice facilities in the heart of Rome.'

He stilled, not trusting her flattery.

'Amazing that you gained such vast success without early investment.'

By *investment* he knew she meant her father's money. The money he'd never taken. Sante had *nothing* to prove. He'd long ago made it a rule not to give a damn what anyone thought and he deliberately kept people at a distance. Their judgement was always instant and always negative, especially if they learned anything about his past—but ultimately he couldn't care less. Mia Lorenti wasn't going to accept the truth so he wouldn't be bothered even beginning to explain. He wouldn't justify. But her very blue eyes drilled into him with an almost insolent challenge.

'I worked hard,' he muttered.

'Really,' she said. 'To go from school dropout to tech tycoon in a decade is pretty unbelievable.'

And she clearly didn't believe he had. She thought he'd cheated. Yet, here *she* was, the one working an assortment of jobs that she didn't stick at for long. She'd had the privilege of an aristocratic upbringing whereas he'd come from literally nothing and no one.

The one time he thought he'd gotten a break it had blown up in his face. He'd left the UK straight after the accident. He'd walked out of school without completing the year, forfeiting the university scholarship before they could rescind the offer. Her father had made it clear that would happen. The police might not have reason to charge him, but Lorenti had contacts and influence in other spheres.

He'd returned to the place he'd been found. Sicily. He'd worked days on the dock as a labourer—picked up any shifts he could until he could afford his own computer. Then he'd worked on his app through the night. The hours he'd put in were insane. He'd gotten interest—yes, investment—that had been *earned*. But he'd retained control.

'You're very humble,' she added, still saccharinely pointed. 'You don't ever want to brag about how you made it?'

Her interest wasn't a compliment; she angled more as if there were something dubious about his achievements.

Sante flexed his shoulders. 'No.'

'But so many people would be curious, hoping to emulate your success.'

'Are you asking me for career tips?' he mocked. 'I can understand your curiosity given you flit from one thing to another so frequently. Is there a reason for *your* lack of reliability?'

That heat in her eyes flared. 'Don't you even want industry recognition?' She ignored his dig. 'Or is it that you prefer no recognition at all?'

'I have nothing to hide, Mia,' he said tightly. 'And I definitely don't need accolades from anyone.'

He didn't need *anything* from anyone. He certainly didn't need her needling him in this way.

'You don't care what anyone thinks?'

'I don't.' He definitely didn't care about *her* opinion.

She was a snob. But somehow, she was closer. Somehow, this was more intense. Somehow, she was the only person in the world.

'You just do what you want,' she breathed.

'Yes.' His mouth dried and he could barely whisper.

'Wow.' She slowly shook her head. 'You have done well for yourself.'

Yet, she made it sound as if his hard-earned liberty were a *crime*. She had no idea the hours he'd worked, the sacrifices he'd made, to ensure his independence.

'Yes,' he repeated huskily. 'And *no one* will ever take it away from me.'

What he had now wasn't bad for an unwanted foundling who'd been bounced from foster home to foster home.

Fury flashed in her eyes but it was nothing on his.

It was bad enough that she was Dario Lorenti's sister. He avoided her brother as much as possible—while their fields had once intersected, Sante's interests were far broader than the fintech space now. His office mostly managed his property portfolio. The coders were a side project—working on the ideas he didn't have the time to dive into.

Mia's presence forced him to remember a time he'd rather forget. The culmination of a series of complete disappointments. Being blamed. Being kicked out. Alone again. She had no idea. Screw her judgement and her questions. He'd had to shut her down when she'd mentioned seeing him at the hospital. He'd been so tired by the time he'd made it there. Mia had just told him that Dario was still in surgery when her father had appeared. The bastard had ignored her because of course he'd wanted to berate Sante. But maybe ignoring her had been normal for the jerk. That would track with everything Sante knew of the guy. Dario certainly hadn't been close to the man at the time, and why was Sante wasting his time now dwelling on this?

Because the level of distraction Mia brought him was outrageous what with her blue eyes and Botticelli beautiful body. He needed more than coffee to sort his head out. That he even gave a damn was shocking enough, but the thought that she'd just looked at him with heat other than anger—

Was only because of his lack of sleep. He would *never* cross the line with an employee. Furthermore, she was a Lorenti and *he* knew what ran in her blood—selfishness, greed, betrayal...*snobbishness*. But he was sure she *had* looked at him like an absolute temptress. One minute she was ice, next moment fire and he needed space to recover.

He stalked out of the office. He'd go one better than a measly pastry; he'd have a long, leisurely lunch—*alone.*

Her eyes gleamed as she watched him walk in early the next day. 'Twice in the one week?' She shot him another saccharine smile.

'I told you I'll be watching you,' he answered abruptly.

'I wasn't sure given you just disappeared yesterday, and of course there's nothing on your schedule.' She shrugged airily. 'But the team will be delighted.'

She obviously was not. Yet, he found himself staring at her. Again. Reading those mixed messages—she was sharply acidic while smiling radiantly, and her gorgeous eyes gleamed.

Sante made the mistake of not closing his office door, which meant not only could he hear her, he could also *see* her. There was no getting away from her when he *really* needed to.

She was on a conference call to the coding team. He knew she was keeping track of them via the project management software but daily personal calls made the difference—well, that was what Adele always said and she'd clearly trained Mia to follow the routine. So why it bothered him now, he didn't know. But Mia was wildly different from Adele. Her voice carried—with its sing-song higher pitch, laced with laughter as she threatened to set a timer on for someone. She radiated a boundless joie de vivre that was extremely irritating. He heard a ripple of soft laughter and then finally there was blessed silence. Until she started humming. Then stopped. Then hummed a little again before she obviously got absorbed in her work.

Sante sat, *his* ability to concentrate obliterated. Restless after less than five minutes, he rose. Hovering at his doorway, he watched her work, intently focused on her screen. He found himself walking to her before thinking, so when she suddenly looked up into his eyes with an intensely attentive expression, he was forced to improvise.

'I'm expecting a package of documents to be delivered

this week,' he said shortly. 'It's essential I get them as soon as they arrive.'

'Of course,' she replied smoothly but a deep colour ran into her creamy complexion. 'Are they late? Do you want to tell me where they're coming from and I can make contact and chase up the courier company if necessary?'

Her immediate efficiency only aggravated him more. As for that uncontrollable blush—it made *his* temperature rise. 'It's confidential.'

'Naturally.' She swallowed. 'Then I'll keep a sharp eye out and bring it to you immediately.'

Sharp eyes were definitely what she had. For a moment he gazed right into their beautiful blue. Satisfaction rippled; he liked having her full focus on him, liked seeing the pink in her cheeks deepen. Until she glanced beyond him and a sudden broad smile illuminated her face. Sante still stared, powerless to do anything but watch as she blossomed with a vitality that was extremely *alluring* and not directed at him at all.

'So nice to see you, Valerio,' she called softly.

Softly. Not the vivacious volume with which she usually spoke. Sante glanced behind him. The new graphics intern almost smiled as he avoided both Sante's and Mia's eyes entirely as he went to his desk. Sante turned back to Mia. She looked surprisingly pleased to see the jeans-and-headphones-wearing guy; her smile had turned almost intimate.

She'd been here almost two full weeks already. She knew his staff. Had she formed *relationships* with those staff—with this young kid who wasn't even on a permanent contract? But then, nor was she. Maybe they'd bonded over that. Which was fine. Naturally. Yet, he was absurdly sensitive to the different receptions she'd given him and Valerio.

Sante stalked back into his office. He jerked his chair forward, determined to focus and finally achieve *something*. But his computer suddenly pinged with a never-ending series of notifications. He went to it and frowned, staring at the calendar with consternation. He didn't pick up his phone. All patience lost, he simply hollered. '*Mia!*'

Mia drew on a defensive smile and headed into Sante's office—leaving his door wide-open behind her and trying to steady her heartbeat. Appallingly, her body responded with increasing chaos to his proximity. It didn't seem to care that he was a heartless jerk who'd betrayed her brother; her body just wanted his near. So she was ignoring her body. Controlling it.

'You've screwed up my scheduling.' He glared at her.

'Where?'

He jabbed a finger at the screen and she was forced to round his desk to study it. Big mistake. There was nowhere near enough of a barrier between them, and she desperately needed to calm her overexcited response.

'You've blocked out a significant portion of my day tomorrow.'

She leaned closer just as he turned his head towards her, meaning his mouth was only inches from hers. It was *searingly* intimate. It would take nothing to lower hers and—

What the hell was she thinking? Why had the idea to kiss him popped into her head? She stared into his brown eyes for three seconds too long.

'That's not a screw-up.' Breathless, she straightened and stepped back. 'It's a lunch meeting.'

If it weren't for Adele she would stalk out of here and not come back.

Was she coming down with some bug? Because Mia did

not mix business and pleasure. She'd done that once and never would again.

'You expect me to have lunch with my employees for two and a half hours?'

Sante looked so appalled Mia had to bite back her smile.

'Not only are you going to have lunch with them,' she said. 'You're going to pay for it.'

'Why would I want to do that?'

'If you want them to come into the office more often, you need to tempt them.'

Tempt. The word hung in the air. She glanced again at his beautiful eyes in time to see *his* focus drop to her lips. They actually tingled in response. She deliberately drew a breath but got a hint of sandalwood instead of the sanity she desperately needed. His soap. It reminded her of his fresh-from-the-shower look, and now her fingers itched as much as her bones ached. For *touch.* She had to have a fever. She *hated* this guy.

'Their pay packet isn't enough motivation?' he drawled softly.

'No. You know they're all super talented. They're capable of getting money elsewhere. They need something a little more special.'

'This is your amazing action plan? What *more special* do you have in mind?'

'Time with you.'

'*I'm* the special temptation?'

'Absolutely.' She couldn't bear to look at him anymore. She dropped her gaze and stepped back, clearing her throat. 'And some food will get them over the line.'

'You're serving me up as the centrepiece of your feast?'

She stifled a chuckle because he was so very appalled as he asked. And the image it put in her mind was irresistible.

'It's a lunch session with you, so yes.' She swallowed. 'They want to work for you. They're inspired by you. *You* are the draw.'

He followed her to the door. 'Is that why you're here—because of me?'

That stopped her. She turned to face him. 'We both know I didn't know you were you when I said yes to Adele. *Adele* is my special reason.'

He glanced past her out to the open-plan office, then back to meet her eyes. 'I have to maintain distance between my employees. I'm not there to be their best friend or…anything.'

Mia suddenly flushed with heat. Did he think he was letting her down gently? Making the boundaries very clear? Had he read her mind earlier? She was mortified. And mad. Because *he* was the one looking at her with that edge of inappropriate interest. She hadn't—wasn't—*wouldn't*. And mortified, mad Mia invariably said things she shouldn't. 'You don't think you can have friends in the workplace?'

It was the way she said it that was off. Unintentionally intimate.

'I don't think any kinds of relationships in the workplace are wise.'

Oh, he was definitely warning her but he definitely didn't need to. She'd already made that mistake with the one relationship she'd actually had and while she'd made many mistakes in her life, she didn't *repeat* the same ones. The public humiliation of that affair had burned common sense into her. Hadn't it? But she simply refused to agree with Sante on this. She squared her shoulders. 'I disagree—'

'Naturally,' he muttered.

She glinted. 'Surely, even you have to acknowledge that employee satisfaction matters.'

And he needed to work on his own boundaries because he'd been the one looking at her in a way that was...just like the way he was looking at her now. *Like he was hungry.*

'Satisfaction?' he echoed.

This time it was the way that *he* said it that was off. Unintentionally intimate. It *had* to be unintentional. She bit her lip.

'What about my satisfaction?' he murmured.

'Your...?'

'What's in it for me?' he clarified.

Mia's irritation mushroomed. Of course there had to be something in it for him. He might not have taken her father's money, but he was still only about himself.

'Increased employee productivity,' she snapped. 'They'll make you more money.'

'I don't need to make more money,' he said coolly but his eyes glinted. 'I can't spend the money I earn from interest alone.'

'Well, you've brought these people together for *some* reason,' she argued, irritated. 'Don't you want them to reach their full potential?'

Otherwise, why did he have them here? If he was ludicrously wealthy, what goal did he have in mind for this group of baby geniuses?

'They're here for you so why not try it this once and see what happens? If it's a failure, then you've your first reason to fire me. What have you got to lose?'

He gazed right into her eyes. 'So when this proves pointless, it's one strike against you.' He nodded. 'You know you only get three.'

'One week, three strikes, you're watching me, I get it.' She rolled her eyes. 'You can't wait for me to fail. Your problem is I'm not going to.'

'No?'

'No. And while we're negotiating, I suggest you have an open-door policy whenever you're actually in the office.'

'A *what*?'

'So you're more approachable.'

'*Why* would I want to be more approachable?' He looked as irritated as she felt. 'I just said relationships in the workplace are—'

'You come across as very intimidating,' she interrupted.

'And that's a negative?'

'When you want the best from your staff, yes. Don't you want them to feel confident enough to toss their creative ideas about without feeling terrified of your reaction?'

'What makes you think they're *terrified*? You've barely seen me with them.' His eyes narrowed when she abruptly laughed.

'Because you're barely here.' She shook her head.

'So you think they require more of my involvement.'

'Inspiration,' she corrected.

Terrified had been too strong a word; they were nervous. They all wanted to *please* him.

'They idolise you,' she acknowledged, her voice oddly husky. 'They want to be you.'

Sante didn't preen. Didn't appear flattered in any way. If anything, he looked angrier.

'They idolise and want my *bank balance*. That's all.'

Two days ago she would've agreed it was his single-minded stratospheric success they wanted to emulate. But the team he'd assembled out there seemed to be as excited about *him* as much as the opportunity to earn money. They were turning up again right now because Valerio had just put out the word that Sante was back in the office again. And they were all smiling about it. And if Sante had really achieved all this success *without* her father's start-up funding, then she could understand why. She was outrageously curious about him; of course they were, too. They wanted to learn from him. But Sante's unwillingness to believe that was weird.

'Perhaps you underestimate what you have to offer,' she said.

He didn't move but that stark, almost lost, expression flared in his eyes. It was the briefest moment, a flash of vulnerability she never would believe if she'd not just seen it. A wave of temptation washed over her—that inappropriate ache to move nearer to him. The man had a *lot* to offer—physically at least, and she was losing her mind because when she looked into his eyes like this, it was as if the world faded. As if there were only them and only—

'Fine.' He suddenly turned away from her. 'I'll be at your meeting.'

CHAPTER FOUR

SANTE GLANCED AT the clock in the corner of his screen and grimaced. He didn't want this meeting but he *had* been absent from the office a lot. He should've scheduled it himself, controlled the environment more. Excluded her. Because the open-door thing was the worst ever. He'd end that little experiment immediately. As a safety net for keeping his interactions with her appropriate, it was a complete fail. When he caught sight or sound of her, he forgot anyone else, anything else, existed. She was fascinating and it was a constant source of frustration because he did not want to be *fixated*. He rose and walked to close the door just in time to watch her walk across the foyer carrying a platter to the boardroom.

She glanced up and caught him staring. She paused. No point pretending he wasn't watching her. He'd warned her he would, so he was justified—yes? But though he should look away, close the door, he couldn't. He was trapped. A slow blush mottled every inch of the creamy skin he could see. Her eyes widened and her lips parted—suspended in that moment of surprise. She was almost a statue were it not for the thrum of her blood giving her away. Undeniable awareness captured them *both*.

With brute strength Sante closed the door. Closed his eyes. Focused on drawing a breath. Mia Lorenti was driving him *insane*. She sounded cool, looked professional, was doing everything perfectly well. But every so often that heat flashed in her eyes and she spoke with a huskiness that made every muscle within him tighten in sensual response. His instincts sharpened, too. He'd think she was playing him if it weren't for the fact that the blushes like that one just now were too awkward, too uncontrollable. They *couldn't* be deliberate. She tried to stop physically reacting to him but couldn't seem to. A feeling he knew well.

He paced in his office but it wasn't large enough to burn the excess energy. He yanked the door open again and stalked out—almost colliding with her on her way back to the kitchenette in the process. Automatically, he reached out, steadying her. That brought him far too close—he caught her fresh citrus scent laced with pastry cream sweetness. He dropped his hands as if he'd been scalded. But he didn't step back. He couldn't. He was frozen.

'Sante?'

He couldn't stand that whisper. Nor that soft inquiry in her eyes. He made himself glance beyond her. There were so many people milling about in the office. Truthfully, he didn't remember hiring them all—or had Adele been on a bigger hiring spree while he'd been travelling? He shook his head, knowing she hadn't. He'd just been distracted with his last property deal, hence his prolonged absence. While he kept a close eye on the programming and project files, he did that mostly from a distance and left Adele to deal with the face-to-face issues like thermostat control, supplies, illness, morale, general interaction…

'It's okay, they won't bite,' Mia murmured.

He glanced back and was immediately lost in the inviting generosity of her looks—the depth of those blue eyes, the endless creaminess of her skin. She was bone-achingly luscious.

Indeed, *he* was the one tempted to *bite*. 'I'm going for a walk,' he muttered, constricted.

'But—'

Getting away from her was imperative. He jogged down the stairs out into the spring day, soon enveloped by throngs of tourists. He would remind himself *exactly* who was boss. That he could do this. He'd dealt with far worse than a damned meeting with his own team. He huffed out several deep breaths. He was fine. This was fine. This was nothing.

He made it back with only a couple minutes to spare. She was hovering outside the boardroom door, her eyes over-bright and alert, and he wished he had the strength to look away from her.

'For a moment there I thought you weren't going to show,' she murmured.

Uh-huh, so had he. But he wasn't going to confirm her worst opinions of him.

He glanced in at the boardroom. Half the team was seated already and emanating a hum of conversation that covered the too-intense conversation he was having with her. Sante's stomach rumbled at the sight of the spread on the back table. An assortment of pastries was in a pile at the farthest end— including some of the cream ones she'd eaten the other day. But he was forced to enter if he wanted one. And he *really* wanted one. So did everyone else. Of course she hadn't done this just for him. She'd done this for everyone.

'You're spoiling them,' he muttered.

Mia looked right into his eyes. 'Doesn't everyone deserve to be spoilt occasionally?'

How was it possible she could sound so cool yet her gaze be so hot? She was a complete contradiction. Seemingly so controlled yet on the verge of combustion at the same time. Or maybe he was projecting his own feelings. Energy surged within him again. That walk had been pointless. How was he supposed to make idle chat with his employees when all he wanted was to look at *her*? When all he wanted was to lose himself in the soft generosity of her form?

'You won't be attending the session,' he clarified crisply.

'No.' That light in her eyes dimmed and her flush deepened. 'I'll pop in only to ensure everyone has everything they need.'

'Good.' He couldn't concentrate when she was around.

Mia hid at the back of the boardroom and tried not to let her hurt anger show. Tried not to watch Sante too obviously. As she'd expected, every one of his coders and creatives had turned up. She'd worked so hard trying to ensure everyone had comfort and space. She'd sourced pastries from her favourite bakery, balanced them out with salads and fresh fruit, but while the spread was sensational, it was clearly Sante himself who was the draw. Just as she'd known he would be. Not that he looked at all pleased about it. Not that he even wanted her in the room. Which was rude enough, and couldn't the guy manage the smallest smile of welcome to his baby geniuses? He put a pastry on the plate he'd taken and turned, encountering her frank stare. He turned to stone. She shot him a wide smile back, damned if she was going to let him know he'd killed her mood. He blinked. Broke eye contact. Frowned harder.

The room was so packed she left the door open so air could circulate freely. So she could eavesdrop. Given the glass and light, she could already see him.

It wasn't a straightforward meeting from the start. There

was no round-up of where projects were at, like the calls she made at the start of each day. He just went straight to it.

'What are the problems?'

Momentary silence. Then Sante glanced to his left. 'Davide? What's the issue stopping the pop-app development?'

Davide coughed, coloured then admitted he had no idea.

'Good,' Sante answered. 'Honesty is good. So let's break it down.'

He clicked to project a file on the large screen. To the right of the code, Mia saw the chat list full of suggestions. Comments from the username 'S' were plastered down the field. The guy mightn't be in the office much but he was all over their files. He hadn't needed the catch-up; he already knew each project inside and out.

Mia didn't catch what someone said but Sante went very still for a moment before suddenly bursting into an explanation, almost frenzied in speed and detail. He paced, energy sparking from him, a marker in each hand, and swiftly covered the glass board behind him in incomprehensible scribble, though apparently everyone else present could both read and understand it. He was a conduit for electricity; the atmosphere in the room surged with energy. Everyone leaned forward, fully focused and hanging on his every word—and there were so many words tumbling from him with speed until they suddenly spaced out into nothing as his brain raced too far ahead of his tongue. Everyone else simply tried to catch up while he amended the mess on the board with more scribble but in another colour. Fascinated, Mia slipped in the back of the room to watch the frenzy of question, answer, deeper explanation—almost none of which she understood.

'The guy's a machine,' one of the coders near Mia muttered. 'I don't know how he does it.'

'Another level entirely,' the guy seated in front of her agreed.

It went for far longer than she'd put in the damned schedule. As Mia replenished the snacks and brought in fresh coffee, she finally realised the disconcerting truth. This disparate brilliant bunch of people Sante had assembled wasn't dreaming up ideas for him to take and monetise; they were here to develop and realise the ideas *he'd* put forward to them. They were in *teams* to dissect and test all kinds of different possibilities because Sante had too many viable schemes to be able to consider fully all on his own. He mightn't appear much in the office but he made notes within their projects on the daily—he knew exactly where each of them were at without needing to ask. The man was on another level in everything—intelligence, drive, strength and yes, looks. Even with his perma-frown and distancing demeanour. She was *fascinated*. But only in the same way as his underlings; it definitely wasn't that she *wanted* him in a sexual way. But the churning feeling in her lower belly begged to differ.

And that was a huge problem. Not only was Sante her brother's enemy, he was effectively her *boss*. She backed out of the room, sternly reminding herself that the last time she'd gotten involved with someone at work she'd blown up her life.

Barely eighteen and only a few months before his untimely death, Mia had fully fallen out with her father and taken a job as a nanny. She'd loved the glimpse into a happy family life that she'd never had. Then she'd met Oliver, the young 'fun uncle' of her charges. Five years older than her, he'd told her she was everything he'd ever wanted. Which was all an attention-starved Mia had needed to hear. She'd *desperately* yearned to be loved and she was such a cliché for being the nubile young nanny who'd slept with someone in her employer's family.

Her father's jaundiced judgement of her as a party girl in high school hadn't been entirely inaccurate. She'd liked to escape school to go out dancing, but actually she'd avoided one-on-one physical intimacy. Deep down she'd been afraid her father was right. That she'd be needy and make bad choices in the heat of impulse—like her mother had.

But Oliver had been patient and persistent. He'd not just wooed her, he'd love-bombed her and eventually she'd believed him. But once she was wrapped around his little finger he'd alternated between attentive or absent. She'd tried harder to be more what he wanted. Tried not to be too much so he wouldn't get sick of her. She'd wanted him to keep wanting her. And in all that emotional angst she'd become distracted. She'd messed up at work—not majorly, but repeatedly in small ways. Until the day she'd found out—publicly—that Oliver had a serious girlfriend. He'd just been using Mia.

She'd been mortified when the housekeeper had watched her exposure with patronising derision. Her colleagues had *all* known. They'd all watched her waltz into it. They'd actually taken *bets* as to whether it would be the father or the brother who had her. When she'd confronted Oliver he'd actually laughed. Was she *serious*? Oh, he would sleep with her but he'd never settle with someone like *her*. She'd left the job that day, her confidence so obliterated she'd avoided intimacy since, choosing to prove to herself that she was capable of working hard and not wrecking her own future by acting on emotional impulse or desire. Now she knew—mixing business with pleasure always ended in a mess. So she was going to do a good job here and now. She would *not* screw up. That meant not screwing with Sante in *any* way. That also meant not staring at him like he was the most beautiful man she'd ever seen—even though he was. She would maintain her professionalism. And she would not provoke him about the past—because she was beginning to wonder whether she didn't know as much about all that as she'd thought she had.

But she never should have suggested Sante leave his office door open. Now she heard him actually laughing and felt stupidly wounded when he didn't treat her the way he did the coders or the legal and accounting staff. And now—at the end of the meeting—he discovered that she'd established an inter-office league with a 'game of the week.' She'd set up a gaming console in the far corner of the office with a couple of controllers, and to her amazement he'd added his name to the property division team and was helping them—*her* team—catch up to the coders' tally before the end of day and it was...too *okay* of him when she needed him to remain a villain. When she needed to stop herself slipping beneath his spell.

When she'd worked on board the cruise liners she'd always rolled her eyes at the guys who'd leered at her. The ones who'd told her they'd taken one look and wanted her. Now *she* was that guy. Driven by hormones and basic instinct. The physical yearning she felt was almost unbearable. It was lust at first look and it was only getting worse. This was different to her experience with Oliver—that had been slow burn and flattery until he'd flipped on her. *Her* reaction to Sante was too strong, too all-consuming. But she could and would shake it off. Except she was parked outside his office nine hours a day. And he was inside it. Constantly.

She glowered first thing Thursday morning when she got in early as usual and saw him lodged in place at his desk.

'You slept in the office again, didn't you?' she said accusingly.

While his suit was fresh and his hair damp and more unruly than ever, he had a burning look in his eyes and his muscular frame was tense. Was he tired after yesterday? She understood the man had introvert tendencies; had it been too much? In which case, why was he still here?

'Why do you need to work all night?' she goaded. 'I thought you were so rich you couldn't possibly spend it all.'

'I work all night if something is so all-consuming that I *can't* sleep until I have satisfactory resolution,' he answered huskily.

Mia stilled, quelling her shiver. The man was *intense*. 'Okay, then have this.'

He glanced at the box she had in hand and his eyebrows arched. 'Why, Mia, are you spoiling *me*?'

'No, it's left over from the meeting yesterday,' she lied.

He pushed away from his desk and walked round to where she was frozen two steps into his office. 'And you don't want it? Are you not well?'

'No, I'm just…'

'Being sweet and putting my needs ahead of yours.'

She gaped at him. He actually thought something nice about her? She didn't trust him and she definitely needed to put distance between them. To get this irresistible magnetism under control.

'No, I'm putting your *staff* needs first, hoping this will even out your mood so we have less of the frowning. You did okay yesterday, so we don't want to ruin the progress now.'

He actually chuckled. '*We*. Wow.' He picked up the pastry, broke it and held half the resulting slightly squished mess out to her. 'Then maybe we should manage your mood, too. Share it with me.'

Mia stared at him warily. Was this a dare? Or was he serious? Serious, apparently. Because he broke it in two, clearly unconcerned about crumbs flaking everywhere. The generosity was unexpected but oddly, she wasn't surprised. She'd watched him yesterday with his coders. And she could act like an adult. So she took the piece he offered, bit into it and suppressed her moan.

'Yes.' His lips quirked. 'They really are exceptional.' He demolished his piece in the one gulp.

Of course he was the sort to simply devour what he wanted. A stray thought escaped her tight control—she wished he'd want her.

'You lied to me,' he said softly.

Startled, she blinked. 'What—'

'That pastry wasn't from yesterday.' He moved closer, his mouth curving. 'That was fresh.'

Was he *teasing* her? Mia's pulse jumped.

'You *are* spoiling me,' he added, almost smirking.

No. She was just being a decent human. Not doing anything special for *him*.

'I didn't know you were ambidextrous,' she babbled.

The corners of his eyes creased and his smile broadened ever so slightly. He was clued in on her desperate deflection. 'Yes, I'm good with both hands.'

Oh, sure. She really shouldn't but she really could imagine all kinds of things he could do with those hands.

An ache opened up within her—mingling with regret. She liked seeing him smile. Why didn't he smile more? Why didn't he tease like this a little more? It was as if she'd suddenly caught a glimpse behind a big grey wall and seen the playful Sante behind it. Why did he hide his humour? Why did he stay so distant and serious? Why was he so very alone despite all this success?

She shouldn't be so curious. She should remain professional. Keep up her resistance—because she realised now just how easily she could slip beneath his spell. But that could mean more than humiliating gossip—he was her brother's enemy, wasn't he?

'Of course you are,' she murmured, unable to resist the fire in this moment. 'You're good with everything.'

Somehow, he was closer. *She'd* stepped closer.

He shook his head and blinked and that smile faded. 'You shouldn't—'

'Sante—oh, sorry.' Paolo cleared his throat.

Mia whirled away, horrified that the lawyer had caught her standing too close to the boss. Being alone with him in his office. *She'd* been leaning in. She'd gotten too close. She'd made that mistake. Of course *she* had.

Always-makes-mistakes Mia; always-too-much Mia. And she was beginning to worry she'd made more kinds of mistakes regarding Sante than in his office just now. She felt forced to reconsider what she'd believed for so long—but he didn't want to discuss it and Dario never would, either.

Sante set his jaw, irritated as hell by his lawyer's interruption but at the same time immeasurably grateful. He'd been about to make a massive mistake—entranced by her interest and attention and proximity. But at Paolo's appearance, Mia had fled. Scarlet-cheeked. Sweet. Utterly unable to hide that responsive light in her eyes. And he was flummoxed.

He'd worked through the night again, desperate to regain his own focus, sparked by the fact he'd struggled to concentrate in the meeting yesterday—hell, he'd gone down a complete rabbit hole with a few of the coders just to pass the time safely, and then sat down and gamed with another couple of them. He hadn't gamed in years and had been rustier than he'd liked. Competitiveness had kicked in. Especially when he'd seen Mia listed as the second-highest scorer in the property team. He'd been both intrigued and compelled to beat her score.

For a moment there this morning he'd thought he'd dreamed her up. But he'd been hanging out for her arrival, and her utterly unimpeachable appearance hadn't disappointed. She was amusingly determined to give him nothing to pull up. But while she was professionally, even conservatively dressed, that long skirt hugged her hips and the neat blouse was perfectly buttoned and he just wanted to—

No. He didn't want to do anything. It wasn't appropriate to even *think* anything. And yet, he'd seen her expression light up when she saw him and then she'd offered him some of her breakfast, and any resolve he'd had evaporated.

And he still couldn't stop watching her. It was like the more he tried, the more impossible it became. Aside from his personal distraction, he had to admit the meeting yesterday had gone far better than he'd expected. Mia had woven through the room a couple of times, keeping an eye on everyone's comfort. She'd gone to a lot of trouble, ensuring everyone was at ease—especially that one coder who struggled most with sensorial overwhelm and Sante had never expected to actually show up. But Mia had enabled him to—radiating positivity, optimism, energy, enthusiasm. She *was* like a damned nanny, getting the best out of her charges. But *Sante* did not want to be babied.

He was supposed to be listening to his lawyer now. Instead, he was locked on watching her walk back to her desk. Vibrant, voluptuous, full of vitality and slightly wild. She was the most devastatingly attractive woman he'd ever seen.

He struggled to focus on Paolo's questions. Struggled for a further two hours. He'd failed to shut his door, which meant he could hear whenever she spoke—welcoming his staff as they came in, answering their fairly frequent stupid questions. Just as he was about to go out and tell them to go do some actual work, she redirected them and got them back on task. She was annoyingly good at managing them and they clearly liked her. Excess energy coiled within him, making his skin tight and his resistance weak.

He could get his self-control back. He just needed occupation. He'd wanted to prove to himself that he still had it. That he wasn't thinking about her all the time. But it was barely an hour before he gave in and stalked out to her desk.

'No sign of that delivery yet?'

She didn't look up, just shook her head. 'You'd have it if it had arrived. I know you're waiting for it.'

Right, he'd been out too often to ask. But he hesitated, unable to walk away.

'I promise I'll bring it to you as soon as it arrives.' She finally glanced up.

He gazed into her soft eyes and realised that she *was* managing him, too. Ensuring he had food, coffee, communicating clearly to temper his expectations. The realisation annoyed the hell out of him.

How was he reduced to asking about a set of plans that he didn't care all that much about? It was a flimsy excuse to engage with her. He was *pathetic*. He'd done too many all-nighters over the years because he was clearly losing his ability to bounce back and redirect his brain. It was stuck on the one track. He just wanted to be near her. It didn't matter that he was playing with fire; he *saw* the awareness in her eyes. He *knew* she felt it, too. That only made it worse. But he was her boss and he wasn't going to be this weak. Why would he be such a fool to get involved with a Lorenti?

But Mia wasn't like her father, nor her brother. She was

far more open. Far more generous with her laughter and warmth.

Screw 'being seen in the office.' He'd been present more this week than he had almost all year. His team was great—on fire, in fact, working hard. They didn't need him. What *he* needed was a break from everything. Especially her. *Immediately.*

CHAPTER FIVE

JUST BEFORE MIDDAY on Friday, Mia frowned at the thick envelope and double-checked the sender's details. This was definitely the package Sante had been waiting on—he'd been at her desk every thirty minutes or less every day this week demanding an update. Now it was finally here but *he* wasn't here to receive it. She glanced at his office but he hadn't materialised in the three minutes since she'd last looked. Her irritation levels escalated. She checked the meeting schedule but there was nothing blocked out in there for him—although he didn't ever fill it in. She phoned him but yet again, it went straight to voice mail. He'd not yet replied to her earlier email, either. She drummed her fingers on the desk and tried not to worry. She would focus on another task. He would turn up or phone in soon enough.

Two hours later he'd done neither of those things. The parcel preyed on her mind—he'd *really* wanted it. But if he wasn't going to bother telling her where he was, then she couldn't courier it to him directly, could she? Bracing, she walked to the lawyer's office.

'Paolo, do you know where Sante is today?'

Paolo glanced up from his computer. 'No, but I'm not surprised if he doesn't show. He's been abnormally present this week.'

Yeah, there were reasons for that. 'Do you know where he's likely to be?'

Paolo's gaze drifted back to his screen, clearly unfazed. 'If he's not answering calls he's probably offline.'

No kidding, Sherlock.

'And where would offline be in Sante's world?' Mia summoned patience. 'I just want to courier a parcel to him.'

He'd said he was going to keep a close eye on her. Now he wasn't here and he'd not bothered to tell her where he was or why, which didn't track given the complete lack of distrust he had over everything she did. But it was Friday, the end of her 'week' and what if this was a test? Sante wanted this document delivered immediately but maybe he'd removed himself to an impossible location to confound her. Just when she'd thought they'd almost reached a cordial working relationship, when she was starting to think he wasn't entirely as awful as she'd long believed. Well, she wasn't failing and he wasn't winning.

'If he's not at his Rome apartment, he'll most likely be at the Sicilian estate,' Paolo muttered. 'Courier won't deliver there before Wednesday at the earliest. You could scan and email the contents.'

There was no way she was opening this envelope. It had 'private and confidential' stamped all over it. 'Can I get the address for both? I'll find a way to get the hard copy to him.'

Paolo clicked a few times and jerked his chin towards the printer. 'If he's not in Sicily, then it could be any of the others on the list.'

Mia gaped at the list of properties that emerged from the printer. Aside from the Sicilian and Rome addresses, there were places in Paris, Madrid, New York—there was even a property in Melbourne, Australia. She was hardly going to circumnavigate the globe to get this to him, but she would at least try the first couple given he'd been banging on about it for days. She would prove herself to Sante Trovato. Because his unexplained absence was aggravating. If she didn't know he regularly went *offline* she might actually worry about him. Okay, she *was* worried about him. He'd worked through the night too many times this week and he'd seemed particularly ragged by the end of day yesterday. What if he was unwell? Surely, all that lack of sleep had to catch up to him at some point.

Mia set an auto-response on her email, picked up the package and set forth. More than eight hours later she stiffly got out of the taxi and stretched out her cramping muscles. She'd gotten no reply when she'd buzzed the door at the Rome apartment, so she'd gone to the airport. Despite her frequent attempts, he'd still not picked up so she'd flown to Palermo and then struggled to find a driver willing to drive her *all* the way here. The trip had taken way more time and effort than she'd expected. Now she stared at the enormous stone wall that obscured any view of the house and garden. It wasn't exactly inviting.

'Do you mind waiting?' she asked the driver.

He immediately frowned.

'I'll be as quick as I can.'

The gigantic gates were firmly closed but the pedestrian gate on the left was slightly ajar. She would hand the wretched package to Sante, turn around, walk out to face another long drive, flight and taxi before finally getting home. She didn't care about working all the hours or proving anything anymore. She just wanted this over.

She trudged up the winding tree-lined driveway wishing she had better shoes than her office pumps. Was this even the right address? That stone wall was deceptive—tall and bland, it shielded a seemingly endless expanse of palm trees, wide stretching lawns, an ornamental lake, even a citrus grove. Between the trees she glimpsed an enormous iron greenhouse and realised it was a vast private paradise. She steeled herself against its beauty but she was reminded of Palazzo di Constanzo, the estate her father had bought to house her mother in Capri after he'd walked out on their marriage when Mia was only a baby. Mia had spent the first few years of her life there—swimming and playing in an enormous garden like this only more neglected, more wild. Nostalgia hit. She'd had a freedom there that she'd never really had since. One she knew Dario missed, too—he'd loved their home in Capri. And she understood how this place would fit Sante—it was a stunning sanctuary in which a lone wolf could freely roam.

Turning the corner she saw the main building and she stopped. It wasn't like the beautiful villas she'd seen on the journey here; it was an enormous palazzo—an imposing structure far too large for a single occupant. The lone wolf ought to have an entire pack.

Finally, she made it to the enormous front door. There would be staff here. The property was too sprawling and too perfect not to be tended by an army of housekeepers and gardeners. She would give the parcel to the first staff member she saw and escape without even having to face Sante. Good.

Brushing her hair from her hot face, she rang the bell. It pealed loudly, echoing long after she'd released the button. Her confidence faltered as no footsteps sounded inside. As no one answered. Steeling herself, she pressed the button again. If Sante wasn't here, she was going to throttle him the next time she—

'Mia?' A harsh voice snapped behind her. 'What are you doing here?'

Mia spun. Sante was standing at the foot of the stairs behind her. She stared, so startled her heart stopped. He was wearing faded shorts, heavy boots and nothing else. Why wasn't he wearing anything else? Why was he sweating? And how had she not heard him walking with heavy boots like those?

'Mia?' he repeated, clearly irritated. 'Why are you *here*?'

He sounded furious but he looked so outrageously earthy, she just snapped right back.

'Why aren't you wearing a shirt?' She clutched the package to her chest and glared at him angrily. 'You should be wearing a shirt!'

'In my own garden?' He stomped up the stairs to glare at her directly in the eyes. 'When I wasn't expecting guests?'

'I'm not a guest,' she argued. 'I'm...'

Fully distracted. He was strong, vital, *physical*—about as man as a man got—oozing testosterone and power. Dirt was smeared on his legs and forearms and the next second his forehead as well as he swept a hand through his already messy hair. As he moved, his muscles rippled. Mia gaped at his abs, his gleaming chest, his broad shoulders. She couldn't drag her gaze away as he stepped nearer and took up all her visual space.

'What do you want?' he repeated huskily.

Utterly thrown by the expanse of bronzed skin and flexing muscles, Mia couldn't think let alone keep her emotions in check. 'What do I *want*? I want you to answer your damned phone.'

'What?' He patted his pocket and frowned. 'Why?'

Yeah, it was obvious he didn't have his phone on him. He had barely *anything* on him.

'So I could tell you this had finally arrived.' She held out the package to him.

An astounded expression widened his eyes. 'You came all the way to Sicily to deliver mail?'

There was grumpy and there was rude, and this was both with his thunderous frown as bonus.

'Given you've spent all week asking me five times a day whether it had arrived, I assumed it was vitally important!' She tossed the package at his feet with a thud. 'So you could at least show a little gratitude. But no, your true colours emerge. You might not have taken my dad's money but you're still a selfish jerk who doesn't care about inconveniencing everyone else.'

She was *pissed*. How dare he be here looking all relaxed and living his best outdoor life and not giving her or anyone else a second thought? And she was doubly pissed with herself for responding to him on such a basic level. Her hormones were activated—it was a raw sexual attraction to the most wildly inappropriate man ever. One who clearly couldn't think of anything worse than *her* appearing on his doorstep unexpectedly.

'How did you even get here?' He ignored her outburst.

'Taxi, plane, taxi,' she shot.

'*Commercial* plane?' He looked at her like she was insane. 'Why didn't you take the helicopter?'

Her jaw dropped. 'As if I would just use an expensive resource without authorisation.'

He sucked in a deep breath and glanced heavenward as if summoning patience. 'I see why you and Adele get on so well,' he sneered. 'By the time I recompense all your travel fees, it'll work out around the same. The last taxi alone—'

'You weren't around for me to ask,' she interrupted, not wanting to think about what the running tab must be on that taxi by now. 'If you'd bothered to answer your phone, then you could have told me that the stupid thing isn't that important and I'd have just left it on your desk for the next time you felt like cos-playing CEO.'

A startled look entered his eyes, then he laughed. Which shocked Mia all over again. She stared—hit by his appalling gorgeousness. When he laughed he was all perfect teeth, bunched muscles, gleaming eyes and sexy-as-hell tousled hair—

It was the last straw. She'd busted her gut to get this stupid package to him and he didn't give a damn. He hadn't snatched it up and torn it open like she'd expected. He simply didn't care. *All* her effort had been a complete waste of time.

Speechless, she stomped down the stairs and began the route march down the infuriatingly long driveway. His lack of gratitude—or even interest—was humiliating. She wasn't staying a second longer. She'd truly thought she'd been doing the right thing but why had she wanted to do a good job for *him*?

'Mia.'

Yeah, no, she wasn't listening to anything he had to say. She was getting back to that exorbitantly expensive taxi, which was only that expensive because his ridiculously beautiful palazzo was miles away from anywhere so everything about this mess was all *his* fault. She bit the inside of her lip, holding back her vitriolic mutter because the driveway was long and she had a hotspot on the back of her heel that was going to be a blister any moment and she *hated* him.

'Mia!'

The day truly couldn't get worse. That driver better still be waiting—

'Mia!' Sante grabbed her arm and stopped her by way of standing right in front of her.

Which meant she got another eyeful of his beautiful body. She forced herself to glare at the tree to the left of him. 'I've not got time to talk. I've got a plane to catch.'

'No, you don't.'

'You can't stop me.'

'Maybe *I* can't,' he huffed. 'But a storm can.'

'What storm?' There was no storm, it was hot and—

'Looked up lately?'

No, she could barely look away from his stunning form. She met his fiery gaze just as a fat raindrop hit her arm. She glanced at it just as another landed. Then another. Okay, the day could get *much* worse. Rain like this was going to soak her in seconds. Glancing up she saw dark grey and deep purple clouds rapidly descending.

'That's why I was outside securing anything that can move. There's going to be high wind, heavy rain, power outages. It's not safe to be out—'

'I'm not going to be,' she growled. 'I'm getting my taxi.' But though she rose on tiptoe, she couldn't see the car waiting on the other side of those gates.

'He'd have left the moment he dropped you,' Sante advised bluntly. 'He'd have seen the clouds and fled. It's hitting sooner than they forecast.'

'I'll be fine.' She was not going back to that palazzo with him. Only now the rain hit harder.

'You're going to walk fifty kilometres to the nearest village?' he asked sarcastically. 'You need to come inside.'

No. But the wind lifted and the tumbling rain became more than torrential.

He gestured impatiently at the rapidly darkening sky. 'How wet do you want to get?'

'I'm *not* going to your house.'

'Too bad. We don't have time to argue.' He suddenly launched forward, grabbing her low and so hard her shriek was knocked from her chest before she could release it. Next thing she knew she was upside down over his shoulder and it was—

'What are you *doing*?' she yelled, even though it was ridiculously obvious. 'Put me down!'

'No.' He tightened his arm around the backs of her thighs and actually sounded happy. 'You probably have blisters from walking up the drive in those shoes already.'

She wasn't admitting to that. 'I'm too heavy for you to carry all the way to the house.'

'I was a dockworker for years. I think I can handle you,' he yelled back. 'You're nothing.'

She was hardly *nothing*. 'You just want to prove yourself,' she muttered—not expecting him to hear.

'That's right. It's the alpha male in me. Isn't that what you'd say?' His burst of laughter was such a shocking sound that it silenced her.

She tried not to be mortified, tried not to like this a little too much—but she completely failed on all fronts. She had the most amazing view of his legs, not to mention an intimate appreciation of his incredible strength.

He didn't climb the steps to the grand entrance of the palazzo but went through one of the arches to the sheltered space beneath. Once there he finally bent, carefully sliding her down his body until she was back on her feet. Her skirt was wet through and so thin it slithered up as she slid down. Which meant she might as well have been naked as she was plastered against *his* heat and his near nudity.

Breathless, she gazed up at him. She was woozy from being upside down, right? Not from this hot, wet skin-to-skin contact. His body suddenly flexed and a bolt of pure electricity shot through her in response. She quaked—a mini convulsion of excitement that was way too intense and intimate for this moment. Mortified, she pushed back in the same instant he released her. Which meant she stumbled. He shot an arm around her waist again immediately.

'You okay?'

Utterly awkward, she smoothed her skirt down her thighs but it still clung to parts that really didn't need the exposure. He kept his arm around her as he opened the door and hauled her through. The furious howl of the wind and rain eased as the door slammed behind them.

Mia struggled to regain her breath. It wasn't right that she was panting when he'd been exerting all the effort.

'You can let me go now,' she mumbled.

He looked wired—more virile than ever as his muscles bunched and gleamed in the wet. For a moment she thought he was about to refuse. Instead, he inhaled deeply and stepped away from her.

Good.

Mia shivered—a belated reaction to his impact on her.

'You're cold.' He glowered.

No. She really wasn't. She reached for an alternate reason. 'That rain was crazy heavy.'

'You need to get dry.' His frown deepened as he stared at her. 'Where's your bag? Don't you have clothes?'

'I was supposed to go straight back to the airport. I'm on the last flight out.' So she only had the small purse slung over her body.

'You're not making that.' He shoved his wet hair back from his forehead and spun away from her.

'I can't stay here,' she declared.

'Not good enough accommodation?' he muttered.

'It's not the accommodation. It's the company.'

'I don't want you here, either, but we don't have much choice.'

She gritted her teeth. 'Is that package still out there getting wet?'

'I don't care.'

'I didn't drag that damn thing all the way here just for you to let it turn to pulp in a rainstorm.'

'You never needed to drag it here.'

'How was I supposed to know that when you didn't tell anyone what you were doing?'

'You know I frequently work away from the office for a few days at a stretch,' he said. 'You didn't need to come all this way just for me.'

'It wasn't for *you*,' she retorted. 'I would go the extra mile for anyone.'

She was not some lap dog leaping to please him.

'Believe it or not I just want to do a good job,' she added defensively as he glared at her. 'I have pride in my work. But you can't just disappear for days at a time,' she said, anger still getting the better of her. 'It's not fair on your people.'

'Not fair?' He looked blank. 'They know I'm fine.'

'How do they know that when you don't bother to communicate with *anyone*?'

'Because I always am.' He cocked his head. 'Track record.'

'That's not good enough,' she argued. 'Adele worries about you—'

'You bothered Adele over this?' He sounded appalled.

'Of course not. Paolo gave me a list of ten properties to try after this—'

'I don't need you to mother me, Mia. You didn't need to trouble—'

'It's not overstepping for any of us to have concerns about someone's welfare,' she argued, losing her shit entirely. 'It shouldn't be a Herculean task to let your team know where you're at. It's common courtesy!'

It wasn't okay to just disappear. Her mother had frequently disappeared from her life before her death. Her father didn't care enough to even bother. While Dario had retreated after his accident. And Oliver had gone silent in his hot and cold games. But even when there were legitimate reasons, it wasn't nice to be kept distanced from someone. *Especially* with no explanation or notice of when they might return. It was *cruel*.

Every muscle in Sante's body flexed but he suddenly stepped back. 'I'll go get the parcel.'

Alone, Mia shivered again, thrown by his rapid retreat. She needed to clear her head but her curiosity mushroomed instead. She circled, taking in the paintings covering the walls, the intricate tiled flooring, the gleaming furniture. The room was beautiful. By rights, a suite of uniformed staff ought to appear with everything she could ever want, but she had a fatalistic certainty that she was here alone with Sante.

Not good.

She wasn't an idiot; she had to stay until the storm passed, but she needed a plan to manage herself around him.

Sante reappeared in the doorway, not holding the parcel but rather a pile of clothes. 'Follow me.'

She followed, waiting a pace behind as he entered a bathroom and set the pile down before quickly backtracking and carefully avoiding her.

'You can't shower, there's lightning,' he said gruffly. 'Rub dry, get warm. There's towel, track pants, top—'

'I'm not wearing your clothes,' she muttered, mortified.

'Then go naked.' He stalked past her.

Compressing her mouth, she marched into the bathroom, closed the door and blinked at the ornate marble and gleaming fittings. It was stunning.

'Be quick,' he ordered through the door. 'Power could go out any moment.'

Yeah, no, she just had to take a moment to appreciate the sumptuous—

'*Move*, Mia.'

Could he see through walls? Grinding her teeth, she peeled her skirt and blouse off. She was sodden—including her bra and knickers, and if she left them on they would only make the dry clothes wet. So she stripped completely, hung her smalls about the room and hoped they'd dry quickly. The track pants were a little loose but such buttery soft fleece she never wanted to give them back. The merino tee was soft as well but it clung to a few curves in a way she wished it wouldn't. She stared at the mirror in horror—it was a vain hope that he wouldn't be able to tell that she wasn't wearing any underwear. Mortified, she turned away. She could be professional. She could control her unruly imagination. She could get through this.

Leaving the bathroom, she followed the faint sounds of activity, pausing in the doorway of a large but cosy lounge. Books were in piles on the shelves, more paintings, thick rugs, but it was Sante hunched by the coffee table who commanded her attention. He glanced up as she walked forward. Her breath stalled but a fireball exploded in the depths of her belly. He'd dressed in faded jeans and tee and both served to highlight his fit, muscular frame.

The lights flickered, then went out. Her breathing quickened as she heard a match strike and he lit several candles dotted on the large low table. And now the room was *far* too intimate.

'Are you hungry?' he muttered.

She was too strung out to even know, but food would *definitely* serve as a distraction. 'A snack would be great, thank you.'

He lifted the lid on a box on the table. In the flickering candlelight she glimpsed the label and struggled not to smile.

'They're from yesterday,' he said as he slid the box towards her.

'I'm sure they're still good.' She picked the smallest pastry and curled up in the nearest armchair. 'They're always good.'

Sante didn't take one. He stared at her, his scowl deepening before he rose and walked past her.

Mia stared at her pastry and tried to regulate her pulse. A soft blanket was suddenly dropped around her shoulders, cloaking her entire body.

'Thanks,' she murmured, surprised.

He sat down in the armchair opposite hers. Truthfully, she wasn't at all cold. She nibbled the pastry but it brought an assortment of associations. All of them dangerous. Desperate to ignore the temptations whispering in her head, she filled the silence. 'This place is beautiful. It must take a lot of people to maintain it.'

Sante wasn't able to speak; he could only stare. What had he done this time to be punished so cruelly? He'd come here to *escape*. Everyone. Everything. Most especially *her*. Today as he'd put furniture away and dug supports for saplings, he'd berated himself for being unable to shake his horrifying fixation on her. Then he'd heard the doorbell and walked around the house to discover he'd manifested her presence. He'd snapped simply to hide his damned delight. But she was Mia Lorenti. Adele's friend. His employee. His former friend's little sister who thought the worst of him. A rich snob to his poor boy. Utterly out of bounds.

Yet, he couldn't blame her for thinking that damned parcel was vitally important given he'd been asking her for it all day, every day. But asking about it had been an excuse to stop by her desk—he'd been getting a fix of her attention. He was *pathetic*. So he deserved to be punished by seeing her swamped in his clothing, her breasts clearly unfettered, the candlelight enhancing her radiance. Flushed and inviting, she looked as beautiful as if she'd stepped out of one of the damned frescoes that decorated the walls. He'd covered her with the blanket but he really needed to grow some self-control.

'Doesn't it?' she prompted.

Doesn't it what? He had no idea what she'd asked him; he'd been too busy drinking her in.

'No staff at all?' she added.

'No.'

He'd sent them home hours ago. Not because he was generous or anything; he'd just needed to be alone. He glanced at the window. Okay, he had wanted them to get home safely before the storm hit. He didn't want to be in any way responsible for their physical well-being. He could barely manage the damned trees, let alone the lives of others. But then Mia had appeared, inappropriately dressed for the weather, arguing with him, all at the worst possible time. The heavy clouds had swept in so quickly, it might as well be midnight.

She picked at a damned pastry and it was torment waiting for her to spill some cream on herself. He grabbed one and tore at the thing. Sometimes he still wolfed his food as if it were going to be the last meal for years so he could be a messy eater, too; and these pastries were meant for fingers and the swipe of a tongue and watching her eat them was always a sensual delight. He willed some filling to spill because he would—

'Why did you come here?' he asked abruptly, furious with himself. 'Surely, it wasn't just to deliver that parcel.'

'Yes it was,' she said stiffly. 'You were so keen to get it but then you just disappeared and when I left messages, you didn't bother getting back in touch with me.'

'So you took it upon yourself to travel all this way?'

'The last thing you said was that you'd be in first thing and then you just didn't show. You didn't even leave a message and then you didn't pick up your phone.' She glared at him.

Sante felt a discomforting guilt curl around him. She sounded like she'd been worried. There was no need for that. He was fine. Always fine. But that she'd travelled all this way?

'I flew last night,' he explained grimly. 'Turned off my phone. Left it inside today while I was out—'

'Preparing for the apocalypse,' she said acidly.

'For the storm that was forecast, yes.'

Desperate for distraction now, he picked up his phone and frowned at the mass of messages and the lack of a few specific ones. Glancing up, he saw her biting back her curiosity and couldn't help explaining. 'I've not heard from my nearest neighbours,' he said gruffly. 'They're elderly. I checked the stop bank for them but they're worried and...'

'You want to be sure they're okay. You should call them.'

He tried, but there was no answer.

'I sent my staff home first thing,' he muttered, filling the vast void. 'We'll be okay up here but if the river bursts its banks, it'll impact...'

He frowned as she lifted the blanket off her shoulders and slung it on the empty chair beside hers.

'What are you doing?' he barked.

'I'm not actually cold.'

Nor was he. And now he was back to staring at her in his favourite merino tee and he could see the curve of her breasts and her tightly budded nipples. He couldn't infer anything about her, but *he'd* never been as aroused in his life.

He desperately needed a drink. If he got blind drunk he'd effectively knock himself out. Trouble was he'd lose self-control along the way and do everything he shouldn't before becoming incapacitated. So he wasn't taking the risk. He'd stay sober. But with no power there was no television. No internet. No radio. The backup generator he had was for the fridge and for emergencies. But hell, this *was* an emergency.

He tried phoning his neighbours again, hugely relieved when they picked up. They were a distraction he desperately needed. He chatted for a while, making them promise to stay inside. 'I'll check on you as soon as the rain stops, okay?'

Finally, he ended the call and put his phone back on the table.

'Do you feel better now you know they're okay?' Mia asked with not-entirely-sweet softness.

He frowned. She might think she was making a point but he'd *needed* to be alone.

'You *can't* just disappear,' she added.

Of course he could. He'd been alone from the moment he'd been born, and he frequently disappeared. Usually, no one noticed. Certainly, no one challenged him on it. But Mia's blue eyes flashed with more than chagrin—had she really, genuinely been concerned? He sank, lost in the blue depths. Of course she had. This was the bubbly woman who'd worked incredibly hard to welcome everyone who walked through his company doors. The caring woman who wanted his staff to make connections with each other and with him. The effervescent woman who hummed in the mornings when she thought no one was there. The woman who tried and who felt everything deeply. She sparkled and she was sweet despite her masking sarcasm. He drew in a steadying breath. She didn't deserve his anger. It wasn't her fault he had such failings. He should try to be a little more human, less beastly.

'I'm sorry I was ungracious when you arrived,' he muttered.

Her eyes widened. 'Was that—'

'An apology, yes. Savour it.'

'I will.' She slowly smiled. 'Honestly, I was starting to think the whole thing was some kind of test—so you could dismiss me sooner.'

'It wasn't a test,' he said tightly.

Her smile broadened and destroyed him—killing his ability to play nice, he simply blurted the truth. 'I didn't tell you where I was because I was trying to get away from you.'

Her face paled. 'Right. Of course.' She blinked and brushed the crumbs from her lap. 'If you could bring yourself to show me to a guest room, then you won't have to put up with my unbearable presence.'

'No. Not good enough,' he said huskily, standing the same time she did. 'I'll still know you're here. And I'll know *we're* alone.'

He watched her eyes widen, darken.

'Then what do you want me to do?' she whispered.

He moved, unable to stop advancing on her, driven to get close. 'You need me to spell it out?'

'I think so, yes.'

'I want you. I've wanted you from the second I saw you half-naked in my office. Every night I fantasise about that pastry cream—' He broke off and caught a breath. 'Actually, I fantasise about you every night and every day. Pretty much every minute.'

She slowly licked her lip. 'That must make work complicated.'

'It makes *life* extremely difficult, but I have my coping strategies.'

Her lips curved gently. 'You mean like a work-from-home day?'

'Today, right.'

'You still should have left a message.'

'I just had to get out of there,' he growled. 'It's impossible to think properly when you're in front of me.'

'Does that mean you're not thinking properly now?'

'Honestly, I'm not sure if you're even here or if I'm just dreaming.'

'You carried me up your driveway. You know I'm really here.'

Right, and his arms ached to hold her again, to place her in his bed, to arrange her so he could kiss her everywhere. 'I hoped you'd let me touch you to prove you're really here.'

'Then why not ask to touch me?'

'Because you're Mia Lorenti.'

'Mia *Simonini*—my family isn't relevant.'

He hadn't the strength to argue that one. 'I'm your boss.'

'What if *I* were to ask you to touch me?' she murmured.

He couldn't breathe. Didn't move. Didn't answer.

But she stepped closer. 'So I'd have to quit, or you'd have to fire me, before you'd consider touching me?'

'Neither of which are going to happen.' He remained still.

'But you want me.' Rampant excitement bloomed in her eyes.

Because he was damned. 'To the point of complete distraction.'

'You know technically *Adele* is my boss,' Mia said gruffly. 'She signed that contract.'

'Semantics,' he sighed. 'You know the money in your pay cheque comes from me. You know that means there's a power imbalance.'

'Not here,' she whispered. 'Not now. Here, there's only you and only me and honestly there's actually no power at all.'

CHAPTER SIX

MIA COULDN'T CLEAR the haze from her head as heat enveloped her body. Sante wanted her, but he wasn't going to *do* anything because of stupid, sane, perfectly sensible reasons. Reasons she would usually agree with but she was here and now and *her* need was too strong.

'I'm not staying,' she whispered. She never stayed anywhere for long. It was better that way. 'I'm not a permanent employee and I don't want to be. I'm only working with you because I promised Adele.'

'I know.' His voice was also barely above a whisper yet despite the incessant drumming rain, she heard him with piercing clarity as if silence had suddenly smothered the storm.

'So it's not as if there's really a conflict of interest because my being in Rome is merely a temporary thing to support someone else,' she added.

He remained rigid but she sensed his soaring energy.

'I don't want to want you, either, just so you know,' she blurted before he could deny her again. 'The fact is I'd like to end this attraction. It's not as if…'

'You'd want to bring me home to your brother.'

That struck hard. Dario *would* mind—he hated Sante, but increasingly she wondered if Dario didn't know everything.

'He has no jurisdiction over my actions,' she said, fiercely rebelling. Sometimes her brother had the controlling tendencies of their father—though with far more loving intent. 'I'm going back to Rome tomorrow so there's only tonight. There's only us. No one else will ever know anything.' Her heart pounded as she edged closer to risk. 'You can keep a secret, right?'

His lips twisted. 'Yes.'

Oh, she liked hearing *that* word from him. But she'd screwed up before, and she needed to be sure she wasn't repeating the worst of her mistakes.

'You keep a very low profile.' She moved so close she could feel the heat, the power, thrumming within him. 'There are no pictures of you online, no info on the company website. I know that's deliberate and I don't want to invade your privacy any more than necessary, but I need to be sure you don't have a girlfriend.'

He gaped. Then growled. 'No girlfriend. I wouldn't be here with you if I did.'

He was clearly miffed but Mia didn't care about offending his moral code; she just needed certainty. 'You *swear* you're single.'

'There's *no one* in my life.' Vehemence deepened his admission, making it more desolate than he'd perhaps intended. He cleared his throat. 'Commitment isn't for me.'

'Nor me,' she muttered.

But she saw scepticism flicker immediately in his eyes. 'Don't underestimate me, Sante.'

'Underestimate you?' He edged closer, his hand slightly brushing hers. 'You're a greater threat to me than anything.'

Yet, that fierce whisper was almost a threat in itself.

'Oh?' Her heart thundered as she tilted her head to maintain their searing eye contact.

He stared right into her soul, but his emotion—though fiery—was unreadable. Was it passion, anger, both?

'You tempt me,' he breathed raggedly. '*Terribly.*'

An overwhelming wave of pleasure washed through her, causing her raw reply to simply escape. 'Then take me.'

He was so still it was as if time had stopped. Then he moved infinitely slowly—tormenting her nerves—so very carefully closing the gap and lowering his head to hers.

Excitement rivered through her but the kiss was a featherlight graze of lip against lip—too light, too intense, too little of what she needed. He lifted, paused, his mouth a millimetre from hers—giving her one last chance to stop this. She inhaled sharply, jerkily, her lips parting in invitation, and with a full burst of excitement she rose to meet him just as he closed in again. They slammed together hard. This time their lips clung, hard and hungry; his tongue swept into her mouth and she curled hers to meet it in an immediate, hungry dance. The sensations shocked her, sending tremors throughout her body and tumbling her towards his. His growl became a groan and he clamped his arms around her waist like bands of steel. She barely noticed as he stepped backwards. She moaned in delight as his grip tightened more and more and he suddenly went down—sprawling backwards onto the large sofa, deftly lifting her in a chaotic sweep, determinedly untangling her limbs until she was across his knee and he was holding her firmly in place. She sank into his hold and tunnelled her fingers through his hair, teasing the silky mess of loose curls and dishevelment that was so very Sante.

She refused to break the kiss. Didn't care if she never breathed again and never saw another thing. Because this kiss was *everything*. She trembled with delight, needing it all—everything *now*. To be naked, to be together, to be sated—but still for this one perfect kiss to never end.

But in the end and far too soon, he broke it.

'Mia,' he groaned, breathless and hot. 'You need to be very, very sure.'

'We have one night, Sante,' she pleaded. 'Make it count.'

Passion flared in his eyes as he gazed into hers. 'I will.'

More than a determined acceptance of the challenge, his reply was a vow that he immediately backed up with action. He claimed her mouth again with intimate, ruthless determination, making Mia writhe and shudder in his lap. *Yes.*

They would destroy this. She moaned and restlessly stirred as he plundered her, revelling in the hard strength and fiery heat of his body and the fierce hold of his arms. She rocked against the erection digging into her side. She wanted that. She wanted all of this. Now.

He increased the pressure of his kiss and unleashed his hands to torment her more. He slipped his fingers beneath the soft tee and the track pants and skated over her skin, unerringly finding her most sensitive places.

'Sante...'

'Your skin is so soft,' he muttered. 'You're so hot.'

'Strip me,' she begged. She needed to be naked, now.

'Soon.'

She was rendered immobile in his hold, in this unutterable delight as he was deliciously focused on her pleasure.

'I like watching your eyes. They're beautiful,' he said, sounding awed. 'You're unbearably beautiful.'

While he was an unbearable tease. She could cry with frustration. Locked in intimacy, they kissed and kissed—the endless lush kisses sent her higher and higher into the stratosphere and his hands kept her there—hovering in a heavenly tortured sensation of want and need and desire.

He groaned as he lightly stroked her slick core, and with a moan she bucked against his hand, desperately needing more—melting in the heat that burned between them. He answered, pressing more firmly, invading her in a rhythm that made her moan louder and longer—*demanding*.

'I like making you hum, Mia.' He nipped her lower lip, then licked it. 'Hum louder.' He whispered his need into her mouth. 'I want to hear you scream.'

She circled and rolled her hips as his teasing fingers became both too much and not enough.

'Sante...'

'Scream, Mia.'

He kissed her with infinite patience and overwhelming intensity. Tormented her as he stroked harder, hotter, faster. She arched, every muscle searingly tight as the sensual tension devastated her. She tore her lips free, her breath caught until with one stroke more he tipped her into a tumult of sensation that blew her mind. She screamed, utterly overwrought as pleasure rocked through her in beautiful, violent waves.

She kept her eyes closed, turning her face into his chest, trying to recover her form. But there were orgasms and then there was *that*. And she wasn't ever going to be the same.

She felt him move beneath her, gathering her in his arms to lift then gently lower her to the plush carpet. She opened her eyes in time to see him kneel beside her and whip his T-shirt off over his head.

Mia's post-orgasmic lethargy—and embarrassment—was immediately dispelled. She stared at him in awe. The candles flickered, casting warm light and secret shadow across his beautiful frame. He was *perfect*—utterly perfect. His shoulders were broad, his chest muscled, his skin smooth and tanned and she avidly watched, willing him to remove his trousers.

He didn't. He sat back and watched her, a slow smile creasing his features.

'Still hungry, Mia?'

'You know I am.' She raked her gaze down his tense frame, taking in the bunch of his muscles. 'So are you.'

His hands slid beneath the T-shirt she wore and up to cup her breasts and then he whisked the top from her body. He lowered his focus and she watched dusky colour deepen across his cheekbones.

'Indeed I am,' he murmured huskily.

He hooked his fingers into the waistband of the tracksuit pants he'd loaned her and slowly tugged them down.

'You're magnificent.' He cocked his head and surveyed what he'd exposed. 'I'm going to taste every inch of you.'

She wanted that, she really did, but she wanted to see him, too. To taste him, too. But he overpowered her completely—simply with the sensations of his lips, of his hands, of the weight of his searing focus. She'd known they had chemistry. She'd been physically attracted to him from the first second she'd seen him in his office restroom. But she'd not been prepared for how intense it would be when he touched her like this. She shivered as he skimmed his palms along her arms, pressing kisses here and there—teasing in a pattern that she couldn't anticipate but that she adored as he moved closer to her more intimate parts.

'Sante...'

She didn't hide her need—indeed, she held *nothing* back. They had only one night and she wanted everything. She would absolutely indulge in her hunger for him.

'*Sante...*'

'One moment...' He sounded ragged as he rose away

from her to pull a square package from his pocket before taking his trousers down and his briefs with them.

Mia's jaw dropped. He was *built*. And he was *hot*. For *her*.

She reached forward, barely getting the chance to trace over his perfect body before he pulled back.

'Don't...don't look at me like that,' he muttered. 'I won't last.'

'Sante...'

Expelling a pained sigh, he braced over her. Mia wriggled in delight, so ready to finally have him. But Sante, the tease, went back to savouring her. She'd not known it was possible to be so tortured and so content at the same time. His mouth was hot and his words sexy. He cupped her breasts, rubbing his thumbs over her tight nipples, rousing her until she rocked her hips towards him over and over.

'Hungry girl,' he huffed approvingly and slid lower.

He was the hungry one—lascivious in his attentions, his touches, until Mia thrashed beneath his hold and gripped his hair. She was going to come again and she wanted him with her this time.

'Sante...'

'I need you ready.'

'I am. I want you, Sante...*please*.'

He lifted his head, his breath blowing hot right where she was most sensitive. 'You want me?'

'*Now. Please.*' Breathless, she arched again and again.

He moved swiftly, abandoning the attempt to tease her more. She cupped the side of his face, feeling his flushed skin, reading the desperate tension in his body as he held her hip firm and still. Their eyes locked and he thrust hard and deep. Mia crumbled instantly, her cry high and loud as ecstasy unravelled her completely.

He growled, his teeth gritted, lodged firm and still, utterly to the hilt, as she shattered about him. As her shudders finally eased, she wrapped her legs and arms about him tightly, so entranced. It was as if eternity was unlocked in that moment. So stupid, so fanciful, but what she was experiencing was just so good. He, too, had a look of wonder on his face.

'*Oh, Sante,*' she sighed, so desperately needing more.

He broke.

'*Mia, Mia, Mia...*' He chanted her name fervently as he thrust hard and fast, utterly unleashed. But in his accent, in this moment, it was as if he were murmuring in his first language—*mine, mine, mine.*

And she was.

Mia blinked, a trickle of desolation creeping in as Sante peeled away from her body. But he immediately held his hands out to her. She automatically took them.

'Come on.' He hauled her to her feet. 'Let's get somewhere more comfortable.'

He tucked her hand under his arm and picked up a couple of candles. For a moment Mia could only watch; he definitely looked like he was ready to continue. *Thank goodness.*

She watched the play of his muscles as he slowly led her up the stairs. The rain struck the windows like bullets. The wind howled, rattling the latches and hinges as if seeking a way to break in and tear them apart. But the wide stone of the house was too solid for the wild weather to breach. She curled her hand around his biceps, smiling at his strength. They were safe in this secret sanctuary, in the dancing, warm candlelight. She saw little of his bedroom, only the vast bed as he set the candles on the small table each side of it, illuminating the vast mattress in the middle. Mia simply crawled onto the soft sheets, ready for him.

He murmured his appreciation as she posed. 'You're an absolute goddess.'

It was such sweet, intoxicating flattery and she tumbled into it with full enthusiasm. 'Are you going to surrender to me?' she murmured, desperate to devastate him the way he just had her.

'Oh, no. Never.' His lips curved into a half-sorry smile. 'But I will worship you.'

And Mia never wanted the night to end.

CHAPTER SEVEN

SANTE WASN'T ABLE to do anything more than listen to the rain steadily falling and will it to continue for hours—no, days—yet, this couldn't be done. He wanted more of her. But time refused to stop and despite the heavy clouds, dawn lightened the room. The only consolation was that he could then see her properly again. Thankfully, he'd had the presence of mind to bring her to his bed. While he was used to staying up all night, she wasn't. She was deeply, beautifully asleep. For a second he pretended that last night hadn't been the best sex of his life, that it only felt like that because it had been a while. But the pathetic delusion didn't stick. It had been the best—sensational. *She* was sensational.

That first time had been too fast. He'd intended to draw her to the edge and back again to torment her for the days of sensual torture she'd put him through this week at the office. But she'd used her breathy pleas and luscious body to sever his will. So swiftly, he'd succumbed to the desire that had been killing him for days.

Now he watched, half-afraid that if he closed his eyes she might disappear. He still couldn't quite believe she'd come after him. No one did that. Not even Adele—though as he sent her a continual supply of work even when he went AWOL, Adele always knew he was alive and well. But he'd not contacted Mia and she'd been pissed about it.

She'd thought if she didn't deliver that stupid parcel he'd have fired her, but her coming here was about more than that. The way she'd *scolded* him for going silent—that he'd been rude and unfair. Ordinarily, he'd never have agreed, but he'd read and listened to her messages. She'd phoned so many times he felt bad about it. Weirdly, he also felt good. She'd persisted. She'd tried so many ways to reach him. And then she'd followed up with action. She was the only person who'd *ever* come after him.

He'd been abandoned at birth. Survived only because he had strong lungs. A foundling—unwanted, unclaimed, unknown. The first foster home had initially been okay but there was never permanence in the system. Soon, it had been another home. A bad one. Then another. Worse. He'd thought he'd secured his freedom and future in the form of a scholarship to an elite school in England…

He went rigid, refusing to think about the time he'd spent over there. The way his past intersected with Mia's would crush what was between them now. But not only had she come all this way to him yesterday, she'd also *unleashed* with him. Because she'd wanted him, and knowing that had evaporated any last resistance he could muster. Hell, his self-control had lasted less than a week and if he'd known they were going to be this fantastic together, he wouldn't have lasted an *hour* before trying to seduce her.

He slipped out of bed and went to the kitchen. Those pastries were good but they weren't enough to live on. He needed a more substantial meal and so did she. He checked the power but it was still out. Fortunately, his backup generator kept the refrigerator going and charged his phone. He scanned the trillion messages that had landed, quickly responded, making one particularly rash decision and eventually clearing the list. Then he pulled food and lit the gas. He was going for a feast—mostly to keep himself busy while she rested. He tried not to recall every moment of the night but his uncooperative brain kept sending images. She'd been so hot. So sweet. He should have stayed in bed, should have waited so he could take more from her—

'Something smells amazing.'

Sante turned. She stood in the doorway and helplessly he just took his time to look. The jut of her breasts against the soft fabric of his tee was torture. Again. And again, he was overcome by the memory of how she'd felt above, beneath, about him. He slowly drank in the sweet curves of her legs. He just wanted to sink back inside her and forget the world. But he glimpsed a mark on her thigh that hadn't been there last night. He didn't remember doing it, didn't want to hurt her in any way at all. This wasn't meant to be that intense.

'Are you hungry?' Amusement gleamed in her eyes.

Hell, he was supposed to be cooking not drooling. He spun back to the pan, quickly stirring to stop the eggs sticking. To stop his brain from spontaneously combusting at the mere sight of her.

'Very hungry,' he coughed. 'Making brunch.'

One look and he'd not just lost his words, but his capacity to think. Again.

'Can I help?' She leaned around him, wide-eyed at the number of pans.

Following her gaze, he conceded he might've gone a little overboard but he'd needed distraction. Apparently, she needed distraction, too—she nosed in the pans and would've taken the spatula off him if he didn't hold it up out of her reach.

'You don't trust me to cook?' He chuckled as her eyes widened with embarrassment.

'Clearly, you can cook.' She gestured at the overloaded cook-top. 'But I don't like doing nothing.'

Right, she was used to being the one who did things for others. It was more than her job. She cared—either as nanny, or manager—ensuring everyone had everything they needed in order to do their job.

'You could just sit down and let me spoil you.' He watched her restless discomfort with amusement. 'Or if you must move, you can find the cutlery,' he added, relenting when she clearly didn't want to remain still.

Sure enough, a relieved expression crossed her face. She set plates and cutlery in position on the table and found juice in the fridge. Sante didn't think he'd ever bothered to set the table when here alone. Food was a scoff-and-be-off thing for him. But she had it looking pretty in an instant. He poured her a coffee and she pounced on it before taking a seat and looking amused as he set the plates of food between them.

'Do you think there's enough?' she teased.

He'd not realised just how much he'd made while she slept; it had just been a way of filling in time. Mia picked up her fork and sampled the pancakes first and he froze, stupidly interested in her reaction.

'This is *really* good.' She swallowed.

'Why so surprised?' And why did he care so much?

'Sorry.' But her giggle undermined her apology. 'I didn't think you'd cook for yourself. I assumed you'd have a private chef.'

'I sent the staff home before the storm, remember?'

'But is one of them a chef?' Her eyes gleamed as he shook his head. 'There's really nothing you can't do. You're a genius at everything.'

Why did she sound annoyed about that?

'I learned to cook thanks to the internet. Utilising scraps. Actually, I worked on an app for nutrient analysis of those meals. It did well.'

'Naturally.' She watched him season the eggs. 'So you do all the cooking when you entertain here?'

Startled, he glanced up. He never had guests stay. This was his personal sanctuary; that was the point.

'Right, no entertaining.' She glanced at the window. 'Which is a shame because you could have the best summer party here.'

'You like parties?' he muttered. She'd organised a mini-party in his office for his staff.

'Sure, sometimes.' She licked her lips. 'But you prefer to be alone.'

'Sure, sometimes,' he mimicked. 'I like the space here. It's calming.'

'Your brain races.'

'Yes.' It overwhelmed him sometimes. 'I work in the garden for hours. It eases up then,' he muttered. While he did manual labour he could put all the ideas in the back of his brain to percolate.

'What about all the other properties on that list Paolo gave me?'

'Most are investments. The property team manages the leases.'

He enjoyed the acquisition process. He was careful and did diligence but ultimately it was a gut decision. Property was tangible—literally solid, and he liked accumulating solid security. But this one was his absolute favourite. Perhaps that was because it was the nearest to the place he'd been found. Though in truth, he wasn't certain he was even Sicilian. His mother could have been from anywhere.

He watched her demolish the first pancake and saw her trying to choose between eggs and yoghurt and felt the oddest need to confess the truth—because he did *not* need to brag to her, right? 'I can only cook breakfast food. Dinner is freezer meals. Nutritious ones a private chef preps back in Rome.'

Mia paused and her eyes gleamed with surprise—and knowing pleasure. 'You should keep a store at the office so you're not starving in the morning and need pastry.'

She was right, of course. Which was annoying.

'Or I could put eggs and milk in the kitchenette and you could cook breakfast for the staff. This is impressive.' She chuckled at his expression, then glanced at the window behind him. 'The rain's pretty relentless.'

'It's forecast to ease later.' He drew breath and broached the topic that'd been bothering him since scanning his messages earlier. 'The helicopter might be able to land later, but the mayor's put a call out for help in assessing damage to the region.'

'Then surely that's the priority.'

Naturally, she would put other people before herself. His body tightened.

'It would mean you couldn't get back to Rome today,' he said. 'You'd have to spend another night here.'

She was quiet and still and looked right back at him.

He coughed. 'For the record, I'm not devastated about that idea.'

'No?'

Oh, he'd needed to see that curve in her mouth. Unable to resist a moment longer, he stalked around the table and grabbed the hem of that tormenting T-shirt with both fists. She lifted her arms, enabling him to have her naked in seconds.

'I know it's terrible to appreciate a personal win when its possibly a crisis for the others, but then, I'm a selfish jerk, right?' he said roughly, moving in close to breathe in her soft warmth. 'I already said yes to them.'

She wrapped her arms around his shoulders and her legs around his hips. 'Good.'

He groaned as she pressed her hot, wet core against him. He'd clearly been wrong about her needing a break. He hoisted her onto the table and kicked off his shorts, immeasurably glad he'd had the presence of mind to shove a condom in his pocket earlier. Her chuckle encouraged him to kiss her wilder, faster. Again.

Which meant he immediately needed another round to prove he *could* take his time.

An hour later he sprawled with her on the sofa, idly watching the rain trickle down the windowpanes, refusing to react to the intense relief streaming through his system. He didn't just have another night with her, but all of this afternoon as well. He ran his fingers through her hair, indulging in constant touch even though they were both boneless. But he would savour her silkiness, take what he could, while he could. Because it had to be enough.

'This place is just beautiful.' She gazed up at the ceiling. 'You have quite the library.'

His biggest collection was here. He could lose himself for hours in either the garden or the books.

'If I were you, I would never leave. Just work from home,' she chuckled.

'I thought I was supposed to show up more?' he teased.

She considered him, those blue eyes glinting like jewels beneath lowered lashes. 'You leave messages for them all the time in the project files.'

He tightened his arms around her, appreciating that she'd acknowledged that. But her comment about never leaving a place like this made him curious. 'You travel a lot—don't you enjoy it?'

'I can save more when the accommodation is thrown in.'

Right. He understood. He'd done the same when he'd first returned to Sicily and needed to claw his way up from nothing. But she shouldn't *need* to save money. Not only did she come from a wealthy family, her brother was also as much of a billionaire as Sante was, so why the hell had he abandoned her?

'Why do you use Simonini, not Lorenti?' he asked before thinking better of such blatant curiosity.

'It's another name from my mother's side of the family.'

'You don't want to be associated with your father?'

She turned her head and shot him a level look. 'You might have some understanding of why I wouldn't.'

He froze, regretting entering this minefield. It would kill the mood by reminding Mia of the enmity her brother had for him. This time with her now was too precious. Too short. But what of Dario? Didn't she want to be associated with him?

Sante didn't blame Mia for believing her father about the accident being his fault, that he'd accepted a pay-off. She'd been a kid. But Dario had known Sante better than *anyone* back then. Sante had even told him a little of his childhood, yet Dario had chosen to believe the worst—that Sante had abandoned him and taken money to stay away.

Sante knew all too well that people generally believed the worst whether they knew about his past or not. He reached for his coffee, scalding his mouth instead of speaking more. Because Sante *was* selfish and he didn't want the past to ruin this moment.

'I don't believe you took money from him,' she said, eventually filling the lengthy silence that had grown.

'After a decade of thinking the worst of me?' His disbelief was immediate and impossible to contain.

Because no one had ever just believed him. Not without solid proof and even then...

Her colour deepened but her gaze remained steady. 'Yes.'

His confusion grew. 'You simply believe my word? Now? Why?'

'It's not only about believing you.' She licked her lips nervously. 'I know my father. He was a bully who did whatever he deemed necessary to get what he wanted. Including lie. He'd have thought nothing of lying about you.' She looked worried, her volume dropping. 'He told Dario you'd taken his money. He didn't want you in Dario's life.'

Sante flinched but she saw. The blooming compassion in her eyes rooted him in place.

'He had very specific plans for my brother and me, and he eliminated anything he saw as a distraction.'

Sante didn't give a damn about Dario now but he found he was curious about what Mia's father had wanted for her. Because he was fairly sure flitting from one random job to another wasn't in that snob's master plan. 'What or who did he eliminate from your life?'

Mia didn't answer. *She'd* been the distraction. *She'd* been eliminated. Not that she wasn't telling Sante that; it was irrelevant and he was only asking to avoid the crux of the conversation. He didn't trust her belief in him. But actually, this *was* exactly the sort of thing her father would have done.

'Did he chase off all the boys who flocked the second they caught sight of you?' Sante muttered.

Her father certainly hadn't liked her getting attention as she'd gotten older. But as she'd not had much from him, she'd liked it. She'd done the inevitable and made a very bad choice mostly because—despite her father's best efforts to squash her natural spirits—she'd been a romantic who believed in *love*. That full-on at-first-sight, deep and irrevocable, no-obstacle-could-ever-deny-it kind of love that only actually ever happened on a movie screen. She'd been so naive.

Mia could see Sante holding back now. In the rare instances that Dario had mentioned Sante since the accident, he'd insisted Sante was a user—only interested in people for what he could get out of them. Dario had referenced all that time he'd spent showing Sante coding and apps—which was why Mia had thought Sante had stolen Dario's idea. She knew that all Sante wanted from her was sex. But that was all she wanted from him, too, right? This was merely a wrinkle in her system that needed smoothing out. Dario would be appalled if he knew, but he never needed to. *No one* would *ever* know.

And *she* didn't need to know more about Sante. Yet, every minute she remained here, her curiosity deepened. The fact that he was so guarded and reticent only aggravated her more. She knew little of his past other than he'd come to her brother's school on scholarship when he was in his teens. But there was nothing about him or his past online—not even anything on his company website—not that there was anything deeply unusual about that; Mia knew super-wealthy people were often notoriously private. So she didn't know where he'd gone after the accident. He'd just vanished. She'd assumed he'd returned to his home town—to his family, but he'd never mentioned any family at all and there certainly was no evidence of family here. There were no photos, no personal 'things.' The only constant person in his life seemed to be Adele. And she couldn't ask her because she was occupied caring for Bruno. She tried to remember more from the summer Sante had stayed at her father's house now. Only there was one moment she couldn't bear to touch on, and the bigger problem was Mia had been so young. The boys hadn't been around her much. Plus, they'd spoken in Italian together—the language had sounded so familiar yet was foreign to her by then. Her loss had made her ache. Her father had banned them from speaking Italian when they'd moved—they were to be English. Mia's Italian still wasn't all that great now. That was partly why she'd agreed to help Adele.

But she *wasn't* going to ask more about Sante's past. She wasn't going to pry over the boundaries they'd drawn. This wasn't anything more than a two-night stand and only about getting this chemistry out of her system. The one pure distraction was to occupy her mouth in another way entirely. This weekend *had* to fix her fascination. Her lust had to be sated because this couldn't be anything more than physical chemistry. And surely, she wasn't screwing up her job because this was only a short-term placement. This was nothing like what had happened with Oliver. She wasn't going to end up publicly shamed and fired.

When she returned to Rome tomorrow, they would move forward and forget all about it. But that meant she couldn't waste a minute on sleep now, nor on talking about things that couldn't be changed. So she turned to him, tempting him, moving with him until she simply couldn't move anymore.

Sante wasn't in bed beside her when she woke early Sunday morning. Heart seizing, Mia immediately glanced out the window. Not only had the rain stopped, the sun had actually appeared. Which meant she'd be able to leave for Rome this morning. Sucking in a breath, she swiftly grabbed her own clothes, showered and dressed. Sante was in the kitchen. He was also fully dressed, not cooking in nothing but boxers this morning. Not cooking at all. Breakfast was ready on the table but it was a cold spread and Sante was on a call. Glancing at her, he ended it and put his phone on the table.

'You must have a bunch more calls to make,' she murmured, avoiding the wariness in his eyes. 'To check on your neighbours and everyone.' She glanced at the phone. Sure enough, it was lighting up with notifications. 'I'll go for a walk in the garden while you're busy.'

He nodded. She took a bowl of fruit and yoghurt with her. She needed some fresh air and some space for herself.

The grounds hadn't suffered badly in the storm—leaves were scattered about the place but the sodden patches were already drying out. She walked the perimeter of the small lake, drawing in the fresh air. It truly was a private paradise—those high, boring walls hid its beauty from the world. But this was definitely the place in which Sante roamed untamed—unclothed even—alone and at peace. And somehow, that thought made her heart ache. The wrought iron and glass summerhouse she glimpsed through the trees was too magical not to investigate. It was unlocked and happily also undamaged. There was some extra furniture stacked in the corner but otherwise it was carefully filled with tropical plants that had flourished through the winter. Someone took huge care of this place. Tired and struggling to keep that unwelcome sadness at bay, she sank onto the plush chaise and put her feet up. She'd had very little sleep last night and she hated the fact she still ached for more intimacy with Sante.

'Mia?'

She stirred, blinking drowsily.

'You okay?' Sante came into her view. 'You're very quiet.'

'Contrary to popular belief, I'm not a twenty-four-seven noisemaker.' She sat up, awkward and flustered.

'Okay.' He moved forward. 'So it's not that you're regretting…'

'There's nothing wrong and I have no regrets. You do more thinking than speaking sometimes. If you must know,

I was napping.' She gestured around the summerhouse, wanting to move the subject on because she'd realised she'd shared too much with him this weekend.

She'd adored having sex with him but she'd liked *talking* with him as well. He was a surprisingly good listener and she'd opened herself up a little too much. She needed to rein it in. She always gave too much of herself to people who didn't actually want it. But Sante challenged the self-protective methods she'd learned to employ far too easily. Hell, he only had to look at her and her defences melted.

'The helicopter will be here in an hour. It's less than a two-hour flight to Rome so you'll be home by lunchtime.'

'Thank you. That definitely sounds better than the trip I took to get here.' She still couldn't drag her gaze from his. 'Are you coming back to Rome today?' She tensed as her stupid voice quivered.

He hesitated. 'I need to check on my neighbours in person.'

'Of course.' Mia stood.

It would be best to leave him here but she kept staring at him, and he at her, and that scorching desire rose within her again. Restless, she waved about the greenhouse. 'This place is—'

He stepped forward and *crushed* her in his arms. With a relieved moan she kissed him back—every bit as hard and as hungry. He was right. No more making polite conversation to fill in the last little time they had left together. This was her *last* chance to touch him. To explore his physical perfection. To make him quiver and shake and shout and she went for it.

'Mia,' he sighed jerkily, trying to catch her hands and wrest back control.

But she ignored him, kissing down his body and wrapping a firm hand around his shaft to hold him firm so she could tease him with her tongue and then suck him in deep and revel in his throaty groans. This was what she wanted—for him to be felled by her. And she got it—until the moment he flipped and paid her back. With interest.

Almost an hour later he pressed her to him, gently stroking her back, keeping her in place against him as they both struggled for breath. She tucked her face into the side of his neck and avoided his eyes and drew in his warmth and scent. With body and soul aching, she appreciated these last moments of intimacy. It was the sweetest embrace of her life.

Which meant it took her a moment to realise the rhythmic noise growing louder was the approaching helicopter. She startled, heart stopping.

'It's okay,' he muttered. 'It'll wait.'

No. It was time to go. The sooner she was out of here now, the better. Mia darted into the beautiful en suite and pulled herself together. Sante walked her down a winding path to a helipad. His frown was back. The square jaw. She just knew the man would say nothing so she made herself smile brightly.

'Um, thank you for…'

He just stared at her. Right. What was she thanking him for? Why feel the need to act polite as if this had been some nice social interaction, not the hottest most intense experience of her life?

She cleared her throat, determined to be resolute and dignified. 'No regrets, no repeats.'

She had to pretend as if this had never happened. As if it had just been a delicious dream.

'Back to work,' she added. 'Back to a professional distance.'

'Of course,' he muttered his agreement shortly. 'Not a problem.'

CHAPTER EIGHT

SANTE FROWNED DOWN at his pen, avoiding meeting anyone's eyes. *Especially* hers. Maintaining his professional distance was an unbearable, annoying, endless problem. He needed fewer meetings. Fewer hours in the office. Better still, none at all if he was going to survive the next two and a bit months. Three days ago he'd watched Mia board his helicopter and told himself it was the right thing.

She wanted them to be done. In truth, in that moment all *he'd* wanted to do was peel her clothes from her and make her hot and soft and his again. Which had been impossible. And it hadn't felt right sending her back alone, either. But it was for the best.

Except it wasn't. Mia had a starring role in his dreams, night after night—fantasies, in truth, given he couldn't actually sleep. He lay awake for hours, staring at the ceiling, wishing she were with him. He couldn't even concentrate on work through the night anymore. It was actually worse than last week and that had been bad enough.

It was appalling. He'd gone for *years* spending every night alone. He'd never had a relationship last more than a few weeks because his date grew impatient with his inability to 'open up.' Because Sante didn't share anything personal ever and he refused to *care*. Except he wanted Mia. *All* the damned time. It was like she'd infected him somehow.

He needed distraction. *More* meetings with *more* people. That was what she'd suggested; that was what she would get. He was insanely careful not to be alone with her. He left every door open so he couldn't be tempted to touch her. Until he *had* to shut his door to try to block her dulcet tones.

He'd heard her humming this morning. She was busy, engaging as ever, clearly not suffering the same way he was. She'd sounded as if she hadn't a care in the world and he'd never felt such resentment. He'd not had a decent night's sleep since he'd first seen her. Now he'd had her, he *craved* her attention—her eyes on him, her touch. And he was jealous of an *intern*. The way she checked in with each one every morning grated. Because she didn't check in with him. She *emailed*. He emailed back. Despite being only fifteen feet away from her. His only respite should have been when she went for her customary walk at lunchtime. Instead, he spent the entire forty minutes glancing out the window, watching for her return.

He was pathetic. He was determined to regain control. But he couldn't so much as look at her while he did. Except his peripheral vision refused to play ball—it sent his brain updates of her in her long skirts and soft blouses that hinted at those glorious curves, her glossy hair in a ponytail or plait. Always stunning. Always looking like the best present a guy could ever hope to be given. But he'd never been given presents at all let alone ones to keep. That didn't stop him wanting to unwrap her, wanting to enjoy her, again and again and again.

He wouldn't so much as look at her. Didn't offer the briefest acknowledgement when she walked into the room. In fact, Sante Trovato was more grumpy than ever.

Mia was determined not to let it bother her. This was the

agreement. They'd had their one night—yes, it had turned into two—but it had ended the second she boarded that helicopter. This was exactly what *she'd* wanted. So she was fine with it. Just *fine*. She wasn't going to daydream about being back in Sicily. She wasn't going to replay every second of the best sexual encounter of her life. She would move forward. *She* would be responsible and professional.

But that he could simply *blank* her? So coldly, so easily? The few times he had to speak to her, he did it without even looking at her. Which riled. Of course she'd expected him to be a little remote but really, the man was being rude.

She began counting off the days on the calendar. They'd had three days in the office since the weekend and there were still far too many to go before Adele would be back.

Her stupid body wouldn't stop aching and her brain *did* unhelpfully replay every moment from the weekend at the *worst* times during the day and rampantly at night. Which meant she tossed and turned and her exhaustion and resentment worsened by the minute. Which was frustrating given she'd been the one to stipulate they could have only that one weekend. That there be nothing more. But his cold, robotic behaviour destroyed the last of her patience. She grabbed a shirt from her wardrobe and buttoned it, pulled on a skirt. She would get through another day. She could do this.

Once in the office she glared at the terse emails and abrupt orders. There wasn't even a please or a thank-you. Absolutely no pretence at politeness. Well, she wasn't replying. He could damned well deal with her in person. But he didn't even look up when she went into his lair to inform him that the team had finished phase one of the synergy project at last.

'Make sure they test it rigorously,' he responded briefly.

'Yes, of course,' she sniped primly. 'Your wish is my command.'

She turned and glided out of his office and back to her desk. Or she would have glided if her upper arm hadn't been grasped tightly—forcing her to veer away from her destination and into the doorway five paces beyond instead.

'What the hell is that?' Sante's growl was harsh in her ear as he pulled her into the small room, pushed her against the back wall and pressed in close. His gaze skimmed down her body, his expression tightening as he saw her budded nipples poking through her blouse.

'You wore that just to torment me, didn't you?' he muttered huskily.

'What?' Mia stared, stunned by the wildness in his eyes. 'Are you ser—'

He slammed his mouth on hers.

'What are you doing?' she whispered when he broke apart but couldn't stop her hips arching forward for more contact.

'I can't sit there looking at you a second longer,' he groaned, sliding his hand to her bottom and pulling her tightly against him. 'I can't stand it.'

'You don't look at me.'

'For good reason,' he explained bluntly, emphasising that very reason with a sharp thrust of his hips. 'In this fucking blouse—'

He kissed her again and Mia was lost. She quivered, all concern fled, all distance forgiven. There was nothing but sweet relief and *heat*. He wanted her still. He wanted her now. And *she* just wanted it all.

'What's wrong with this blouse?' she half laughed as he kissed across her jaw.

'Cream.'

She was blank for a moment before realising it was the

shirt she'd worn that morning he'd arrived. With a groan she flung her arms around his neck. 'You've been so stand-offish—'

'I've been so *restrained*,' he argued, sliding his hands beneath said blouse. 'You have no idea—*how* could I look at you? Everyone would know what I want to do to you. I can't control my own thoughts.' He pressed against her with shockingly fantastic intimacy. 'Tell me it's the same for you.'

Mia tried to recover her reason but in the same instant she leaned fully against the wall, her legs trembling. 'Sante…'

'Maybe I'll just find out for myself.'

His kiss was hungry, his tongue rapacious, but it was his hands that were truly greedy. They went straight to her secret treasure and discovered *exactly* what she'd been thinking of for days now—with only a few strokes he made her shake.

'Sante.' She gasped and they both knew it for the approval it was. 'Sante,' she repeated, shuddering as he caressed her.

'You're *so* ready for me.' He looked at her with savage approval. 'I'm turned on so tight all the damned time, Mia. I just want to—'

He didn't say, he showed. Kissing her neck as his fingers teased. Excitement poured through her, heating her all the more. He stopped the stormy kisses and defiantly stared down at her as if daring her to stop him when he could feel for himself, so intimately, just how much she wanted him. How close she was to—

'*Sante*.' She struggled to catch her breath and slow them down because they were at *work*. 'This is the cleaner's closet,' she breathed, even as she rocked her hips a little, encouraging his skilful fingers to assuage that horrible ache inside.

'Yes.' He skittered and circled her slick sex in a wicked

tease. 'Because someone thought it was a good idea for me to have an open-door policy and if I'm with you in there, someone could walk in at any moment.'

That was...*true*. She suddenly smiled. 'You have to admit a lot of the team has been more present in the office this week.'

'They won't get out of my face. Which is frustrating. Because do you know where I really want to put my face?'

'*Sante!*' she squeaked as he dropped to his knees before her.

He lifted her skirt and tugged her panties down just enough for him to graze her upper thighs with his lightly stubbled jaw. She slumped all her weight back against the wall and surrendered, spreading her legs and arching towards his hungry mouth.

'*Please...*' she pleaded, then moaned as he stroked her. 'Oh...'

She didn't need to beg. He was already stirring her higher with a rhythmic sweep of his tongue.

'*Oh...please!*' she sobbed, rocking against him. She ached for the release that was suddenly so close.

But as her arousal soared, she gasped, eyes widening as she neared the pinnacle. But it gave her the briefest glimpse of their surroundings. Of *reality*.

'I can't.' She clutched his shoulders even as she rocked against him, simultaneously panicked and shuddering and turned on even more. 'I'll be too loud.'

'I like you best when you're loud,' he said deeply.

Desperately, with her last functioning brain cell she rationalised—the others were in the meeting room so surely they wouldn't hear her from here? And with another stroke of his tongue she was too far gone to care.

'Be loud. Come on, Mia. Let me taste you. Let me hear you again.'

Oh, my. She almost crumpled as he double fingered her and fastened his hot mouth to suck her off strong. She bucked but he just worked harder, lashing his tongue over her. Oh, she wanted him. This. Now. *Always.* They were both starving and now unleashed, there was no stopping either of them. His stubble burned like an intimate fire against her sensitive skin, stirring her higher. She was so completely his.

'You're so hot, so fast for me,' he muttered. 'Come on me, Mia.'

His commanding growl unleashed her entirely. She tunnelled her fingers through his hair, holding on in sheer joy as he devoured her, pulling her over the precipice into velvety decadence. So quickly. She closed her eyes, convulsing as waves of pleasure washed through her.

'Oh, Sante.' She gasped and pressed her palm to her mouth to muffle the sobbing scream as her orgasm rocked her.

When she finally opened her eyes she saw triumph and demand glowing in his. But he shook his head as he rose and he drew her hand away from her mouth.

'You should never silence yourself,' he muttered roughly.

That was nice and all but there was reality to face. 'We're at *work*.' She shivered.

This had been a mistake. A gorgeous, desperate, but definite mistake. Work and home and life might be one and the same for him but it wasn't for her. There were people out there. People who could have walked in on them at any moment. Who could have heard. People whom she wanted to respect her—not talk and whisper behind her back. She bent her head. This was lust. Nothing but lust. And she couldn't let herself be carried away by it.

Leaning close, he tilted her chin, forcing her to meet his

fiery, intent expression. 'We're not done,' he breathed. 'You *know* we're not done.'

As she could feel his hard erection pressing against her bare thigh, she'd pretty much grasped that fact, yeah. And her own arousal was building shockingly quickly again.

'Not *here*,' she whispered fiercely while she could still think. 'I'll sleep with you again, but *not* at work.' She couldn't stop herself capitulating, but she needed this bargain. 'This can't encroach here at all. Not again.'

He drew in a breath. 'Then come to my apartment tonight.'

She shook her head. She couldn't be seen with him. 'Discreetly, Sante.'

'We're the last to leave work anyway. No one will see us. We can order in.'

So he assumed they'd dine together again as well?

Mia avoided his eyes by straightening her clothing, trying to haul together her scattered wits and regain some control over this. The fact was animal instinct had already won.

'Okay.'

She was doing a good job here and she could keep that as a separate thing. The fire between her and Sante was far more difficult to manage. So she wouldn't spend the entire night with him. She would have what she wanted and then return to her own place. The reality was this affair wouldn't last the duration of her contract. Sante was fast moving and would likely get bored—so she needed to take what she could, while she could. And as she was leaving in a few weeks, the lapse in professional judgement wouldn't matter. This was a private thing between her and Sante—one they needed to burn through. Because it was one she simply couldn't deny. But she was determined to do an even better job of managing the office. She would have nothing said against her work ethic. Ever. And as she now felt the best she had since the weekend, she could actually focus. She sat at her desk and pulled out the raft of notes she'd made from Adele's day.

'You realise it's an hour since everyone else left?'

Mia jumped, spinning her chair slightly, startled to see Sante standing just behind her.

'What's so absorbing?' His attention had flicked to her screen. 'A new software?'

'I'm updating the onboarding manual with some of the notes Adele gave me. As she knows everything about this place, I figured it would be helpful if everyone could access her usual processes.'

'You mean you've devised a way to stop the coders asking you stupid questions all the time.'

She smiled slightly. 'It's just an online reference as backup.'

He reached across and flicked through a couple of the files she'd created. 'It's simple, easy to use, pertinent information. You're really good at this.'

'Is that so surprising?' Mia asked.

But his attention had dipped to her blouse. He lifted a finger, pushing to release the top button of her vee, taking her from perfectly appropriate to provocative.

'Sante?' she whispered.

'Mmm?'

'Do you think because I've got boobs I can't have brains as well?' she murmured. 'As if it's possible to have only one or the other?'

His gaze shot back to her face and he flushed. 'Of course not.'

Mia giggled.

Sante gaped for a split second, then laughed. '*I'm* the one with no brain. I apologise. I got distracted.'

'Maybe try keeping your eyes *up*.'

'It's very difficult.'

'We're in a work setting.'

'*Empty* work setting. And it's still difficult.' He watched as she closed down the computer systems. 'Why didn't you go to university? Surely, your family has been going to Oxford or Cambridge for years?'

Mia stiffened, surprised he'd asked her something personal.

He chuckled. 'Relax, I'm not some higher education snob. You know I don't even *have* a degree.'

She didn't know that actually. She knew very little about his past other than that he'd been on scholarship to her brother's school for a couple of years.

'Didn't you go to some elite boarding school like Dario—surely that would have set you up?'

She swivelled in her seat, looking up as he leaned against her desk. He had his sleeves rolled up and his expression was relaxed and open. The most tempting man she'd ever seen in her life. Desperate to stop herself launching into his arms again here at *work*, she answered. There was no better way of cooling her jets than by thinking of her father.

'My father certainly felt I should've been more grateful for that investment, but boarding school wasn't for my benefit. It was for his. I didn't fit in. Sang too loud to make the choir. Laughed too much to be studious enough for the advanced class…but he didn't want me at home much. I spent almost every holiday being taken on school trips that I was "lucky" to go on.'

Admittedly, the extracurricular excursions had given her a bit of a travel bug.

'You were home the summer that I visited,' he said.

'Because he was away for most of it.' She watched him. 'I didn't like you,' she admitted huskily. But she'd been *fascinated* by him.

'No?' His eyebrows arched. 'I wasn't the right kind to fit in?'

'No, it wasn't that. You guys didn't even notice me,' she elaborated slightly. 'You were so busy with all your plans and I was alone.'

His gaze narrowed and his mouth opened and suddenly she didn't want to talk about what had happened towards the end of that summer. The day her father had come home unexpectedly and trampled her heart. She'd been a stupid, lonely kid who'd once again acted on a foolish impulse. But hopefully, Sante didn't remember because he had been so busy with Dario.

'Of course he wanted me to go to university.' She redirected the conversation just in case. 'He also wanted to dictate where I went and what I studied. He threatened to disinherit me if I didn't go, while at the same time moaned about having to make a donation to the university to wield enough influence to ensure my acceptance. I told him to cut me off.'

'Did he?'

She shot him a look. 'You know he was transactional. Do what he wants and he'll pay. But if you don't, then he'll withhold.'

'Not just money, affection and attention, too?' Sante said.

Yes. '*Everything* with him was conditional. And when I couldn't do what he wanted, didn't dress the way he wanted, I wasn't the right size, I didn't speak properly, and when I did I was too loud. The pathetic thing is even when I tried to do as he wanted, I could never get it right. I could never fit the mould he wanted. I tried so hard, but I'd only last a few days and revert to type—I'd laugh too loud, take another biscuit, sing too much. I'd been free at my mother's, maybe a little wild. But Westwick was so cold and I don't mean the weather. If I partially succeeded, he'd become more strict, constantly shifting the boundaries so I would always fail. Eventually, I realised I was *never* going to be what or who he wanted. He said it himself. I was too much like my mother. He'd never wanted me and he didn't like me. *I* was the distraction so I was eliminated. And in the end I rebelled—deliberately became "more." Too much. When I was seventeen I took myself right off the rails just to provoke him into pushing me away completely.'

Mia stopped, stunned that she'd just unloaded all that onto Sante of all people. It took less than two seconds for embarrassment to smother her.

'See?' she tried to joke. 'Too much. Like that. Always.'

He was clearly stunned, too. Silent and frowning. Sante slowly drew breath but she prattled on before he could offer any awkward platitude.

'Anyway, I'm starving,' she lied. 'Shall we go?'

He simply nodded.

Sante's car was powerful and utterly comfortable, but not flashy, which made her smile. Music played the second he started the engine but he flicked it off.

'Leave it on if you want. I love that song,' she murmured.

It would help cover the cringy silence enveloping them.

'Yeah,' Sante muttered.

She glanced at him as he put it back on. His cheeks were slightly flushed but he said nothing more. She'd discovered his apartment was only twenty minutes from the office when she'd tried to track him down last Friday, and again she wondered why he crashed at work as often as he did given it was so close. She bit the inside of her lip so as not to ask. Not that nor the other billion questions flooding her mind.

Like the palazzo in Sicily, his apartment block was outwardly imposing with an impenetrable brick facade. But once inside, Mia was hit with colour and comfort. The place was larger than it appeared from the outside and filled with bright furnishings and lush plants, and shelves straining beneath the weight of books with no curated orderly sense. They were piled haphazardly with no discernible cataloguing system whatsoever. Mia grinned, certain he'd be able to find whichever tome he wanted regardless. She was absurdly pleased that he had a sanctuary space here, too. She studied the series of photographs forming a massive feature wall. They were landscape shots. She recognised one taken in the grounds of the palazzo. He clearly loved that place. But the others—an ocean view through an archway, a mist-filled forest, a waterfall—they were all beautiful.

'No family photos?' she murmured.

There'd been none at the palazzo, either—only those beautiful frescoes on the walls. She kept a gallery on her phone but she always travelled with a framed picture of her mother.

'No.'

His finite response was typical closed-book Sante, but she'd offloaded earlier because he'd asked a personal question; maybe she would reciprocate and balance the scales the tiniest bit.

'None of you, either.' She faced him. 'You don't like having your photo taken?'

Sante just stared back at her. His silence was both pointed and prickly. But as he remained there—still and silent—she saw heat build in his eyes.

Right. So much for balancing the scales. They were only about a *physical* affair and she needed to reel in any other interest in him.

'Not going to send me any nudes then, huh,' she noted, covering her frustration with a little tease. 'You realise that means you don't get any from me, either.'

His stunned expression made her yelp with laughter.

'Don't want any,' he declared, stepping forward and pulling her into his arms. 'I'll settle for nothing less than holding the real thing.'

CHAPTER NINE

SANTE PRESSED HER CLOSE, sharp satisfaction rippling through him from having her in his arms again. He'd hated what she'd told him about her childhood. He remembered her as a scamp of a girl. Loud, yes. Full of laughter. Forever singing. Until her jerk of a father had come home. Lord Westwick had briefly called in twice that summer. Dario had turned resentful and silent each time his father had appeared, but it was the second visit that had particularly hurt Mia. Sante hoped she'd forgotten but she likely hadn't and he wasn't about to remind her. He knew better than anyone that there was no fixing the past.

So he kissed her, knowing he could make her feel good in that one way at least, barely restraining the urge to haul her straight to his bedroom. *Patience.* The food he'd ordered was about to arrive and she'd said she was hungry, so he forced himself to relax and release her.

'Another enormous sofa!' Mia laughingly gestured towards it with a flourish. 'I know you work almost all of the time, but when you drag yourself away you really know how to relax.'

'You think I should live in some kind of medieval prison—all hard stone and discomfort?' he asked dryly. 'Is that what I deserve?'

She shot him an arch look. 'What do you think you deserve?'

He smiled. He liked her coy and playful. This way they could avoid untangling the knot of personal information she'd offloaded in the office. She obviously didn't want to talk about it more. Her father was an absolute jerk. So was her brother. End of story. He and she were here now only for physical release together. No feelings. No sharing of anything more than their bodies and enjoyment of food and superficial things. That was all this was.

'Clearly, I think I deserve to lose myself in soft, warm things at the end of the day...' He walked back to her.

The sharpness in her eyes heated and he abandoned any idea of patience—

The doorbell rang. Expelling a rueful sigh he whirled away to fetch the food. He forced himself to slow down—actually put the succulent lamb on plates for them to savour.

'I don't get to try the freezer meals?' she chuckled.

'They're just fuel. This is more of a feast.'

Her smile widened. 'Sounds wonderful. What did you order?'

'It's a surprise.' He was oddly nervous about pleasing her.

She set the table—fossicking in his kitchen without asking. He was absurdly happy to let her. After all, dining with her was a tormenting sensual pleasure of its own and he liked taking the time to appreciate it with her. She was as much of an enthusiast as he—just a little more audible, and her appreciation of the creamy sauce only added to his building desire.

'Oh, that's goooood,' she moaned as she tasted the sharp bite of the blue cheese sauce.

He smiled. '*Sì.*'

She eventually sat back with a resplendent sigh. 'I *was* really hungry.'

'I still am,' he muttered bluntly, rising to pull her out of the chair.

He was an absolute hedonist when it came to Mia. She unleashed every appetite he had and better still, she met his with her own. He ignored the plates and mess. It was his turn to explore. Her curves. Her heat. Hands-on and hungry, he wanted her in his bed *now*.

'Rules,' he said huskily while he could still remember that he still needed boundaries.

'Rules?' She blinked. 'What—'

'You're only sleeping with me for the foreseeable future.'

Not that there was a future. This was not forever. This was only now.

'Ditto, obviously,' she said haughtily. 'And it ends when my contract ends.'

'Obviously,' he echoed her bite.

'And *nothing* more at work.'

What did that matter when she was leaving in only weeks? Every scruple about being her boss was long burned by lust, but he agreed anyway. 'If I know you're going to be in my bed every night that'll make that easier.'

'Every night?' Her eyes widened. 'Then you won't be pulling all-nighters at work anymore.'

'You work from home with me on Fridays.'

'Home?'

'Sicily.'

She frowned. 'You mean I do a four-day week because let's get real, I won't be working.'

'You work long hours already. Consider it time in lieu.'

Enough negotiation. There was only one thing he could do now because there was nothing he liked more than making her limp and speechless, pink cheeked and panting with that stunned-but-sated dreaminess in her big blue eyes.

He worked her hard, savouring her warmth and strength until at last she lay sleepy and quiet, snuggling close. Her beautiful smile pulled his own from him. *Sì*, rendering this beautiful bundle of positive effervescence into a speechless heap of lax limbs was about the most rewarding thing he'd ever set his mind to.

She sprawled over him like a soft blanket. 'You really like a landscape.'

Sante fiercely protected both his privacy and autonomy. He never wanted to factor anyone else in his decisions. He was selfish. But being free to make his own decisions, not to be constrained or have judgement poured over him, was as essential to him as breathing. Yet, Mia's genuine appreciation, the fearless interest in her eyes, touched him.

'The one on the far left is the view from my property in the South of France.'

'Ooh la la.'

He chuckled. 'They're views from all my various properties.' He liked having the gallery here to remind him of what he'd achieved when he was working hard. And that he had places to go should he need to. Always.

Mia lifted her head and studied the frames. 'Is there more than one view from each, or one from each property?'

'You think there's too many? That I'm greedy?'

'No. When you've known deprivation or uncertainty, then you need as many as you can hang on to.'

'Deprivation?' He stiffened. Had Dario told her about his childhood?

'Are you saying you had everything you ever wanted in your childhood, Sante?'

'No one does,' he deflected with a generalisation. 'You didn't.'

That silenced her. For a moment.

'So it's pictures of places not people.'

He combed through her hair gently. Curious thing she was.

No people because he had no family. He had no pictures of himself even—why would he ever want to dwell on his past?

'There's more permanence with places.' He opted to keep it light. 'Most of them are investments.'

'Investments. So you don't invest in people?' She shook her head. 'Your tech incubator is important to you,' she added. 'You want them to feel comfortable.'

'So they make me more millions. Isn't that what you said?' he murmured.

She turned to look down into his eyes. 'I think underneath the isolationist exterior you're still a team player.'

'That was the only way to get ahead back then. I had to play the game until I was wealthy enough not to have to bother.'

'So because you're ludicrously wealthy now you think the rules no longer apply to you?'

'I don't go around just doing anything I want at any time.'

'No?' She actually giggled.

'No. I'm being incredibly restrained right now.'

Her eyebrows arched. He rolled, pinning her with his body. Yet, instead of distracting her, his own curiosity was engaged.

'Don't you want a home of your own?' Why didn't she have cosy sofas with blankets and books when she clearly appreciated them? She should be the vibrant chatelaine of some vast manor, all cashmere sweaters and surrounded by adoring dogs. 'What happened to Westwick?'

Presumably, her father's estate in Wiltshire was now Dario's.

Mia stiffened beneath him. 'I don't want to be tied to one place.'

He didn't believe her. But he understood why she wouldn't have fond memories of that place.

'Everyone wants their own space they can feel safe in.' To have things that brought comfort or peace. For him that was space, greenery, solitude—a *view*. But Mia had too much heart to settle for that. She would need company of the canine kind at least. He inhaled, about to ask her—

'That's usually just my bedroom. Speaking of, it's late. I should get home.' She wriggled, trying to get out from under him.

'The agreement was every night.'

'But not *all* night,' she said. 'We only have that in the weekend.'

Huh. Sante never normally acknowledged weekends. Every day was the same. Sleep. Wake. Work out. Work. Eat. Sleep. In whichever of his abodes he felt like at the time. But now he *lived* for the weekend. For having day time with her again that wasn't constrained by workplace etiquette or a finite few hours in the evening.

The first Friday through Sunday was a pure romp—sex followed by food followed by a teasing debate about music, and then she'd tried to trounce him on the gaming console he'd brought with him. It was fantastic. But still not enough.

Despite knowing she would be in his bed every evening, the days at work became an annoyance. The brief moments he was unable to touch her caused a slow rising sense of panic in him. But then she was beside him again and he relaxed.

They quickly fell into a routine. He discovered that he could cope better at work if he spent more time in the open-plan area—so he could see her, not just hear her. But by the last half hour he was so hopelessly distracted, he had to seek space in his office again so he could choose which restaurant to order from, while she made 'end of day conversation' with his recruits as they left. He knew this fascination would pass, but he was ridiculously glad she was contracted for a couple months yet.

* * *

'Sante?'

He glanced up and saw Mia standing five paces into his office, wide-eyed and waiting for him to answer some question he'd not even heard. He just gazed at her, absurdly pleased to see her even though it had only been minutes.

'Did you hear me?' Paolo said.

Sante blinked. He'd not only failed to hear his lawyer, he'd not even *seen* him, either.

'Sorry.' He frowned, swiftly dealing with Paolo's query.

Mia lingered in his office until the lawyer left.

'What were you thinking?' she muttered the second the main door banged shut.

'How much I want you.' The embarrassing thing was that was *all* he was thinking almost all the time.

'Well, stop.'

'You think I haven't tried?'

'Not hard enough.'

He walked around his desk. 'Let's understand what's hard, shall we?'

'Sante…' Shaking her head she backed away.

But she was smiling and he wanted to make her hum.

'Surely, everyone has left now,' he muttered. 'Come on, let's go.'

He drove her home. She set the table—it was a little ritual now. Twenty minutes later dinner arrived. They were working through the best restaurants in Rome but Sante was increasingly tempted to *take* her to one—he wanted to sit opposite her, take time over five or so courses—not being able to touch her as intimately as he wanted would be a delightful torture, seeing her savour the fine food another pleasure. *Sì*, he was a masochist.

Hours later she stirred. 'It's late.'

'It is.' Right now he didn't think he could move. Didn't want to. And he really didn't like her leaving his bed in the middle of the night.

'I don't have your stamina. I can't stay awake all night. The shifts on the boat are too long as it is.'

It was good she'd not had to work twenty-four or more; it wasn't healthy. He'd done it out of necessity—coding his first app through the night, working on the docks during the day. It had become habit. In truth, working all hours had been a salve. It helped him avoid the midnight demons that haunted him. Because he remembered nights in his life when he'd been utterly alone and unbearably afraid. He closed his mind to those memories and focused on Mia. She was a far better salve than work. He kissed her gently, slowly building her up until she shuddered in his arms and sighed—wanting to make her sleepy and lax and *unable* to move. But when he pulled her close after her release, he felt her summon resistance with a deep breath.

'I *really* better go,' she sighed.

'I don't want you to.' He felt a lurch in his chest as he muttered it. He wanted to walk it back right away. But it didn't matter; she was shaking her head.

'You'll be sick of me sooner if we don't have some time separately.'

'What?'

She laughed. 'I'm a lot. You know I can be a lot.'

'A lot in a good way.'

She rolled her eyes. 'Trust me, you'll have had enough, soon enough.'

He remembered what she'd said about not fitting her father's mould. 'You don't seriously think people get sick of you?'

'My mother, father and brother all did at various points

and it's been a continuing theme. Which is truly pitiful, so it's really better if I—'

'You know you're perfect,' he muttered.

'*No one* is perfect, Sante. Especially not me.' She slid out of his bed and pulled on her top. 'You don't need to flatter me. I'm just tired.'

Then she should stop getting dressed and just lie down with him again. He frowned. 'I know your father was a jerk, but your mother? I thought—'

'I loved her,' Mia interrupted, instantly defensive and fully regretting her casual admission of what was actually a deeply vulnerable truth. 'Absolutely loved her.'

And she'd loved this last week with Sante, too. But she didn't want to stay the night. She didn't want anything in their arrangement to change because she didn't want it to end too soon. She avoided his frowning gaze and talked. Her mother was a good diversion while she dressed.

'She was full of vitality,' she rambled. 'Lovely to everyone and everyone loved her. Vivacious and larger than life with a laugh that was infectious—'

'She sounds like you.'

Mia smiled sadly. That wasn't quite the compliment he'd maybe meant it to be. 'I'm the spitting image of her. Not good in my father's view. He took one look at me and the lectures began. *Don't eat so much, you don't want to get fat like your mother.*'

Sante's jaw dropped. 'Mia, you're—'

'I know, it's okay.' She smiled.

She'd worked hard to overcome the shame and guilt instilled by her father. The belief that she was too greedy, too big. He'd constantly berated her for not being slim—that she wouldn't make a desirable match if she was overweight. Because a desirable match was all she was good for. Yet ironically, the bigger she'd grown—at least those particular parts of her, the breasts, the hips, the butt—the more desirable she'd seemingly become. But that attention hadn't been the 'desirable match' kind. It had been lascivious and basic.

Yes, this affair with Sante was purely a physical thing but she revelled in his appreciation of her—it was different. Where other men had expressed attraction it was often by leering, voicing unwanted requests for photos and crude comments—seeing her only as a body. And aside from Oliver she'd kept every one of them at a distance. But Sante savoured her in a way that was so tender it was utterly shattering. Aside from the time he'd totally lost control in the office store cupboard, he was slow and careful and such a tease. And while that cupboard moment never should have happened, it was the hottest experience of her life, and again he'd been all about pleasing *her*.

'Apparently, I took up too much space and I made too much noise.' Mia cleared her throat. 'He said my mother was an addict—to food. Alcohol. Drugs. Sex. And that I was going to be the same what with my addictive personality. I needed to tone down. I was too loud, too raucous, too curvy, to be taken seriously. *Don't overindulge like your mother. Don't be a slut like your mother.*' She paused. Then conceded. 'I mean, my mother *did* like a party. She would host all the time at our place in Capri. It was beautiful and sunny and possibly hedonistic.' She remembered the house being full of people—of *men*. Lots of laughter and doors closing on more laughter. 'Looking back I realise now she was masking unhappiness. But she needed her time out from me, too. She would get Dario to take me away to the gardens.'

She'd probably had headaches, jaded from partying all night. But as a little girl, Mia had only seen the sparkling gowns and smiles and she'd wanted to stay. It had hurt to be denied.

'And then she overdosed.'

Right. He knew. Dario would have told him.

'You moved to England.'

'To cold rules and impossible expectations and boarding school.' She nodded. 'I got in trouble at school, too. So then to another more strict one. Basically boot camp. And I was still too loud. I've been told to be quiet or go away too many times in my life to count.

'He tried to starve the love of life out of me but I can't compress myself into something I'm not.' She sighed. 'The irony was I *did* listen to some of his rubbish. I kept my virginity for years until...'

She trailed off. She'd not wanted to have her worth determined by her ability to secure a man. She'd not wanted to be 'too much' and rejected again.

Sante's eyes widened comically. 'Until?'

She sat on the edge of the bed. 'I was a naive fool. You have my permission to laugh.'

'Why? What happened?'

'As soon as I left school I got a job as a nanny. I figured it was a good match—use my "too much" energy to entertain small children. Plus, it was live-in, which meant I could leave home. There were loads of staff—maids, gardeners, drivers, secretary—the works. Two children. The parents were nice. The father had a brother who would visit sometimes.'

'And he wanted you,' Sante guessed.

'He pursued. It was very flattering. I liked the attention. I thought it was true love. As I said, I was very naive.'

'Because it wasn't true love?'

Mia bit her lip. 'I fell *hard*. I wasn't discreet—blurring boundaries between my work and personal life. I was unprofessional and distracted and young. All the staff knew we were sleeping together. What I didn't know was that all of them also knew he had a girlfriend. And all of them watched while I found that out in a public setting when he brought her to a family dinner and I had to sit there and take instruction and—'

It had been the most humiliating, shameful moment of her life. Worse than anything before. But she saw the anger in Sante's eyes and spoke before he could. 'I was a fool, Sante. It was my fault.'

'How? For thinking he cared for you?' Sante looked tense. 'He *lied* to you. And your colleagues were awful for setting you up. They were *bullies*.'

She'd thought so. But she'd also realised that she wasn't someone anyone wanted forever. Her father had said she was just like her mother—'fun for now,' not forever. Her father certainly hadn't wanted her. And sure enough, Oliver had only wanted her for *fun*. She was a good-time girl who actually hadn't had that many good times and who'd been more naive than people would have believed. Because she'd also realised that it was her pride that was hurt more than her heart.

'I fell for the *attention* he gave me,' she said. 'For the fairy tale he spun. I thought I'd found a family I could fit into. Instead, I wrecked a job I'd actually enjoyed before getting so giddy I failed to perform. I can't let that happen again.'

But now she'd had a taste of true sensual passion, she wanted more. Her father had always berated her appetite. She was voracious, wanting more than was proper or *allowed*. She didn't want anyone putting limits on what she could or couldn't have. Maybe she would take what she wanted. Claim it for herself. She shouldn't have listened to her father—shouldn't have equated lust with shame or her value with her virginity. That appetite—*any* appetite—

was a bad thing. She should have let herself indulge in all pleasures *including* sex. Because it was so very good. And maybe if she'd had more, she wouldn't be making more of *this* now with Sante than what there actually was.

'Now you never stay long in the one place,' Sante murmured.

It was better not to stick around anywhere for too long. But there were other reasons for her choices. 'Travel enriches my life. I like meeting new passengers and crew. I like the variety.'

'You could still travel *and* have a home for yourself, so you're not living out of a few bags.'

'I like a nomadic existence.'

'No. You're saving for a *reason*.' He leaned up on his elbow and looked into her eyes. 'You should be living on some vast country estate with a bunch of dogs around you.'

Mia froze, *horrified*.

'I remember,' he whispered. 'You brought that stray puppy home that summer the day your dad came home unexpectedly.'

She'd really hoped Sante *hadn't* remembered that—hoped he'd been too busy with Dario to have paid much attention to an episode that had been utter heartbreak for her. But this was Sante and he had a brain bigger than Jupiter. 'I don't want to talk about that.'

She walked to the door but in seconds felt Sante gently take her arms from behind and pull her back against his warm body. 'You loved it.'

She'd wanted to.

Mia bent her head. She'd been such a fool. She'd wanted a friend. She'd wanted something to love. Something to love her back, too. That puppy had been *so* precious and she'd thought it could be hers. It had come from the farm down the road. She'd convinced the farmer's wife that her father would let her have one. The woman had always been kind to her. But Mia had lied—she'd been naive and impulsive and she'd thought she could keep it hidden somehow. But her father had arrived home unexpectedly that very night.

'*That half-breed mutt isn't staying in my house*,' Sante quoted her father, sympathy roughening his voice. 'For a moment I'd thought he'd meant me.'

Mia closed her eyes, horrified.

'He was so mean to you,' he muttered, turning her in his arms and carefully pulling her closer still. 'I heard you crying half the night.'

'You know me, never quiet.' She swallowed, tried to smile. Failed. 'Dario came and checked on me.'

'We should have done better for you that day.' Sante pressed her against his chest. 'I'm so sorry, Mia.'

'There was nothing either of you could have done. Nothing would have changed his mind. He only ever wanted his posh tweeds and pure breeds. Hunting dogs in the kennels not the house and he never wanted…'

Her, either. And definitely not some cute mutt that she'd loved instantly and unconditionally. But her father had taken that puppy and she'd never seen it again. It had just *disappeared*.

'Mia.' Sante stroked her back so tenderly. 'You should have everything you want now. You should have a big home filled with dogs.'

No. Losing her puppy had hurt too much. She wasn't doing that again.

'You shouldn't be taking jobs with accommodation included so you can save more. You should have inherited far *more* than enough to buy yourself a home in a place you love,' he said harshly. 'What happened? *Why* didn't you get your birthright?'

She straightened and looked into his face, reading his frustration. 'It's not that straightforward, Sante.'

Her father spared a little more time for Dario but that was because he was the son and heir. Her father hadn't just disinherited Mia. He'd made those threats to her brother, too.

'Isn't it? Dario inherited the world and made his own fortune, yet he's left you with nothing. *How* is that possible?' Outrage burned in Sante's eyes.

In this past week they'd not mentioned her brother by tacit agreement. Apparently, now there was no avoiding it.

'I didn't *want* anything from my father and I didn't want Dario's help.'

'Not good enough. He should have insisted. If I had a sister there's no way I'd let her have nothing while I got everything.'

'If you had a sister you would know how difficult it would actually be, because she'd be even more boneheaded than you,' Mia fired back. 'The fact is Dario had strings as well.'

Her brother didn't trust her entirely, either. And as she was fooling around with the man he hated, maybe he'd been right to doubt her.

The ire in Sante's expression simply grew.

'He *cares* about me.' She tempered her tone and shrugged. She didn't have many memories of her life before her mother's death but she remembered a couple of times when Dario had kept her distracted. 'He protected me when we were young.'

'Not just your father. You mean in Italy.'

She nodded. She hadn't understood the extent to which Dario had protected her and that it was hard for him to let that habit go. 'We were young when she died. In England we were separated for school and most holidays so we didn't spend much time together. And then…'

'The accident.'

'His recovery took a long time,' she said softly. 'He became distant.'

Mia had been kept away from Dario—she was 'too loud'; she would impede his convalescence. So she'd felt she was little more than an annoyance to her brother as well.

'So with all that happened, we're not as close as you might think.' Not as close as she would like. 'He's used to making all the decisions and when my decisions aren't the ones he'd make, then he struggles. I would have burned anything he gave me and he knows that.'

Sante frowned. 'Mia…'

'*No one* will control me,' she said. 'And I don't need rescuing. I can manage perfectly well on my own.'

'You shouldn't have to—'

'I don't need *billions*. I don't need to acquire an infinite number of properties to feel secure. I just need to feel free to be myself.'

His lips twitched. 'For the record, accumulating an infinite number of properties is a hugely satisfying endeavour.'

'Money and power aren't what really matter. *People* are.' Mia gazed into Sante's suddenly stiff face.

Looking at his physical perfection, no one would believe he'd ever been in an accident where the car was completely smashed. There wasn't a visible mark on him but there were scars on the inside, and her brother would always be a shadow between them. But she braced. 'I know you didn't want to leave him in the car. I know you tried everything you could to help him…'

He froze. Then moved. Stepping back and releasing her. 'You wanted to get home.'

She stepped forward. 'I *know*, Sante.'

'A week ago you thought I was a monster.'

'I saw your feet,' she said, bullishly not moving a muscle so he couldn't get past her. 'I didn't connect the dots until recently. Your shoes were worn. Your socks were bloody. You'd run for *hours*.'

'Run *away*, according to your father.'

'You *never* would have done that. I think you ran to try to get help.'

He stood, completely silent. Mia watched the shadows deepen in his eyes. Had she taken this too far? She was good at that but she wasn't going to apologise for it this time. Sante had such a *closed* life.

His lips twisted. 'I went in the wrong direction. I was disoriented. I didn't know where I was—'

Sante broke off. He'd not intended to discuss this with her again. Before her he'd not discussed it with anyone since the relentless interrogation in the police car when he'd been picked up. He'd run through the night. In the dark, cold, terrified. Devastated at leaving Dario. He'd hated that he'd had to leave him. He'd never wanted to leave someone he considered a brother. Not *again*.

'You were in shock. You'd probably had a knock to the head. Did anyone even check you out?'

'I was fine,' he muttered dismissively.

'No, you weren't.' She moved forward, planting herself right in front of him, her eyes wide and beseeching and beautiful. 'You ran for hours trying to get help for your injured friend.'

He couldn't hold that gaze. Couldn't stop the whisper from escaping. 'I thought he was going to die. I couldn't get him free. I didn't want to leave him.'

'You've never told him any of that?'

'I couldn't get to see him.'

'Dario didn't regain consciousness until two days later,' Mia explained quietly. 'He was in a bad way for a long time. Alone a long time struggling with it. My father told him you'd taken his pay-off. That you'd bargained the amount upwards to go quickly and quietly.'

'You're able to believe that your father would lie about it. But Dario still believes I would do something that awful. He never tried to find out my side of the story. He just accepted it as fact.'

Dario was like his father—entitled and ruthless. Able to just cut someone out of his life, no matter how they'd been treated. No matter that Sante had trusted Dario more than anyone in his life at that time. Dario had done it to Mia, too, hadn't he? By not supporting her.

'*You've* never talked to him about it, either. You're *equally* stubborn,' Mia pointed out. 'Maybe you should tell him the truth.'

'It wouldn't matter what I said.' Sante shook his head. 'It's easier to believe the worst of someone than the best,' he said. 'Everyone always does that.'

Mia looked at him sadly and he braced. He didn't want to hear whatever she thought she could say to make this better. There was no making it better and he didn't want to revisit this ever again. He didn't want to see compassion in her eyes. He didn't deserve it. He hadn't abandoned Dario, but he wasn't worthy of her belief in him being a decent person. Because he'd failed before.

He stood, frozen. Driving her home felt impossible. He could summon a driver, but that was an admin step too far. And now he needed to silence not just her, but the memories swirling in his head. There was only way to blank out the world. The best way. He pulled her close and to his immense pleasure, she melted.

CHAPTER TEN

Sante spent the last hour of the workday gaming with a couple of the younger coders, desperately filling in the time before he could touch her again. He'd not gamed in so long—he'd stopped when he'd left the UK and had just worked all the time. He'd forgotten it was fun—though in this moment it was basic distraction and barely working. Work was impossible—he couldn't stop dwelling on what Mia had said last night. He was furious with her family for crushing her spirit and making her feel flawed. She wasn't. She really—

'Did you learn to code at school, Sante?'

Sante glanced at Roberto, momentarily stunned. He would talk product, programming or problems, but the personal was irrelevant and every other employee knew it.

'Was it at school or did you pick it up yourself?' Roberto added. 'I mean, did it just come easily?'

'Sorry to interrupt.' Mia appeared behind them so quickly she had to have been hovering. 'Roberto, I need you and Davide to fill in this sheet for me before you go, okay?'

Sante avoided Mia's eyes, knowing she wasn't sorry at all. Both techs immediately followed her before Sante had the chance to drum up a vague but finite response for the guy. He stayed slumped in the gaming chair long after they left.

Any other evening he'd be considering what to order in for dinner back at the apartment. He'd ordered in from a selection of restaurants every night this week and not tried to stop her leaving early again. Now he understood her deep need for independence, he didn't want to make her feel controlled. He'd long had his independence, but she'd long been denied hers. It riled him more than anything. He loathed controlling bullies like her father. Yet, *her* boundaries around their affair chaffed. He didn't like being told what he could and couldn't do, either. He *wasn't* like that jerk she'd had the affair with. Sante would treat her—a restaurant, a walk through the city, a trip to…anywhere. But she insisted on absolute discretion, determined not to be seen with him outside the office. He knew his annoyance about it was ironic when he was the privacy freak. But he wanted to sit opposite her and take time over their meal. He wanted to dance with her in a club, not just on the patio at the palazzo or in the glasshouse. She would glitter. She always glittered. His pilot Jerome knew they spent the weekends together and while he was discreet, Sante knew it was only a matter of time before others in his office became aware of their routine. Would it matter that much if people did?

Because if they didn't have to be secret, they could go to Paris or Barcelona for a few days—preferably *during* the week because the weekends in Sicily felt sacrosanct. He didn't want to miss having her there.

He heard her humming and smiled, knowing the office was now empty. She'd brought music back into his life, too.

'Were you protecting me from prying questions?' he asked when she sank into the second gaming chair, certain he'd not imagined that hint of proprietary care in her interruption earlier.

She shrugged. 'I know you don't like to share personal things.'

He kept watching her. Waiting.

'No one knows anything about you.' She picked up the controller, selected a game and pressed Play. 'You're a reclusive, elusive genius with no personal details on your website. Not even the name of your company has any obvious connection to you. I had to ask the guys why they wanted to work for you. They all said the same thing.'

'The money.' Sante clicked, selecting his avatar, ready to best her on screen at least.

'You really think your value is only in your bank balance?'

He leaned back in the chair. 'I prefer not to discuss my background because then there will be fewer preconceived judgements or ideas about me and, therefore, my work.'

'You like to let the product speak for itself.'

That had been the money he'd taken and run with. 'It was a means to an end.'

'Freedom. Security. Property.' She leaned forward, eyes narrowing on the screen as they raced. 'So why create this incubator for other genius misfits now?'

'I have too many ideas. I want them to take them off my hands. Personal questions invariably lead to judgement. Someone finds out you were a foster kid, there's automatically the question *why*. What was wrong with me to be in foster care?'

Mia fumbled, accidentally tripping her character. 'You were in foster care?'

Sante hit Pause on the game. 'You really didn't know?'

'How could I?' She tilted her head towards him as she realised. 'You told Dario. He never said anything to me.'

Sante supposed he should be grateful the guy hadn't told the world about his past. '*Sì.*'

She moved forward, turning his face so she could look

into his eyes. 'Sante, you can't think anything was wrong with you,' she whispered.

'Don't you wonder what was wrong with you that your father didn't want you?'

'I don't need to wonder. I know. Because I was like my mother, he couldn't stand to look at me. It spiralled down from there.'

'You reminded him of heartbreak. It made him angry.'

'You assume he had a heart to break. I don't think he had one.'

'Maybe not, given how he treated you in life.' He sighed. 'I wonder what it was that I reminded my mother of that made her want to put me in a cardboard box and leave me at a church gate.'

'Sante...' She stared at him, clearly shocked. 'You don't have to tell me anything else. Some things hurt too much to be stirred up and discussed.' She suddenly blurted, 'I don't need to know your past to know what kind of person you are now.'

He stiffened.

'Seriously, you're no mystery to me,' she added. 'There's plenty I know about you. You don't have to open up to me or anything.'

Sante smiled ruefully, appreciating that she was trying hard not to pry and accepting his reticence instead.

'What do you think you know?' He leaned back.

'I'm not talking about knowing you in the biblical sense.' Her smile was tinged with sadness. 'I'm talking about knowing you here.' She reached across and pressed her palm on his chest, right over his heart. 'You're quiet. You like to watch and observe.'

'How astute, Captain Obvious.'

'But you can't quite separate yourself completely.' She

ignored his dryness. 'You care about people. You care about your coders and creatives. You care about Adele and Bruno. And your neighbours. You can't stop yourself caring completely. I know you're loyal. You're willing to put yourself at risk to help another. Especially someone you care about.'

His eyes widened. He didn't have relationships based in anything emotional. Dario was right; he was transactional. Furthermore, his interactions with others were invariably temporary. Which was how he liked it. Even this now with Mia was only temporary and only sexual. But she was arguing differently. Wrongly.

'You're aware of the needs of others and you're receptive to change.'

'Is this the open-door policy?' he drawled, trying not to take any of this seriously.

'And the shared lunch, yes, it is. But it's also phoning your neighbours to make sure they were okay in the storm.'

'That was just being...' He cleared his throat. 'It's better for my property if the ones next door are well maintained.'

'It was giving "kind human." One who has connections even when he pretends to himself that he doesn't. I don't need to know everything about you to know that you're a decent person.'

'You're a blind optimist. I have faults, too.'

'Oh yeah, heaps.'

He cocked his head, suddenly amused. 'Such as...'

'Ego,' she chuckled. 'Impatience.' She leaned close to whisper. 'Insecurity.'

'Is that a fault?'

'It can be. When it stops you believing you can do things.'

'You think I lack self-belief?' he scoffed.

'No. I think you lack belief in *others*. That they'll truly be there for you.'

He stilled. 'Maybe you're projecting.'

'Probably. Maybe we have more in common than we'd first have thought.'

'More than an insatiable sex drive?' he teased but he didn't really feel like laughing.

She shook her head.

And weirdly, her lack of intrusion loosened his tongue. She cared about everyone. She was caring enough *not* to ask even though he knew she was curious. He wanted her to know why he wouldn't ever…couldn't ever…have anything more than something like this.

'My early childhood was okay.' He found himself reassuring her. 'I mean, I wasn't wanted by my birth parents. I was found in a box and after a night in hospital went straight into the system. My first foster family already had an older child but then they'd had a baby pass away, so at first I was…' He sighed. 'I was a gift, I guess. But when I was four, my foster mother unexpectedly got pregnant with a real gift. Twins. That meant it was a high-risk pregnancy and she needed to rest a lot and I didn't really understand. I was just…'

Mia's eyes widened. 'A *child*.'

'I came home from nursery school and found my bags packed.'

'They couldn't get help for your foster mother—she had no family support?'

'I guess I wasn't really part of that family.' He'd been with them almost five years and then there'd been *nothing*.

'That was a huge betrayal, Sante. I'm so sorry.'

Sì, Mia knew what it was like to be completely uprooted and forced to go to a place where you weren't welcome. That was the only reason he kept talking. She was one of the few people in the world who would actually understand.

'I didn't last long at the next placement. They'd told me that if I caused trouble, I'd have to move. I ran away, thinking they'd send me back to my first home.'

'But that didn't happen.'

There were rational reasons for difficult decisions, but there was core rejection that couldn't be healed. Nothing to be said to assuage it. Mia looked at him—her expression open. She could be so full of joie de vivre but on the flip side, deeply considerate. And compassionate.

'Did you get placed with another foster family after you ran away?'

'I was at the third home for a few years. They had several foster children. Very strict foster father. He was an athletics coach. He had high expectations of himself, his wife and all of us.'

'Expectations that you would have met. You won that sports scholarship to Dario's school.'

All-rounder scholarship, actually—the academics had been the clincher more than the sporting strength, but he wasn't in the mood to brag.

'I know. So his routines didn't damage me. I could handle the intensity. He wanted to make something of us. We were nothing, but we wouldn't always be nothing because he would help us get there but we had to work for it.'

'He told you that you were nothing?'

'It was five-mile runs before breakfast. Weight training. Things were withheld unless you hit your daily targets.'

'Things?'

'Food. Rest. You had to keep pushing.'

'Oh, Sante.' She looked stricken. 'It was abuse.'

She immediately saw what he hadn't realised for too long.

'I was lucky,' he muttered. 'He set the challenge and I wouldn't give him the satisfaction of beating me. But I'd been blessed with a strong enough body to be able to endure it. But Luca wasn't.' He dropped his gaze. 'He'd been there about a year and he struggled. One weekend I was away at a meet. The foster father would normally come on those trips. He liked to watch me win. It was good because it gave the others a break from his supervision. But my foster mother was unwell and he had to stay home. Which made him frustrated and when he was frustrated, he would blow the whistle and demand more effort. Other times I was able to distract him—ask him to spot me for my weights routines. Ask his advice. Flatter him.'

'You played him to protect the others,' she said. 'But that time you weren't there. What happened to Luca?'

'They assessed him at the hospital. Aside from the broken ribs there were all kinds of overuse injuries. They shut down the home. The foster father was charged with cruelty. But I was the success story. He used me as the model to prove his strategy worked. The social workers challenged me. Why hadn't I said anything? Or done anything to stop him? She said I was selfish because I could do it and show off and that I was as bad as he was.'

'Sante, you know that wasn't fair.'

He bent his head. 'She was right.'

'You were a *child*. You tried to protect the others by taking the attention of your foster father the one way you could. Sante, *none* of it was your fault.' She paused. 'What happened to Luca?'

'I never saw him again.' He glanced up. 'I was sent to a group home and a new school. The principal there helped me apply to that school in Wales.'

'Dario's school. It was supposed to have changed your life.'

'Get me a full ride to an elite university, *sì*. Make connections with the right people. The principal was delighted for me.'

'Were you delighted?'

'You know how hard it is to leave the place you've lived your whole life and go somewhere wildly different. When you don't speak the language all that well...'

'It's hard,' she said. 'Especially without anyone to support you.'

'I met Dario,' he muttered.

Her brother had become a friend. The one person he could speak in his own language with. They'd joked about creating apps that would make them billions. But Sante had always been serious. Dario was as smart. As sporty. Idealistic. He'd been a friend and competitor. Dario had wanted to do big things, to make a difference. He'd been a damn idealist. But he'd had a backstop. He'd had a family. Money. Entitlement. He could *afford* to be idealistic. For Sante it had only been about *survival*. Of course he'd wanted to make money. He'd wanted to create security for *himself*. He'd wanted personal freedom. Never to have to perform for anyone again. Never be told what he could or couldn't do. Never feel trapped and helpless. Never have to suck up to powerful people or feel as if he were the change in a transaction. Never rely on anyone—never make the mistake of letting anyone close ever again.

Certainly not the baby sister of the guy he'd felt betrayed him most.

'But then you had the accident,' Mia said softly after a while. 'You tried to help Dario. You just ran the opposite way to which help came.'

'I failed,' Sante said harshly.

'You still tried. That matters, Sante.'

No. Failure sucked. It had ended that friendship. He

would fail her at some point. He couldn't sustain relationships. Once again, he'd failed to protect someone he'd come to feel close to. He wouldn't be close to anyone again.

'For what it's worth, Dario shut everyone out. Even me,' Mia said.

Dario had believed Sante had abandoned him when he was hurt. Abandonment was one of the worst things that could happen to a person. He would never have done it. That Dario believed he had just said it all.

He was blamed again—everything about the accident deemed to be his fault. Going to the music festival had been Dario's idea. Sante had never been to one and he'd thought it would be fun. But Dario's father had blamed him. The police had shamed him. He'd taken one look at the principal's face and known to withdraw as a student before he was expelled. As he was seventeen they didn't bother to try stopping him. That had ended the scholarship offers for university.

He'd always been discarded. If something or someone better had come along. Or if there was a problem—if *he* caused any problems. For any arbitrary reason. Any trouble and Sante was blamed first. Judgement lingered. Assumptions, negative expectations, were what stuck with him, never people.

The moment anyone found out about his past, their perceptions shifted. His achievements were marvelled at—as if somehow it was a miracle that someone like him could do anything beyond the norm. He wasn't letting anyone reject him again. He took control of everything. Always.

'After the accident you came back to Italy?' Mia asked.

'Like you I took jobs that included food and accommodation so I could save everything. Worked through the night on my app.'

'You must have been exhausted.'

'There wasn't any other choice.'

'You could have taken my father's money.' She smiled sadly. 'I know you didn't. You're not big on taking help from anyone.'

'That wasn't help,' he said gruffly.

She nodded. 'It's hard to ask for help, let alone accept it, when you've been let down by people in the past and almost everyone let you down.' She fiddled with the controller, her voice going husky. 'Until Adele. She's been constant.'

'I needed someone to take the phone calls and do the admin. She stays because I pay her well and she has financial stresses that require her to remain. Her loyalty isn't personal.'

'You know that's neither fair nor true. She cares about you. She just knows better than to *let* you see it. Her desperation to get me to handle the office wasn't just about Bruno. It was for you, too.' She lifted those lashes and gazed at him, emotion blooming in her blue eyes. 'And I bet you've never told her about your past. So it's not pity, Sante. You know that and it goes both ways. That's why you've been helping her by paying for Bruno's new specialist.'

'You know about that?' He frowned. 'Does *she* know about that?'

He'd pulled some strings—made a donation. Because Mia was right. Adele had been constant and he'd been compelled to help even if it was only in the one way he could—financially.

'Of course not. I guessed when she told me they'd gotten a referral to the top guy in Rome. I knew I was right.'

'Want to lean on her to accept a cook and cleaner as well?'

'Leave it with me.' Mia nodded but her smile was sad. 'The reason you don't have personal photos is because you don't actually have any, isn't it?'

'Why does that bother you so much?' But she was right. No family. No photos. 'The photo on my file is like a police mugshot. But it doesn't matter. I don't want reminders of that time.'

'Did you ever try to find your biological parents?'

'There were no DNA matches in any databases at the time and I don't want to find out now. They didn't want me. I don't want them.' He fully imagined the worst.

'You don't have to have DNA answers to know who you are, Sante. You're a good person.'

'Am I? My genetics might be flawed. I might have inheritable diseases in my body or brain—undesirable personality traits or—'

'We all have messy genes. We're not clones of our parents. You're still you. You're in charge of your destiny—you've proven that beyond doubt. But I'll admit you're not normal, Sante,' she said. 'You're *exceptional* in so many ways.'

'Mia—'

'I stand by what I know,' she said softly. 'You're aware of others. You help. You *care*.'

'Don't start thinking I'm something I'm not,' he muttered, rejecting her innate positivity. 'I'll only disappoint you, Mia.'

'Lots of things in life are a disappointment.' She shrugged but then shot him a loyal look that lanced. 'But you never will be.'

CHAPTER ELEVEN

Mia walked on her lunch breaks—a half hour of sunshine and solitude. Sometimes she checked in with Adele—who'd finally accepted the additional support that Sante had been desperate to supply—but mostly she processed the time with Sante, trying to lock it into her memory so she could savour every sensation. Somehow, two weeks had passed since that first weekend in Sicily. The time had passed in a dreamy blur of sizzling sweet torture in the office before the too-quick delights of nighttime—dining in his apartment, debating over the best songs of the century, destroying each other on the gaming console before teasing higher stakes games in bed. The weekends in Sicily were slower, lazier, decadent. She caught up on the sleep she'd missed through the week while Sante worked in the garden or read. He still worked so hard so she liked to play with him—putting on music, dancing naked in the glasshouse, reading, eating…and spending hours in bed. Her adjustment to helicopter flights, fridges full of delicacies and walking into perfect homes prepared by discreet staff was shamelessly effortless. Every aspect of this lifestyle was utter luxury but her most favourite thing was the attention from *him*. Sante spoilt her in the best possible way—with his focus and time. It was so good she was struggling about missing it even before their affair was ended. Because this *was* an affair and she reminded herself of the fact daily.

She didn't like to open up emotionally. It was simpler to live lightly, never scratch beneath the superficial. She enjoyed a job, or a new place but moved on before anything went wrong—but she kept in touch with many people, revisited places. She just was always careful not to stay too long.

Sante preferred not to open up as well—he retreated to his sanctuary, not letting anyone past his guard and given what he'd been through, she didn't blame him. And while he'd opened up with her, it was partly only because of their shared past. His isolation increasingly bothered her. She remembered that summer back at her father's estate when she'd been jealous of and fascinated by her brother's best friend. She remembered hearing their banter, their competitiveness, their laughter.

For all this time since, Dario had kept the sad facts of Sante's childhood private and now Mia couldn't understand why he'd believed their father about Sante's behaviour after the accident—why he would accept that Sante hadn't just abandoned him but taken money to stay away. Their friendship hadn't just been severed, but Dario still seethed with resentment. Her brother's awful injuries still caused him pain and it must've been hard to see his former friend succeeding back when he was so broken. But Dario had worked stupidly hard to 'catch up' on the time he'd missed. He *still* worked stupidly hard. So did Sante. Initially, they'd created complementary products but despite their past closeness, 'doesn't play well with others' was stamped across both their report cards now.

It shouldn't be. They'd been on the same team once, and while Sante mightn't agree, he was effectively building himself a team here in Rome. He and Dario had so much in common. If they could clear the air maybe they'd see they *weren't* each other's nemesis. Knowing the truth about Sante—that he hadn't taken any money—might lighten her brother up. And hiding her affair from him felt wrong to Mia. Because this was more than a physical thing. She *cared* about Sante and she didn't want either him or her brother to be so *alone*. Maybe she could make a difference to them. Maybe she could bring *them* together.

Impulsively, Mia pulled out her phone.

'Mia?' Dario abruptly answered on the third ring. 'What's up—is everything okay?'

He sounded so concerned—did he think she'd only phone if something was wrong?

'Everything's fine.' Her pulse accelerated. 'I just thought it had been a while since we caught—'

'I figured you've been working on board somewhere sunny,' Dario said.

'I was, but I've taken a temporary position in Rome. Funny thing, actually.' She squeezed her eyes shut and went for it. 'I'm working for Sante Trovato's tech incubator.'

For a moment there was no response. Then she heard a door slam.

'Can you repeat that please, Mia?' Dario's voice suddenly sounded much nearer, much softer, much more serious.

Mia immediately overcompensated—smiling to inject lightness into her voice. 'I'm working with Sante Trovato. You remember—'

'Of course I remember.'

Mia tried to soften her own tension and remain calm. 'I didn't realise when I took the job that he—'

'Mia!' Dario groaned. 'Listen to *me*,' her brother added urgently. 'You need to stand up and walk out of there right now.'

'I can't do that.'

'Yes, you can. He has no hold over you, Mia. He's bad news.'

But Sante did have a hold—on her heart. 'If you really want to know, I'm involved with him.'

'*What?*' Dario's question cracked like a whip.

It was just like the way their father asked whenever she'd screwed up in his eyes. Because that was what she did, right? Messed up. Was too impetuous. Was *stupid*.

'Are you sleeping with him?' Dario almost choked. 'Why would you fall for his false charm?'

Which showed how much Dario actually knew because Sante was *not* charming. He was guarded and prickly with *everyone*.

'No, Mia,' Dario added. 'You know he's a user. You know he'll just take what he wants, then leave. No goodbye. No backwards glance. He's only interested in what he can get out of people and then he's gone.'

Mia would have agreed with that assessment only a couple weeks ago but working with him, being with him, she'd gotten to truly know him. 'You're wrong, Dario. He didn't abandon you that night. And he never took money from Dad. He cares about—'

'About *his* needs,' Dario argued. 'He's using you, Mia. It's a cheap double win—he gets what he wants from you *and* he gets at me.'

Cheap. *Sex*. She stiffened at the implication that that was all a man could want from her.

And Dario believed he was the true target in Sante's interest in her—why? Because he was more important? The firstborn with the balls and the brains and thus the title.

Dario got horrible attention from their father, too, but he *was* valued more—he was *wanted* if only to be the heir—and that still hurt.

'Maybe what's going on between him and me has nothing to do with you,' she said.

'It has *everything* to do with me. He wants to score points against me and he's using you to do it.' Dario scoffed again. 'Don't be this naive, Mia.'

Actually, she wasn't. She'd been thriving just fine on her own for the past few years. Travelling, working hard, managing the money she earned. But her brother still didn't think that she was *capable*.

'What do you think is going to happen here, Mia? You can't trust him. I don't want to see you hurt—'

'I won't be,' she defended fiercely. 'And if you met him—'

'That's *never* going to happen.' Dario's disbelief streamed through the phone.

'Not even if I ask?' she murmured. 'Dario?'

There was silence down the phone.

'The only way I'd meet him is on the day he marries you,' Dario said brutally. 'Is that going to happen, Mia?'

'No, because that's not what I want,' she shot back. 'You know I *like* my independence. There's nothing more important to me. I just thought *you* should know that he's not the awful man you—'

'He's *worse* and—'

'Can't you trust my judgement?' she interrupted. 'Can't you consider this for me?'

Dario sighed heavily. 'Mia, I can't. I know you. You're so like Mum—too generous, too impetuous. You dive headlong into situations that don't serve you—'

He broke off and she heard him cursing beneath his breath.

Right. He thought she was screwing up her life. He was tarnishing her with their mother's failings just as their father had. Mia's anger sparked. 'Maybe I'm like her in daring to enjoy—'

'Mum was an *addict*, Mia. You don't know—'

'*You* don't give me any credit for being able to understand anything, but *you're* the one who doesn't understand subtleties and shades of grey and that reality might not be as binary as you'd like it to be. I'm *not* a child anymore. And I'm *not* Mum. I'm capable of evaluating evidence and making rational decisions—'

'Sleeping with Sante Trovato isn't a rational decision. Please, Mia. He's using you.'

Using her to hurt Dario. Using her just for convenient sex. Dario couldn't consider otherwise. *Mia* couldn't possibly be wanted for anything other than her connections or her body.

'I'm sorry,' she muttered, and she was because she heard the pain in her brother's voice. 'I shouldn't have talked to you about it. I shouldn't have tried to—' She broke off with a jerky inhalation. 'Don't worry, okay? I *am* leaving here soon and it will be over so just forget I ever said anything about it.'

She ended the call before he could reply and shoved her phone into her pocket. She was in control of herself here, wasn't she? But Dario's cynicism didn't seed doubt, it made her fully face her own actions. Her own feelings. She *had* been impetuous in starting the affair with Sante and she was under no illusions that *she* had started it. It should've been a short-term fun fling—not heavy or serious. She'd not meant to feel anything deeply for him. But now she saw she'd not been daring to enjoy physical pleasure with him; she'd dared her *heart*. She just hadn't realised it. And now it was too late.

She *liked* him. She more than liked him. And she didn't want this to end.

But Sante had never hinted that he'd want anything more and it was insane to think he would given they'd only been together a few weeks. The truth was he hated her father and he hated her brother and he couldn't overcome that past any more than Dario could. Her wishing for a different future was pointless. They *would* end.

She was a fool for having given in to her desire in the first place. But she couldn't regret it.

Heart aching, she turned back to walk towards the office. The streets were crowded with both tourists and workers and she was carried along with them back towards Sante's building. She was relieved to get inside and into the cool stairwell. She heard voices just above—others climbing the stairs ahead of her.

'…they both stayed late the other night. You know they're always last to leave so who knows what happens when we're all gone.'

Mia stilled. There was someone on the landing above; despite talking quietly their words carried down the empty stairwell towards her.

'Carla went in the helicopter the other day and saw the last few flight logs. Apparently, Mia's been a passenger on the weekend trips to Sicily. She's not been in the office the last couple Fridays. You know they're not working all weekend.'

Horrified, she pressed back against the wall. They were talking about *her*. And Sante.

'No *way*,' Davide scoffed. 'I don't believe it.'

'You watch—you'll see the way she looks at him.'

Shame slithered over Mia's skin.

'No!' Davide was in full disbelief. 'They're total opposites. He wouldn't. She's far too—'

Mia didn't hear what Davide said but the men's laughter streamed down the stairwell. Amazed. Amused. *Derisive.*

'He's a guy, isn't he? He'd totally do it. Wouldn't you?'

'Yeah, but—'

Mia closed her eyes and covered her face with her hands, blocking out the rest of what they said. She'd been *obvious* and the colleagues whom she thought respected her clearly didn't. They were discussing her as a sexual *option*. Staying working here now was untenable. She couldn't—knowing they were watching her. *Mocking* her. She simply couldn't live through the humiliation of an exposed workplace affair.

But their *laughter* shook her. It hurt more than her brother's concerns. Dario believed Sante was using her—that he didn't really want her. But these guys knew Sante far better that Dario now did and they saw the truth. *Mia* was the misfit in the relationship. She was too…*something*. She didn't need to know exactly what—it was always the same. Too much in one way, too lacking in another. She wouldn't ever be considered a serious match for Sante Trovato.

And it was devastating.

Sante restlessly prowled around the open-plan area knowing he was freaking the coders out but he couldn't stop pacing. Mia wasn't yet back from her lunchtime walk. She wasn't normally gone for this long and he couldn't help lingering—watching, waiting, his nerves shredding more by the second. He wasn't even able to focus enough to have a crack at the game of the week for her league table. Because he'd done something impulsive. He'd made a Mia-like plan. Or so he hoped. He'd wanted to do something nice with her—*for* her—and the trip he'd booked definitely ticked those boxes. They'd have to take a couple days more away from the office, but she'd not had a holiday since starting here and he couldn't remember the last time he'd had a holiday that wasn't simply a trip to his estate. Nor could he remember the last time he'd felt this nervous.

It was a good idea. It was. She'd love it. She would smile and her cheeks would flush and they would have fun.

The door opened and Mattia, the property junior, walked in with Davide, one of the coders. Disappointed, Sante turned back and kept prowling round the room. Ten minutes passed before the door opened again.

Sante stilled. Mia looked pale and her eyes were downcast as she went to her desk. There was no smile or gentle greeting to anyone she walked past—which was weird. He immediately headed back to his office via her corner.

'Do you have a minute, Mia?' He nodded towards his door.

She didn't answer but after a moment rose and followed him into his office. She didn't close his door behind her. She didn't meet his eye. Sante took in her visible attempt to hold herself together. She was quite literally clasping her hands tightly in front of her. While they weren't hands-on in the office, they were friendly. They made eye contact.

'Are you okay?' he asked quietly, moving closer to her.

'Of course.' She still didn't meet his eye; instead, she glanced at the window.

'I, uh…' Awkward discomfort licked through him. He was so unpractised, he didn't know where to begin. 'I've booked some tickets. For a concert. In London.'

Not just any tickets. Most expensive available.

'*London?*' She looked at him then and her eyes widened. '*A concert? What?*'

'We'd have to take—'

'Sante,' she interrupted. 'Is this a work thing?'

He blinked. No, it wasn't. What did that matter?

She bit her lip. 'You know the rules…'

Did those rules still matter? Really?

Her wariness raised red flags in his head. He'd wanted to take her away. He'd booked for the band who sang her favourite songs. It was the final concert of their world tour and the timing was insane and he'd thought she would *love* it. That they both would—she'd liked dancing with him in the palazzo… But now Mia's creamy skin paled, even her full lips whitened. She almost looked ill. Was it London that spooked her? She would have friends there from when she grew up. Others from her aristocratic background. The school she went to. The jobs she'd worked.

She checked the window again. Sante glanced at it, too, and saw a couple of coders walk past towards the kitchenette—both of whom looked in.

Sante turned back to Mia. Now her cheeks were mottled crimson and she actually took a step back. '*Please*, Sante.'

Mia—his lovely, enthusiastic, effervescent, loud Mia, *whispered*.

She didn't want to be heard discussing anything personal with him. She didn't want to be *seen* with him in a personal capacity. And if she couldn't handle being seen with him here, there's no way she'd agree to be in the VIP section of one of the world's biggest concert arenas, rubbing shoulders with celebrities and the toffs she went to school with.

'We can't talk about this now,' she added.

They didn't need to talk about it. Her answer was obvious. It was going to be no. And he didn't want to hear it. He *couldn't*. She'd said they came from different worlds and she didn't want them to mix. All of a sudden he wasn't Sante Trovato, billionaire. But Sante, the foundling—unwanted, parentage unknown, *problematic*.

'Right,' he said brusquely.

He was a fool for plotting this—for ever imagining she would walk out with him anywhere public. She would never want anyone to know—certainly not her brother. Hell, Sante hadn't been to a concert since the night of their accident, and there would never be any way he could make any of this work.

'Sante...' she muttered. 'Please—'

'Sorry—oh, am I interrupting?' Paolo paused in the doorway.

'No, come in.' Sante jerked his chin at the man and flatly dismissed her. 'We're done here, right, Mia?'

She escaped wordlessly.

His pulse pounded. She'd rejected him. She'd not needed to say a word; he'd read it in her eyes. It was his mistake. He didn't want to be a secret. Not her source of shame. He'd felt so much shame in his life. And now he'd exposed himself—made himself *vulnerable* to that rejection. He'd not allowed that possibility in *years* but he'd just let her slice the ground from beneath his feet and he was *falling*—

'What is it, Paolo?' he asked harshly.

Desperate for distraction, Sante fell on the info that Paolo had brought in with him. A contact had just informed him about a property coming to market in Monaco. That sounded good. Sante had been considering acquiring one there.

Breathing hard, Sante nodded decisively. He'd go see it for himself. Make the decision on *full* information. This was important. Work was the constant. Work was the only thing that mattered. He would head there. *Now*.

CHAPTER TWELVE

MIA COMPLETELY UNNECESSARILY sent a document to the farthest printer simply to have reason to get away from her desk. As she walked back, she used peripheral vision to see Sante still intensely talking with Paolo in his office. She let her glance sweep the room and saw Davide watching her. She dropped her lashes and went straight back to her desk.

He knew. Which meant they *all* knew. She was such a fool to have let this happen. She desperately needed to talk to Sante *privately*—as in off-site—so she could explain exactly why she'd not wanted to talk about his plans here. She'd thought he would understand given he'd been empathetic about what had happened with Oliver. And what had he meant by tickets to a concert in *London*? Who and what and *why* had he done that? She *ached* to know now but ten minutes ago she'd been feeling trash with Dario pitying her, hearing those guys laughing about her and she'd just needed him to stop.

He'd done more than that. He'd shut down. His dismissal—that they were *done*? That had sounded final.

Five minutes after she'd left Sante's office, Paolo exited—Sante just behind him. He walked past her, jacket and bag in hand. Mia didn't look up; she couldn't. She checked the schedule but nothing new had been added. She heard the bang as the main door closed behind him but she couldn't chase after him given the curious gazes of the coders.

Instead, she faked being busy—clicking windows on her computer screen as if her life depended on it and overthinking everything. She was totally thrown by that invitation—it was thoughtful and generous and what had he meant by it?

She willed the workday to end. Willed Sante to return. Wished she could get to a space where she could be alone and think. But she couldn't just leave. She couldn't go away to London with him and have everyone know it.

An hour later a message pinged on the company-wide message board.

Gone to investigate a property. Back soon. Keep pushing *S.

It was more information than Sante usually offered the team when going away but Mia felt hurt that there was no message directly to her inbox. Nor her phone. She braved up and sent him a text—saying they needed to talk, asking when he'd be back.

Two days later she was still waiting on a reply.

Three days later she'd accepted the reality. She'd thought he'd get in touch and while he responded to work emails and updates—briefly—his message was clear. He didn't want *her*. Those tersely worded work instructions made her feel worse. He sent them only because he'd *had* to. Otherwise, he would've severed all ties—on a personal level he had, no texts, no calls. He'd walked out and never looked back.

That was what he'd done to Dario after the accident. What he'd done with that school. And with his foster placement. It was how he dealt—he walked away, stayed away, stayed silent.

'Are you okay, Mia?'

Mia glanced up and saw Valerio quietly standing near. She couldn't even interpret his question—whether he, too, knew and was asking with gossipy intent or whether he genuinely cared.

'I'm fine, thank you,' she lied.

She wasn't fine. She was furious. And even though she knew it was horrible to simply disappear from people's lives, at 11 am on the third day of Sante's absence she closed down her computer, shoved her spare blouse into her bag and walked out of the office without a word to anyone.

As soon as she was out in the bright sunshine she grabbed her phone and tapped the screen. Her call was answered almost immediately.

'Adele?' She checked. 'I'm so sorry.'

Sante's thundering pulse deafened him to everything. Nothing within him would work properly. He couldn't even get it together enough to bother walking around the stunning building overlooking a vast coastline. He just stood in front of it and felt like crap. Alone. Again. Again. Again.

He'd gone straight to the airport—so desperate to escape he'd actually flown commercial. First class, but still, it was cramped and crowded. He'd walked through the apartment in Monaco and gone straight back to the airport. Restless as hell. He'd felt a biting drive for space and distance and so he'd gotten onto another flight; this time Melbourne, Australia. He'd spent more than fifteen hours in the air all up. Which gave him plenty of time to think. To *stew*.

He'd thought he'd visit his favourite properties, remind himself what he liked, what he'd achieved, what was most important to him. All that had happened was that he'd wished Mia was with him. At every moment. Every place.

He'd wanted her with him. He'd *missed* her. And he was an idiot because she didn't want to be seen with him. She didn't want to talk with him in private. Never wanted to leave his apartment in Rome or the estate in Sicily. Half the time she didn't want to stay in his bed the entire night. She wanted to have sex with him, but anything more?

It hurt. Especially because he knew damned well she was an 'all in' person—with impulsive warmth, generous with her self, her soul. It wasn't hedonism—there was a deliberate direction in her choices. She'd turned her full-bore attention to him but it had been *confined*. She'd wanted him but only if it was *quiet*. And he was furious with her for that. Furious with himself for *still* wanting more. And his fury surged—unabated, unanswered. He wanted to know *why*—to hear the trash reasons from her mouth. To watch her eyes as she answered. And he needed to tell her how much *she* bothered him.

He'd made a mistake in running away from the fight. He needed to have the fight with her to be able to *forget*.

It was days before he got to her apartment. There was no answer when he rang her doorbell. He glanced at his watch and cursed his idiocy. She would be at work by now. The emails had still been coming but she'd not offered anything personal other than that one text he'd not replied to.

He stalked through the office, stopping at her empty desk and glancing around. Why wasn't she here already? The main door opened and he whirled to face it. Freezing when he saw who'd entered.

'What are you doing here?' he muttered huskily. 'You can't be here.'

Adele merely raised her eyebrows at him.

'I thought you were taking three *months*, not three weeks,' Sante added.

'Apparently, my fussing is driving Bruno up the wall and he'll do better with a break from me. The specialist you got for him is amazing, the cleaner is amazing and his best friend is dropping in. So he's in good spirits and I'm needed here.'

Why? Sante's chest felt hollowed out by a spoon. 'Where's Mia?'

Adele got busy unpacking her bag at Mia's desk and wouldn't look at him. 'I'll be in the office three days—'

'And Mia the other two?' Sante interrupted.

Adele straightened and looked him in the eye. 'No, Sante. Mia's gone.'

He shook his head. 'She wouldn't have done that. She wouldn't let you down.'

'*She's* not the one who's let me down.' Adele paused.

His heart thudded and instinctively he pressed his lips together. She was scolding him—about the only person he'd take it from.

'Mia's a generous soul,' Adele added quietly. 'I'd hoped you might see that.'

Of course he had. The problem was he wanted too *much* of her generosity.

'She was right about you,' Adele added.

Meaning what, exactly? But Adele didn't say more.

Sante drew breath, softening stiff muscles enough to be able to speak. 'Where can I find her?'

The older woman sat at her desk and didn't answer.

'So, you know we're...' He trailed off.

'Everyone knows you're together,' Adele said calmly. 'Isn't that part of the problem?'

He frowned. Everyone? Already? In his head that had been inevitable, but while he didn't care, the thought bothered Mia. A lot. 'Did someone say something?'

Adele looked at him like he was an imbecile. He frowned. Had they said something off? Was that why Mia had been so uncomfortable that day? Then why hadn't she said anything to *him*?

Because he'd not given her a proper chance to. And she *had* said something—she'd said they couldn't talk *here*. In his office with all its windows and open-plan space. And he really was a fool. He'd taken her hesitation so badly—so *personally*. He'd immediately assumed her reluctance was regarding his invitation. He'd been so *insecure*. So he'd backed off.

He'd disappeared and then *she'd* disappeared. And wasn't that what he'd wanted? He'd known his silence would hurt her. He'd known his *disappearance* would drive her away. He'd been horrible because he'd felt not good enough for her and couldn't handle the prospect of her rejection. Now he felt even more horrible because driving her away wasn't what he'd wanted at all. It was the complete *opposite* of what he wanted. He'd been such a coward. He'd hurt himself. And he was still so damned insecure he didn't know how *badly* he'd hurt her.

But he did know that Mia was empathetic and loving. When she'd first realised who he was, she'd sided with Dario's version of their past with almost blind loyalty because she loved her brother deeply. The magnitude of Mia's emotions had always attracted Sante—he wanted her to feel deeply for him, too. For him most of all. He wanted every ounce of her generosity—both body and heart. He'd wanted it so much he'd gotten scared and pushed her away instead of speaking up. But Mia needed love, too—the certainty of that body-and-soul kind of love. She'd never had it and she feared rejection as much as he did. She walked out when she felt that she'd been too much—but she could *never* be too much for him.

'I get that you're angry with me. *I'm* angry with me,' Sante said to the woman who'd been better to him than almost anyone. Because now he understood that she'd chosen Mia to help, oh *so* deliberately. 'I screwed up but I can't fix it if I don't know where to find her.'

Adele looked up, her gaze serious. 'Do you actually want to fix it?'

A desperate, desolate ache swept through him. 'More than anything,' he admitted hoarsely. 'But she's the one who needs to hear why. Though admittedly, I might need help with how.' He leaned against the wall and ran his hand through his hair. 'Please, Adele, I know you know where she is. Will you tell me?'

CHAPTER THIRTEEN

Adele told him a little more information—by the end, Sante was feeling small but hopeful. Also desperate. Also grateful to the woman—she'd been more loyal than he deserved and she'd put up with more of his flaky behaviour than she should have.

The only person to call him out on it up to now had been Mia.

But he'd apologised and gone straight back to the damned airport. The irony was too much as he boarded another endurance-test flight. Mia had gone even farther than him—not to Australia, but New Zealand. Of course she had. Which meant it would be almost another day before he could see her. Adele had given him her new number and the address she was staying at. He didn't phone ahead; face-to-face was the only way. He needed to see her; hopefully, make her listen somehow.

She was staying in a small hotel on the waterfront of a suburb not too far from central Auckland. Sante went straight from the airport, knocked on the door of her unit and got no reply. Frustrated, he stepped back and sucked in a breath. He'd wait. He'd sit on one of the beachside benches by the water where all the people walked their dogs along the sand. He'd wait and watch her door for as long as it took.

But that was where he found her. Sitting on one of the

beachside benches, watching the dogs gambolling over the sand. For a split second he thought he was hallucinating because it was the Mia he knew from Rome—wearing the same blouse and skirt from the day he'd met her. It was as if she'd been plucked from there and transported here in a blink. No pastry, though. No spark. No smile.

'Mia?' he barely muttered as he walked up to her.

She glanced up and a shocked expression flashed on her face. '*No.*'

He wasn't hallucinating, then. His entire body weakened and he sank to the other end of the bench. 'Mia—'

'I don't have time to talk to you right now. I have an interview to get to.'

'Job interview?'

She nodded, crushing his lungs.

He dragged in a breath. 'Well, can I give you a lift there?'

Reproach flashed in her eyes. 'No, thanks.'

'Can I walk with you?'

'No.' She shook her head. 'I'm not making this mistake again.'

Then he would wait right here until she returned.

But she hesitated, staying perched on the edge of the seat. 'What do you want?'

'To talk to you.'

'You could have talked to me anytime in these last few days.'

Sì. 'I was travelling.'

'You could've called from your plane.'

'You've changed your number and I wanted to look you in the eyes when I talked to you.'

She didn't move and he watched the blue deepen. A small bubble of hope flickered through his blood.

'What did you want to say?' she muttered.

All those hours in the air and he still didn't have it straight. Didn't know how or where to start something so vitally important.

'Adele told me you overheard a couple of our guys talking in the stairwell,' he huffed.

She tensed. 'I don't—'

'I talked to Davide about it.'

'You *what*?'

'Davide said he'd told Mattia you were far too good for me. I think you missed that bit. They were laughing about *my* unsuitability for you. And he's right, by the way.'

'What?' Her whisper was inaudible.

'I shouldn't have tried to talk about the trip to you at work. I was nervous and I made a mess of it. You'd told me you wanted to keep our relationship quiet at work but I started feeling as if you didn't want anyone to know because you were ashamed of me.'

'*What?*' That time, her voice was like a whip crack.

Sante almost smiled but the distress in her eyes smote his heart. He really had been a fool. 'Mia…'

'No.'

Mia couldn't do this. She couldn't believe he'd spoken to Davide—of course the guy had spun it that way. Ordinarily she'd be more humiliated only *nothing* could overwhelm the agony she was already suffering this second.

Sante looked *outrageously* amazing and she couldn't stop staring, drinking in every detail. His tan had deepened and his hair was messier than usual, the curling ends utterly roguish. Even in casual trousers, heavy tee and soft leather boat shoes he quietly screamed wealth. He looked as if he'd spent the past week lounging on a private super yacht. Maybe he had been; what would she know given his complete *silence*? They'd had *weeks* of intense intimacy and he'd just left. She'd made a massive mistake in getting involved with him. She'd thought they could have a small secret fling—that there would be no real consequences—but she'd had so *much* to lose.

Once again she'd wanted more from someone who didn't want to give to her. Once again she'd been an 'amusement' only to become an annoyance—someone to be sent away, or simply avoided. But that wasn't the worst of it. The worst was that he'd taken her *heart*—and all her hopes and dreams—with him.

She made herself stand. He immediately rose and she realised her mistake. He was so tall and so handsome, he didn't just block her path, he dazzled her.

'I've been a coward, Mia,' he muttered. 'But you need to know that I will follow you. I will fight for you. I will face my own stupid fears for you because they've been stopping me...'

Mia froze, desperately wanting to believe him, but she knew Sante never stayed for a fight—not a *personal* one. He just stepped back—unwilling to put himself on the line, and she almost understood that given how rough he'd had it in the past. And her own hurt rose in an unstoppable wave. 'You just *disappeared*.'

'So you left.'

'I'll never stay where I'm not truly wanted,' she whispered. 'You of all people should understand that.'

And he did. She realised that was why he'd done it. He'd known just how cruelly that action would strike.

'You're *wanted*,' he said roughly, stepping forward. '*I* want you. And I don't want anyone or anything but you.' His eyes glinted with ferocity. 'I promise you, Mia. I won't walk out on you ever again.'

She shook her head slightly. She couldn't believe him.

'I'm so sorry, Mia.' His voice broke. 'So sorry. Please, *please* forgive me.'

Mia stilled. Sante never stayed for forgiveness, either, and that broke her heart. Did he think he could never get that? Did he think he would always be kicked away after one mistake? Did he think that he needed to protect himself from everything and everyone including *her*?

She desperately summoned some semblance of calm but the tears she'd been trying to stop spilled down her cheeks. She gulped but couldn't suck her sob back. She was in utter chaos.

'Mia.' Suddenly, Sante stepped forward. He gently cupped the back of her head and pressed her forehead to his chest. Instinctively, she clenched her fists and pushed them against his chest. She *wasn't* just falling into his arms. She would keep some distance because this was…this was…

She didn't know what this was. She didn't want to hope. But hope was a boundless thing that ignored reality. She clenched her fists more tightly, still unable to speak.

Sante didn't fight her stiffness; he didn't try to press her close. He lightly cradled the back of her head, gently stroking her hair while *she* hid her face in his shirt. Because her tears now streamed.

'I'm not letting you go. I'm not. I can't. You're mine,' he breathed. 'Or at least, I'm *yours*. Please forgive me, Mia. Forgive my silence. I freeze. I retreat. I say nothing. It's always been safer that way. But safe isn't living. It's not loving. And I love you so I can't be silent now. I can't walk away from *you*.'

Her fists unfurled and she spread her fingers over his warmth and strength.

'I was such a jerk,' he said. 'I thought you were going to say no and I regressed in an instant.'

'You wanted to do something nice for me but you—'

'Asked you in the office. With the door open. Maybe I wanted to see if you'd say yes anyway or if you'd freeze. I think maybe everything was getting so good that I got scared and I found a way out. I've pushed people away all my life, Mia, before they can push me out. But that wasn't fair on you. My only excuse is that I've never felt this way about anyone and I was fucking terrified. But I'm even more terrified now.'

'Me, too,' she whispered, collapsing against him completely.

Beneath her cheek his chest rose and fell faster as he pulled her closer still.

'I'd talked to Dario,' she admitted. 'He made me doubt—'
'Me?'
'No. Myself and then I heard Davide talking.'
'Our guys think the world of you—'
'It doesn't matter.'

'It does matter. And they do think you're wonderful. You've made the office so much better. You've made my life incredible.' His arms tightened. 'You know I listen to the songs you hum in my car so I feel near you even when I'm not. I scour menus online because dining different every night with you is so much fun. You make every moment sparkle. I went away this week and spent the whole time wishing you were with me. I've never wanted to share anything the way I want to share *everything* with you. You enrich *my* life. You're generous and warm and welcoming,' he muttered. 'You're the most loveable creature on earth and these last few days have been the worst.'

They'd been the worst for her, too.

'I know you're afraid to trust me now and I don't blame you for that, but here's the thing, Mia,' he muttered directly into her ear. 'You're not too much, not for me. You're *perfect* for me.'

Mia trembled.

'Please,' he whispered. 'Be mine. My Mia.'

She lifted her face and saw his expression was utterly intense and determined. 'Oh, Sante—' She lifted her chin and caught his lips with hers.

Passion shot through her in an electrical surge so powerful she could only cling while his hug became so tight she could barely breathe. But it didn't matter. He was back and he was *hers* and she was never, ever letting him go. Fortunately, he clearly wasn't letting her go, either.

'*Mia, Mia, Mia.*' He kissed her breathlessly. 'Can we get to your room? Now?'

She chuckled as her blood fizzed and her brain jumped all over the place.

'I need to cancel the interview,' she babbled. 'It was with an agency. I can't just not turn up.'

He shot her a rueful smile as he took her hand and laced his fingers through hers. She made the quick call as they walked to the room she'd booked at the little hotel. The moment they were inside he turned to her and she threw her arms around his neck. It was with both laughter and tears that they tumbled together onto the bed.

'I've missed you,' he groaned. 'Having you in my arms, by my side, every moment of every day, I have *missed* you.'

Engulfed in joy she fumbled trying to get his tee up before he swore and took over. Getting naked, being together, was everything. But the relief of seeing him again, when she thought she'd lost him forever, was overwhelming. Her hands stilled and her eyes filled and all she could do was stare at him mistily.

'It's okay,' he said, seeing her torn between distress and

delight. 'It's okay.' He pulled her close, gently sweeping his hands over her trembling body. 'I'll never leave you again,' he vowed. 'Never ever let you go.'

He tenderly undressed her with gentle slowness, caring, calming her until the heat flowed back into her body. Until she truly believed. And then she moved—she arched towards him, her hands impatient and her mouth hungry. She needed him inside her—to share that ultimate intimacy with him—*now*. 'Sante.'

'I'm here.' As he sank deep inside her, he closed his eyes briefly and his voice hitched. 'Don't leave me again, either.'

'*Never.*' She trailed her hands down his back and pulled him even deeper into her. She never wanted to hurt him. She hadn't understood that she could. But now she knew she had his heart the same way he had hers. 'Love me, Sante.'

'I do. Will. Always.'

They lay together for a long time after, breathlessly whispering words of love and forgiveness, sharing soft, sweet laughter. But he suddenly rose up onto his elbows and gazed into her eyes even more intensely than he had just before.

'What's wrong?'

'Nothing at all.' He swallowed. 'I just…will you marry me?' he asked shakily. 'Preferably as soon as possible?'

'*What?*' Mia's heart stopped and started all over again—at thrice the pace.

'I love you. I want you. I never want to be apart from you again, and I want you to know and believe it, too. I want you to be mine and I want everyone in the whole damned world to know it. I'd be so proud to be your husband, Mia.'

'Isn't it too…' Mia studied the vulnerability in his eyes.

'No. It's not too soon. Not for me,' he whispered. 'I love you.'

He'd just offered the future she'd not yet dared dream of.

'Yes.' But she was so stunned her answer was soundless.

'Was that a yes?' His eyes gleamed.

'Of course yes!' she screamed.

Sante laughed and rolled, flipping her so she was above him. He swept his hands up, cupping her breasts as he gazed up at her adoringly. 'Then let me love you again, my gorgeous fiancée.'

An hour later she still couldn't stop smiling. 'So you want to elope?'

'No. I want a big wedding.'

She yelped. '*No.* You're too private. You would never want—'

'Okay, so maybe it won't be that big,' he conceded. 'But we need Adele and Bruno there, right? Definitely the coders and creatives.' He chuckled at her cringe. 'I need to prove to them I'm good enough for you.'

'You already are.' Despite her smile, Mia's eyes watered again. 'And your neighbours in Sicily.'

'We could marry there. Everyone could stay. Big party.' He stiffened slightly and cupped her face, looking directly into her eyes. 'Including Dario, if you want. I don't want to come between you and him. You only have each other—'

'You're not the one coming between me and Dario. It was our father who did that.'

'So invite him. I know you'd like to be closer to him.' He lowered his gaze. 'Family matters.'

'It does. He'll have to get used to you being mine.' She held him close.

'I'd like to build a big family with you,' he whispered.

'I would love that. Dogs, right?'

He laughed but his voice softened. 'And children. Three or four? Five or six? You pick.'

She giggled, too, and wriggled beneath him. 'You know I'm a little greedy.'

'And you know I love that about you.' He breathed in shakily. 'I'll try, Mia, but—'

'We'll make good lives for them,' she assured him. 'We'll never abandon them. We'll never make them feel…'

'Unwanted.' He rolled and pulled her to lie on his chest. 'We'll give them—'

'Love,' she breathed, adoring him with every fibre of her being. 'All our love.'

CHAPTER FOURTEEN

SANTE ARRIVED SLIGHTLY later than planned but he had good reason—one he couldn't wait to share with Mia. He ran up the stairs to fetch her, but stopped just in the doorway and blinked. The palazzo was full of people—cleaners, catering staff, florists—all being overseen by a very efficient, equally terrifying, wedding coordinator that Adele had hired. The older woman had become quite smug about her hand in their whirlwind romance.

I knew you'd be perfect for him, Mia.

She was, of course. But right now his perfect woman wasn't in sight. He snaffled a pastry from the pile on the counter, ignoring the combination of smiles and frowns the theft earned him, and backed out of the chaos and onto the balcony to look across the gardens as he quickly ate. A flash of colour clued him in. He went back to the car and carefully lifted out his precious cargo and walked towards the wrought iron summerhouse.

He heard her humming but couldn't see her from the back of the plush armchair. Carefully, he set the load down behind her and stepped around so she could see him.

'You found me.' She was curled up in one of the plush chairs.

'You knew I would.'

'I was just checking the place was ready for Dario and his fiancée.'

Her brother had accepted the wedding invitation they'd sent him a fortnight ago. Mia was nervously pleased about it. Sante was pleased she was pleased, but he didn't entirely trust that Dario wouldn't try to interfere. He was mentally rehearsing self-restraint—determined to stand alongside Mia should that happen. He wanted Mia to have everything. To marry him and still have a relationship with the brother she deeply cared about—even if things had been distant between them for a while. If Dario actually loved her, he would accept Sante's relationship with Mia for what it was. Genuine. All-encompassing, all-consuming love.

He hunched down before her. 'And got distracted? Needed a minute?'

'It's very busy in there even for me,' she said.

Sante had discovered that sometimes his effervescent, kind-to-everyone, sweet humming sunshine girl needed some space. She smiled but her eyes filled.

'Hey.' He cupped her face in both hands, frowning at the tears sparkling in her eyes. 'What's up?'

'I'm nervous,' she confessed. 'I don't want to have the night apart from you.'

Relief washed through him. 'I thought you said it's tradition,' he teased.

'Screw tradition. It was a stupid idea…' She bit her lip. 'Are you sure about this, Sante?'

Oh, his bride still didn't believe how much he loved her.

The past three weeks had been the best of his life. They'd returned to Rome—to a party atmosphere in the office when they'd made the announcement. They'd taken the week off—gone to the concert, gone out to dinner, gone back to Sicily. He'd found her a ring and they were only just getting started.

'So sure,' he promised. 'You have my heart, Mia. Be gentle with it.'

'I'll hold it close and treasure it always.' Her smile went a little coy. 'Though I might not be as gentle with other parts...'

Chuckling, he leaned closer. 'I'll be with you tonight and every night that follows. I *never* want to be apart from you. I want you with me for the rest of my life. You're my anchor. My everything.'

Mia wrapped her arms around his neck and pulled him down to her. It was everything she'd needed to hear because the old insecurity was hard to overcome today. Sante could have *anyone*—yet he'd chosen her and she wasn't used to being wanted. Unbelievably—devastatingly—nor was he. But they would spend the rest of their lives loving each other. Completely.

'I can't wait for tomorrow,' he groaned. 'You'll be my *wife*.'

She loved that he shared his dreams with her. 'And you'll be my husband who right now tastes of—' She paused. 'Did you hear that?'

'What?'

'Scratching?' She wrinkled her nose. 'Oh no, do you think there are rodents in here?'

'No.' He smirked. 'I have a present for you.'

He drew her out of the chair and led her round to the oversize box sitting behind it.

'Are you going to unwrap it?' Sante prompted when she just stood staring at it.

Her heart raced because there was definitely something moving in there and she didn't want to guess in case she was wrong.

The paper was loose and lifted away at the first tear. It

wasn't a box, but a wire crate and inside it was a floppy-eared, trembling-limbed puppy.

'Oh, Sante...' She dropped to her knees and drew the little darling out, her tears immediate and fast. 'He's *ours*?'

'Yes.' He crouched down with her, slinging a firm arm around her. 'He's ours. Always.'

Mia buried her face in the puppy's fur.

'I was going to research some dog breeders but there was an animal shelter not far from the airport and they'd just taken in a litter and—'

'And you rescued him.' She lifted her head and her heart swelled.

'Couldn't leave without him.' Sante shot her a sheepish grin. 'Figure we could start building our family right away.'

'Oh, yes. He's gorgeous.' She cuddled the puppy close, chuckling as it licked her jaw, when something dangling from the crate caught her eye. She reached for it and her laughter deepened. 'You got him a very blingy collar.'

'Actually, that's an extra little present in case you didn't like the dog—'

'How could anyone not adore this dog!' Then she shot him a look. 'You got a collar for *me*?'

'Look a little closer.' He winked.

She studied the tiny collar looped around the top rail of the crate, gasped as she realised the 'bling' was actually a pair of sapphire-and-diamond drop earrings. 'Sante, they're stunning.'

'You don't have to wear them tomorrow. I just wanted to give you—'

'*Everything.* You've *already* given me everything.' She bent her head and breathed in the puppy's sweet scent again. 'They're beautiful and he's beautiful and you're *wonderful.*' She craned forward and pressed her mouth to his.

'Mmm.' He chuckled as she almost toppled over.

'Actually, I have a gift for you, too.' She had her present wrapped and hidden in here—it was the real reason she'd come in here before getting distracted by insecure thoughts.

He paused. 'You do?'

There was that hitch in his breath that she'd come to recognise—a hint of emotional vulnerability.

'It's hard to buy for a billionaire who could get himself whatever he wants, whenever he wants, but I thought of something. I think. Will you take him a minute?'

Sante took the wriggling bundle into his arms and cradled him close. Mia watched as the puppy sank against his chest and promptly fell asleep.

'He knows he's safe with you,' she whispered.

Sante looked at her and she fell in love with him all over again.

'Whereas he just wants to kiss you,' Sante chuckled softly. 'He and I have that desire in common.'

He carefully put the sleeping puppy back into the crate and tucked the blanket around him before turning back to her.

He unwrapped the present slowly, not tearing the paper the way Mia had, but taking care with it. Mia sat on her hands and refused to hurry him despite her nervousness. He was savouring the experience because it wasn't one he'd often had—a fact she intended to change.

The frame was facing down and she held her breath as he flipped it. He studied the black-and-white photograph she'd had printed for a long time. She was just about to ask when he cleared his throat.

'This is just before the concert and you insisted on a selfie.'

'To remember the moment, yeah,' she whispered.

'It's beautiful,' he muttered, still looking at it. '*You're* beautiful and we're…'

'Happy,' she said. 'I know it's just a selfie, but we're *us* in this and I thought it was time for you to have some family photos. We can have a house full of family photos. A house full of family.'

'There's nothing I'd like more. I love it. Thank you—' He kissed her.

But Mia broke away to giggle at a sudden, silly, *happy* thought. 'We'll need to have another taken with the puppy.'

'He can always be the ring bearer tomorrow,' Sante murmured through kisses.

'Oh, yes!' She laughed, joy bubbling up from a spring deep within that he'd filled. 'Oh, I love you, Sante.'

'And I adore you.' He bent his head to hers and pulled her into his strong arms. 'I always will.'

* * * * *

If you just couldn't get enough of
Enemies Until After Hours, *then be sure*
to check out the next instalment in the
Enemy Tycoons *duet, coming soon!*
And why not explore these other stories
by Natalie Anderson!

My One-Night Heir
Billion-Dollar Dating Game
Their Altar Arrangement
Boss's Baby Acquisition
Greek Vows Revisited

Available now!

MILLS & BOON®

Coming next month

BODYGUARD'S ROYAL TEMPTATION
Abby Green

She felt incredibly delicate and yet he sensed a latent strength.

He had a feeling he shouldn't underestimate her. After all she'd managed to ditch her bodyguards and avoid her brother.

He looked down at her and she lifted her face. She smiled. It made something inside Ares ache. Why was she so smiley? So perky? She was a princess way out of her depth. She could have been unconscious somewhere now if it hadn't been for him. But again, he had that sense that perhaps she would have surprised him by managing to get out of that predicament. She was using a false name to avoid detection.

Then his gaze went to her mouth. It opened slightly and he had a glimpse of pink tongue. White teeth. A fire started raging in his blood. He'd never been more tempted by a woman. By a woman who was so far out of his bounds that –

Before Ares could formulate another word, she'd reached up and pressed her mouth to his, a chaste and surprisingly sweet gesture. But any thought of *sweet* fast dissolved as *sweet* morphed into burning hot *heat* and intense need. Ares couldn't resist.

Continue reading

BODYGUARD'S ROYAL TEMPTATION
Abby Green

Available next month
millsandboon.co.uk

Copyright ©2026 Abby Green

COMING SOON!

We really hope you enjoyed reading this book.
If you're looking for more romance
be sure to head to the shops when
new books are available on

Thursday 26th March

To see which titles are coming soon, please visit
millsandboon.co.uk/nextmonth

MILLS & BOON

FOUR BRAND NEW BOOKS FROM
MILLS & BOON MODERN

Indulge in desire, drama, and breathtaking romance – where passion knows no bounds!

OUT NOW

Eight Modern stories published every month, find them all at:

millsandboon.co.uk

TWO BRAND NEW BOOKS FROM
Love Always

Be prepared to be swept away to incredible worldwide destinations along with our strong, relatable heroines and intensely desirable heroes.

OUT NOW

Four Love Always stories published every month, find them all at:

millsandboon.co.uk

LET'S TALK
Romance

For exclusive extracts, competitions and special offers, find us online:

- **f** MillsandBoon
- **X** @MillsandBoon
- **◉** @MillsandBoonUK
- **♪** @MillsandBoonUK

Get in touch on 01413 063 232

For all the latest titles coming soon, visit
millsandboon.co.uk/nextmonth